THE ALPHA OF GRAVE HILLS

DRAGONKIN

BOOK II

KATHRYN MOON

For my mom,
who gave me wings.

Contents

About the Book

This story was originally shared with chapter by chapter updates in rough draft form on my Patreon in starting in March of 2025. It's currently being removed.

While this series is made up of standalone romances in a series, I do strongly recommend reading the series in order. The events of this book happen simultaneously alongside those of The Alpha of Bleake Isle. I did have to make a minor change to Bleake Isle, where previously Torion had defeated his father. In this book his father has just passed away.

Content Information:

It's always best to check my website kathrynmoon.com for a thorough list of content information

This story deals with past trauma, including past relationships between minors and adults, and a large part of the story deals with a past miscarriage, and infidelity. There is in book pregnancy and birth.

Chapter One

BRIGID

aggie's eyes widened as the dragons' screaming flight overhead rattled the walls of my cottage.

"Don't fidget, Mags," I murmured, once again blowing an impulsively shorn lock of auburn hair out of my eye, ignoring the rallying cry of change in the sky above my thatched roof.

"You know what that means, Miss," Maggie said, fussing at a tear in the skirt of her smock.

I kept my eyes on her ankle as I massaged the salve and gently encouraged old bones and weary muscles to turn under my hands. I did know what it meant, although I was too young to have ever heard the betas roar in unison before. Lachlan Feargus had risen as alpha when my mother was still a girl, had nearly matched with her for his second rut—although that might've been another of Mother's tall tales—until he met his omega on a quick trip to Skybern. And from Skybern to Grave Hills, Omega Feargus had remained at our alpha's side, and for many years after. Lachlan had doted on his omega and seemed quite in love with her, sometimes to the exclusion of his care of the hills, or so the betas claimed.

Omega Feargus had died in the spring. Our alpha withered at the loss.

And now he had reunited with her.

My hands worked, rubbing strong circles around Maggie's ankle, turning her shin, stretching and soothing muscles that tended to want to tangle and tighten, shortening the old keep maid's stride. I wondered what it was like to have been so cherished by the alpha, to have held a man so tightly in one's grasp, shared him with no other. Sweat dripped between my breasts, and the salty, overripe scent of myself made me snort.

Omega Feargus had been a beautiful woman, with a black sheet of hair that draped down past her hips and warm brown skin that gleamed, always smiling up at the ruddy and redheaded bear of an alpha who beamed proudly at her side.

I was certainly no comparison for such a jewel of a woman. Perhaps I had been once, freshly of age, cheeks still full of youth, and smiles for everyone. But no, I had a beak for a nose—that had always been the case. The years had hardened and chipped away at me, my cheeks sharpening and hollowing, my body losing its softness for the strength it needed to survive...on my own.

"Who do you think it'll be next?" Maggie asked, her hands twisting in her lap.

"It hardly matters," I thought aloud, and then realized the source of Maggie's worry. "I'll fix you up, Mags. You know that keep like the back of your hand. Whoever rises, he'll see that straight away," I offered.

I wasn't sure that was true. The alpha's keep was huge, and Maggie was wearing herself down, running through its halls from morning to night. I doubted she was keeping up with the other humans she worked alongside, but it had been her home since she was a child. At the very least, it would break Maggie's heart to be cast aside. At worst, it might leave her homeless.

"Perhaps it'll be the little lord. He couldn't covet the role as alpha while his da lived, but now..." Maggie mused.

I smirked at the thought of Torion Feargus being referred to as "little" by anyone, let alone Maggie, who barely reached my own chin. But the alpha's son had likely been raised under Maggie's eye, and while he was a giant like his father now—and as handsome as his mother—I suppose he must've been a child once.

"Would he make a good alpha?" I asked Maggie, just to keep her talking.

"Aye, I think he might. Bit of a scamp, he is. But I think his heart still belongs to the hills, like his father's did before it caught sight of the omega."

"He'll have to take an omega himself," I pointed out. "Perhaps it will be captured then."

"Perhaps. But if she's a good girl from these parts, then...it won't be so bad."

I hummed indifferently. Some of the locals—especially the local dragonkin—had taken it personally when Lachlan had chosen an omega from outside the territory, and blamed her for our alpha's attention straying away from the care of the Hills. Personally, I thought men had a tendency to be inconsistent. Omega Feargus had just been lucky enough that it hadn't been *her* the alpha had lost interest in.

I SHIVERED as I rose from the river, wincing as I ran over the rocky edge and twiggy slope, up to the large boulder where I'd laid out my things. The dip had done me good, and not just because I'd started to smell. I'd grown indulgent with myself, cooped up in my cottage too long, forgetting what the sky looked like as I busied myself turning the last of my dried stores into salves and teas and tinctures. It would be time to start gathering new growth soon, and then I would be out of my cottage more than in, but it was past time for me to shake the winter bear off and remember how the world's embrace looked and smelled and felt.

I dried and dressed, taking my time on the rock to let its heat sink in and thaw the rousing chill of the river, lifting my face up to the sun, knowing the freckles that had faded would brighten again at the attention—freckles I'd worked so hard to hide when I was younger.

I was tying up my boots when the neigh of an indignant horse coming from beyond the brush froze me. Someone was at the cottage. The only reason for someone to arrive this close to evening was if it was an emergency, or if they were so at their own leisure that they didn't have to prepare someone else's dinner. And other dragonkin were rarely the folk who came to knock at my door.

A little bead of dread—the one I always carried with me— snarled and grew in size, zipping nervously from the pit of my stomach, racketing through my heart, and then lodging itself in my throat.

He would've traveled for the flight, I thought, worrying my lip between my teeth as I tried to double check every bit of me, from my soaked and tangled hair to the buttons rising up the back of my dress. Nothing I could do between here and my cottage would change the obvious. That my clothes were wearing thin, and there were lines creasing my forehead that never seemed to smooth away. That I was thirty-two, not seventeen, and my age had never mattered anyway. I'd never been beautiful enough, even at my best.

With a humph of irritation and a shake of my trembling hands, I marched toward the tangled brush of young oaks and snarling blackberries. There was a small opening marked with two rotting posts, just barely keeping the wild growth back enough for me to pass through, and I made it to the border of my property when the horse I'd heard rounded the corner of my cottage.

"Lightning," I greeted, and the proud white gelding warned me from my approach with a haughty head toss. "It's my house you're haunting," I volleyed back, forgetting my own nerves for a moment in the face of my old adversary.

"Brigid?" a muffled voice called from inside my cottage.

I stiffened. I supposed it was too much to hope that the horse had found its way to me without its master. I took a moment to brace myself, to steady my breath and harden my heart, to buck my chin high and refuse my gaze a wince, and then strode forward.

Malcolm had to duck to appear in my cottage doorway, so my first glimpse of him in three years was the crown of his head. There was new gray in his hair, and less hair overall. My heart was split in two at the sight—a petty glee burning brightly at the sight of him losing just a little of his perfection that I'd coveted for over a decade, and a darker, sweeter ache, the old fondness, the dreams I'd once savored of us aging together, of my maturity catching up to his in time.

He stood straight, and that small peek at his vulnerability vanished as he blocked the narrow, slightly crooked entrance to my home. He stared at me, a subtle appraisal, and I hid my quaking hands behind my back, knowing he would find more changes in me than I saw in him.

"You look well, omega," he greeted, low voice gentled to be tempting when I knew how well it could thunder with rage. His mouth quirked, but it wasn't a smile. "Still bathing in the river like a girl of sixteen?"

"What are you doing here, Malcolm?" I asked, relieved my voice was strong and clear. I wanted to retreat to the safety of my cottage but refused to step closer to him.

"The alpha passed this morning," he said.

"I heard."

He nodded, his slow, unending study of me making the hair rise on the back of my neck. "We voted to settle the matter. Tomorrow at dawn, we battle for a new alpha."

"I wish you luck," I said.

Malcolm's humored lines deepened at the corner of his eyes, and I ignored the pang of my old bruised heart. "You think I'll compete? Did I seem so ambitious while Lachlan reigned? So discontent?"

I opened my mouth to tell Malcolm all I had seen, his deep bows and the smiles that didn't reach his eyes, the way his fists clenched behind his back when he lied to our alpha's face, the way he used me roughly at night when he'd conceded to Lachlan's decisions. It was too much to share. It would've been like trying to tie our lives back together when I'd worked so hard to sever the false connection.

"Yes," I said instead, shrugging.

Malcolm laughed, but his eyes narrowed on me. "You always were too observant for your own good."

The words stung, just as he'd meant them to, and my eyes skidded away from him, flinching, before I could steel myself. He was likely right. I might be happier today if I'd failed to see what was going on under my nose. Perhaps I might still have some pride intact if I'd never discovered the other women. But there was no mistaking Malcolm's lack of feeling for me, and I'd fooled myself for as long as possible. A girl of sixteen was easy to charm. After ten years under the same roof, that woman of twenty-seven was a touch harder to fool.

At thirty-two, I was tired.

"I intend to fight," Malcolm said, and I nodded.

"You'll take a new omega," I said, meeting his eyes again. I didn't care now what he saw on my face—indifference or injury, it didn't matter. We would be done with another, well and truly.

His head tipped, and a cold trickling warning ran down

my spine. "If I rise, yes. But Lachlan's son will be a worthy opponent, as will the others."

I froze. "I've left, Malcolm. I'm not coming back. If you want another bed warmer for the rut—"

"I can find a new omega easily enough, Brigid. But this cottage is mine by your father's agreement—"

"It wasn't his to give! Not like that. She left it to *me*."

"And she left you to him. And he left you to me. And with you, the cottage. You signed the contract."

A trembling hand covered my stomach. I'd signed that contract at seventeen. Signed it before the cottage meant anything to me, before it was my sanctuary, my escape.

"Malcolm—" I started, but my voice was rasping, and I wasted time trying to clear the fear away.

"You can come home to me for the rut. Or you can give up your rights as my omega and vacate my property."

"You don't *want* the damn cottage!" I cried out, my temper snapping free.

Malcolm's eyebrows rose, and there was laughter hidden behind feigned sympathy as he stepped forward. My body swayed as I fought to keep still, to keep from rushing closer and drumming my fists against his chest, or running back to the river and diving deep, as if it might wash away the memory of him. It wouldn't. I feared nothing would.

"I don't, you're right. But it's a fine property and close to the alpha's keep. I could build myself a second home here, for myself and my omega, somewhere to stay. If I'm not the next alpha, I'll have work to put in once more. And if it's Lachlan's son, he's young. He'll appreciate an older influence." Malcolm approached, and I shook with the rage that would do nothing against him. I wasn't very tall, and while I was strong, he would always be stronger. "As you did, dear Brigid."

I'd been sweet once, a perfect daughter, an ideal omega, nearly lovely if not for a slightly ambitious nose. Malcolm had put his lips to me when I was sixteen, and he'd sucked my sweetness out as if I were a ripe orange, until I was only dry and tough and bitter.

I spat at him as he passed me, something an old washer women might do to keep a curse at bay, and he was too busy looking forward, smug humor written over his handsome face, to see the viscous glob land at his shoulder.

"You always enjoyed yourself, Brigid. There's no use claiming otherwise. And there's still a chance you might get with child. Third time's the charm—isn't that what they say?"

Malcolm was nearly to his horse, but I didn't wait for him to leave. I ran for my cottage, too low to be embarrassed, slamming the door behind me and feeling it shake on the hinges. I pinched my lips tight as my body started to jerk. My eyes squeezed shut, the ache of the pressure a distracting relief. But as the sound of horse hooves receded, I unleashed myself. A dark sob tore free of my throat, clawing through me as it escaped. I staggered toward the table at the center of the room but couldn't make it into the chair before my knees gave way. My fingernails dug into the wood grain as my mouth opened on a wail, a long, mourning sound for the love I'd lost, over and over again. The love Malcolm had fooled out of me once, twice, three times.

And the love I had cultivated in my most heartsore moments, the love that had grown in me, the love I could never bury or run from but must carry without a source, just the memory of an idea of the child I'd carried too briefly.

The child I'd sworn to bring into the world, and then failed. I wept for him and for myself, and vowed a single, certain thing.

I would not go back to Malcolm Barr.

Chapter Two

TORION

The air was thick with rich incense, but it mingled with another fragrance, sour and heavy and uncomfortably sweet—the rot of death shrouded in ceremony. My eyes were sore, fixed on the still figure in the bed, covered to his chest in a white sheet, body limp and sagging. My father had been *all* life, all movement, all laughter. Was I sitting vigil at his side, waiting for some hint of him to return, or reconciling myself with his absence? He'd been gone for hours now. This body, all that remained of him, bore no resemblance to the man I'd loved, respected...and sometimes resented.

A knock thudded softly at the door frame, and I moved slowly, taking in the massive figure that waited just outside my father's room. Waited and did not enter, because another alpha was not permitted at the deathbed of one so recently departed.

"You should've slept," Seamus de Roche, Alpha of the Craven Sea, called to me from the hall.

I braced my hands on the arms of the chair and lifted my

stiff body from its seat, swallowing the groan as my limbs and muscles resisted movement after so long in one place. I didn't need to prove him right.

"I'm sure I slept some," I said, my mouth dry and words cracking.

Seamus turned for the stairs, leaving room between us as I followed him, shutting the door to my father's suite behind me. It was too early for dawn and the hall was dark, but the candles by my father's bedside had burned out sometime in the night and my eyes were already adjusted. And I knew these halls well, knew the uneven trip of the steps down from the tower, knew the feel of the stone that grazed under my trailing fingertips.

"You don't have to do this, you know. You could buy a boat, join my fleet," Seamus said, wearing a half-hearted smile. He already knew my answer.

I'd spent a fair amount of time on the sea with my friend, avoiding my father's rut cycle with an extended stay on Seamus's ship, visiting as emissary and for fun. It would be an easier life to sail the sea under Seamus's rule than to try and establish my own here in Grave Hills. But this was my home, and while time with Seamus had always been enjoyable, there was still that slight pressure, the faint chafing, of being *below* someone. Seamus might offer me freedom on the sea, but he wouldn't step aside and let me rise as alpha in his stead.

This was my chance.

It could only have arrived on the heels of my father's death.

Seamus was right. I should've slept.

"Don't waste your breath turning me down," Seamus said as we reached the second story of the keep, the balcony that overlooked the great hall and front doors.

"It's more tempting than you might realize," I admitted.

"But it's not rising as alpha," Seamus said with a shrug. "I wouldn't give it up, either."

I nodded, even though in truth, I had no idea what it would mean, what it would feel like. I only knew that for decades now, my body had seemed too small, too tight; that I'd been stamping down the instinct to snarl at my father, to snap and challenge him. I loved him, loved the memories of him from my childhood, the gentle smiling man who had one arm around me and one around my mother, but as the years had passed and I'd grown, my love had been sprinkled with frustrations and the urge to push him forward or out of my way entirely.

The sorrow of his passing, so deep I already felt buried even before his grave had been dug, was tempered with an eager relief. Finally, there was room for me. I only had to claim it.

"Do you think I can do it?" The words appeared on my lips before I could stifle them, further proof that I'd spent the night sitting vigil and stuck in my head when I should've been resting and preparing for the battle to come.

Seamus clapped his hand on my shoulder and guided me to the stairs. "Only you can decide that. But for what it's worth, I think you'd make a good alpha. So does Cadogan. Worthington has said the same. When you rise, you'll have us in your corner."

When I rise.

I nodded and straightened, leading the way down the stairs, stopping at a familiar old face as it exited the kitchen. "Get me water and coffee."

"Yes, milord, and breakfast?" the old woman asked.

I shook my head, not sure I'd be able to keep food down this morning. Certainly not in the fight to come.

Seamus cleared his throat. "Speak for yourself. I'll take a

heap of breakfast." I glared at him, and he only grinned. "A good alpha is generous to his guests, my friend."

I rolled my eyes and found an open spot between tables to do my morning stretches, ignoring the alpha's lazy, large frame as he dropped into a chair by the fire.

I RELEASED a burst of fire in the face of the dragon whose snarling maw tried to catch me by the ankle. He screeched and turned away, barreling into another beta on its way to me.

Damn cowards.

Beating my wings hard, I turned in the air and searched the sky, surrounded by rivals. I'd grounded two betas so far, smallish dragons who had no business being in this fight. There was only one dragon worth fighting.

My eyes narrowed, and I let out a roar that thundered through me, lifting my chest and swiping out at the first beta who neared, my patience wearing thin enough to draw blood against a foe who was no foe at all.

Distractions. They were all distractions. Betas with no chance of surviving as alpha, swarming me, *wasting my time*, as the only true potential threat waited just out of reach. It was a smart ploy. Annoying and impotent as these dragons were, they were still dragons. There were a half dozen of them to one of me. I'd been lucky so far not to have them all manage to hit me at once, to whittle away their numbers. No doubt, the large rusty brown dragon waiting for his turn expected them to wear me out and make me easier to down when it came time for us to fight.

Malcolm Barr, I'll remember you after I rise, I vowed.

His plan might work, but it showed me just how scared of me he was. Unfortunately, it also proved that he had allies.

Allies he'd been forming behind my father's back—a risk I'd never been willing to take.

A jaw caught me by my tail, rousing me from my musings. There was a simple way of settling this. If these other betas were here to assist Malcolm, they would fall away when he was defeated. I let the dragon's jaws hold me as I swept my wings up, losing the air resistance and dropping hard and straight down. The yank on his bite burned, but I was stronger, heavier, and I'd caught the beta by surprise, pulling him along with my fall as we vanished from the circle I'd been trapped in.

I was released, the dragon who'd had hold of me scrambling to gain air, but I flipped in the air, rising to catch him by his belly, drawing blood. I was done being polite. If it took blood to ground these dragons, then blood they would have.

I *would* be their alpha.

Turning in midair once more, I released the dragon in my talons, sparing a brief breath to watch it flail on its way down to the ground, unable to catch air, before narrowing my frame and racing toward my quarry. To his credit, Malcolm's dark dragon didn't race away at my approach. Perhaps even to him, that would be too clear a sign of cowardice. He'd bought what time he could for himself. Now we would see which of us was stronger.

It would be me. I'd come to this battle determined but reserved. I would do what I had to to claim my position as the alpha, but this game they'd devised against me had shattered unknown reservations. Now I *relished* their defeat, a new brilliant heat burning in my chest, my wings broadening to keep height and then snapping back for momentum. Malcolm was flying to meet me, but my sudden speed made him falter—a moment of consideration as he decided whether or not to allow the collision. The moment was too much.

I had no hesitation, no fear for myself, as I crashed into him, tail and talons swiping, knocking us out of flight and into descent. Malcolm roared, flashing fire at my shoulder, and it bounced off my scales back into his own snout. He scratched at my belly, and I ignored the searing sensation. I might bleed, but I *would* rise.

The ground rushed up toward us, and Malcolm twisted frantically. His dragon was huge, as big as mine, and he was able to jerk us but not turn us over completely. On our sides, neither one of us was able to stop the race of our descent. If we hit the ground, we would both fail in our goal.

Malcolm tore himself free of me with a scream, turning fast, trying to gain air again when we were barely above the ground, giving me his back.

I was already starting my own flight, curling my tail up under my belly before it could disqualify, stretching forward, reaching for him.

My jaw snapped on his wing, tearing through tough hide, gouging ruthlessly, ripping it open. I clawed my way up his back, scratching at every step, forcing him lower, his injured wing weakening his flight. I braced myself on top of him, crouched, and then leapt, pushing him below me as I rose up into the air. I kept my head high, my body streaking back into the sky as I listened to his roar of defeat, the thunderous collision of his body against the craggy hills below.

I BRISTLED at Francis Keane's hearty laugh in my ear and forced myself not to flinch as he clapped a hand on my shoulder, my eyes scanning the tent. Malcolm Barr had gritted out his congratulations to me and had no qualms about leaving the celebration early, but some of his little helpers were doing their best to make up to me now. I was sick to death of it.

Even Worthington was getting on my nerves. Had he always been so patronizing?

"Indeed, Lachlan's lad will follow in his footsteps well," Keane said, too cheerily.

"I have my own footsteps in mind," I bit out.

Keane just chuckled. "Of course you do, my boy, of course you do."

I opened my mouth to remind Keane exactly who I was now—his *alpha*—when someone knocked into me from behind.

My snarl escaped before I could stop myself, but when I spun to face the man, I found de Roche winking at me. "Pardon me. Bit of drink?"

I rolled my shoulders out but made sure not to sigh with relief.

"A toast," Damian Worthington declared.

"No toast," I said, holding up my hand but not turning back to the man. "But a dram, yes."

Unable to make a scene of it, Keane and Worthington turned to one another, making it easy for me to retreat to the edge of the tent with de Roche.

"I've got my men on a bit of a plot to get the others out of here," Seamus murmured in my ear.

I opened my mouth to ask what kind of plot but decided it was better not to know, as long as it *worked*. I was sick to death of the pomp. I'd thought I'd be excited at my success, but instead, I found myself impatient to move on from celebrating. There was work to be done, and damn, but did I need to *sleep*.

Ronson Cadogan, Alpha of Bleake Isle just a flight north of here, rose from a high backed chair to face us. He'd seemed tense today, and I'd started to worry he might have changed his mind out of favor of supporting me, but he greeted me with a wry smile.

"Ready to tear your own skin off yet?" he asked.

I let out a rough breath. "How'd you know?"

He shrugged. "It's how it feels. It will settle eventually. After the rut, if not sooner."

I accepted the glass from Seamus, and Ronson raised his own, black eyes glinting with dark humor. "To your rise, Alpha. And all the trouble it brings with it."

I didn't care about the trouble. I drank deep with them.

Chapter Three
BRIGID

I watched the dragons in the air from a safe distance away, hidden under a large pine, my breath caught in my throat and my hand pressing hard over my heart as a pair of massive forms wrestled in the air, a bright flash of blood bursting and glittering in the sunlight. My fate was tangled up in those two dragons, and it didn't seem fair that they were there in the air, together, without a thought of me —because I was sure Malcolm's mind wasn't sparing a worry over his wayward omega in this moment—and I must simply stand on the ground, watching and waiting.

At least I didn't have long to wait. A glimmer of bitter rust went crashing to the ground, and the other dragon, the Feargus son, dark as pine needles in winter, rose into the air with a roar and a burst of fire.

It was wrong to be sorry that Malcolm had failed. He'd make a terrible alpha, and in spite of his threats, I was likely no safer if he rose than if he tried to take my cottage from me. It was just the only hope I had of keeping my home. Now that hope was gone.

I caught a ragged breath, crossing my shawl around my

front and tying it behind my waist, then started marching forward. The alpha's keep was still a good hour's hike away, and I would need to speak to him before morning if I had any hope for myself, my future, my *freedom*.

I hoped Maggie was right. I hoped Lachlan Feargus's son would make a good alpha. But even that might not mean he would help me.

<hr>

I STARTLED in the large chair at the sound of footsteps approaching, a masculine grunt and a soft laugh following. My eyes blinked at the large fire in front of me, my head shaking. Had I fallen asleep in the alpha's keep, or had I just been sitting here so long, in the quiet and the dark and the heat of the fire, that I'd sunk into some kind of trance?

There was a man all but falling through the cracked doors of the keep, tipping forward and then stumbling upright. I wrinkled my nose at the scent of whisky, gassy and sharp. I'd never liked the smell of it, nor the nights when Malcolm came to bed stinking of the stuff.

The man chuckled, a low, warm sound, and then righted himself, straightening so perfectly, walking forward in such a direct line, you might never have known he was drunk, except for the smell and the lazy hood of his eyes. Dark eyes, dark curling hair, and broad, brown shoulders. Lachlan Feargus's son, and now...

"Alpha." The title came out of me roughly, surprised and foggy from the long day of traveling here and then sitting still by the fire.

For a moment, Torion Feargus seemed to not have heard me at all, busy heaving the heavy doors of the keep shut behind him on his own, his bare shoulders flexing in such a show of strength that I lowered my eyes in reflex before deciding I'd rather watch. Then he stiffened and turned, eyes searching the room in uneven sweeps twice before finally finding me. He stepped, swayed again, and then corrected.

He was huge and handsome and entirely unsober. I found myself tongue tied at the sight of him and also at the reckoning of what I'd done, what I'd come here to do. But I *was* here already. And the new Alpha of Grave Hills was staring at me, waiting for me to speak...or perhaps trying to decide if he should know who I was. I could run out the doors now, and he might forget about the strange woman who'd been standing in his keep the night of his rise as alpha. I would lose my cottage. Or I would lose what was left of my heart and my freedom back in Malcolm's house.

I stepped forward and, as if in unison, the alpha and I both took a breath, his lids a little heavier for a moment in an almost desirous look. Then he frowned and blinked, his head tipping as he studied me from top to bottom.

I resisted the urge to squirm. "My name is Brigid Grant."

His frown deepened, lines carving over his smooth forehead, and all at once he looked less like a young wayward son of the Hills and more like what he was—the alpha. A power and heat radiated from him, one I could almost taste on the back of my tongue, a shivery warmth running down my back.

"Malcolm Barr's omega," he said, the words dark and sharp, his eyes narrowing at me.

My own jaw hardened, fists balling at my side as I lifted my chin. "I was. I have been. For several years, I've been living in a property my mother left to me—a cottage just to the southwest of here. The property backs up to the river."

He was moving suddenly, every step seeming to move the stone floor beneath us, shrinking the room as he grew closer, swallowing up the light of the fire into his dark wings, all of it glinting back in his stare. I never lost my ground, not even when Malcolm came to the cottage, but I fell back a step reflexively, and he paused. "Did he send you?" the alpha snarled.

"He? Malcolm?! Fang's fire, no," I spat out, dizzy with the accusation.

The alpha was quiet for a moment but continued before I could gather myself to speak. "Then you want me to intercede on your behalf? Demand Barr takes you back into his home?" he asked.

"No—" I snapped, and my hand covered my belly at the nausea that suddenly gathered there. It was a reasonable question. It wasn't uncommon for betas to evict a chosen omega from the home when they felt the woman no longer had any chance of bearing them a son. I swallowed down a bitter flavor at the idea that I was so past my prime. Certainly I would be no prize at a choosing ceremony, but plenty of women my age had delivered sons and daughters.

I cleared my throat and glanced down to the floor, hands rising and crossing to hold my elbows, trying to still the shaking in my hands. "That is to say, yes, I want you to intercede, but I don't want back in Malcolm's home. Quite the opposite. My mother's cottage was included in the contract my father drafted. Malcolm demands my return for the—" I didn't want to speak of the rut, but I didn't have to. The alpha nodded for me to continue, his stare still too keen to meet, too clear, considering he'd entered the keep swerving drunkenly about. If this was him drunk, he'd be a terror of intensity sober. I shook myself and continued, "He says if I don't, he'll evict me from the cottage and take a new omega."

A soft growl snarled through the air, and I was surprised by the small burst of heat in my belly at the sound. The alpha cleared his throat, and the sound vanished.

"Do you have the contract?" he asked in a milder tone.

I thrust a tightly rolled paper between us, darkened with age and wrinkled with my own frustrated attempts to make sense of my situation. He reached to take it, and for a moment my grip tightened. What I was doing would have consequences. Even if I succeeded, even if the alpha stepped in—*especially* if he did—Malcolm would be furious.

"It's late," I rasped out, wishing I could turn back the hours, that I might remain ignorant in my cottage, as if none of this would matter by morning. "I didn't think, there's just—"

"You won't be evicted from your home," Alpha Feargus said.

The words drummed through me, beautifully certain, a reassurance and a command all in the same statement. I straightened myself. I was not a coward, and I forced my shoulders to relax, surrendering the contract to the alpha. I meant to move away, to leave the keep perhaps, but I found myself meeting the alpha's stare. He had a surprisingly warm gaze, shades of copper and chocolate. He seemed to surround me, even from an arm's reach away, and once more I was in a kind of trance, one of safety and heat.

"How far did you travel to get here?" he asked, his words rousing me.

I blinked and tore my eyes from his, the heat I'd felt a moment ago now rising up into my cheeks. "I'm just an hour's ride from the keep," I said, and I tried to smooth my skirts, hide my worn and dirty boots from the long walk here. If I'd had a horse, it would've been an hour's journey. On foot, it had taken all morning and some of the afternoon.

His eyes narrowed, not missing a detail. "The night is too late now, even for an *hour's ride*. And you might've guessed from the state I was in when I walked in, there's been revelry outside of the keep. Many betas are still outside, and not in their best behavior. We'll find a room for you," he said, and I opened my mouth to refuse but wasn't given a chance to speak. "I'll have a solution to your problem in the morning."

I crossed my arms over my chest and glared up at him, because glaring reminded me not to fall back into the hypnotism of his gaze. "By 'the state you're in,' I'll assume you mean the whisky you reek of."

He grinned, and it took all my control not to lose my breath. Boyish beauty and charm struck me hard in the form of a man who towered over and around me, who swallowed up light and warmth and then shone it back at me.

"Good whisky," he corrected before subduing his smile, but not the brightness in his eyes. "You came to your alpha, Brigid Grant. You're my responsibility now. Come." He held his hand out to me, not touching, but offering to guide.

His confidence was a horrible temptation. I reminded myself that he was drunk tonight, cheerful on the success of his rise as alpha. In the morning, he would recall this vow to me, an omega who'd been seemingly discarded by her beta, and decide it might be better to wash his hands of me. But it was late. And Malcolm might be outside the keep. I stepped into his wing, caught the brief sound of his breath, and then we moved together toward the stairs.

The keep was old, had been here for many generations of dragons, but I'd been here once years ago with Malcolm, and it'd been busy and full of life, gleaming and ancient and proud. Sometime in the past decade or so it had started to show its age, dusty tapestries hanging from the balcony wall, a cobweb here and there.

Alpha Feargus hailed a maid on the upper floor, and she scowled for a moment before approaching us.

"Show Omega Grant to a guest room," he said, and then seemed to consider something for a moment before leaning in with more authority. "I trust you to know which might be best ready. She'll need a fire, and fresh water for bathing."

"That's not—"

"Did you eat?" he asked.

I wet my lips, prepared to lie and say I had a full meal. Maggie had managed to smuggle me scraps at least.

"Some food as well. There should be plenty left over from the feast," he said.

"Of course, milord," the maid said, not looking at all pleased with her assignment of me. I had a feeling my water would be cold and my food thin, but since I hadn't expected either, I didn't mind.

"Goodnight then," the alpha said, with a sort of silly smile on his face and a bow that wobbled.

I sighed, realizing the man was too good at faking sober, and that meant there was no real promise for what would happen in the morning. "Goodnight, Alpha."

He stood straight at that, his eyes darkening, his body seeming to swell, the word conjuring the reality out of him. For a moment, his hand twitched at my back, finally touching, almost grabbing. Little pinpoints of heat appeared on my spine. And then he stepped away, turning in the opposite direction of us, heavy wings in shadow turning the hallway into a black void.

"This way, if you please, madam," the maid said reluctantly, and with a bit of impatience.

My fate was up in the air, spinning wildly in front of me, and I had even less of an idea of where it might land in the morning than I had before coming here. There would be no sleep for me tonight, but there would be a bed at least. I followed the maid to a musty but otherwise fairly decent guest room, the sound of men's shouting voices from outside the small window convincing me to stay. I would wait and see what the new alpha might have in store for me.

Chapter Four
TORION

I glared back at the sun streaming through my bedroom window, far too high in the sky for my body to feel so leaden and my eyes so wooly. I needed to give the keep staff new instructions to wake me earlier. As the alpha's son, it had been easy enough to get away with sleeping until I woke naturally. Now there was too much to be done, too much that my father had let slip off his plate after my mother's death.

First and foremost, however, I had to deal with the matter of the omega in my keep. A hazy vision rose from the night before—a petite woman in shabby, too large homespun clothing, but with clear bright eyes, handsome features, and a heavy braid shining like a ruby in the firelight. I scrubbed my hand over my unshaven jaw, thinking of the woman. She'd been prickly and sharp and nervous, and every word she said had sobered my mind with a new, unfamiliar urgency to *act*. I'd thought at first she might've been another trap set by Barr, but the spiteful way she'd spoken of him had been too convincing. She needed my help. As alpha, it was my duty to do something for her.

That was the cause for my determination, naught else. I was alpha now, and it was my responsibility.

It had nothing to do with that first breath of her, a fresh scent, like a clear day in the hills, the sharp promise of rain in the air, and then a deeper sweetness, a syrupy and yet almost savory note, like molasses. She smelled like the very definition of home.

The problem of the land dispute might be simple enough, provided good land was all Malcolm was really coveting. I could negotiate a parcel for him on his terms. But there was spite in the position he'd put his omega in, and that spoke of a more complicated twist. I wanted the woman away from his machinations, but that would mean putting another woman, probably a younger one, in his way.

I rolled away from the sun with a groan, planting my hands in my bed to rise up, when the sound of a distant male shout, nearly a bark, echoed through the keep and to my door. With a cold shock of warning, I leapt from the bed, scrambling into a pair of leather trousers—there wasn't time to wrap my plaid—and throwing open the door, nearly scaring a maid into dropping a jug of water.

"Who is that downstairs?" I asked, snapping the words a little too hard.

The maid gaped at me, and I shook my head, pushing past her.

"A local beta, my lord. His omega is—"

Brigid Grant. It didn't matter how drunk I'd been—fairly, but not terribly—her name was as clear and firm in my mind as her voice had been, as the hard little tip of her chin as she'd stared stubbornly back at me.

I ran down the stairs, the stone hard under my bare feet, cold morning air nipping at my bare chest.

"Going behind my back—"

"You cannot take my home from me, Malcolm!"

The beta snarled something too low to hear in answer just as I made it to the balcony that overlooked the great room. There were a few betas that lived near the keep watching the scene, watching the large man reach for Brigid Grant, her spine stiff as she leaned back but refusing to give quarter by stepping away from him.

All at once, the worst and simplest solution rose up in me. The idea I'd toyed with and rejected a half dozen times in the night before falling asleep with it rooted in my imagination.

"I know you aren't about to touch my omega, Malcolm Barr."

The room stilled into a tableau of outraged shock, every man and maid freezing in place, aside from one. Brigid stepped out of reach of the beta who'd berated her, moving toward the stairs. I took slow steps to meet her, keeping my eyes on Barr, pleased with the silence of her acquiescence.

"Alpha Feargus," Barr said, turning my name into a curse. Someone had tended the scratch my dragon had delivered to his right wing, plastering it to give it time to heal. He wasn't up for another fight with me. "Brigid may not have been at my side at recent events, but you cannot be unaware—"

"You cannot be unaware that the alpha has the right to take the omega he chooses. Whoever she may be," I said, descending the stairs.

Of course, it would be akin to declaring war to claim another man's omega.

"I have not lived under your roof for five years," Brigid murmured.

Malcolm raised a brow and glared at her. "In fact of contract, you have."

"In fact of contract, that roof now belongs to me," I said, raising the signed papers in the air. "'And to whomever she is bound, she brings with her the assets left to her.'"

There was more, and I wondered if Brigid had seen it

there, or if she'd taken Malcolm at his word. Her freedom was nearly in the contract. It would take someone to argue her case, but it was possible.

My current solution was simpler.

Barr's upper lip curled with menace, but he focused that stare on Brigid rather than me. He'd always been obsequious with my father, and that facade was failing to stand in the face of this betrayal. Which was what this was. I wasn't a fool. He probably thought I was doing it out of spite for the way he'd orchestrated the other betas against me in the battle yesterday. For that reason alone, I'd searched for a different solution, knowing too well how much it would cost me with my new position to steal an omega away from one of the betas. It wouldn't please the other men for me to appear so pettily vengeful on the back of a victory.

"She's barren," Barr spat out.

Then again, he's a bastard, I thought, all remorse vanishing.

Brigid flinched, a sharp catch of breath and a faltering step. But I'd reached the main floor, reached her, and as she swayed back, I caught her waist in my hand. For a moment, her weight leaned into me, surrendering. Smug, dark satisfaction unfurled through me, my wings spreading around us.

This was a terrible plan. I'd have Barr and the other betas at my throat for years at least, a clear line drawn between us. I'd fight them tooth and nail for every proposal I issued.

It was right too. Brigid gathered herself once more, body lean but strong, and made no move to pull away from me.

"Then you will have the opportunity to find a more fruitful partner," she said, chin lifting. She had a long, graceful throat, and she hadn't replaced the shawl tucked into her dress this morning, so the lines and shadows of her clavicle were on display, elegant and a little too pronounced.

"We can discuss land. There are—" I started, knowing any consolation would be too belated an offer now.

The beta growled, hands fisting at his side and jaw working under the heavy dark beard. "Keep your pity parcels. I'll keep my anger, *Alpha* Feargus. Don't show weakness now, not when you led with force."

I restrained my sigh as the older man turned to the door.

"Good riddance to you, Brigid Grant," he called back.

She turned toward me at the insult, face too blank to be unaffected. I let my low growl echo across the stones of the hall.

I took in the state of the room. There were five other betas, and only one left with Malcolm Barr, both northerners. Barr had been obnoxiously loyal to my father, but the other man had often been a dissenting opinion, arguing against the few reforms my father raised. Seeing them together told me enough of my suspicions of Barr.

"Wait here," I told the other men, two of whom looked wary but nodded. The third, an old competitor of my father's, settled into a chair with an amused expression.

Brigid responded to the slightest nudge of my fingers on her back, and we turned up the stairs together as if we were of one mind. My father's office was at the end of the far wing, underneath his old suite. I took her there, closing the door behind us, pausing in place at the sight of one of my mother's colorful shawls still draped over the back of my father's chair. I should've buried it with him, but I was grateful to see it here now. I'd mourned her loss too, although my own feelings seemed pale in the wake of my father's grief.

"You didn't think that through," Brigid said, pulling away from me at last, turning to face me. She stood with the sun at her back, igniting her hair, outlining her slender frame. I didn't understand the immense force of her allure, but it rang down to my bones all the same.

"I did," I said, leaving out that I'd decided against it until the sudden impulse that struck while seeing her at Malcolm's mercy.

She turned her face, lifting her chin, putting that strong nose in profile. "Then you should know I'm not barren."

I took in a deep breath. "I've no intention of—" Now that we were alone, I could explain the clause in the contract.

Brigid folded her arms in front of her and shook her head. "You can't claim me in front of them like that and then set me loose. It's one thing to wield your power to take what you want, and quite another to do it solely to spite a beta."

I raised an eyebrow. "That's what I've done, though."

Her lips twisted in a bitter frown. "That's what they suspect, but you'll make them sure of it if you turn around and find another omega after dropping me. I can give you a son. I made sure Malcolm Barr's home was the most hospitable in all the Hills, including your father's keep. I'm a good omega. The only way they'll ever forgive you, ever trust and respect you, is if they believe you claimed me because you *wanted* to."

I fought my smile. She'd called herself a good omega, but I was fairly sure that direct speech would've persuaded most of Grave Hill's betas to keep her out of their homes.

"But I want daughters," she continued, stiffening to raise herself taller. I leaned back against my father's desk, crossing my ankles in front of me, and watched her eyes flick to my bare chest. "I want to raise my children. If I agree to stay as your omega—"

Don't laugh, Torion.

"—you'll promise not to toss me out, cut me from their lives. And the cottage will go to the girls."

"By my count, we're having three children?" I asked, unable to resist teasing the woman.

"At least," she answered baldly.

I understood the cause of the heat in my loins at her

answer. Brigid Grant was an attractive woman with a scent I wanted to bathe in, and she was asking—no, demanding—to be bred. Plentifully.

I'd expected—and slightly dreaded—the prospect of choosing an omega. Ronson Cadogan had avoided choosing his own for decades, afraid of showing favor to the wrong family too soon in his reign. It'd bit him in the ass, making him look weak and indecisive. I wouldn't make that mistake, but I understood his reticence. He had one now, at last, and I wondered if she'd bossed him into it the way this woman was doing with me.

Because Brigid was right—I'd look both an idiot and a petty ruler if I yanked an omega out from one of the men who'd fought me for position as alpha, and then turned around and claimed an entirely different woman.

Especially when this one was strong, confident, and powerfully appealing.

"This is what you want?" I asked.

Brigid let out a sound that was meant to be a laugh, and in it I heard all the nerves, the fear she'd hidden so well. "I wanted my cottage, my life there, the peace I thought I'd been promised when Malcolm let me leave his house. But you aren't the only one he'll take this out on. I need your protection. And you need *me*."

I should've been ashamed of the truth that she spelled out so clearly. Instead, I was itching to reach for her, to draw her against me and coax her into telling me again how many children she wanted me to give her.

The promise of a son was a dangerous offer from an omega. Birthing a dragon's wings could cost a woman her life, and for all I knew, Barr had been telling the truth and she was lying to me.

I didn't particularly care. The fun was in the effort of

production, and it was a prospect I'd let myself entertain last night before I'd fallen asleep.

"Then you are mine, Omega Feargus," I declared.

She blinked at that, going pale, and then flushed. Her arms dropped to her sides, stunned, as if it was all occurring to her at once too. If Barr had hurt her in the past, or she showed any qualms in being intimate, I would find another solution, I realized. I wanted the bossy little queen in my bed, but I wouldn't drag a desperate woman looking for safety there.

"Good. Good. Then I'll speak to the staff," she said, transforming once more under my gaze, shoulders drawn back and hands smoothing at her skirt.

"The staff?" I asked.

"There'll be a nest to build, order to establish. My cottage..." She trailed off, scanning the room, then darting around the desk.

I stood, watching her take control of the space, sliding easily into my father's seat.

I had allies with other alphas in other regions, but any I might've established here in the Hills would've looked like a preemptive move against my father. I would need an advisor, or at least men who trusted me, who could speak with other betas.

"I'll need some of my things," she continued, wetting a quill and marking her full bottom lip with a line of ink in the process.

"I ought to send someone to keep an eye on it, make sure Barr doesn't retaliate," I said. Her eyes widened, and she nodded.

"And someone to let the patients who come to see me know where I am now."

"Patients?" I echoed, studying her, perversely pleased with the way her attention refused to turn back to me.

"I'm...something of a healer," she muttered, scratching words over a loose sheet of paper. How had a woman who claimed to keep a perfect house for one of the Hill's most prominent betas become 'something of a healer'?

I would need others on my side, it was true. But at least I found myself with an assertive omega. It was a start.

Chapter Five

BRIGID

What have I done?

I chewed on the corner of my thumbnail, counting the bricks in the wall in front of me, until a steaming roll appeared in front of my face. Queasy as I was, I snatched it from the gnarled hand that held it and took a rough bite, chewing frantically.

What have I done? I wondered once more. *Nothing*, a stronger voice reminded me. This was *his* decision, his bold declaration in front of a half dozen betas from Grave Hills. His madcap plan that I couldn't really believe he'd considered thoroughly, in spite of his claim.

And then I'd encouraged him, promising him *children*, demanding years at his side!

What have I done?

"What a stroke of luck this is, lovey," Maggie declared, patting my hand as I tore the roll to little pieces, stuffing them into my mouth one by one until my cheeks were swollen. "That you should be Grave Hills' omega. And a fine one you'll be for the lad."

Lad. As if the enormous man, devastatingly attractive, brooding one moment and smirking gently the next, could be called a *lad.*

Alpha Feargus. *Torion,* I corrected myself, because "Alpha Feargus" brought to mind his father, and aside from their size, they bore little resemblance.

I had told that man I would bed him. Not so directly, but it'd been implied when I'd demanded several children, of course. And he'd...agreed.

'Then you're mine.'

Fang's fire, what have I done?

I'd come to the keep yesterday wanting to plead for the alpha's intervention, *not his bed.* But I'd arrived too early, left sitting in the great hall with barely a word from any of the servants who passed me. I'd had to beg for water and a bite to eat from Maggie, and still, I'd waited hours longer. Long enough to grow tired and forget my entire speech I'd prepared.

Instead, I'd found myself startled by the new alpha, handsome and young and warm with that cheerfully loose way of men who'd been drinking. I'd stammered out a request and been tucked into what must've been a fine guest room at one point, but was now dusty. And then when I'd tried to leave this morning, too embarrassed by the turn of events, I'd run into Malcolm, who'd known immediately what my presence in the keep meant.

"It's likely too soon to say so, but his old lordship had a little too much mind for his wife and not enough for the keep, let alone the Hills," Maggie continued in her ramble, the speech rousing me from my panic.

"Mags," I chided, glancing around the room. We weren't exactly alone in the kitchens, but the other staff were certainly keeping their distance.

From me.

Because I was their alpha's omega now. And I was *hiding* in the kitchens like a servant who'd been scolded.

"You're just a practical girl, if you don't mind me saying. And he's an eager lad, was always trying to bend his father's ear about some local problem or the other. You'll be a good pair for us," Maggie murmured.

Her speech was a little too familiar, now that my position had changed, but I was grateful because it was just what I needed to hear. There was work to be done, and I was accustomed to work. I gathered up the crumbs from the table and then straightened my skirts. I'd worn my best to see the alpha, but my best was from the time before I'd left Malcolm and was now worn enough to be serviceable to the day.

"Right. Show me the worst of it, Mags," I said, taking my shawl from my shoulders and wrapping it around my waist.

"We'll start with the cook," Maggie hissed in my ear, and I flinched.

"Second worst, in that case," I whispered back, eyeing the brawny old man pounding a cut of meat with a mallet in the corner of the room.

Maggie snickered and led me out of the kitchen. "Better give you a look at the linens."

THE LINENS HAD BEEN LEFT to molder, the wool blankets were moth eaten, the pantry and stables were both infested with mice, and there was a hole in the roof that was leaking into two of the guest rooms. Thankfully, not mine.

"I don't understand," I said to Maggie hours later as I watched men and women racing across the main floor and past me in the upper halls. "There's plenty of staff."

"Been no supervision, has there?" Maggie said with a shrug. "Not since the housekeeper left after the lady herself died."

The housekeeper had come to Grave Hills with Lachlan's omega, and had apparently been quite eager to leave after her mistress's passing. With no direction from the alpha in mourning, there was no one to replace her, not in any official capacity. The cook kept the kitchen and the stables managed themselves, but no one had offered to rise up in the maids. In fact, near as I could tell, most of the maids seemed to go to great lengths to undermine one another.

I glanced out of the corner of my eye at Maggie, who was looking smugly and cheerfully down at the activity of the keep. She'd dragged me from top to bottom, and while she was starting to look a little worn and her limp was showing more than it had at the start of the morning, she seemed bright-eyed and flushed with renewed energy.

"Could you manage them, Mags?" I asked gently.

I halfway expected the woman to jump at the chance, but she frowned at the question and gave it a good time to mull over.

"I expect I could. I've been a maid for two alphas and their omegas now, seen the keep at its best, I think. You'll find someone better suited to the work soon enough, but I won't shy from helping now."

I sighed and nodded. "Get us through the rut, at least," I said, and she hummed in agreement. "Bring any argument to me until they know better than to not listen to you."

I wasn't sure how long it would take for Torion's rut to take hold. He'd only just taken the mantle of alpha, and the general idea was that a new alpha was vulnerable for a time until their first rut, when the power truly set in. It was also said that a good omega could bring a rut on faster.

I wasn't sure what constituted a good omega, in spite of

my claims to Torion that I was one. I'd been told I was when I was young—pretty and sweet and raised to manage a fine house. And for a time, Malcolm had shown himself as pleased with me, certainly long enough to woo and choose me, to rut me. But I imagined a good omega would be able to keep her beta's attention, keep him from straying to other women's company.

I knew better than to assume faithfulness now, but I had wrought the promise of children to love and a home to share with them from the alpha.

Maybe not *wrought*, I thought. He hadn't seemed to have any reservations when it came to agreeing to the deal.

Which was even more suspicious. If I'd asked him to keep only my company in bed, he'd no doubt have had more objections to give. Which is why I hadn't asked. Expecting indifference from the alpha was better than having my heart seduced by Malcolm once more. Having it broken again.

"I'd like to see the alpha's quarters. I have a nest to plan," I said, turning my mind back to the present.

Maggie smacked her lips and nodded, but asked, "Do you mean where he sleeps now, or where the alpha's meant to sleep?"

A strange flare of panic rose up in me, and I tamped it down quickly. "Meant to," I said. It was no business of mine where the alpha was sleeping. I'd promised him a son, and that meant we'd have to wait for his rut to arrive for any proper bedding to commence.

Malcolm had blamed our not waiting on why I'd failed to conceive a child during our first rut together. And I'd never told him the second had been a success, however briefly.

I followed Maggie down a central hallway and then up a spiraling set of stairs. There were two doors at the top landing, and she opened the one on the right.

As a heavy, oily scent hit my nose, mineral and dark, I

realized what Maggie had meant when she said this was where the alpha, Torion, should be sleeping. This was his father's room. It was thick with an unpleasantly rich odor and lingering traces of something cloyingly sweet, like honeysuckle.

"Needs a bit of dusting," Maggie said.

Which was certainly true, with dust motes shining and passing by tall, sunny windows. It was a beautiful, large room, but I itched to back out the door. Being here with Torion would be too uncomfortable, the scents too strong. I couldn't build a nest here.

"It needs washed top to bottom." And I wasn't sure even that would do the trick. I backed up as I spoke and then jumped as a warm and heavy pair of hands settled on my shoulder.

"No." The word was hard, and Maggie, who'd ventured deeper into the space than I could stand to, startled with a squawk.

I took a deep breath, expecting to brace against anger, and instead found myself unwinding slightly. Which was concerning on its own.

"Not yet," Torion Feargus said from behind us.

"No," I agreed, keeping my own voice gentle as I turned. The alpha was close, my shoulders hitting the solid strength of his forearm. He had a shirt on now, loose and dirty at the cuffs, covering the broad expanse of bronze muscle he'd been showing when he'd claimed me in front of Malcolm and several others. The muscle I'd done my best to ignore as I'd bargained out a life with him.

"No, we won't touch this room yet," I said, soothing the words.

The tension that revealed the brutal strength of the alpha in this man—a man who transformed so quickly from lackadaisical to intent, mercurially serious and then youthfully impulsive—eased slightly. He backed out of the doorway, and I followed the urging of his hand gratefully.

"I know it will have to be done at some point," he said, frowning.

"Perhaps we could...open the windows for a few hours each day?" I suggested.

For a moment, he grimaced, and I opened my mouth to dismiss my own words. "That would help, yes," he said, looking to Maggie over my shoulder. "Not when it's raining."

"'Course not," she said carelessly, hurrying over to a window.

He turned away, the hand on my left shoulder sliding down and taking hold of my own hand. His was warm and large, heavy as an anchor. "You've been busy," he said bracingly.

I hesitated, wetting my lips, ducking my head as we turned in a slow circle down the flight of stairs.

"It's good," he said, not waiting for my answer. "I've been out, checking on the flock and cattle. Too much has been left untouched since my mother's passing. How are you with numbers?"

My head reeled at the way his speech seemed to turn from one subject to the next.

"I've kept household books in good order," I said, not mentioning Malcolm's name.

"I expected as much," he said, flashing me a wry smile over his shoulder. I caught myself before my slippered foot missed a step. "Careful, every sixth is shorter. It's meant to be defensive, but I think it causes more injuries to those of us in the keep than any who might try and invade it."

You are a little too handsome for your own good, I thought. Or at least for *my* own good.

But attraction made the prospect of the rut easier to face. In fact... I ducked my head to hide my blush. I could look forward to the rut. Malcolm was right that I'd enjoyed myself in bed with him. Heartbreak had soured the memories, but sometimes, I craved faceless company to help me revisit those moments safely. I'd lain awake plenty of nights on my own, daydreaming of some unknown lover, imagining what it might be like to lie with someone new, just for the fun of it, for the closeness of the moment. For the sensations without the emotions.

"There should be money to spend where you need it," Torion continued. "But I've no doubt we'll have some reckoning to take stock of."

"I've put Maggie in charge of the maids for now," I said.

"The old woman? She ought to manage. She knows the keep well enough, certainly."

I glanced over my shoulder, but there was no sign of Maggie following us. I hoped she hadn't helped herself to working on the old alpha's suite too much. It would need to be done, but I knew how it felt to want to hold onto a parent after their passing.

"She might not be up to the physical work for much longer. We should...think of what we can do for her," I said, wondering if I would've stepped beyond my place here so soon.

Torion stopped at the bottom of the stairs and turned to me, not smiling, but somehow expressing warmth all the same. I shied from his open stare.

"Good. There are cottages on the keep estate. Many need repair. I'll speak to the steward and the groundskeeper so we're ready." His fingers squeezed around mine. "I'm lucky you came to me for help, Brigid."

My voice caught in my throat, no answer ready, and Torion released me.

"You keep the staff busy in here. I'll keep seeing to the estate. We'll eat dinner together. The books are in my father's office," he said in a rush, heading for the stairs down to the main hall.

I wiped the heat of his touch on my makeshift apron and turned in the direction of the office, my chin held high and eyes refusing to look back.

Chapter Six

TORION

I stepped into the keep late, a little too aware of the smell of sheep shit on my boots...and other even less desirable places. I braced myself for—perhaps even relished the prospect of—a disapproving sniff from my new omega, but aside from the glowing and crackling fire in the hearth of the main hall, there was no sign of life in the keep. She hadn't waited for me for dinner.

Not that I could blame her. From what I'd seen so far, Brigid was an imminently practical woman. My own mother had been wonderful, sweet, soft, and somewhat ornamental. She'd played the part of the alpha's omega well, hosting events with the region's prominent betas and omegas, taking baskets to the poor and elderly on holidays, and orbiting beautifully around my father. She'd never been spotted covered in dust with an apron around her waist, sweat on her brow and a determined squint in her eye.

I'd wanted to both kiss Brigid's rough knuckles and rumple her already untidy skirts when I'd left her earlier.

No doubt she'd waited exactly five spare minutes before sitting down and enjoying her own dinner. Hopefully, there'd be some cold cuts on a tray for me in my rooms...unless she was the punishing sort.

Strangely, that idea brought a grin to my face.

But it was not a cold covered tray I found in my rooms, or even the absence of one.

Brigid was bent, pouring a kettle of hot water in the largest copper tub I'd seen outside of the one in my parent's personal rooms. She looked to me in the doorway as she poured, and her lips twitched.

"I heard you were rolling about with the animals, but I thought they exaggerated," she said, an attractive crackle in her low voice that made me shift in place.

She straightened and set the kettle aside, gesturing to the tub. "Undress. I'm playing handmaiden."

My hand clenched on the doorknob of the bedroom, and for a moment my thoughts flooded with heat, a senseless hunger. But my vision cleared, and I caught the subtle twist of Brigid's fingers before she hid her hands behind her back.

"I'd offer to help, but then we'd both be covered in muck and the tub's really only big enough for one," she said, voice rising brightly.

I could've argued that point. I would certainly have been able to find a way we both might fit—tangled together—but I cleared my throat and turned to shut the door behind me.

My mind tripped over stray questions. What exactly was she offering? What motivated the offering? My body flicked the questions away, desire demanding the majority of my attention. Not all of the lust I felt was even for the woman waiting by the tub. I was sore and dirty, I stank, and there was a steaming tub of hot water ready and waiting for me. I wanted to be soaking in that steam as soon as possible.

I reached to my collar and then had to force myself not to startle as I found Brigid at my shoulder, unfastening the plackets around my wings, stirring warm air over my skin.

"I take it you're staying," I said, holding my suddenly restless wings still so they wouldn't knock into her.

Her hands faltered in their work, knuckles brushing at my spine, a shiver of pleasure at the careless touch racing up to raise the hairs at the nape of my neck.

"Unless you'd prefer I go," she said.

I'd been managing my own baths just fine for forty-odd years, and Brigid was virtually a stranger. But she'd done more for the care of the keep in a handful of hours today than anyone had bothered with in a year. She was my omega. We'd have to grow used to one another soon enough.

"Stay," I said, reaching for the front of my trousers. "Tell me about your day."

"My day? Yours looks to have been more exciting."

"I wrestled three sheep who'd found themselves a hiding spot up by the crags, got knocked into shit, and perhaps broke a toe," I said, shrugging free of my shirt with her help. I pulled away and sat down, reaching for the heel of my boot and then raising a hand as she stepped forward, expression gamely serene and ready to help. "No, you're clean and let's keep it that way."

"Careful of your toe. I'll take a look at it once it's had a soak," she said. "Are the sheep back with the flock?"

"They are, though this isn't their first escape."

Brigid snorted at that, and I watched her out of the corner of my eye as she stirred some sort of oil into the water with her hand.

"I ordered fresh linens for the nest," she said, and I grunted as I managed to free one foot from a muddied, mucked boot. "And I sent a boy to speak to the local thatchers for the roof. I considered putting maids to work on the rooms that have been damaged by the leaks, but..."

"It's sure to rain tomorrow," I said, and she murmured an agreement.

The moment struck me strangely hard, domestic and awkward but somehow easy too. Had she spoken with Barr like this? But that wondering burned in my chest, and I nearly growled, swallowing the sound down quickly before I could startle her.

"There's food, if you're hungry."

I was starving, but I rose to the sideboard at the far side of the room and washed my hands and arms before nudging my loosened pants and smalls down my hips. There was a hitch of breath by the tub, and a small smile curved my lips. I wanted to turn and see where she was looking. Was she still staring at me, or had she blushed and turned away?

I spun to face her and found her kneeling by the tub, a cloth being wrung to a rope between her hands and a shock of color across her cheeks that darkened as I approached. Otherwise, she looked perfectly calm, her eyes focused on my face, pointedly fixed above my bare hips.

Which was good. Hopefully, she wasn't noticing my cock stirring just at the thought of her looking fully at me. Was this a seduction? It didn't seem like one, but it was doing the trick all the same.

"We always speak of the value of an omega to an alpha, but I hadn't considered the full scope. From managing the home to the...well, body," I said, hissing as I stepped into the water. "Haven't I gotten as much in the way of you remaining in your cottage as Barr would have?"

"No," she rasped harshly, ducking her face away from my stare as I sank into the water. "That is... The cottage was not my only concern."

"Did he hurt you?" I growled out, and my hands tightened around the rim of the copper tub as she remained silent. I could ban Barr from taking another omega. I *would* if he posed a danger to the Hills' women.

Then Brigid sighed, leaning into the tub and meeting my

gaze with a weary smile. "Not in the way you mean. Lean forward. Let me wash your wings."

I rested my chin on my knee, my arms looped around my legs, and listened to the rustling of her skirts. My eyes shut, and a rough purr rumbled in my chest as she gently spread one wing, her hands sliding along the top spines. Her touch was confident, and I ignored the jealous throb of understanding that she had done this before for another man.

"I...I enjoy my independence," Brigid said softly.

"I don't mean to take it away—" I started, but she cut me off, using the now soaked cloth to sluice water down the expanse of my wing.

"But I like helping others. I want to be a helpmeet to you."

I blinked, the words on my tongue to tell her that this was the first time I'd ever purred for anyone. The sensation was pleasant, vibrating through my chest and out my limbs. I wondered if she liked it too.

And then her hand rested on my back, and she let out a soft sigh. I leaned into the touch, my own heart pounding in my ears, the purr growing louder. It wasn't the only reaction I had to her touch, but I didn't plan on drawing her attention to *that*, at least not just yet.

"My things arrived this evening, thank you," she said.

I cleared my throat as she went back to work on washing my wings. "It's nothing." And then, thinking of her words, I twisted to catch her eye and added, "I would be your helpmeet too, Brigid."

She froze in place, her hand clenched around the washcloth, water dripping down my wing as she stared back at me. I reached for her hand, holding her gaze, but she stirred with a deep breath, rising up on her knees and leaning in. Her scent dizzied me, clear but full of nostalgic memories, wild heather and rainy days of flying around the hills, chasing little downpours. Her face neared mine, knowing and serene, and her hand landed on my shoulder, stroking slowly over my chest.

"Show me how to please you, alpha."

The words were heady, and for a moment my head spun and my eyes shut, purr roaring through my chest. My cock jumped in the water, eager to greet the woman so boldly touching me. But the picture of Brigid that appeared in my mind was stepping back, eyeing me warily, refusing to flinch from Malcolm as he railed at her. As much as every cell in my body wanted to arch toward her—and many already were—my head called out a brief warning.

I rested my wet hand over hers just as it reached my stomach, which twitched beneath her palm, but I noted the way her fingers trembled. "You don't have to do this," I rasped, my eyes opening and tongue going numb as I found her just a bare inch away.

And then several inches away, all at once, her hand yanked from beneath mine as if I'd scorched her with dragon fire.

"Of course, my lord," she murmured, folding her hands over her stomach and rising.

I gaped, the sudden cold of the room surrounding me, and she made it a few steps away before I realized my blunder. "Brigid, wait, I—" I scrambled to rise from the tub, but the water was slippery from the oil she'd added and my foot skidded out from under me, my ass landing hard and my words interrupted by a rough grunt.

"I'll leave you to rest. It's been a long day."

"Brigid, I only meant—" Water sluiced down from my body as my puzzling omega all but ran for the door, her braid drumming against her spine. What had I meant? Only to be *sure* that she was acting out of desire rather than duty. And now, at the slightest question, she was disappearing. I paused, and she stopped with one hand on the door handle, glancing back at me with a soft smile and a shrouded gaze. She waited for a moment, and I realized I was standing naked and half erect, but the pause of considering my nudity wasted the second she granted me.

"Goodnight, Torion."

I caught my breath, raking a damp hand through my tangled curls as she slipped out of the door, shutting it silently behind her.

"Goodnight, Brigid," I huffed out.

Chapter Seven

BRIGID

I winced as I opened my bedroom door and found the alpha in the hall. He was smiling broadly, but it faltered at the first glimpse of me, and I considered slamming the door in his face.

You're embarrassed. Get over it. You can turn tail and run back to the cottage, or you can see this through.

"Good morning," he said, smile stretching once more. He moved suddenly toward me, and I jumped back in place, the pair of us freezing and staring at one another.

He was too handsome. It made me want to tear my eyes right out of my own head, just to spite the effect his alluring looks had on my good sense. It made me bold and nervous, trying and failing to seduce a man who'd offered me charity in a moment of impulse. Malcolm would've laughed right in my face last night and then let me fumble my way through giving him a cheap release. Torion had simply dismissed the notion entirely.

I should know better than to try and secure a dragon's affection.

Slowly, Torion reached for me, large hands cupping my shoulders and drawing me a step closer, meeting him halfway.

I held my breath, but he inhaled deeply as he bent over me, that dark, rich purr rising once more from his chest, smoother this morning than it had been the night before. The sound sunk down into my own chest and then glowed its way out through my limbs, like a sip of brandy. His nose brushed my cheek, and my body trembled, startled by the intimacy. My blood thrilled, a plucked string vibrating with an eager note. Warm lips caressed over the spot, and I squeezed my eyes shut, suppressing their sudden stinging.

"Good morning," he said again softly into my ear, the heat of his breath brushing over the lobe and down my throat. I couldn't make my own voice crack to answer him, but he leaned back and continued. "I'd like to fly us around some of the region today. Introduce you officially."

I nodded. It made sense. Better not to tuck me away as if his claiming me was an accident. It was what we'd discussed, after all.

His hands smoothed down my arms, squeezing gently at my elbows before releasing me, drawing a sheath of fabric off his shoulder. "I brought you this to wear. It was my mother's. It should keep you warm and make a good statement, I think. If you like it."

He held it out in front of him, letting the fabric drape open. My eyes widened. It was the same plaid he wore around his waist, blues and browns and greens weaving together but with an incredible wealth of embroidery covering the surface —unfamiliar animals crawling down a line of gold, birds soaring across a broad map of blue wool, vines twisting through the pattern of the Feargus family colors.

"It's beautiful," I murmured, taking it from his hands. "She did this herself?"

"Much to the local dragonkins' consternation," Torion said wryly.

I huffed. I'd worn Malcolm's colors until I'd spilled wine

on them one night at dinner and he'd declared me too clumsy to be trusted with them. Embroidery as decoration would likely be considered desecration, but it was lovely and further proof of the former alpha's devotion to his omega.

Devotion that certainly didn't exist between Torion and me, and yet my hands were lifting, greedy fingers reaching for the fabric. It was a kind gesture, and a smart one, and probably meant as recompense for last night's rejection.

I took it from his hands, stroking the fine wool between my fingers, the silk of the embroidery smooth and gleaming. I wrapped the length over one shoulder and around my waist, my breath catching as I looked up and found Torion much closer than before, a worn leather belt in his hands.

"And this was my father's," he said, not hesitating this time to circle me in his arms, fastening it tightly around my waist with a tug that drew me closer to him, too close to catch my breath. Except I must have, because my head was full of that warm, ashy scent of his, like burnt cinnamon. "When he was a boy, his father made it for him, and he passed it down to me."

Being so close to Torion's body was like standing in rays of sunlight, heat soaking into my skin with every passing second, leaving me drowsy from my sleepless night and content to remain in place. It was such a pleasant feeling that I barely noticed as one large hand reached for my chin, taking it in a gentle grip. My heart stuttered in my chest as he grazed his mouth over mine, soft and almost polite, if not for the slight gust of minty breath that slipped between my parted lips.

"They'll know you're mine," he said, stepping back before I'd made up my mind whether or not to kiss him back.

I knew enough of men to recognize the approval in his gaze as he looked me over. Was it simply seeing the mark of his family on me, or...?

"Come," he said, clasping my hand in his and then tucking it around the inside of his elbow, towing me down the hall at his side, nodding his head in greeting to every man and woman we passed on our way down to the main hall. "Have you eaten already?"

If I said yes, I might escape this sudden attention from the alpha and my own foolishly awkward response, but the truth was I'd eaten poorly the night before, too nervous with anticipation for my attempted seduction, and not at all yet today.

"If you have, I'd claim your company anyway, if you can spare it," he continued.

"Why?" I asked, and then realized it was the first thing I'd said to him today. I thought I caught a slight darkening of his cheeks, and he swallowed hard, revealing a flash of nerves before clearing it away with another smile.

"I want your opinion on some of my plans," he said, shrugging, as if that wasn't a shocking announcement from an alpha to his omega.

I stopped him with a tug on his elbow, glancing around and finding us mostly alone, aside from a servant waiting by the far door. "You don't need to make up to me," I said softly.

He shifted to face me, and I ignored the strange impulse to arch as I stared up at him.

"Make up to you?" he repeated, not bothering to temper his volume.

I swallowed and noted the eyes of the servant on us, as well as a couple others from the balcony above.

"For last night," I whispered, keeping my eyes lowered to the floor. "You don't need your omega's opinions, and you don't have to..."

Torion cleared his throat, and even with my stare off of him, I could catch the way he seemed to swell briefly before relaxing once more. "I do. Even if you're just humoring me by listening, it will help to think things through out loud."

And then his hand settled at the base of my waist—did he tuck two fingers beneath the belt or was I imagining the gentle pressure of his touch there?—and ushered me to the table by the fire, laden with a modest collection of covered plates.

"We'll talk about last night later," he added, barely breathing the words into my ear.

"Oh, let's not," I gusted out.

He laughed but didn't speak until we were settled side by side and he'd piled a plate high with steaming rolls, thick slices of ham, a few sausages, a generous scoop of coddled eggs, and a heap of roasted vegetables. I gaped as he set it in front of me.

"Eat as much as you can stand," he said, and then paused, frowning. "Unless you think you're likely to get sick on my back."

"I beg your pardon?"

"Flying," he explained with a grin. "Do you get carriage sick? It's not the same, but it's the best I can think. Or did Barr ever fly you—?"

Oh. "I'll be fine," I said, trying not to think of those few moments of flight, so many years ago, when I was dizzy with love. Or perhaps just dizzy with the rush of flying. Had that been part of Malcolm's illusions too?

"It seems easy until you have to do a full day of it," Torion said. "My mother didn't get sick, but she'd spend the next two days in bed with all sorts of aches. Do you ride much?"

Do you want me to eat or answer a dozen questions? I wanted to ask.

"Not since I left for the cottage," I said, carefully stepping around Malcolm's name, my past. "I rode a great deal when I was a girl, however."

Torion nodded and looked thoughtful. "Well, it's a bit like that. I'll do the steering, you just need to keep your seat. Would you like to choose a horse from the stables? Or we could buy you your own. Perhaps there's a young—"

"Torion," I said, picking up my fork and knife in tight fists. "Tell me one of your plans so I might eat some food."

I immediately regretted the words, the bite in my tone, knowing I'd stepped wrong and been disrespectful. I braced myself for a harsh whisper, a dark scowl, something worse perhaps?

Torion just laughed, loud and easy, not quite booming like I'd remembered his father, but an open and hearty sound that brushed away my nerves.

"YOU'RE MORE than welcome to take a room here, Feargus," Lord McKinney said, for the third time since we'd sat down at their table to supper with them.

Word must've been traveling fast through Grave Hills because we'd clearly taken the first two betas by surprise with our visit, but by the time we'd circled Torion's territory and reached McKinney, he'd produced his entire family—and the man had managed to get his omegas with three sons over his lifetime, so the family was sizeable—to join us for dinner. It was a noisy affair at the end of a noisy day of people pretending to be pleased for Torion when it was perfectly apparent that they were just happy to have a bit of gossip to share with their neighbors.

I wasn't sure if we'd given them an adequate dose, really. Torion kept me close to his side, grazing his hand over my back or waist or shoulder, and occasionally I'd found myself caught in his stare, receiving a purr in my ear or a brush of his lips over my cheek or the crown of my head.

It had me on edge. Although the edge wasn't...unpleasant.

I hadn't been touched so much, nor spent time with so many people, expected to smile and laugh and respond sweetly, in *years*. I was exhausted and wistful, longing for the safety of my cottage well out of anyone else's way, unless they needed me for healing.

"I thank you for the offer, but we're not so far from the keep," Torion said.

His arm came around my shoulders, and instead of feeling oppressive, the weight seemed to steal some of the ragged tension out of me. I was too tired to stiffen or brace myself, so I leaned into Torion's strong frame, using his body to prop myself up.

"But your lady looks as if even a short distance might be too far," Lady McKinney said. She was a simpering girl who'd been batting her lashes at Torion all night, as if trying to tempt him into stealing *her* away from her beta too.

I opened my mouth to object, trying and no doubt failing to appear young and hale and full of a stamina that had been sapped out of me on our third flight of the morning, but Torion beat me to answer.

"And she'll rest better in our nest," he said.

Perhaps it was good I was so weary, because I didn't have it in me to startle at the words. Lady McKinney giggled and blushed at the implication.

"A nest so soon? My, Omega Ba—*Feargus*, you are industrious. Or perhaps this has been something in the making for a time, eh?" Lord McKinney said, silky tone heavy with meaning. "That cottage you've been hiding away in isn't so far from the Feargus keep, is it, now that I think of it?"

I was too slow to catch on, but Torion was quick. "Near to my favorite hunting grounds, in fact," he said.

"Hunting indeed, young man, hunting indeed! And why

should she go to waste out there on her own?" Lord McKinney laughed, his eyes bright with excitement.

Ah. Now *here* was gossip. Before the week was out, it was sure to reach every corner of the region that Torion had been wooing me out from under Malcolm for some time. And Torion had planted the seed.

It was a clever lie. I turned my cheek away from their stares, turning exhaustion to shyness and giving myself a moment to smile into Torion's warm shoulder. He was young, *boyish* even by beta standards, but he was smart. Not even Malcolm would know if the rumor was false or not.

"We should take our leave," Torion said, and I lifted my chin, not hiding my smile, not caring that I probably looked half in love with him. I was fully in love with the idea of getting somewhere quiet.

"Before your omega is too tired to keep her seat as we fly," I agreed.

Torion's dark eyes flared, and that eager purr rattled in his chest, although I didn't know why that should please him so much.

I did my best to keep my smile on and my voice gentle and patient as we said our farewells to far too many people. Had some of the young ladies gone round the back of the line and taken a second turn? Torion kept his arm around me, which was good and kept me upright, but even he walked out of the McKinney front door and down the drive with a not entirely disguised eagerness.

"His line is far too prolific. There must be some way of keeping him from taking another omega after this one," Torion whispered in my ear, drawing out an unguarded snort from me.

And then a squawk as he scooped me up in his arms, my hands clutching hard at his shoulders as his wings beat and he lifted us from the ground.

"You're flying!" I cried out. The night was cool and dark enough to hide my blush at the silly words.

"It's not quite as fast this way, but my bones are tired of shifting back and forth," Torion admitted, and then he grinned at me. "And this way I'll be sure not to let you fall to your death."

"It would be a waste after that clever story you spun of us at dinner." I rested my head on his shoulder and closed my eyes, mostly to keep from noticing how close his face was to mine, chin still smooth and cut with such lovely angles, ones that begged to be studied by some form of touch. His mouth had a very full bottom lip, one I'd been looking forward to sampling last night...before he'd opened it.

"Ah, I was hoping you'd approve. I imagine McKinney will expand on it nicely. I suppose I got injured on a hunt somehow, crawled my way to your door, and fell in love with you as you nursed me for days on end. Maybe even weeks? Granted, I haven't gone missing that long, but who really likes facts in gossip?"

"You haven't seen my cottage. I'd have nowhere to put you."

"You shared your bed with me," Torion said easily, and I hoped he mistook the sudden jerk of my body for me adjusting my position. He continued, eyes focused ahead but a sly smile curling at his lips. "I would've been too weak to take advantage, of course. At least for the first couple nights."

I let out another snort, glad the wind and cold night could explain away the color no doubt flooding my cheeks. My bed was a loft above the work table of my cottage. If it *did* hold both Torion and I together, it would do so only in the closest of terms—body to body, and not an inch to spare between us.

"Does it bother you to sound disloyal to Barr?" Torion asked, all the teasing rinsed from his voice. The keep loomed, tall squared frame traced in silver moonlight.

I choked and found myself tangled up in Torion's dark gaze too quickly to shield myself against its potency. "No. Fang's fire, no. It's... I doubt Malcolm was bothering to talk of me as his any longer."

"I never paid much attention to him until my father's passing. He hid his ambition well," Torion mused.

"Aye, he liked hiding things," I snapped.

Torion fell quiet at that, and I cursed my bitter tongue. His arms tightened around me, hands hot on my hips and waist, chest a comfortable furnace to lean against. Every so often, the wind would catch one of his black curls and brush it against my cheek or forehead like a playful feather. I wanted to close my eyes and fall into this man, because I missed the way that felt, being safe and held up and surrounded by someone you trusted. But I didn't feel safe and I didn't trust this man, and I didn't want my body fooling my heart into letting its guard down.

"About last night..." Torion started.

"Oh, don't," I said, too tired to be meek and agreeable.

For a moment, I thought he'd let it die, but then he cleared his throat. "I only sought to be sure it was what you really wanted. You don't owe me your body, Brigid. Regardless of any bargain we made, that's your choice."

You don't have to do this.

Torion's throat flexed with a swallow, a brief shimmer of buried scales glinting at me, the muscle and heat of him enveloping me. In this moment, it was easy to imagine putting my lips to that throat, letting my tongue flick out, the sound he might make. I'd been a shy but eager participant in bedsport with Malcolm, and it was the celebration and release of the act that I still missed. But last night I'd been thinking of my place at the alpha's side, thinking of the risk of surrendering my body to another man, what he might take along with it. My hands had shaken, and it hadn't been desire coiling in my belly. Had Torion sensed that?

"You dismissed me," I said, trying to put things back in place.

Torion's feet touched the ground in front of the keep, but he didn't release me. "No, I wasn't asking you to leave. You took the opportunity, though."

I flinched and pulled myself out of Torion's cradling arms, but his hands caught me at my waist, keeping me in the halo of his heat, his face lit warmly by the fire inside the keep, the doors opened and awaiting our return.

"We don't have to rush anything," he said, body bowing over mine. And perhaps it was some alpha nature influencing mine, or perhaps it was my body still craving the memory of a long lost sensation, but I arched in his hold, stretching up to him. His mouth found mine, slightly parted, our first kiss made of our shared breath. My blood rushed through my veins as his feet bracketed mine, one hand sliding up my spine to hold me in that swoon, his lips pressing gently. His purr vibrated through his entire body, thrumming into mine, and even with my eyes closed the world spun.

Too much, my mind cried, but my fingertips pressed to Torion's chest, barely gripping. I flicked my tongue against that tempting bottom lip, finding the burn of whisky and an appealing salt. I had a sudden ravenous hunger to consume this man, to devour him in a feast of touch and taste and violent desire. It made my entire body throb and my good sense rebel.

That way led carnage. That way led me leashed to another man who didn't love me, my own feeble heart foolishly trying to find purchase.

Torion's hand on my waist moved away and I took the opportunity to spin out of his arms.

"You will—" I was embarrassingly breathless, and I shook

my head, stumbling another few feet safely out of reach. "You will have to tell me when your rut approaches, my lord."

"Brigid?"

I glanced over my shoulder and the sight of him, enormous and beautiful, hands still reaching and legs spread, a perfect structure to throw myself into, made my knees weak. I needed to run.

Better a coward than a fool.

"Goodnight, Torion," I said, rushing into the keep.

Chapter Eight
TORION

For three days, I caught flashes of Brigid around the keep, always darting around the corner of a hall. I'd tried calling out to her twice but received no response, and the pointedly averted gazes of our servants was too galling to continue the process. Had she changed her mind about our bargain? She only needed to say so.

Lie.

I blinked, staring down at my muddied fingers, my arms and shoulders and back aching from hauling stone. I'd been standing out in this field, burning under the sun and mulling over my wayward omega too long.

Was she skittish? Shy? Reluctant?

Whatever the answer, if she *did* ask me to be released from our arrangement, I wasn't sure how readily I might agree. Not that I would force her to remain my omega. But I might try to *persuade* her to stay.

If I could get my hands on her.

My hands on her waist and soft hips, fingers digging into thick auburn locks, teeth nibbling at a long pale throat.

Grasses rustled behind me as someone approached, and I

cleared my throat, putting another rock on the wall I was rebuilding.

"This is fine work for our new alpha," a rattling old voice greeted me.

I grinned and brushed grit from my hands before turning to face old Ned MacIntyre, my father's former advisor for many years and as close to a grandfather as I'd ever known.

"Don't tell the betas vying for my wings, but it's the kind of work I prefer, truth be told."

Ned huffed and held out a waterskin in one hand and an open flask in the other. "Expected as much, since you're out here yourself rather than sending folk as you ought to do. Not that you ought—"

I stopped him, taking a quick draught of water and a grateful sip of whisky. "I'm doing just as I ought, and what my father should've taken care of years ago."

Ned only grunted at that. My father had told me stories of his youth, following Ned MacIntyre about, constantly underfoot, and when my father had risen as alpha, he'd credited Ned's support and guidance to his success. Ned had served as my father's most trusted advisor for decades, even when they were at odds. But when my mother'd grown ill and my father's already tenuous attention to the territory had turned exclusively to his omega, Ned had finally delivered the harsh dressing down my father refused to heed, and they'd parted ways. Ever since I'd reached my majority, I'd found myself wanting to push my father in new directions as alpha, then wanting to claim the position for myself, but I'd never been so disappointed in his leadership as when he'd abandoned his oldest, closest friend.

"My herd isn't so large as to matter," Ned reasoned, helping himself to a seat on a partially finished wall. His yellow sage wings hung a little loose and low these days, and I expected they wore on him because he stood stooped now.

They certainly wouldn't support flight, even for his bony old frame. "You'd be better served to seeing to the Roberts blocked well."

"I sent folk to him this morning," I said, grinning as Ned chuckled. I joined him on the wall, passing the flask back, staring out at the rising green and gray landscape in front of us, speckled with the warm rust of Ned's herd of cattle. "I like your lands. You have the best views."

There was a long sloping falls running down the rocky hill that bordered his estate, and it turned into a stream that cut through his property, where I'd spent hours catching newts and toads as a boy. I'd wash there later, before flying back to the keep to try and fail to catch another glimpse of Brigid. Maybe I could even be lordly and demand she join me at dinner. It'd be worth it to see her annoyed at least, that snarl that caught her upper lip that she always tried to hide away.

"I'm too old to be serving you up advice like I did your father—"

"I didn't ask for any," I said, laughing, knowing there was more coming, and it would certainly be advice.

"—but I can't say as I would've advised you to claim another dragon's woman. Even if he was doing a piss poor job of keeping her."

I grimaced and drank more water to avoid the conversation. "I'll admit it wasn't my most well thought out decision."

"She's a fine looking creature. I don't fault you that," Ned said with a shrug.

And Brigid was, indeed, fine looking. She was soft one moment and dagger sharp the next, which I found appealing, like I was preparing for potential battle just to kiss her but might instead find unexpected treasure in her sweetness.

"It wasn't about that. She came to me for help in avoiding him," I said.

Ned sighed. "Ah, was afraid that might be it. You'd be better off not to take after your father in that way."

"My father?"

"Aye, falling into a woman who needs you when your people need you more."

I stiffened at that. Ned had always been polite to my mother, although he'd also always pushed my father to be more attentive to the Hills. But was there more to it than that? More resentment than I'd been able to glean as a child?

"Brigid's...independent. She might need me to avoid Barr, but she doesn't need *me*," I said, frowning. *Doesn't want me is more like.*

Ned stared at me for a long time, long enough to have me squirming like a boy again. "Ah, I see. You're a fool then."

I huffed, crossing my arms over my chest. "Ned, I thought you didn't want to give me advice—"

"Well, if you can't see the obvious—"

"Ned!"

He rolled his eyes dramatically and took a long helping of whisky before I grew too impatient and stole it away from him. He hid his grin, but poorly.

"A woman who's been so thoroughly scorned by the man who shares her bed will take a special touch, a little extra assurance, before she trusts the next man," Ned said slowly.

"Scorned?" I asked, sitting up straighter, trying to ignore the irritated heat in my chest at the mention of Brigid and Barr together. It was distant past, according to her.

Ned met my eyes, his own rheumy wet blue ones astonishingly keen and sharp. "Barr was a fine dragon, well into his prime and already having dismissed two omegas from his house, when he set his eye on that girl. And girl she was. He had his scent on her by the time she was sixteen. Her father was only too pleased to arrange the match, and she looked at that man like he hung the moon just for her each night."

I swallowed the fire in my throat and focused my stare out at the streak of white water rushing down between the hills.

"But Barr's never been satisfied. I don't know how long it took him, or if he never was faithful to that girl, but I could see the moment she *knew*, and it wasn't even a year since she'd been claimed."

I startled at that, blinking. "He had other women?"

"Doxies, widows, other men's omegas, servants, you name it. He bedded any willing woman he could find. All while she kept his house, and hosted his guests, and looked like her heart had been kicked from here to Skybern."

My fists clenched on the stone, little pieces crumbling under my grip. I could imagine my words in the bath to Brigid now, why she heard dismissal rather than concern. I'd been assuming she didn't really *want* to bed me. Replaying our words in my mind, the conversation sounded more complicated now.

"They reconciled for a time. Barr wants an heir, of course, and she was still young and ripe. But he wouldn't have kept true for long, just through a rut cycle, and this next time, she left him for good."

She'd been betrayed twice by the same man. "She's not going to trust me easily," I said.

"Surely not. Likely doesn't trust herself, either."

I thought of the kiss, how careful I'd tried to be, how gentle, how she'd melted for a moment and the wild victory that had made me tight and eager, just before she'd torn herself away. I turned to Ned, and I didn't even care that the old man looked smug.

"What do you suggest, Ned?"

He took in a deep breath and set his hands on his old knees, frowning and pretending to think, when I knew full well he'd already decided exactly what I needed to do.

"Be patient, of course. Listen when she has a mind to

speak. But don't be afraid to show that woman you want her. Barr was a small man that wanted to feel big, and I think he did so by crushing that girl—her heart, her spirit. You ought to see what happens when you do the opposite."

I sipped at the whisky flask, enjoying the heat burning its way from my tongue down my throat and into my belly, like dragon fire. Like desire for a woman.

"I'll see what I can do," I said.

I STARTLED at the sound of the knock, wincing as water splashed from the tub onto the floor. *Get it together, Torion.*

"Come in." I cleared my throat and rolled my shoulders and wings, settling back into the hot, shallow water. I'd taken Ned's advice, mulled it over for a night and a day, and come to one slightly self-serving conclusion. A plan, to be exact. I would rewrite the night I'd erred with Brigid.

The door creaked open, and a sharp silence that rang in my ears. Her voice broke it softly. "You asked for me?"

I turned my head just enough to get a glimpse of her out of the corner of my eye, resisting the urge to drink her in fully. I'd have plenty of time for that later if this went well.

"I did." I only watched her enough to know that she closed the door and approached me in the tub, giving myself a last moment to catch my breath and prepare for my plan to go terribly awry or...not. When she reached the side of the tub and remained standing, I looked up, catching her eyes fixed on the water, on what it distorted and revealed. "You've been avoiding me, Brigid."

That roused her enough, her cheeks warming with color even as she straightened and hiked her proud little chin. "I've been busy taking care of the keep."

We remained silent for a moment, me staring at her and her staring anywhere else.

"I'm not going to summon you to my rut, omega," I said softly, and my chest twinged as I watched her swallow, eyes blinking.

"I see," she said, her voice a little rough. I knew exactly how she would take the words, and I waited for any glimpse of relief. She only guarded herself more tightly than ever. I hated making assumptions, preferring a simple bald truth, but she was not going to give me that—not yet, at least. "What does that mean for me?"

I resisted the impulse to smirk. "It means I have need of you tonight, Brigid," I said, and her eyes flashed to mine, openly surprised. I continued before she could misinterpret me again. "I expect I'll have need of you tomorrow. And the day after. My hope is that by the time my rut arrives, I won't have to *summon* you, because you'll already be in my bed. But that decision is up to you."

I wanted to rise up from the water, rub my cheek against the heat in hers, nibble at those parted lips and slide my tongue inside her mouth before she could respond. It took a tight grip on the ledge of the tub to hold myself in place, waiting and watching. This track was a gamble. As much as I strived to rise as alpha, I wasn't naturally imperious, especially not with a woman. I couldn't make myself *demand* Brigid in my bed, but I would be as direct as possible about wanting her there. If she ran now, I wouldn't chase her—that would be her real answer on whether or not she was ready to be mine.

"I see," she said, and this time as her eyes slid over my body, she didn't hide the appreciation. I leaned farther back in the tub, because I'd seen the way women looked at my chest. Brigid's lips curved slightly at the corners, and she knelt slowly, stare fixed on the dark shimmer of my cock in the water. "Like this?" she asked, reaching for me without hesitation.

"Fuck!" I gasped as her hand found me in the water, and my own flashed down, wrapping around hers before she could pull away, holding her in place. I felt her twitch in my grip for a moment before stilling, holding me just below the head. "Y-yes, but come closer, witch."

Her gaze met mine, wide and unguarded for once, and she shuffled close enough for her knees to touch the outside of the tub, her arm in the water bending at the elbow. My free arm wrapped around her back, stroking up her spine, her breath catching sweetly and her body shivering as I cupped the back of her neck.

"Witch?" she asked, with a furrow on her brow.

"You had me hard with just a look that night," I admitted in a whisper.

Her eyes grew dark, fastened to mine, and I pressed gently on the back of her neck, pleased as she followed the touch without resisting, until our lips were almost touching.

"And tonight?" she asked.

I grazed my nose against her jaw, breathed the scent of her in, forced my hips to remain still rather than pump myself into our still hands. "My imagination was busy as I waited for you," I said, and then helped myself to caress of her mouth, so soft and open to me.

"Mm. Who did you think of?" she asked, the playfulness cracking under the faintest hint of nerves. I would've missed it if not for Ned's revelation earlier.

I would have to kill Barr.

"You, Brigid," I said, taking care with her name. I kissed her again, savored the ragged breath that rushed against me. "It's been you since the night you arrived."

She huffed, a sound of disbelief, and I swallowed it with a

rough kiss. I gripped the back of her neck tightly to hold her to me and stroked my tongue against her mouth to plead for entry. She surrendered with a muffled moan, answering my hunger with her own, leaning into the tub. I squeezed her hand on my cock, reminding us both what she held, and she stroked me once. I groaned, caressing her tongue with mine, and then leaned back, pulling my hand from hers to reach up and cup her jaw.

"It's been so long. I won't last this first time," I admitted, gasping as she twisted her hand over the head of my cock.

She frowned, puzzled, and I hid nothing from her, bucking up into her touch, my eyes falling shut and head tipping back. Her sweet fist pumped down and then released me, finding my balls and drawing a loud moan from me, the plea of her name.

"Do you want me to draw it out?" she asked, her voice unfairly clear. Not that it was likely I'd have her panting and moaning when she was doing all the work.

I shook my head, forcing my eyes open. "I want to come. I want you to make me—guh... Yes, like that."

I would've liked to say that I was loud, eager, easy to please because I wanted her to feel confident. The truth was that I couldn't stop the sounds I made, the pleas and groans of approval. It had been years since I'd had anyone else touch me, to enjoy this with, and Brigid wasn't hesitating or teasing. She wasn't shy. In fact, she was merciless, confidently working me into a quivering heap in the water.

"Faster?" she asked.

I growled, sitting up abruptly and pulling her mouth to mine. I didn't want her speaking to me like a doctor, damnit. Better to keep her occupied, make her as mad with lust as I'd so readily been. I needed her too far gone to run away when this was done.

She whimpered as I nipped her lip, and my growl turned to a purr. I shifted in the water, and she never released me, just squeezed and pumped my cock as instructed. I rose to my knees, and her free arm slung over my shoulders, fingers clutching and body leaning into my side, the bath water soaking into her dress. Her mouth opened, tongue searching for mine, curling, a dark sound of satisfaction rising from her throat and sinking into my chest. I thought I might be able to pull her right into the water with me and she wouldn't notice.

I wanted her wet after all.

I pulled away, hiding my grin against her throat, licking over her pulse and then sucking at the spot with teeth and tongue.

"Is-is this g-good?" she stammered out, her hand barely moving as I rutted into her grip.

I licked my way up to her earlobe. "You have me nearly there, witch," I snarled into her ear, pleased with the way she shook, her fingers tangling into the curls at the nape of my neck. "Play with my sac again if you want to make me wait. Or tighten your hand around me to finish me off."

She hesitated for a moment and then leaned back in my hold, her chest heaving with breath, eyes flashing over my face. Her hand tightened, and my own eyes fell shut, mouth falling open with a cry of surprise. She worked her hand over me, warm and soft and still easy from the water, taking care to squeeze hard around the tip and then slide down to the base.

"I need both hands," she mused.

I opened my eyes to find her staring at my face in wonder. *She wants to watch me as I come, wants to see she's pleased me.* A warm glow rooted in my chest. "Don't you dare let go of me," I ground out, my arm around her waist tightening.

She smiled, a rare unguarded expression, delighted with her own success. "Come for me, alpha," she said, voice all velvet and sweet.

I was hers to command.

Chapter Nine

BRIGID

I had never heard that weak, pleading sound from a man before, almost a whine, a laugh of relief, and then Torion was gasping, moaning, shuddering as his cock jerked and heated in my hand. I wanted to look down, to watch him spurt. Would it splash up to his belly or into the water? Some hit my hand, scorching and dribbling down to my wrist, but I couldn't tear my eyes from his, the beautiful transformation of surprise, relief, gratitude, and something like fear.

"That's it," I said, still stroking him, the mess sticky and slick, coating my palm and his thick length. "That's good."

"Brigid," he rasped, crackling with awe.

Heat shivered through me, pooling in my chest and in my core. His eyes fluttered shut, and he forced them open, as if he knew I needed to see him falling apart. He moaned, and it was almost pained, another little gush of release escaping him. He leaned into me as if he couldn't support his own weight, as if he needed me to hold him up as I milked him dry.

"Better?" I asked, softening my touch to more of a pet, enjoying the way he jerked and trembled.

I wanted his answer, but instead he fell on me with a strangled sound, his mouth covering mine for a messy, deep kiss. He bent, and it pulled him free of my hand. I needed to wipe myself clean and then him, but Torion's arms had me surrounded now, almost hugging me as he kissed me hard, over and over again, more and more weight from his body falling into mine.

Before I could warn him I was about to fall backwards, a wet slap hit my skirt, soaking through immediately, and then I was falling backwards, with him following, never stopping kissing me.

"Torion!"

"Brigid," he said, growling out my name, crawling over me, soaking wet and huge. My back hit the floor, but one of his hands cupped my head. The other was rucking up my skirt. "Are you wet?"

"I am now," I bit out.

Torion pulled away, rearing back, and I finally got a good look at his cock. It had felt huge in my hand and I'd been right, but it was beautiful too, dark and dusty, a purply red at the tip. Then the damp fabric of my dress was raised between us, hiding him from view, shoved up my legs. I had a brief moment of confusion—he'd just come; what was he doing raising my skirts? Except he hadn't looked like he was softening just now, and he was an alpha, so perhaps...

And then the confusion returned, doubly strong, my mouth hanging open as Torion scooted back on his knees, upper half lowering until his face hovered just above my thighs. He breathed deeply and then let out a long, satisfied groan, a proud sound. It was the kind of sound Malcolm had made at his finish, not that beautiful crumbling cry I'd just heard.

"You're soaked," Torion said, the words somehow both reverent and triumphant.

I squeaked as he bent even lower, trying to brace my feet on the floor without absolutely exposing myself. "Wh-what are you doing?"

"Having my turn, witch," he said, and then his hands scooped beneath my thighs, lifting my hips from the floor, my dress sliding down toward my chest, unveiling my sex.

I opened my mouth to ask what he meant by that, what he was doing *down there*, when his own mouth opened, releasing a hungry sound. I gasped as he drew me to his lips like I was some kind of wild game to feast on, but even as he did so, I never imagined he would—

I shouted, a garbled sound of shock and the hot, giddy pleasure of lips and tongue between my legs, and then slapped my hand over my mouth. What was he doing? Why? What purpose did it serve?!

Torion's eyes glared at me, even as the warm, wet tip of his tongue dipped inside of me, killing all my frantic thoughts with the divine sensation, tender and gentle and explicit. I whimpered as he pulled away, his brow furrowing.

Had he not meant to do that after all? Could I persuade him to try it again?

"Don't keep your sounds from me, omega. I didn't hide mine from you," he said.

And then he returned, licking a line up my slit with that wicked tongue. Shuddering relief lasted a moment before it was layered with tense need as Torion focused on the little bud between my lips. I made another sound, but he was right and I didn't want him to stop again, so I moved my hand from my mouth to cover my eyes, the view of his handsome face between the V of my legs too beautiful to stand staring at another second longer.

Was this...was this something only alphas did?

No, even I knew that was too silly. A sharp spark of spite and anger with Malcolm rose up in me, but Torion smothered it just as he did my core, with a drugging, heady pleasure. It was better that I'd never known this existed. I might've forgiven too much.

Torion grunted, shifting, and then I was lifted higher, my toes barely brushing against the soft fur below us.

"You taste so good," Torion mumbled against me, licking at me for a few moments. "Do you like this?"

I wanted to lie, because telling him how good this was felt like handing him a weapon. But Torion had been cautious with me before. If he believed I didn't like it, he might stop, and that would be a tragedy.

"Yes," I whispered, finding his hand on my hip and covering it with my own.

"Good. I want to always have a taste of you on my tongue," Torion said, stealing my breath from my lungs and then returning more enthusiastically to his work. I went hot at the sound of a slurp, wondering if I could die of shame when I was feeling so wonderful. I hoped not.

Slowly, tentatively, I lifted one foot from the floor, peeking through my fingers as I rested it onto Torion's shoulder. He purred into me, and I shuddered as the sound echoed into my core. Shyness was impossible in the moment, and my body loosened, the foot touching his back helping me brace, rocking my sex into his mouth. Torion groaned, his eyes meeting mine as I flung an arm behind me. He nodded, sucking at me.

In that moment, Torion wasn't a stranger. He'd shown me something of myself I'd never learned, offered me something I could never have discovered on my own.

"Alpha," I breathed, whining at his answering purr. He narrowed his tongue, curling it up to flick over my clit once more, and I gave in. "Yes, yes, that's so good. Oh, I'm so close. Please, T-Torion."

Torion's fingers tightened on my hips, lips pursing around my bud, and I started to shake, to make new sounds, broken little shards of sweetness cutting through my vision. If I spoke, it was nonsense, and Torion never tore himself from me, just a few stray licks as if to make sure he didn't waste a drop of me before going back to suckling at the same perfect spot.

I came with a sob of his name, with hot tremors racing through my bones and a spiraling shiver in my blood. Torion slipped one hand from my hip, stroking two fingers into my core and rubbing in and out, giving me something to clench on, teasing new tracing pleasures out with his touch.

"Beautiful."

I heard the word but blocked it out easily, rocking into his fingers, his gentling kisses.

"So good. Mmm, yes, just a little more," Torion whispered, lapping at me, circling his tongue around his own fingers. "I don't care what else we do until the rut. You just have to give me a taste of you every day."

A soft laugh slipped out of me as I sagged. I opened my eyes just in time to watch Torion pull his fingers out of me, rising back up onto his knees and rubbing my release onto his rigid length. My legs lay limp and parted wide as he scooted closer, staring down at me. He'd just wrung me out, and now he was kneeling above me, stroking himself with my wetness, looking like a starving man.

"Give me just a moment, and I'll do that again in bed," he rasped, jerking his hand over himself quickly, his cock pointed at my belly. "Can I finish on you?"

A faint voice at the back of my mind balked at the suggestion, but it was quickly drowned beneath the roaring rush of something entirely new—a mix of lust and pride and...dark victory. I gripped at the hem of my dress, arching off the rug to pull it over my head, a smug heat joining the blush on my cheeks as Torion groaned and stared down at me, panting as he worked himself.

"Yes, alpha," I murmured.

I PUSHED Torion's hand away from my sex, his laugh vibrating from his chest where my head was resting.

"Sorry. I just like the way you feel," he said.

Damn you, be quiet, I wanted to cry out, irrationally angry at him for saying something so...pleasing.

"I feel numb," I bit out. "I can't take anymore tonight."

Torion had kept to his word, finishing himself off with an almost charming swiftness before hauling me and the mess he'd made on my stomach into his large bed, where he'd proceeded to feast on me through two more ecstatic releases. I wasn't actually numb, but I was oversensitive, a sharpish sensation warning my body that I couldn't take another round.

"Mm, sore?" Torion said, kissing the top of my head and rubbing up and down my back.

I wanted to push away from him, stomp my way out of the room, maybe slap him on the way out. But for what? Being wonderful?

I took a deep breath and let it out slowly. "No, not really. I wasn't expecting the rut to hit so soon, though. Were you?"

Torion barked out a laugh, rolling us in the bed. His curls were a riotous tangle, combed and snarled by my frantic clutching, but they tickled softly at my cheeks and throat as he leaned over me, one leg settling heavily between my own.

"This isn't the start of the rut, Brigid," Torion said, grinning.

I wet my lips and froze as Torion's gaze caught the slight movement, eyes darkening and a purr thrumming out of him and into me. "You—*we...three* times, Torion," I pointed out, lifting a hand to brace it against his chest, as if I could keep him from unraveling me for a fourth time.

Will he spend in the sheets again? I wondered, recalling the glowing churn of his back and hips as he'd reached his own finish on the bed while driving me to mine.

I frowned up at him, considering. "Is that normal for you?"

He closed his eyes with a snort of laughter and grew heavier against me, more relaxed. "Youthful vigor, perhaps? It's... There's not a lot of comparison to offer, truth be told." He twisted onto his side, propping his head in his left hand, leaving his right to trace patterns on my skin, between my breasts, down my ribs, and over my hip, then back again.

If I was understanding him correctly, his claim was unreasonably attractive to me. "And this...*comparison* is where you learned to...?" I trailed off, finishing the thought by simply pressing two fingers to his mouth. His cheeks darkened, but his eyes crinkled with more laughter.

"You liked it?"

I huffed and raised my gaze above his head. "Obviously," I snapped. My body was still charged with pleasure.

Torion just sighed and nuzzled against my chin. "I'm glad. It's all I've been able to think of for days. You tasted better than I imagined. And how wet you get? I—"

I jammed my elbow into his side before he could use that wicked mouth to talk me into wanting him again. Torion grunted, but the damn man was still smiling. "You didn't answer my question," I said.

He frowned for a moment, looking away. He'd genuinely grown distracted thinking about what we'd done, and I found it unreasonably charming, flattering even. "Oh, where I learned—? Yes, I suppose so," he said.

"You suppose?" I pressed.

He looked a little sheepish as he shrugged. "It was presented as a means of readying a woman, a courtesy to help ease the start."

"Readying?" I asked, frowning.

Torion stared at me, and I tried not to fidget in the silence. He cleared his throat. "Making her wet, eager, needful. So she might welcome a man more comfortably," he said, watching me for a beat and then continuing. "I was young and impatient at the time. I hadn't considered its potential as a...full and pleasurable course on its own, if you will," he said, grinning once more, and then waggling his brows. "One I would want increasingly more helpings of after every sample."

What a fool, I thought, but I wasn't sure if I meant his antics or the eager little leap in my chest at his teasing. I rolled my eyes just to look away from him and slapped my hand over his mouth.

"Enough," I said, and his laugh vibrated warmly against my palm, running down my arm and into my core. I pulled my hand back roughly and turned to my side away from him. "Who was she?"

Torion stilled and then settled close against my back, his legs curling into mine, an arm over my waist cuddling into my chest in order to draw me closer to his. I couldn't fight him, I told myself. I was too tired, too limp from so much pleasure. And he was so warm.

I must simply...accept how good it felt to be held once more. Acceptance was fine.

"You really want to know?" Torion asked.

I nodded. It would be good to imagine him with another woman. It would cut these little tendrils of feeling that the intimacy we'd shared had allowed to take root.

"She was..." He let out a rough sigh that ruffled my hair. "She was an omega, a beta's omega."

I stiffened, but Torion didn't release me, simply adjusted me in his arms, combing my hair back from my cheek so I could see him out of the corner of my eye.

"My father took me on one of his tours when I was nearing my majority. I wasn't supposed to think of usurping him as alpha, and we never spoke of it, but I'm sure he expected my ambition, so this was a way of teaching me something about the duty. We stayed at one of the lord's estates for several days, negotiating I don't remember what. The lord was quite old, he's since passed. His omega was still young, a few years older than me, but—"

"How old were you?" I asked tartly, fisting my hands in the sheets as I twisted to get a better look at him.

"Sixteen," he said, and the word struck me hard. I turned back to face the wall, found his arm against my middle and held it tight in my grip. "I was an idiot too. It wasn't that women hadn't started turning my head yet, but I'd no notion I was being seduced. She had to appear in the bedroom one night before I realized why she was being so solicitous."

I ground my teeth. Solicitous indeed.

"If I'd been a few years older, even untried, I would've had the sense not to let it happen. It was just the one night, but... I could've caused a world of trouble for my father, for that woman—"

"She'd be perfectly responsible for her own trouble!" I snapped, finding myself suddenly sitting up and facing him once more. "I suppose she wanted you to claim her?"

His smile was wry as he shook his head. "I don't think so. I've not sought her out to ask her. She left Grave Hills after the beta passed. I imagine she was just being selfish, taking something for herself. He wasn't a pleasant man."

I chewed the inside of my cheek as I stared down at

Torion. He was so beautiful. He'd probably been charming and silly and gloriously good looking at that age—and so, so young. I could not forgive this omega, whoever she was. Just like I couldn't forgive Malcolm for claiming me when I was that young, or my father for letting it happen.

Torion reached up and touched my cheek, the one I was abusing, drawing me back to the present. He was lazing against the bed, his wings stretched out to hang over the edge, body shamelessly on display for my gaze.

"You enjoyed yourself?" I asked, arching a brow.

He laughed. "It was my first time with a woman. Yes, I enjoyed myself. Embarrassingly so. Thankfully, we left the estate early the next morning before I could've given myself away to the old man. My father, however, scented my folly immediately. Gave me the ear scorching lecture of a lifetime. Scared me soft for a few years."

He was being light just to set me at ease. His eyes were also fixed to my breasts.

I crossed my arms over my chest, and his smile was knowing. "There were others, though," I said.

"Women?"

"Omegas," I said.

His eyebrows rose and then, astonishingly, he shook his head. "No. I'm a quick learner. She may only have manipulated me for a night, but I realized that wouldn't always be the case. I've behaved myself in the Hills since then."

My eyebrows rose. He would've lived like a monk for decades—

"In the *Hills*?" I pressed. I was mad for digging this up, for demanding to know every instance, every woman. If my reaction to his first experience was any indication, it would *not* serve to make me less charmed by this man. My alpha. *My* alpha.

Torion laughed and covered his face with his hand. "You're a bloodhound."

"As you might've assumed, I've only ever had one man in my bed and—"

"Don't mention Barr," Torion growled, pulling his hand away to reveal a storm over his features.

"—I'd never experienced what you—what we—I just—" I scowled as I stumbled over the words, not even properly sure I knew what I was trying to say, but Torion's expression softened all the same.

"If I tell you, will you let me wake you up with my face between your thighs? Or sucking on those lovely little breasts you're trying to hide from me?" he teased.

I shivered and pretended it was a bristling irritation that made me sit up straighter, my thighs clenching together. "If you must."

Torion's smile was dark, and he sat up momentarily, one wing shifting so they were spread flat across the top of the bed. "I avoided my father's ruts by spending a month or so around those times on the Craven Sea with the alpha there. But last cycle, I returned when it should've been safe and... felt as though I was experiencing something like one of my own. Not quite so mindless, but still risky. I spent a few days at a brothel in Skybern," he said.

My eyes widened, surprised to find I wasn't outraged but curious. "A brothel?"

Torion blushed and nodded.

"For days?"

Torion fought his own smile. "That's why I think it was something like a rut."

"And there you..."

"Brigid!" he laughed, rubbing his hands over his flushing face.

"With one woman?"

He groaned and threw his arm over his eyes.

"Several, then," I said, finding my own lips smiling. "And you were more vigorous there than you were tonight?"

His laugh grew louder, even muffled beneath his beautifully sculpted arm.

"If you learned what you did tonight from the omega—"

"I did not *learn* to fuck a woman with my tongue, Brigid, I simply *desired* to do so tonight," he bit out, moving his arm out of the way to show me his glare—an effect ruined by the crinkled humor around his eyes.

"I cannot imagine what you might've learned from *several* women at a brothel over the course of *several* days."

Torion was quiet for a moment, staring at me. And then in a low, purring tone he asked, "Would you like me to show you?"

This is fun, I thought, a little wistful. It would be easier later if I could avoid enjoying Torion's company so much, but I could already tell that would be impossible. So perhaps it was better to let myself savor him. Surely small, careful doses would be safe.

"Yes, but not tonight," I said, bracing my hands on his chest and then settling back down at his side.

He hummed, his arm curving against my back. "Do you really want a son? I don't mind either way," he said. "If you do, we'll need to be careful until the rut."

I rested my palm over his heart, feeling the steady pound there. "I want to give you an heir."

"I don't care about the specifics of our bargain, Brigid. I won't dismiss you if we don't have a son," he said, so beautifully gentle with every word.

It was sweet and might even be true. I hated to tell him that it would bring me a dark, cruel joy to give Torion the heir that I'd failed to deliver to Malcolm. I knew what an ugly impulse it was.

"Ten years might take away another chance," I admitted, even though it stung to do so. "We should at least try. Do you mind?"

Torion laughed, kissing the crown of my head. "Do I mind fondling, kissing, touching, and pleasuring my omega in any manner of ways that might keep her from getting pregnant until the rut? No, little witch. I relish the prospect. When may I start?"

Torion had been delightfully creative tonight. Malcolm had never really wanted to enjoy anything but the most rudimentary of sexual activities with me, although he'd made me put my mouth on him to ready him. I'd never considered the gesture might be returned. Men were ready when their cocks were hard. If they weren't, touching or mouthing made them ready. No one had ever suggested a woman might want to be prepared too.

Wet, eager, needful.

"In the morning," I said, resisting the impulse to begin now.

Chapter Ten
TORION

'd only meant for it to be a kiss.

In spite of my promise to Brigid that I'd be needing her every night and every morning, I'd spent the past three days visiting the many crofters, arranging the repairs of roofs and fences, new irrigation, and the exchange of animals. I'd returned to the keep each night weary, hungry, filthy, and found my omega waiting with a hot bath and a cold meal, my eyes barely keeping open as she reported her own progress around the keep. And then, witch that she was, she'd offered to massage my shoulders and oil my wings, working her sorcery to lull me asleep with those perfectly magical hands.

She wasn't sleeping in my bed. I thought I'd made it clear it was where I wanted her, but I'd also made it clear it was her choice. And she was choosing to return to her own modest room each night. Out of my reach in the morning. Out of my sight throughout the day.

So when she'd appeared in the stables with three hand pies and a jug of ale for my midday meal, I had a mind to remind her what she was missing by not letting me wake her.

Just a kiss. A *good* kiss, but only enough to tease her.

I groaned into her mouth, arms wrapped tight around her back, trying to pull her into me as she rocked over my lap, grinding herself down over my covered cock. She panted into my mouth, her breath sweet and fresh, herbs and honey. I licked against her tongue for more of the flavor, bucking my own hips up. I was too close. She felt too good, her skirts hiked up as she straddled me, the heat of her thighs bleeding through the wool of my kilt.

"The-the others?" Brigid gasped, pulling from the kiss, her head tossed back to reveal her throat to my greedy nibbling.

If the other men who'd been working in the stables had any sense of what was good for them, they'd stay out of the stables until they saw Brigid and me emerge. They'd left on the signal of my slight head jerk. I thought Brigid would appreciate the privacy, even if it was just a kiss.

It was never going to be just a kiss.

No, now that I'd had a taste of my omega, I would likely never be able to settle for something so chaste and simple. She was too rich, too sweet, too heady, like mead made from heather honey.

"They won't interrupt us," I rasped, and then licked a line up the side of her throat to tease at the lobe of her ear.

The sound of her whine made my balls grow heavy and ready.

"Bellfry's ballocks, witch, you've got me sprung tight," I hissed.

Brigid moaned and covered my mouth with hers before I could suggest that she let me lick her, touch her. Her hands were in my hair, holding me close, her hips working with such a sincere urgency over mine it made me wild. I wanted to lift her from my lap, toss her down into the hay, and mount her roughly, fill her lithe, hungry body with my length and send us both over the edge. And yet...having her use me this way, squirming and whimpering and kissing until we lost our breath? There was nothing like it.

It went right to my head. And then right to my cock.

"Brigid, love, let me—" I tried, too aware of my own release near at hand, fighting it with every little nudge of her hips, the way the warmth and dampness of her arousal was soaking through fabric to kiss against my stiff length.

It was a mistake to pull away from the kiss. It gave my little witch an opportunity to work her magic.

I grunted as her fingers tightened in my hair. Her eyes were dark and her lips swollen, marked red from the stubble I hadn't shaved this morning.

"I can feel your cock twitching, Torion," Brigid said, her voice low and ragged. "Are you going to come for me?"

And like an untried youth, with her eyes glaring down at me and her body churning not for *her* relief, but mine, I did just that, a loud, broken sound escaping me at the shock of it.

Brigid's stern expression fractured with a whine, and she swallowed the sounds I made with a deep kiss, moving unevenly, frantically even, meeting the rough thrust of my hips with her own unsteady grind.

Hot release coated my cock, and no doubt the inside of my kilt, but I didn't care about the mess. Not when I had this enchanted creature in my arms. I turned us roughly to the side, cradling Brigid in one arm as she landed in the loose hay, shoving up her skirts with the other, exposing her swollen, wet sex, almost pulsing with need. Brigid arched and twisted as I pressed two fingers inside of her core, her eyes wide and unseeing, the tight channel clasping on my digits, soaked and dripping down to my wrist.

"Oh, Torion, I—"

"You'll make too much noise if I kiss your cunny now, omega," I growled, grinning as Brigid shuddered and started to fuck herself on my fingers. "But I expect to have you rinsing my tongue tonight. No scurrying away to that other bed. Swear it," I said, pressing my thumb on her clit but holding still, not rubbing.

"Torion," she whined, almost near to tears, the pretty creature.

You have all the power over me, I wanted to tell her, but I waited, imagining the soft clench of her on my fingers was around my cock instead. It would be, soon enough. For now, I would relish the pleasure of watching this woman fall apart at my touch.

"Go on," I coaxed, circling her clit once, her eyelids sinking closed with a groan.

"Oh, I swear it. I swear. I—ah! Torion, yes, I—"

I swallowed her cries with another kiss, leaning over her as I stroked her fluttering cunt through release, Brigid's arms flung around my shoulders to hold me close, her teeth biting roughly on my bottom lip as she strangled the sound of her own pleasure.

"That's it, love," I whispered as she settled, shaking through the aftershocks, blinking drowsily up at me, her long braid mussed and cheeks flushed red. "There now. That's better, hm?"

Her gaze skittered away as she tucked her face into my shoulder. She got so shy in the aftermath, body tensing as if to run and then softening again as the relief of a release soaked in.

I kissed her brow, feeling her stiffen and then relax, her sigh rushing down my throat.

"Are you hard again?" she asked, one of her arms dropping from my back to reach between us.

I pulled my hand free of her and caught her wrist before she could find me as stiff as ever. I wasn't sure I ever really *stopped* being hard when Brigid and I were touching. I'd taken

Ned's advice to show her how much I wanted her, but that admission felt a little too great.

"I'll be all right. Until *tonight*," I said, just to remind her of her promise.

She blushed, eyes fixed to my chin. "I wasn't trying to *avoid* any...morning advances. It just seemed silly to stay while you slept."

Malcolm didn't sleep with her, I'd bet. I shoved the thought away, brushing a slow, grazing kiss over her forehead, ignoring the triumph as she cuddled into me.

"It's not silly when I like to feel you next to me. Do I snore?" I asked, sitting back and pulling her up to join me.

She smiled, and something in the picture of her—straw in her hair, pleasure coloring her features, and the gentle, fond expression—struck me hard in the chest. "No. Sometimes you purr. But I like that sound," she admitted, looking down at her own lap.

She snored. I wouldn't tell her. I wasn't that stupid. And it was just a little sound, a low and quiet chuff and drone, like a cat dozing in the sun. I wanted to hear it again.

"I...I like this too," she murmured, fiddling the leather ties at my collar.

I didn't regret the turn my "simple kiss" had taken this afternoon, but I wanted us entirely undressed at the next possible opportunity. "Cuddling?" I asked.

She blushed and frowned at the same time, opening her mouth for a moment and then closing it and shaking her head. "Never mind."

I tightened my arms around her waist. "Oh, no, you don't. Tell me, or I'll guess."

"There are men waiting for me to leave so they can get back to work," she huffed, pressing at my shoulders and not gaining an inch of ground. "What a bully you are."

"You like rutting like a couple of youths in an empty stable stall?" I tried.

She looked away from me and hummed, shrugging. "Something like that. Go on, let me go."

"You like making me gush inside my own kilt and make a mess of myself?" I continued.

She laughed at that. "I do, as a matter of fact. There. You have it."

I sighed and released her, watching her smooth her skirts down over her hips, waiting until she'd turned her back to me to pick another piece of straw from her braid without her realizing.

She paused at the door of the stall and glanced back at me over her shoulder. "I missed...lust. And I like feeling it with you, Torion Feargus."

Her words nailed me to the spot until long after she'd left the stable, the rise of male voices approaching stirring me from my stupor. She had not said she liked *me* exactly. Just that she liked lusting after me.

I grinned like an idiot all the same.

"AND WHAT IS your intention for the summer drought?"

"You've certainly neglected to see to my broken dam long enough."

"Let's discuss a real issue. How do you expect to keep our omegas from being smuggled out of the territory?"

I blinked and took a slow breath, eyeing the betas surrounding me each in turn, until their squawking settled into an expectant silence.

"Gentlemen, the drought comes every year. We are no less prepared now. Campbell, your dam *is* being seen to—a fact you would've been aware of if you ever looked to the west end of your estate." I paused as Mitchell Sterling tried to cover his laugh with a cough. "And as for the omegas...I intend to do my best to ensure that their home, these hills, is a safe and comfortable place to live for them. So they might choose to stay."

The men in front of me, the men who'd cornered me on my way into the keep, when I was still covered in dust and dirt and no doubt less savory substances, shifted warily at the vague claim.

Francis Keane cleared his throat, two unruly gray eyebrows rising. "You've already denied them the greatest honor of presenting themselves to you for the selection ceremony."

"And denied the people of the Hills the celebration of wishing you and your chosen omega well," another chimed in.

I frowned as the men all seemed to sharpen their stares. "You're concerned about the lack of selection ceremony?" I asked, searching the open hall of the keep for someone with sense. Preferably Brigid.

"There are some...disputes that might be settled at the event," Mitchell hedged carefully.

"I see." I did not entirely see.

"And of course, you might discover another young maid to...strike your interest," Keane said slowly, gaze too fixed to miss my jerk of surprise. "Not to say you aren't certain of the Barr woman—"

"Grant," I snarled, before settling myself, "And now, Feargus."

"But a mark of spite against a man like Malcolm Barr will only get you so far. You need an heir and—"

I took a breath before I might suddenly release fire on these men, raising a hand to pause the insulting ramble. "If you all think that the Hills are in need of a ceremony, then we'll have one. At soonest convenience."

Only Mitchell had the sense to look wary.

"If you'll excuse me," I said, barely managing the polite response as I turned away from the group, charging forward toward the stairs. A flash of copper above me caught my eye —Brigid, pulling back into the shadows, a fleeting glance of her face tangled with worry sending me leaping up the steps two at a time.

Still, I didn't catch up with her until I reached my bedroom door. She gasped as I wrapped an arm around her waist and dragged her inside with me.

"What are you going to do?" she whispered.

I shut the door and then pinned her against it. "What I'm *not* going to do is go back on our bargain," I said.

"I didn't think that," she said, too fast, her little sharp chin lifting in defiance. She softened in my hold, and I settled contentedly against her, my purr thrumming out as her hands came to stroke over my chest and shoulders. "But you have an idea."

Only the start of one, I admitted to myself. "I bet you hate surprises."

"I do," she said firmly, glaring at me.

My hands slid down over her hips, her ass, down to cup the back of her legs. "Too bad."

She screeched as I lifted her up and spun us, hauling us in a stumbling march toward the beginning of the nest she'd built us. I smiled as she broke into laughter, then set about striving for her moans.

Chapter Eleven

BRIGID

You are so dangerous to me.

My hand hovered above Torion's sleeping face, tracing the shadow of stubble that'd grown over his jaw in the night, down to the long tendon of muscle in his throat. The sun hadn't risen over the horizon yet, but night had eased away enough for me to make out the thick of his lashes, the lock of hair that plastered to his cheek, engraved there by his pillow.

His wings were stretched out behind him, and his bare skin was pressed to my side, heating me through my shift. I'd woken with my toes still tucked against his calves. His arm was heavy over my belly, elbow bent so his hand cupped the outside of my breast.

We'd fallen asleep still kissing.

This was terror and temptation, so easy to fall into it made my heart thrash in protest. Was it too late? Had I already let myself enjoy this man too much to brace against the disappointment when it came?

Biting my lip and eyeing the first rosy glow out the

window, I started to twist away, inching to the edge of the bed.

Torion's arm tightened around me, hand shamelessly squeezing my breast.

"No," he growled, his other arm snaking under my hip, tugging me back into the long stretch of his body. His cock prodded against my bottom, but he didn't grind against me.

"It's time to get up," I said, fighting the urge to wiggle into him.

"I know, but...no," he answered, burrowing his face into my hair, his hands moving over my belly and arms wrapping me in a tight hug. "Another minute like this first."

I squeezed my eyes shut. He was too sweet. It crushed me. It showed me all the ways Malcolm had truly demonstrated how little interest he'd really had in me.

"I'm sorry," Torion sighed out, and I flinched. "You're so tense. I shouldn't—"

"No," I blurted out, covering his hands with one of mine, forcing myself to relax against him once more. "You just... surprise me sometimes."

Torion hummed, but I was grateful he didn't ask me to explain myself for once. His chin tucked over my shoulder, breath stroking down my chest, our fingers tangling together beneath the sheet.

"I'd like there to be a feast at the keep after the selection ceremony," Torion murmured, his voice so deep and soft, it sank into my bones, into my core, warming me from the inside out.

The selection ceremony. Where he promised not to choose an omega to replace me. I tried not to care.

"I'll make sure we're ready," I said. "But I... It's time to gather certain herbs from the woods. I know I might not be doing so much healing lately, but I would still like to be prepared. I usually gather near the cottage, but I think I could find some of what I need nearby."

"Let me fly you," Torion said.

I tried to look at him but ended up just bumping our noses together and receiving a soft peck of his mouth against mine. "Don't you have something you need to do?"

He huffed a laugh against my jaw, nuzzling his scruff into my throat until I shivered. "I've been busy because I like to be. Today, I can be busy helping you. Besides, you should check on your cottage. I've had a man visiting, keeping an eye on it, but you'll know if there's anything else that needs doing there."

Please don't, I thought. *Please don't be so kind. Please don't help me. Please don't make me spend the day so close to you.*

My daily reprieves from Torion's tender company had been keeping me sane, keeping me from sinking into the ease he created between us. But flying would save time, and I had been gone too long. And I needed to plan a feast here at the keep now too.

"Brigid?"

"Hm?" I was frowning as he pulled away and rolled me gently onto my back, my head still trying to stomp away fondness and feelings as he appeared above me, perfectly handsome and rumpled.

"There's something *I've* been meaning to do too," he said.

I blinked at him stupidly. He grinned and tossed the sheet back.

"Spread your legs for me, omega."

My breath caught in my chest. I hadn't really thought he'd meant the promise to start a morning kissing me between my legs. I'd been almost afraid to let him do it again, afraid of how good it felt, how much I liked his mouth there and his eyes staring up at me.

But not so afraid that I hesitated for even a moment to do as he asked.

"Is this—"

"That's poisonous," I snapped, huffing as I straightened up from my work to glare at Torion.

His hand hovered just inches away from the flower.

"Did you already touch it?" I asked, scowling at the alpha who stood there, sheepish as a boy.

He nodded slowly, lips twitching, the sun dappling through the trees to gild his hair and shoulders. He looked like a forgotten idol here in the woods, divine and charmed. Golden light clung to him, dazzling me. My temper rose as I resisted the pull to move closer, touch, taste him.

"Go wash your hands in the river then," I said, trying to soften my voice and absolutely failing as I added with a mutter, "again."

"I'm of better use out of your hair, aren't I?" Torion asked, laughing.

I bit my lip to keep from answering. Torion couldn't tell the difference between a dandelion leaf and a thistle.

His boots crunched carelessly over the ground, and I stiffened, tense and trying not to frown as he approached. With arms wide to keep his hands away, he leaned in and kissed my cheek, leaving a warm sparkling spot on my skin.

"Come find me when you're ready," he said.

I sighed as he retreated, leaving me to my work. I straightened from my crouch, letting out a small groan and resting my shoulder against a sturdy tree trunk. Gathering herbs was always harder work on the body than I recalled, but I'd never come to the work already sore. Sore in the hips from stretching myself over Torion's lap, my stomach muscles tired from clenching as I churned myself against my alpha.

I was getting old.

"Brigid?"

I shook the thoughts away and turned towards Torion's voice, just barely able to make out the deep shadow of his wings through the trees.

"Can I go for a swim?"

My lips twitched, and I rolled my eyes.

"I'm not your keeper, alpha!" I called back, having to fully fight my smile as Torion laughed. *Damned cheerful man.*

"Thoughtful," I muttered, as if the compliment were a curse. I knelt down once more to pick more of the delicate pink mushrooms that could be steeped for a strong tonic.

Heat rose to my cheeks as I recalled the slow morning in bed, the unhurried time Torion had spent with his mouth studying every inch of me. "Talented," I added on a breathless pant.

There was a bright whoop in the distance, a sudden splash, and then a howl of surprise as Torion met the sharply cold water of the river.

"Absurd," I added, smiling.

Then I scowled and focused on my work.

We'd flown to the cottage *after* Torion had left me so deliriously satisfied in bed, I'd barely been able to contemplate moving. Which is likely why I hadn't protested when he'd gathered me up in his arms at the front doors of the keep, in front of all the staff and the passing dragonkin. I'd assumed we'd fly with him as a dragon, but instead, he'd held me and chatted with me, remaining closer to the ground, acting as if carrying me in his arms for at least half an hour hadn't cost his strength in the least.

"Infuriating," I caught myself saying before snapping my lips shut.

I lost track of time, filling two baskets to carry by hand and a third I would strap to my back. The light had changed and my stomach was growling by the time I turned and headed for the sound of water.

Torion was stretched out on the large boulder by the river's edge, naked, sunlight glittering on his skin, catching the faintly hidden emerald scales, turning him into that jeweled divinity again, like one of the old dragons come back to the earth.

I shivered, hidden in the shadow of the small woods, but he turned his head, eyes opening unerringly on me, and a smile stretched his wide lips, wicked and knowing.

A part of me crossed into the sunlight, climbed the boulder, and sat astride his lap. A part of me let him peel my dress over my head so I would be equally bare, equally alight in the gaze of the sun. A part of me took him inside of me then, joined as we were meant to be joined, a union of flesh and breath and our eyes feasting on one another.

But that part of me was my imagination. I cleared my throat, dropped my gaze, and spoke only loud enough for him to hear.

"I just need to get these inside and do what I can to preserve them."

"Can I help?" he asked, sitting up with his hands braced behind him.

"Absolutely not," I said, more afraid that if he came too close to me right now, I might make my fantasies a reality, there on the stone, or in the water, or on the grass. Anywhere, really.

Torion just snorted and returned to his sunbathing. My gaze slid back to him, the long endless lines of his legs, the shadow and soft flesh between them, the beautiful hooked muscles at his hips. My throat burned with thirst as my eyes searched for a drop of water I might lick from his skin, and I hurried back to the path, to the bramble fence, to my home.

But I couldn't outrun my craving for the alpha.

Chapter Twelve

BRIGID

I rubbed my thumbs into my temples and stared down at the cobalt blue gown spread over the bed.

"It's fine silk, my lady," said the young maid, Vera, while eyeing me watchfully.

"Aye. And likely fifty years out of date," I murmured.

The maid hummed noncommittally. The gown had been my mother's, wrapped carefully in more fine silk tissue, and then paper, and stored away in her cedar chest that I'd tasked Torion to fly back to the keep with us. Conveniently, it had required him to shift to his dragon, keeping me from having to make conversation while cradled in his arms.

It was the morning of the selection ceremony, and between planning the feast, running wild through the keep to get rooms ready for guests, and bullying the workmen to get the stage ready in time, I'd gone half mad preparing the alpha's keep. Now was the first chance I'd taken to even consider how I would prepare *myself*.

I'd enjoyed gowns and jewelry when I'd been Malcolm's omega. I'd enjoyed presenting myself as his, knowing I was beautiful, or at least understanding I could convince others as much. My lip curled now as I thought of what a pretty little trophy I'd been, how *willingly* I'd made myself as such.

Malcolm had kept the jewels, of course, but the gowns had been mine. I'd tried to keep them in good condition at first. And then slowly, as spite warmed me at night rather than a good fire or a large man, I'd taken joy in wearing them thin, staining and patching and tearing them down to rags for a more useful purpose than ornamentation.

So now I had an ancient gown of royal blue silk and no time at all to make it into something fashionable.

"Is there a lace fichu?" the maid asked.

I shook my head. "There's only this, I'm afraid."

She shrugged. "A well made gown on a handsome woman can never go so wrong, my lady. Let's get you dressed."

Her words, so matter of factly presented, made me blush and fall silent. I remained docile as she pulled the robe I'd donned away from me and hurried to ready me.

Already, the keep was buzzing, the volume outside Torion's bedroom door rising by the minute. Betas and their families had started arriving the night before, the men camping outside while the young women—the omegas who would be standing on stage—piled into every available guest room by the double.

The door to the bedroom opened, but Vera had me by the hair, tight braids working back from my temples.

"Not too much up," Torion said, appearing in the mirror, the maid squeaking assent as he reached and caught a long lock of my hair between his fingers. "It's sunny today. Your hair is going to shine like amber from our seat."

I bit my lip and studied his sporran in the mirror. "Won't I be on stage?"

Torion had been tight lipped about his plans for the ceremony. I wasn't sure if he intended to make a show of choosing me in front of dragonkin and all gathered or had some sort of perverse plan to auction off the other omegas, but I dug for hints at every chance. Surprisingly, Torion had uttered not a clue. For such an open man as he was, he kept a secret well. I tried not to let him see how much it bothered me.

He knelt down, Vera scrambling to follow as he turned me and the stool I perched on to face him.

"Neither you, nor I, will step foot on that stage, omega," he said softly, holding my gaze too fiercely for me to look away, fire rising in my throat. "We'll have a nice view of the proceedings, where we might be admired as the lord and lady of these hills."

I huffed, and Vera patted the braids she'd finished before curtseying and fleeing from the room.

"Then what—" I started.

My question was cut off as Torion surged forward, cupping my face and drawing my mouth to his, a hungry purr roaring out of his chest to burn against my lips.

"You'll see," he rasped, nibbling my bottom lip. "My rut is near, Brigid."

His mouth covered mine once more, tongue thrusting in eagerly as I moaned, my arms settling around his shoulders to keep him close. A breeze stroked against my ankles, and I realized he'd pulled a hand from my cheek and was now rucking my skirt up, scooting on his knees to fill the space between my thighs.

"Are you ready for me, Brigid, hm?" he asked, barely parting our mouths.

"But I—the nest isn't—" My voice hiccuped as a warm hand pressed the inside of my knee, a path of heat moving up my inner thigh. My personal dress wasn't the only thing I'd neglected. I'd been putting off building the nest we would need for Torion's rut, as if that might keep the event at bay too.

"You'll have time to finish the nest," Torion said, voice

low and quiet, the keep strangely silent all of a sudden. "That's not what I meant, though. Are you ready to have me, *here?*"

Two fingers stroked down from my clit to my opening, not hesitating a moment before pressing inside. I caught my breath, my eyes opening to find Torion so close, watching me, all his easy charm now sharpened into dark intent.

"Are you ready to take my cock into you, omega? It's all I think about. I can barely walk straight," he rasped.

I opened my mouth to answer, to pant out a yes, but he swallowed the word with another probing, licking kiss, his fingers settling deeper as my body eased the way with slippery welcome.

"To root myself in you." Torion's teeth scraped over my jaw, his bold, hot words ghosting over my throat. "To fill you for days on end, seeking only our release. Over and over again. For the love of flight, Brigid, I can barely stand not to start now."

I shuddered, the stool thumping faintly against the floor as I started to roll myself into his touch, fucking myself on his two fingers. "We could," I offered, not thinking straight.

He groaned, the sound broken by a ragged laugh. "You've no idea how tempted I am. I'm so hard just touching you. I'll come when you do. The sound of you always makes me burst."

"T-Torion, please!" I gasped, suddenly desperate to have him inside me, to satisfy us both. Only a little of the reason, just the smallest kernel, was due to how much I dreaded presenting myself as his omega to all of Grave Hills dragonkin.

"Mmm, no. We must see this farce through. And then we fly to the other alphas," he muttered. "And the nest, omega. You need to build me a pretty nest."

"The alphas?" I squeaked out, startled, thrown by the suggestion.

"The flight approaches. But first—"

His touch inside me grew urgent, his mouth on my throat biting gently and then suckling hard over my pulse, a spot I found so sensitive. I moaned, my hands scrabbling over his shoulders, hips rising off the stool until only his arm around my waist and his fingers inside of me kept me from hitting the floor.

"Torion, I—"

"Don't beg, Brigid, I can't stand resisting you," he said, and the words were so rough, so earnest, that I sobbed and obeyed, pleading only with wordless sounds, with the unsteady thrust of my hips into his touch.

It didn't take long. Torion knew the path to my climax too well by now. When my toes dug into the floor and my hips arched high, his thumb found my pleasure point, circling twice and then rubbing firmly on the right side.

The damn man had figured out too much of me.

I came with a shout, his teeth and tongue holding firmly at my throat, his arm around my waist steadying me as I started to fall. He pulled me to his chest, settling me in his lap. He pulled his fingers free of me and then brought them up between us, stuffing them greedily between his lips with a lewd, wet sound as he sucked and licked them clean. I watched with wide eyes as he let out a long, low cry, his eyes rolling back and fluttering shut as he shuddered beneath me, sagging forward so we were propping one another up.

I gaped at him, wondering what we'd just done, why it felt like so much and so little at the same time, but he only nuzzled my cheek and sighed.

"That's the best I can do until we deal with the next two days of duties," he said, kissing my cheek.

He stood with a soft grunt, lifting me to my toes in the

movement, turning to set me at his side. On the floor, a spatter of Torion's opaque seed remained. My mouth watered at the sight, and I stiffened, strangely struck by the urge to crouch and lap away the evidence of Torion's desire for me.

I twisted away from the sight, a little appalled with myself. Torion hummed, searching the room quickly before reaching for a spare washcloth, wiping the mess away.

"Come, they'll be waiting," Torion said, tossing the cloth into a basket of linens to be washed and guiding me toward the door with an arm about my waist.

"Wait," I cried, spinning back to the nest. I grabbed the plaid Torion had gifted me and hurried back to the mirror, gaping at my reflection. "You marked me!"

I had a large red and pink welt on my throat where Torion had been suckling. A matching flush covered my cheeks as I spotted his handiwork, and Torion huffed a laugh behind me.

"I like that spot," he said unrepentantly.

I sighed, lifting the plaid and trying to arrange it over that shoulder, bunching at the top like a collar that might hide the love bite.

"No," Torion said, the word low but gentle, his hand settling over mine, taking the plaid away and then rearranging it to his liking on the opposite shoulder. "Let them see."

It was childish. I'd seen girls who'd been marked by their young sweethearts, maids with stable boys who could not resist the possessive claiming, omegas whose young betas had wanted to make a statement. Malcolm had never felt the need.

Malcolm had been a cold but accomplished lover, and I'd never known the difference, I told myself, grazing my fingers over the now sensitive spot on my throat.

"It's silly," I murmured, catching Torion's eye in the glass.

"I know," he said, shrugging. "But I like it."

Ignoring the soft heat that bloomed in my chest, I turned

away from the mirror, stepping into the shelter of Torion's wing and following him out of the room.

"What did you mean about going to the alphas?" I asked, trying to sober myself from the giddy high of release.

Torion's head tipped as he led us through the halls. The keep had been cleared out, everyone moving outside to where we'd set up the stages and tents for the ceremony. My legs were still weak from the unexpected and swift lovemaking, and Torion was warm, wrapping his arm around my shoulders and tucking me close to his side.

"The flight of the alphas," he said, catching my eye, saying the words as if they ought to have meant something to me. "Didn't I mention?

I shook my head. "Weren't they just here?"

"For my rising, yes. But this is an event that takes place regardless. We try as a group not to step on each other's toes, keep our laws and our trade agreements equitable. It gets sorted out after we fly together. But it takes place between here and Skybern this year, so it's a quick trip."

"If your rut is near, and the nest isn't finished—"

"Brace yourself," Torion warned before throwing the doors open.

We stepped out of the keep together to a rousing cheer from the crowd, and I caught my breath, blind in the sudden bright sunshine, blinking at the mass of people ahead of me with blessedly no clear faces. Torion led us easily through, bodies shifting out of our way, and a bite of relief rushed through me when we turned away from the stage, walked past the risers of dragonkin nobility, and over to the smaller plat-form where a private seating arrangement I'd planned for just the two of us waited.

To the left, hovering near the high stage, a cluster of young women perfumed the air, tittering as Torion and I passed near them. My good sense warred with my curiosity, and I leaned around Torion to study them. They were a pretty bunch, and a few had keen gazes as they eyed us, but mostly they looked...young. Fang's fire, some of them looked like children, and it made my heart pang.

"Do you know who you would've chosen?" I whispered, looking up at Torion, who seemed to take no notice of the group.

His brow furrowed as he gazed down at me, and I wondered if he could hear me over the murmuring roar of the audience around us, but then he looked briefly over to the girls. One real beauty, a tall and gloriously curved creature with long black hair curling down past her waist, smiled with too much knowledge and tossed that wealth of hair.

Torion shook his head and smiled at me. "Haven't the faintest, really. I made sure to steer clear of them," he said, an easy grin on his face. Then he bowed his head and whispered against my ear, his breath hot and stirring inside of me. "I'm going to shock them, Brigid. And in truth, I wanted to surprise you. But be united with me, yes?"

We stopped at the foot of the stairs. I'd requested two chairs for us to sit in and watch whatever proceedings Torion had planned, but found instead a cushioned bench waiting for us. Torion was taking my hands in his, staring down at me, waiting for my answer. All around us, humans and dragonkin watched us. Had the rumors, the truth, and everything in between reached them all by now? Was there anyone who didn't know that Torion had claimed me in defiance of Malcolm Barr? Was Malcolm here today? Would I watch him claim my replacement?

My eyes slid to the gathering of young omegas, wondering who it might be, when I caught the eye of the dark haired beauty once more. She was looking at me now, not Torion, and I didn't understand the expression on her face, only that it wasn't jealousy or spite but something like...admiration.

Torion's fingers squeezed mine, drawing me back.

Be united with me.

My heart hammered. With fear. With hope.

"Always," I said, nodding.

He beamed at me then, releasing one hand to cup my jaw and lift it higher to accept his lips as they lowered to mine. I did, and the gentle warmth, the tender press, blocked out the cheerful cries that surrounded us.

Chapter Thirteen

TORION

My omega was rattled. It had started in our bedroom... No, it had started the morning we'd finally woken in bed together, but I'd certainly caught Brigid off guard with my desire today. Her gazes were shy and wary, occasionally faltering into an open wonder that made me throb head to toe.

Yet she stood at my side, proud spine straight and demanding little chin high, the hidden clutch of her hand at my back the only outward proof of her nerves.

I wanted to gather her up into my arms and fly us back to my room, bury her in blankets to make our nest, and then bury myself inside of her. Presenting her in front of so many, especially so many betas, made me want to roar a warning. I searched the crowd in front of us and found Malcolm Barr on the farthest edge of the risers of dragonkin, but he watched us every bit as much as the rest of the audience, with a sneer on his lips and narrowed eyes.

You lost her, I thought, gleeful and furious at the same time. *You lost her, and I claimed her.*

And soon, once this was done and I'd done my duty by

the rest of the alphas, I would make her mine even more fully. If I was lucky, I'd give her the time to build our nest first, but in truth, I wasn't sure I cared if we only had the bed. I was constantly swollen and aching with my need for her. The base of my cock had a constant pulse, like it was just biding its time before I could tie her to me with my first knot—an alpha's gift to his omega. We'd make our heir together. *The first of many*, I thought, offering a grin to my omega, who blushed and returned my smile with a scolding glance.

"They're waiting for you," she muttered, nudging me gently in my stomach.

"They're admiring you," I countered.

She huffed at that and tried to pull away, but I refused to release her, leading us both up the few short stairs.

I raised a hand, waiting for the cheers and the rumbling conversation to die to an expectant silence. "Thank you all for joining us today. I know my...impatience to claim my omega came as a surprise to many of you," I said, taking a special kind of pleasure in rattling the crowd's interest and Brigid's nerves by savoring a long pause to stare down at her until she started to squirm. When she shot a subtle glare up at me through her lashes, I indulged myself with a soft kiss on her forehead, reveled in the way she eased into me, and then turned back to the gathered company.

"I don't mean to be contrary. I have loved and lived in these hills for all of my life. It has long been a wish of mine to stand before you all as your alpha." I smiled through the hurrahs, my body swelling proudly as Brigid's hand rested against my chest. I covered her touch with my own, steadying us both.

"I took my omega in an unconventional manner, it's true. In some ways," I added more softly, so the crowd had to hold their breath to listen, "it felt as though she claimed me first."

Brigid arched a brow at that, eyes just barely narrowing.

I ran a finger down her spine, and the irritation melted into awareness. I wanted her. I *needed* to be inside of her. The itch and burn of the rut had never been so demanding. I'd left the bed before dawn this morning, too aware that we might not leave it at all if I let myself wake her in the manner I wished.

"I will be a good alpha to you all," I said, but I held Brigid's gaze. "I have the best of omegas to make sure of it."

Her eyes flinched, her hand tightened at my back, and her lips parted, barely mouthing my name. If I pushed her any more, she might break in front of our audience, and that would certainly not soften her to me. I knew her that well, at least. Brigid was beautifully proud. Her dignity was armor—armor I hoped she might unburden herself of someday. But not here in front of the crowd.

"In honor of her, and because today's proceedings were never going to go traditionally," I said, pausing for the soft huffs and faint laughter, "I propose a curious twist on the event."

The omegas stirred, eyes widening, looking nervous. In the risers, betas grumbled. I turned to them, smiling, barely hiding my disdain. Perhaps not hiding it at all.

"Gentlemen. I am sure many of you are eager to claim a fine woman of your own. No doubt you have your mind set on one. I *hope* you've done all you could to convince her to feel the same," I said, low, not straining to be heard. I knew they were listening. Then I straightened and called out, "Will any beta who seeks an omega to claim, or desires to take a new companion, please make their way to the stage, so our omegas might admire you better."

"Torion, what—" Brigid breathed, but her voice was stifled under the cries of objection, shock, and a few easy laughs of those who thought I was joking.

"I suggest you be quick. As we are all so aware, there's

quite a few more of you than there are eligible women," I called out above the rabbling conversation.

There was a stutter, a few familiar faces looking nervously at one another, and then a strapping, young beta strode down from the middle of the pack, chest puffed and golden wings stretched proudly at his back. He grinned at the crowd of omegas, tipping his head in deference, and made his way calmly up the steps to the stage.

"This is...madness," Brigid whispered, her eyes darting back and forth as more betas hurried to join him, their protests toppling at the prospect of being left out of the proceedings.

"Do you object?" I asked, bending my head to hers, hiding the words in the curls of her hair, my body stiffening and swelling at the brush of those soft strands against my lips.

Brigid's lips were pressed flat, and I wondered if I'd blundered, angering her and the betas at the same time. Her hands covered my arm around her waist, her grip tightening with surprising strength. She twisted only slightly, enough for me to see a kind of wild joy in her eyes, almost entirely hidden by her blank expression.

"I heartily approve," she gasped out, one hand stroking meaningfully over my forearm. "I will demonstrate as much when we are alone."

I wanted to kiss her, and the soft scratch of her nails told me she was thinking the same. But if we did, I wasn't sure we would make it off this stage without thoroughly exposing ourselves, and that was not the show I had planned for the day.

"This must be from you," she murmured, and this time as she pulled away, I let her go, allowing myself the moment to savor the regal glide of her form onto the bench where she could wait for me.

She'd appeared in my house on the day I'd risen as alpha

like a boon granted for my success, like some wild, enchanted creature sent by the old dragons. My little witch. *My woman.*

I turned back to the gathering, not bothering to hide my smug satisfaction from the betas glaring at me from the stage. I looked down to the young women waiting with wide eyes to hear my next instruction, and then over to the women who had been left standing on the risers, staring at the betas who had chosen them a handful of years ago, now taking their chances on a new match. There were some men who'd berated me only days ago, wanting their chance at choosing a new omega, who remained standing next to their own claimed woman, probably wise enough to realize what I had planned. There was a young woman alone now, wiping tears from her eyes at being abandoned. I didn't know her name or who had been her beta, but she lifted her chin with a mulish determination and turned to glare at me.

"Omegas," I purred into the expectant quiet. "Take your pick." I swept my arm toward the crowded huddle of men waiting on the stage and watched their expressions freeze, their eyes go out in many directions to the crowd, their faces flush.

For a moment, all was stillness, omegas gaping at me, the betas on the stage feeling the first flash of panic regarding their fate. I wondered if any regretted their choice to leave their last omega behind.

And then a bright, delighted cry came from the ground, a young woman with long black hair shoving her path clear as she raced for the stage. An equally young man, one I recognized as the youngest son of a prosperous beta, shouted from the back stage and forced his own way toward the stairs. The pair united with a clash of bodies, their arms tangling around one another, mouths meeting in joyous relief. Behind me, Brigid sobbed out a laugh, and I indulged myself with a glance at her, seeing her eyes shining and her mouth covered to hide her happiness for the couple.

The dam was broken, and a clamor of women charged for the stage, shouting at one another, shouting at the men waiting for them. Some didn't wait, a few betas leaping down to meet their lovers halfway. It was likely for the best. The stage had been designed for a dozen or so young women, not the stampede that was taking place.

A warm hand clutched mine, and I stepped back to join Brigid on the bench, our shoulders resting against each other.

"Look." She nodded toward the tearful woman I'd noticed a moment ago.

"Do you know her?"

"Mhm. Emily Anderson," Brigid said as the woman who looked to be a little older than Brigid herself stepped slowly down the stairs.

My eyebrows rose at that. I hadn't ever met the woman, but I knew who she was. "Cameron Murray's omega?"

Brigid nodded, her stare following Emily's progress toward the stage. "She made that man rich with her family's shipping business. Malcolm always said it drove Murray mad that he couldn't lay claim to the business himself, only the money. I suppose he decided he had enough of it now to last him."

"If it's her business that makes him prosperous, why look for another omega?" I asked, watching Brigid's expressions twist and shift.

"No heir," she murmured. "They had an affair."

I frowned. "Her beta and—"

Brigid shook her head, eyes bouncing quickly now between the stage and Emily Anderson. "Malcolm and Emily. For a year or so. She was the first woman I caught him with."

I stiffened, following her gaze finally and realizing what she watched. Malcolm stood center stage, and his eyes tracked the fluttering, giggling swarms of omegas like a predator, but he seemed to take no notice of Emily, who was only just mounting the steps. The crowd was loud and boisterous, arguments and joyful unions taking place throughout the field. One young girl stood nearly wrapped around her lover, as two older figures, clearly her parents, pleaded at her oblivious back.

I'd made a mess of the local dragonkin. But my focus was on my omega.

"Do you hate her?"

Brigid turned to me then, looking genuinely surprised at the thought. Color flashed in her cheeks, and she settled, leaning more fully into me. I wrapped my arm around her shoulders, now interested to see how things would play out on the stage.

"I did at the time," Brigid admitted softly. "When I was foolish enough to think Malcolm might've been true to me if not for the seduction of another woman. It didn't take long to realize that was never the case."

Malcolm stiffened as Emily neared him on the stage, as if suddenly realizing the *possibility* of being claimed, but she passed him without a glance.

"Who do you think she will choose?" I asked Brigid.

Her brow furrowed as she scanned the stage and her frown deepened. "I'm afraid she will go back to Murray."

"After he took his chances looking for a new omega?" I asked, startled by the idea, now searching for the man on the stage. He stood in the corner, clearly disgruntled by the absolute lack of interest of any of the younger women. He was an old beta, albeit a wealthy one, but it seemed the young woman who'd first claimed her handsome beau had set the tone for the afternoon. The omegas were making *their own* choices, and the winners of the day appeared to be younger betas of various standing.

"Sometimes, it's easier to forgive," Brigid muttered, wincing as she shrugged. She froze, and then her expression cleared, eyes widening slightly and lips curving up at the corners.

Emily Anderson had stopped, but not in front of Malcolm or Murray, or any of the other older beta gentlemen who might've been amenable to a companion rather than a woman young enough to produce an heir. She stood now in front of a very tall, very surprised, and somewhat shabby looking young beta. I didn't recognize him, but he had more of the look of a human farmer than a member of dragonkin nobility, if not for his almost comically large black wings. Perhaps he would grow into them. Either way, he stared down at the petite and lovely older woman. Dragonkin males' ages might be deceptive, but it was clear this lad wasn't very long past his majority, somewhere in his twenties. He was young for a beta, but then again, he was a great deal closer in age to Emily than she had been to her previous beta.

He spoke to the omega, having to hunch to reach her ear. Brigid's hand squeezed mine as Emily rose up on her toes, one hand resting on the young dragon's shoulder, her lips whispering back into his ear. He nodded, obviously eager, eyes wide and earnest, and Emily offered him a small smile.

And then the young man snatched the woman off her toes, one arm wrapped around her waist, the other hand catching her at the back of the neck. Brigid huffed a laugh as Emily Anderson was kissed by her eager new beta.

"She'll make him rich," Brigid said to me, with a smile in her eyes that I usually only saw after thoroughly pleasing her in bed. "And I expect she'll enjoy his...youthful vigor?"

It looked as though *many* of Grave Hills' omegas would be enjoying youthful vigor. It also looked as though I was going to have a fight on my hands from some of the older, more established, more *powerful* betas.

I should've cared. I should've regretted my plan for the day.

But two delicate fingers were sliding up the back of my neck, twisting a lock of hair at my nape. A soft breast pressed to my arm, and warm breath caressed my ear.

"If we leave now, we can have the keep locked before the dust settles," she teased.

Some of the betas, the ones who'd won eager omegas today, were wisely considering the same, fervent couples making their way out of the crowds, hopefully soon to find their way home.

On the stage, still at the center, Malcolm Barr remained standing alone, glaring daggers not at me, but at my omega. I swallowed the growl in my throat and turned to Brigid, lowering the arm over her shoulder to wrap around her waist.

"I'll have to bear their complaints," I said, and then to soften the rejection before she could misinterpret it, I added, "And truth be told, if I go to bed with you, omega, we may not make it back out for the Flight."

I caught the wince of her features, but Francis Keane—who had not subjected himself to the humiliation of the stage—was marching closer with a warning glare, and I didn't have a moment to quiz my omega.

Chapter Fourteen

TORION

❦

"You're lucky there are still some mercenary women in the Hills," Francis Keane muttered in my ear as the great hall of the keep roared with activity. "As it is, you've angered every middling lord from here to Gillifenn."

"There isn't a lord without an heir who went slighted by the omegas today," I pointed out. It was a stroke of luck, really, but I was grateful for luck. "And as you mentioned, the richest men came away with a prize as well."

Keane opened his mouth, no doubt to blister my ear with his cautions and warnings and chastisements again, when a rickety old tenor sounded behind us.

"Give it a rest, Francis. We're more likely to see a healthy crop of newborns in the next ten years than we have in a century. The young couples can barely keep themselves from mounting each other here in the hall," Ned McIntyre announced.

I choked down my laugh, and Francis Keane let out a bluster of shock and irritation.

"You should make your rounds, soothe the ruffled feathers. Your omega, while *not* a wise choice, is certainly doing her part," Francis said, and then left at last without a word to Ned.

"He's a pompous prig. Shows what comes of breeding our stock with Skybern's."

"My mother came from Skybern," I said, smiling at Ned as he took Keane's spot at my side.

"Aye, and look what a mess you've made today," Ned shot back, grinning.

I looked out over the room at the young men and women who were, indeed, snuggled and cozied and in some less polite positions too, all looking deliriously happy at claiming one another. I also glanced at the "middling lords" who were scowling and clustering together, no doubt plotting against me now that I'd caused this slight to their egos, and at the smug wealthy men who sat with new omegas at their side. And finally, I let my gaze linger on the slim figure encased in vivid blue, with coiling and gleaming copper running down her back—my omega, who went from one couple to the next, offering congratulations and smiles.

I scanned the room for the hundredth time, searching for Barr. There were more revelers outside with musicians and dancers by a brilliant bonfire that tossed wild sparks into the air and food stalls supplementing the feast Brigid had arranged in the keep. So far, Brigid's former beta hadn't stepped foot inside. I was relieved and suspicious. He'd been chosen by an omega, one who'd been left standing alone on the risers. The woman had looked young enough to still be prepared to give him an heir, although she'd been plain and had shook hands with Barr like they'd made a bargain between them.

If I could've prevented him from having any woman claim him, I might've, but even in my most frivolous plan, that was too extreme a slight. I could only hope the woman had known what she was getting in her choice.

I wondered now how today would've gone if I'd had no omega. If I'd been one of the men standing on stage. I wanted the fantasy that Brigid would've claimed me like the dark-haired young woman had claimed her beta, with a race to the stairs and a cry of joy. But I knew the truth. Brigid would not have run onto the stage, not for me and not for any other man. There'd been no omega standing unpaired at the end of the tussle today, but there likely would've been if my omega hadn't already been claimed by me.

Strangely, I found myself smiling at that.

Brigid wouldn't even have left her cottage for the ceremony.

I'd found the one omega in the Hills who'd have taken a one room cottage and a shabby living of caring for others, rather than the company of a male dragon. No, she found me.

And yet... I caught her eyes across the hall, watched her cheeks blush at the heat in my gaze, her lips quirk.

And yet, I'd made her want me. In bed, at least.

"Lovesick fools, the pair of you," Ned huffed at my side.

My smile was half-hearted. "She doesn't love me yet, Ned."

He chuckled and patted me on the shoulder. "I meant you and your father, lad."

My chest panged uncomfortably, as if I'd been hoping he might contradict me. "Ah. You think I've made a mistake today too, I take it."

Ned hummed at that, helping himself to sitting on the arm of my chair, our wings brushing together. "I think you were wise today. It wasn't just the omegas on that stage who were happy with your boon. There were young girls in the audience that took hope from you granting their kind a choice, young and old mothers too. You might have convinced our women not to leave the Hills for greener pastures today."

I sat straighter at that, and Ned rolled his eyes at me.

"Doesn't mean the betas will recognize as much," he added drily.

I sighed. "I'll take what little victory I can find."

"You rose as alpha, lad. You have an omega. You've not been challenged yet," Ned listed, nodding firmly. "Those are victories. Remember and count them. And here's another. Your lady approaches."

Ned and I both rose, but he beat me to greeting Brigid, taking her hand and bowing lower than I would've guessed he could manage. "Sir Edward McIntyre, my lady," he said, shockingly gallant.

"Ah, you match my mother's description exactly, my lord. She spoke very highly of you in her journals," Brigid said.

I watched, awed, as Ned stood taller, his cheeks bright with a blush. "Ah. I am surprised she mentioned me. I was well beneath her notice. You take after her. Beautiful women, true to the Hills."

"I don't believe you're beneath anyone's notice, Sir Edward," Brigid said, smiling and still holding Ned's hand.

"Quit flirting with my omega," I teased Ned, delighted when he reddened further.

But he shot me a sharp glare. "Mind you not give the lad too much leeway. He's a foolish pup, no matter how fine his taste in women is."

Brigid laughed as Ned stomped away from us, and then gasped as I caught her hand and tugged her against me, drawing her into my lap. A few cheers from nearby dragonkin went up, but I ignored them and turned Brigid's face to mine.

"This is the finest feast the keep has ever seen," I said, my voice low and private.

Brigid sighed, leaning into me, and some of the mask she

must've been wearing slipped to reveal her weariness. "I'm glad it pleases you."

"Even the men who can't stand to look at me tonight are enjoying themselves," I added.

Brigid glanced in the direction of the slighted betas. "How serious is the damage?"

"I don't know, and tonight, I don't care. When can we retire? We have an early morning tomorrow." And I'd been considering a few ways we might touch tonight that wouldn't prove too tempting to give into the rut.

But Brigid frowned and looked down at her lap. "I was thinking I ought to stay here at the keep while you attend the Flight."

"Stay here?" I echoed.

"I haven't finished building the nest and—"

"Brigid, your place is with me."

She stiffened in my arms, and I swallowed hard, wondering why the words bothered her and what I could do to change that.

"I know that's true, but with all of the other alphas?" she asked with a demureness that set my teeth on edge. Where was my bold witch?

"Those with omegas will have them in attendance," I said.

Her eyes winced, and she turned her face to the room at large, conjuring a smile, pretending to be enjoying herself here on my lap. She *should* be enjoying herself, or at least that was what I wanted for her.

"It just sounds...oppressive," she said through her teeth.

"Oppressive." Why did I keep repeating her?

"All those alphas together at once," she whispered.

I found her hand in her lap, some of the unease softening as she tangled our fingers together without hesitating.

"Do you find my company oppressive then?" I asked, trying to keep my voice light, teasing.

She huffed and turned back to catch my eye. "No," she said, her tone impatient, like I ought to have known better. I sagged a little with relief, but she continued, "But you certainly can be overwhelming at times."

With her on my lap, there was hardly anywhere else to look but at her, but I focused my gaze over her shoulder, doing my best to keep my expression blank.

"Not in a bad way, necessarily," she murmured.

Necessarily.

"Torion," she coaxed, and it was clear she knew she'd injured me.

Which somehow made the injury feel worse. I reached for her face with my free hand, drawing her mouth down to mine for a slow kiss. It lacked our usual heat, a gesture meant to console one another.

"I'll leave tonight then," I said.

"Tonight?" she asked, eyes widening. "Torion, I only— I didn't mean—"

"It's not that," I rushed, because I didn't want an apology for her honesty. "Since I am co-hosting the event, it will be best for me to be there in the morning to help prepare. I just didn't want to fly you through the night."

She frowned, her fingers fiddling with mine in her lap. "Are you sure?"

I nodded, pulling her chin—stubborn, sharp, and proud, like her—back for another quick kiss. "I'm sure. Stay here. Prepare the nest."

Her hands framed my face, and it was difficult to meet her eyes at first, and then painful as they caught mine, saw too much, told me too little in return.

"I will look forward to your return, Torion," she said, slow and simple. Honest. She meant the words.

But I could be honest with myself too. Brigid would not have chosen me if I'd stood on that stage today. Not if I'd stood tall in the sea of other betas. Not if I'd stood there all alone.

I GROANED, stretching in the tent reserved for myself and my company—company I hadn't brought with me to the mountain flight. Because Brigid had asked to remain at the keep and I didn't trust a local beta well enough yet to bring one as my second.

Canvas fluttered, and I glanced up, sighing at the sight of Seamus. "Had enough of harassing Cadogan and his omega?" I asked.

"For the moment," Seamus said, grinning and helping himself to one of the seats, conveniently located next to a decanter of wine and a plate of meats and cheeses and fruit. "Why did you rise to Worthington's bait about your omega?"

I sighed and rolled my shoulders, ignoring Seamus's presence as I arched forward and bent down, doing a routine of movement I'd learned from my mother. "Because I flew here at night. Because I'm nearly in rut. *Because* I realized that my omega likely would've preferred I'd not claimed her but left her in peace in the wilderness."

Seamus grunted. "Women."

Considering the man had been Alpha of the Craven Sea for a century at least and had never taken an omega, I wasn't sure what he could know about the subject.

"She hates you then?" Seamus asked.

I straightened too quickly and then forced myself to take a slower, deeper breath, raising my arms high above my head. "No, she doesn't hate me."

"You don't please her in bed?"

I rolled my eyes and ignored his goading. "We do very well together in bed."

"I like Cadogan's little omega," Seamus mused, filling his mouth with too many grapes.

"You've made that very apparent," I said, raising my eyebrows.

He grinned and waved his hand. "Don't *warn* me, Feargus. I've no intention of making trouble with Bleake Isle. I just haven't ever met an alpha's omega who struck me as...the sort of omega I might be tempted to take. They're usually...you know..."

"Omega Worthington?" I said, thinking of the pinched and prim woman from Skybern.

Seamus grimaced and nodded. "But she suits him."

I sighed, shifting my legs apart, spreading my arms ahead and behind me, my wings to match. "She does. I should've noticed sooner."

I'd thought Damian was my ally, but after his needling and nagging today, I realized I was simply a more available ear to Damian than my father had been. If I wasn't going to cooperate with his plans, he certainly wouldn't stand by me against a challenge.

"And your omega? Does she suit you?"

I didn't hesitate. "She does. In fact, I think she has the spirit of an alpha. She's proud. Stubborn. Smart. She cares about the people around her."

Seamus watched me. "She sounds very serious. Does she make you very serious too?"

I stared into the distance. I thought of my choices since I'd risen as alpha and of my time with Brigid, the things I would do or say to make her smile.

"No, actually."

Seamus clapped his hands on the arms of the chair. "Well, that's a relief. You get unbearably maudlin when you're taking yourself seriously. Like now."

I laughed at that, and the way it rushed through my chest lightened my limbs.

Seamus shrugged. "If she likes you well enough, enjoys you in bed, surely you can sort out the rest of the issue."

The rest of the issue was that I had started to fall for my omega, without waiting for her to join me in the descent. But Seamus was right. Brigid's words at the feast had hurt me, but they hadn't been designed to do so. I wasn't sure why she'd balked at the idea of coming to the Flight, but in the middle of the keep, surrounded by dragonkin, I hadn't taken the time to coax a real answer out of her. I'd just...left. I grimaced at myself, trying and failing to hide the expression from Seamus.

"It's your first alpha rut," Seamus said calmly, taking on that deep stillness he sometimes had that I'd found so calming when I'd joined him on the sea. "It's normal to have uneven moods. I imagine it grows more complicated when you have an omega at hand."

"Why haven't *you* ever taken an omega?" I asked.

Seamus grinned. "Oh, I've considered it. Every time I set foot on land, enjoy an evening with a welcoming lady, I think it might be time. But I'll never give up my life on the sea. Not until some brave upstart can take it from me. And it doesn't seem to suit the gentler sex."

I hummed at that. To my mind, omegas hadn't been given much choice in the matter. Most were kept strictly in their homes, in their territories. A rare few managed to escape, and even less of that number was recovered.

"Have you ever come across a fleeing omega on the sea?" I asked, thinking of the many women who'd gone missing from the Hills over the decades.

Seamus shifted forward, elbows resting on spread knees, eyes shifting to the barely parted curtain of my tent and glaring farther out into the setting sun. "No, in spite of what the others might think. And I've searched. Not for the alphas' sakes, but for the omegas'. It's not the easiest mode of traveling."

"I recall," I said drily, thinking of some of the storms where I'd been sure we wouldn't survive the struggle.

"Either those women have a shepherd who knows the waters better than I, or..."

Or perhaps they'd been lost in the effort. Given what I'd experienced with Seamus in our travels, I thought it likely the latter. We shared a moment of pained quiet.

"I expect you and Cadogan will do your bit to lose fewer women from your territories," Seamus murmured.

My lips twitched. "As a matter of fact, you might like to hear what I pulled off in Grave Hills yesterday."

I would return to Brigid soon, make up for my sullen exit, and in time, I thought I might win her over properly. I knew it wouldn't be easy, but she'd already proven she'd be worth the effort. I just needed to be patient.

Chapter Fifteen

BRIGID

I huffed, wiping the sweat from my brow with the heel of my hand as I stepped back against the bedroom door to examine the nest in front of me. A tall tent of sage green velvet now took up the majority of Torion's bedchamber. With its opening barely parted, I could just see the large copper tub we often used. Sliding inside, the space grew hazy in the light low, and another peaked sheath of thin cream linen hid the bed from view. I'd had local carpenters fashion half walls of cedar, topped with an attractive scrollwork design, and I'd set them up a few feet around the mattress and then filled in the gaps with feather pillows and wool bolsters, expanding the mattress in every direction.

It was a nest fit for the alpha.

I chewed at the corner of my thumb, glancing through the parted velvet to the window, where the sun was just starting to drop from the sky to meet the horizon.

I should've gone with Torion, I thought as a now familiar turning sensation, heavy and sour, rolled in my chest. Defiance kicked back hard, and I pulled my abused thumb away, fisting my hand at my side and bucking my chin.

I might've gone with Torion if he'd given me more than a day's notice. If I hadn't spent weeks toiling to bring the keep back into shape, or gone mad in the past few days preparing the festivities for the selection ceremony. If I'd known to have the nest ready by now.

I sighed. "You knew," I muttered to myself, shaking my head, opening the curtains around the bed and reassuring myself with the sight of heaping pillows and soft sheets.

I'd known from the start that the rut would come. That I'd bargained my way into being the alpha's omega, a role that required me to play a part once more—supportive and sweet, welcoming to all who arrived at the door. I hadn't realized how attached I'd grown to my place in the woods by the river, hadn't braced myself for how shocking it was to step back in the shape of being a man's woman, and this time on an even grander scale.

I'd worn a decades old dress for the selection ceremony, for goodness' sake. Most days since I'd arrived, I was better suited to being one of the keep maids than I was the alpha's omega, dusty and sweaty and up to my elbows in a task.

Because I'd chosen to be.

A knock sounded behind me, and a bright pleasure spiked in my chest before quickly burning away. Torion wouldn't be back yet, and he wouldn't knock on his own bedroom door.

"Yes?" I called, retreating from the nest.

"My lady, there's a beta in the old alpha's chambers," a maid answered from the other side of the door. They were now under orders not to step inside the room, so that the only scents present would be mine and Torion's.

"A beta?" I echoed, marching for the door. I hurried out into the hall and found one of the younger maids nervously wringing her hands.

"Miss Maggie is with him, milady, but he's talking around her and not leaving as asked."

Dread ran icily through me. "I'll go deal with the situation. Send up a couple of the big lads to stand outside this door. No one is to go in. Especially not this beta."

Whoever he is, I thought, afraid I might already know.

The maid dipped a low curtsey as I rushed for the tower stairs. As a beta, Malcolm's scent was milder, but it still provided enough warning for me to brace myself, to reach the doorway with my arms crossed and my eyes narrowed, a sharp word on my tongue.

He was expecting me, arms spread and face skeptical. "He hasn't even taken the alpha's quarters? That ought to say enough."

I wiped my teeth with my tongue and changed tack. "He is the alpha. The alpha's quarters are wherever he chooses. Regardless of that, you have no right to be here, Malcolm."

He scoffed, his eyes studying every inch of me. "You look more like his washer woman than his omega."

I blinked, lips quirking, surprised and pleased to find the words held no sting. "You're being childish, Malcolm. You should find your way home. You don't want the alpha to find you harassing me *here* when he returns."

Malcolm's jaw tightened, and he stepped forward, eating up the space between us too quickly. "What are you going to do, omega, when you fail to deliver the alpha's heir? You and I both know your body is a disappointment in that way," he said in a low, too sweet whisper.

I swallowed the urge to tell him about the heir I'd nearly given him. He didn't deserve to mourn with me, so I did my best to keep my expression blank.

"Your body was a disappointment in many ways," Malcolm continued, with a more leisurely glare caressing over me. That look would've stirred me once, regardless of his bitter words. I felt nothing now, at last, and that realization made it easier to breathe as he continued, "Why do you think I had to seek succor elsewhere?"

My brow furrowed, and Malcolm's eyes glinted in victory, gaze tracking my tongue as I wet my lips.

"I have realized, my lord, that you lacked the understanding to draw out the best of what I have to offer," I said softly, thinking of Torion, of his mouth and hands, of the way he glowed, watching me come apart in his arms.

I was too focused on the thought of my alpha, too slow to dodge, and Malcolm caught me by the shoulders in a tight grip, his eyes blazing with fury and also a hunger I recalled but didn't feel the echo of now.

"Is that *so?* Maybe you had better—" Malcolm's snarl died as I pulled a pair of shears from my apron, ones I'd used to cut the velvet and linen for Torion's nest. They were sharp, and they left a pale indentation where I pressed them to Malcolm's throat, my slim arm reaching up easily between us.

"Are you mad, Malcolm Barr?" I hissed, trying not to let my voice quake. I hadn't been prepared for him to touch me, grab me, and it made my heart pound too hard and too fast in my chest, but my hand was steady where it pressed the sharp point of the shears to my former lover's throat.

His grip lessened and then released, face shuttering to its usual coolness. I kept my weapon in place.

"Leave here. Collect your new omega. Return home," I gritted out, one word at a time. "Pray I don't tell the alpha you dared to touch me."

Malcolm stepped back slowly, and I tried not to crow as I watched his shoulders droop, his breath slipping out on a sigh. He kept his eyes on the tip of the scissors, and I wondered if he would have the sense to be wary of his own washer woman in the future.

"I beg your pardon, Omega Feargus," he said, delivering a

too brief and stiff bow before sweeping around me to retreat out the door.

I waited until I could no longer hear his footsteps down the stairs before gusting out my own sigh and dropping my scissors back into my apron, falling backward to lean against the doorframe.

I needed to bathe now, to wash any trace of Malcolm off me, for my own sake and for Torion's rut. I needed to eat, to prepare myself for the coming rut, when there would be less opportunity. But as I stood, shaking, catching my breath as if I'd run a mile, the only thing I *wanted* was Torion to appear before me, gentle and sweet and a shield against the past and the rest of the world.

When my trembles settled, I stood straight and returned downstairs, pleased to find two strapping human men waiting at the door to Torion's bedroom.

"We watched the man go out the front door of the keep, milady," one lad announced before offering a belated bow at the hips.

I flattened my hands over my hips and nodded. "Thank you both. Please have someone send up the hot water for bathing. And all the provisions for the alpha's rut." They started to depart as I reached the doorway and I turned, calling out to catch them at the last second. "And ask those outside to be sure that any lingering dragonkin depart soon. As politely as possible, mind you."

The men hurried away to do as asked, and I entered the bedroom, tugging at the strings of my apron, pulling off the handkerchief I'd tied around my hair.

Torion would return soon. He'd said his rut was near. Rather than wait for it to come on, I would draw it out myself.

A dark determination came over me, petty revenge and

selfish passion snarling together. I knew Torion better now. I knew he wanted me. I would conquer his desire and build it up into the demand of the rut.

The alpha would be mine tonight.

Chapter Sixteen

BRIGID

***

Morning light was gently dulled inside of the nest, but I greeted it all the same with an irritated glare, knowing full well that I was alone.

Torion had not returned to the keep in the night, a fact I was sure of because I'd left the nest a half-dozen times and asked the guard stationed outside of the front doors.

I huffed, sitting up in the bed, a flow of pillows toppling from where I'd shoved them to land behind my back. I was exhausted, annoyed, and fighting a nauseous worry that made me even more annoyed. Torion hadn't strictly promised to return last night, but I *assumed* his eagerness to reunite with me, or at least the call of his rut, might ensure the trip was short.

Maybe it would've been if you hadn't insulted him on the way out, I thought, groaning and scrubbing my face with my hands.

A low murmur, deep in the keep, rumbled through the velvet curtains, dulled but familiar, and my hands dropped to my lap.

Torion.

It was still early morning, which meant he would've departed at dawn.

Grinning, I wrestled against blankets and pillows to reach the foot of the bed, snatching up my robe and nearly putting it on backwards in my haste to get out into the hall. It wasn't until I was opening the door that I heard the second voice.

A soft, husky feminine laugh echoed up from the great hall of the keep. "Are the beds made of stone too?"

Delusional hope flared for a moment. Maybe not all of the visiting dragonkin had made their way home yesterday. Maybe that hadn't been Torion's voice I'd barely heard, but another—

"Certainly not. Didn't you see all the sheep on the way here?" Torion asked, his voice so easy I could hear the smile he was wearing even before I'd reached the balcony.

"You sleep on sheep?" the woman teased in answer.

My heart sank, dead weight now, as I looked down to see them together, and my stomach turned. She was pretty and windblown, with dark brown hair hanging in braids over her shoulders and down her back, buxom and tall and womanly. Not a young omega, but younger than me, I expected.

"It's a better rumor than what's usually said," Torion muttered with a crooked smile, his face starting to lift, to turn in my direction. I would duck behind a pillar and then retreat to...where? The room I'd taken when I'd first arrived? My cottage?

"Quit flirting with my omega."

I froze, and Torion's gaze found me, but my own flashed toward the three men entering through the keep doors, where the words had come from. A handsome figure with dark eyes and hair and deep umber wings took long strides to reach the woman Torion had been speaking with.

"Quit accusing your friends of flirting with me," she volleyed back.

"I will when they stop flirting with you," he said, his smile lascivious and hungry as he wrapped an arm around her and drew her to his chest. But the kiss he placed on the crown of her head was tender and chaste.

"Ahh, this must be she," called one of the other men, the largest of the group, with long hair and ragged clothes but a confident sonorous voice, and I realized I'd been spotted.

Torion was still watching me, and the jealousy that had struck me hard at the sight of him with a beautiful woman sizzled away into nothing at the blatant hunger in his stare, the hope and expectation. I caught my breath and turned for the stairs. I was wrapped in a robe over my nightdress, but there was an ease amongst the group that spoke of genuine friendship, and they were all clearly just landed from a flight.

Torion reached me halfway up the stairs, the heat of his hands branding against my hips as he caught me, bending slightly to press his nose to my temple, the rustle of his breath as he scented me making the fine hairs on my body stand at eager attention.

"We woke you," he said, low enough for only me. I could see the others watching us over his shoulder, but I gave into the urge to close my eyes.

"No. Just drew me out of bed." *When I heard your voice. Because I've been waiting for you.* "Should I get dressed first?"

"We'll all go up together to freshen up. Come say hello first?" He leaned back, brow furrowed. "There are two alphas."

And I had said I found alphas oppressive. "And friends of yours?" I asked instead. I did not excel at sounding *sweet*, but I was fairly sure I'd managed to be less temperamental than I had the night he'd left.

"Yes, but don't let that prejudice you," he said, smiling now and stepping back, his hand finding mine to guide me down. "I...offered them all a place to rest tonight."

I resisted the urge to laugh at myself, at my silly plan to seduce and tease and bed Torion straight upon his return to the keep, but I let my smile bloom and turned it to our guests.

"We have rooms refreshed from the selection ceremony. We're well prepared for welcome guests," I said. Torion's fingers squeezed around mine.

He made the introductions—the Alpha of Bleake Isle, his omega and half-brother, and the Alpha of the Craven Sea, who winked as he bent over my fingers and kissed them until Torion let out a growl.

"We'll do our best to make sure our visit isn't too taxing for you," Alpha de Roche said, eyeing me carefully, ignoring Torion's glare.

I ignored the warmth in my cheeks and tried to think of something kind to say, but Torion snorted and turned us away. "You're the only one she needs to worry about, so just mind your manners, de Roche."

"I imagine they're harder to come by when you're spending all your time on a ship with a bunch of unruly men," Alpha Cadogan said, following us in our wake, his omega tucked against his side.

At the back of the group, Niall Cadogan's voice was just barely heard above our steps. "Look, you've given them some-thing to bond over."

"What's that?" Alpha de Roche asked.

"Wanting you to keep your eyes off their women."

"I hope the lot of you find something to do today besides bicker," Omega Cadogan murmured.

Torion waggled his eyebrows at me, and I realized I could take my time finding my footing amongst this group. They managed the conversation fine on their own.

We met a group of servants at the top of the stairs, split-ting off from one another in the direction of private rooms. I tried not to be pleased by the way Torion's hand tightened around mine, pulling me urgently in the direction of his bedroom.

"I didn't mean to stay the extra night away," Torion said, his voice low as he shouldered open the door. "Oh!"

I inched closer to his back, eyeing the curtains of the nest over his shoulder, rising on my toes for a peek of his arrested expression. And then he was tugging me inside, pushing me back against the door until it clicked shut, and I was trapped between it and his large frame. My breath hitched as his hands mapped my hips and waist, urging me onto my toes so his hips could better fit between my thighs.

"Little witch," Torion growled, bowing his head. I raised my mouth, expecting his kiss, and then moaned as he settled against my throat instead, nipping and kissing, suckling over the fading bruise he'd left behind. "How did you magic us up a nest so quickly? If I'd known it would be ready, I never would've invited guests over. Oh, the things I will do to you in our bed, Brigid. I can't even speak of them, or I might just start now. Let's tell the others to leave. They can finish their flight home today."

I arched in Torion's warm hands, trying to remember the short speech—an apology, really—I'd prepared. Not that Torion seemed to require one. His welcome of me was *warm* to say the least. Instead, all I managed was a garbled, "Diplomacy."

Torion snorted, softly kissing his way along my jaw, almost sweetly if not for the way his hands were groping my ass, spreading the cheeks suggestively as he nestled the ridge of his cock against my sex. "They're allies, but they're friends. Cadogan only just made it through his rut, and he still can't keep his hands off Mairwen. He'll understand."

But his arms circled around my waist and his weight pressed still and comforting against me, our faces cheek to cheek so his breath teased warmth against my ear. I realized too late that my own hands were cupping his ass through his kilt, as if to urge him to move against me, inside me. I cleared my throat and moved them up to rest beneath his wing roots.

"I should've gone with you. I'm sorry I balked," I said, relieved at how much easier it was to say when I didn't have to look him in the eye.

Of course, that didn't last long. Torion leaned back, one hand reaching between us to lift my chin and force my gaze to his. "I like you," he said.

I jerked in his arms, the words striking me like a sharp arrow.

His lip quirked up in the left corner and he ducked, grazing a kiss over my lips. "I prefer you telling me when you don't approve of something, or don't want to do something. Even if I may not take it very well at first."

I couldn't speak, a small, strange sound rising in my throat, and Torion released me, let me hide my face as he stood straight and led us over to the opening of the nest. I winced at the sight inside—the bath I'd had waiting, now cooled, and the covered platters of food ready. Torion took it all in, purring and approaching the linen around the bed. He parted it and stilled. His wings shrouded him from my view.

"Is it...all right?"

His wings spread briefly, and Torion let out a low groan, bending forward and bracing his hands on the built up mattress I'd fashioned. "Come here, omega."

Wisely, I backed up.

Torion glanced over his shoulder, his grin feral, his laugh low. "It only needs one thing," he said.

That made me pause, my brow furrowing. "What?"

"The scent of your release all over the sheets."

My face went hot and I ducked out of the tent, fighting my own smile as Torion let out another laugh.

By unspoken agreement, Torion and I didn't touch again, each taking our turn out of sight of one another to dress, not lingering in the bedroom together when we were done. After a brief luncheon as a group, Torion left the keep with the other men to give them a tour of the Hills. I didn't mind sitting the expedition out, but I'd forgotten what it was like with these sorts of social situations. I was the lady of the house. I had another woman to entertain.

Thankfully, that woman was Omega Cadogan.

Mairwen was not what I expected of another alpha's omega. She was shy, suddenly quiet at the departure of the others, but not so much so as to leave things awkward between us. She let me lead for the most part, asking just enough questions to keep me busy as I led her first through the keep and then out to the grounds, more interested in the farming and grazing lands than in the silly little castle folly and rose garden.

And when she accidentally stepped in a bit of sheep dung, she just let out a low laugh and shrugged, scraping her boot off on a rock.

"I'm surprised there is so much land to farm, when it seems like everywhere else is so rocky," Mairwen said, busy petting a young lamb who'd decided to use her to prop itself up.

"Only because the rocks were dug up, likely used for building border walls or even outbuildings," I said. "Every so often, the hills will spit another little boulder up through a field. It gets set aside until there's a use for it. I'm sure there's a pile around somewhere."

Mairwen finally relented, lifting the lamb up, ignoring the smears of mud it left on her fine gown as she cradled it to her chest. "I know they're for eating, but as long as this one's not my dinner, I'm going to coddle it," she said, smiling.

"I'm waiting for Torion to notice, but he's been settling for mutton over lamb since I arrived," I said, wrapping my arms around myself, turning back toward the keep's herb garden. "How was the flight of the alphas?"

Mairwen hummed, taking her time in answering. "Interesting. I wasn't there for any of the alphas' real conversations, of course, but just watching interactions was enough information."

I watched her wet her lips, stare into the distance. She stopped as the lamb squirmed, realizing it'd wandered as far from its herd as it might want to. She let it down again with a pat and then glanced briefly at me, eyes dropping to watch her step over the craggy ground.

"I think Ronson and Torion might be the start of a...tide turning, so to speak."

My eyebrows rose. "Really?"

She shrugged, as if to make her words carry less weight. But Mairwen struck me as a woman who *watched* things, and most people in my experience tended to underestimate how much they really allowed themselves to be seen. It had taken me too long to learn to look.

"There are some betas who seem on the brink of rising, I think," she said softly. "I can't speak to their nature, of course."

I hummed, and we carried on in a companionable quiet. It'd been so long since I'd spent time in this way with another omega, and even this was different. When I'd been a girl, other omegas had been both confidants and competition. I was raised to understand that a good match with a powerful beta was my most important duty, my sole goal. After

Malcolm, *during* my years with him, I'd spent far too much time blaming the other women. And then, when I'd finally freed myself, I'd taken to the woods, taken to a role where I was still only one thing to anyone but myself—helpful, but isolated.

I scowled at the horizon, at the patterns of my life.

"I sometimes wonder if men can really be the answer to the challenges we face," I said, without thinking about who I stood with.

Mairwen made a soft sound of agreement, and I found her smiling. "Ronson is always so surprised when a new injustice occurs to him," she said fondly. She looked down at the edge of the herb beds we reached, her lips parted to speak, when her eyes widened. "I know this plant."

She knelt in front of a thick patch of blue sorley, fingers stroking the fine leaves between her fingers. Her brief glance up at my eyes, a searching look, told me we were both familiar with its properties. It had taken me far too long poring over my mother's notes to understand the clues she'd left, to understand the *need* omegas had for this herb. I wondered now, with Torion on the brink of his rut, if there were women in Grave Hills drinking the tea already.

"My mother was an herbalist—her notes on the flower..."

Mairwen rose slowly, nodding to fill in my words. She knew. Blue sorely flowers could be dried and brewed in a tea to help prevent a pregnancy, even during a rut.

"Many women come to me looking to promote a son. And many of the women who've survived giving birth to a son come for blue sorely," I said, and we fell into step together.

Mairwen sighed. "There has to be another way."

I grunted my agreement. Not that it mattered. I did want a child. I wanted to keep my vow to Torion. I wanted to prove to Malcolm that he was wrong about me being worthless now. I accepted the risks.

Chapter Seventeen

TORION

I panted and thrashed against the blaze that burned over my limbs and up my throat like fire surrounding me, about to burst from my lips. Sharp blades scratched over my chest and down my back, stabbing my heels and fingertips. I groaned, trapped in a dark shroud of flames. I searched around me, groping desperately, certain there'd been shelter here at one point, a safe haven, soft and full and scented like—

A cool shiver doused the scorch marks on my chest.

"Shh, it's all right. I'm here now."

My eyes opened to a gray view of rising linen sheets. "Brigid?" I rasped out.

Another cool touch soothed away the sting and ache of my right hand, and I watched my omega lift my hand to her mouth, kissing the center.

"You're feverish," she murmured, stroking her cheek against my palm, a strange tension leaving my fingers as if they'd found what they'd been searching for.

Of course they had.

"The rut," I said, and the words came out in a growl.

She nodded, releasing my hand and crouching over my bare body, bending to trace her mouth over the hard scales that were trying to rake their way out of me. At the first touch, the pain vanished, along with the urge to tear myself open. Claws I hadn't noticed receded from my hands and feet.

"I just saw our guests off," Brigid said, and then stretched her glorious frame over mine, dressed in a thin nightgown that only did the faintest job of hiding all the lines and curves, swells and valleys, the full map of her I was so obsessed with.

I groaned, rocking up into her, face going hot at the immediate drip of fluid from my cock, pooling on my belly between us.

"De Roche said if he stayed another second—"

I snarled, rearing up and catching Brigid's mouth with mine, drinking the muffled words, the silky taste of her, flavored with honey and tea. I didn't care what Seamus said. I didn't care if they were still here, or if they were halfway back to Bleake Isle. I'd suffered three nights without Brigid and woke up with the rut racing through me like an inferno. Only one thing mattered now.

I rolled us in the bed, Brigid's nightdress tangling and getting in the way of me sinking between her thighs. I released her only long enough to reach for the hem and tear it open.

"Torion," Brigid called, clasping my face in her hands. I moaned. Every touch from her was like dipping into a cool stream at the height of summer. "It's all right. It's time. I'm here."

The soft feel of the inside of her thighs as they spread and welcomed me in their cradle was so beautifully tender, so complete, it drew another flood of readiness out of me. I reached between us and pressed the head of my length against her sex so I could help slicken and ready her. Even there—usually so brightly hot against me—was a relieving contrast to my fevered desire.

"Tell me you want this. Tell me you're ready," I pleaded, rubbing myself against her, eyes fixed to her tongue as it flicked out and wet her lips on a panting sigh.

"I want a child, Torion," she said.

My mouth formed a feral smile, my teeth sharp. The words were sharp and commanding, my bossy little witch. They weren't romantic. They weren't even lustful. But they were honest.

Still, I wanted a little equality between us. I gripped at the cotton, grinned as her eyes narrowed, and finished ripping her nightdress apart, baring her to me. She growled, and the sound made me answer in kind, bowing over her lithe body, taking a breast in hand and the other pert nipple between my teeth. Brigid arched with a groan, and my purr rushed out, not low and gentle at all but an urgent roar.

"I want—" She gasped, and I traced my tongue around her nipple, then suckled, the refreshing taste of her sliding down my throat and cooling the dragon fire that waited there. "I want to feel you inside of me, alpha."

I moaned against her and stretched until she was pressed deep into the soft cushions of the nest beneath me. Her feet dug into the back of my thighs, and I smiled at the scrape of her callouses. My omega was not soft. She had sharp angles and a tart tone.

"I like when you call me Torion," I said, because it was still so new to be *alpha*, to have the title be mine rather than my father's.

"Oh," she said, and I propped myself on my elbows on either side of her shoulders, so we could look into one another's face. She smiled, shy and sweet enough to make my heart pound. "I prefer Brigid to omega. Witch is nice too."

My forehead rested against hers, and the rut granted us a moment of closeness, friendship. But the way her body was already opening to the tip of my cock rose up in my consciousness. The little graze of her nipples against my chest where my scales were eager to rise. The taste of her on my tongue, like brandy and ice.

"Don't look away," I whispered.

Her hands held to the back of my neck, fingers twisting around locks of hair, eyes widening with the first nudge. Fang's fire, there was nothing like it. I'd been young and inexperienced the first time I'd been with an omega, and everything was panic and excitement and urgent movement. I hadn't been aware of anything other than *enjoying* myself.

Brigid was so wet, hot and cool at the same time—or maybe it wasn't about temperature at all, but that she was what my rut demanded, the only possible succor. She seemed to suck me into her, like lips grasping and swallowing me deeper, and it took every ounce of effort in me to keep my eyes open as I'd demanded of her. My brow furrowed as I tried to catalogue every sensation, every individual moment. Her hypnotic stare, the way our breaths pressed us closer, the snag of her fingernails tightening at the nape of my neck as I filled her to the root.

We paused there, my head empty and too full all at once. And as if our physical union created one of thought too, we both smiled, laughed, shuddered against one another as we held in place. I sipped at her lips, kissed her cheek, her jaw, and thought I might stay like this forever, dizzy and grounded.

"Torion." My name was a plea, whimpered in need.

I was meant to act, wasn't I? There'd been a rhythm to it in the past, one that went too fast. But this was better than those fading memories. Just the simple act of being inside

Brigid was more than anything I'd ever experienced before. It was enough. It was overwhelming.

Brigid huffed, moving beneath me, and the silk and squeeze of her was a heady shock, the way she pulled sound from my chest and pleasure from my bones. She shifted into me once more, and I lost the strength in my arms, in my neck, falling into her.

"Yes, Torion, I need—"

Yes, that was it, that was what I was meant to be doing, moving with her, rocking and joining and rubbing against her until we both fell apart. But it was too good, the pant of her breath on my throat stealing the air from my lungs, the way she moved against me, taking what she wanted.

Taking me with her.

With a groan and a surge of effort, I turned us back on the bed, keeping Brigid fixed on my length, watching her catch her breath and balance, spread over my lap. She didn't hesitate. Her elegant hands, worked and marked with scars and callouses, braced against my chest as she rose and fell, swallowing me up and then stroking me with heat and slick arousal.

"Torion, I—you feel—"

"Don't stop, witch," I managed through gritted teeth, watching where we were joined, the incredible spread of her lips around me, the tight grip she held me in, welcomed me with.

I looked up and groaned as I found her watching the same point, her mouth open on a moan. I wished her hair was down, curtaining around us, but her throat was exposed, lean and strong, and my mouth watered at the sight of her swallowing a cry. I bucked and purred as the sound escaped in answer, bright and sweet and pleading.

"You're getting—" She grunted, eyes widening. "You're getting bigger. Oh, Torion, I want—"

A stony ache was building at the base of my cock, and every time Brigid bore down the feel of her rubbing against it made me want to shout, to claw the bedding apart, to spread my wings and fly hard into the sun. The spot grew swollen, a dark and violent shade of red—my *knot*. My hands caught Brigid by the thighs, tugging her harder against the growing knot, watching her spread wider over it and then retreat again with a soft cry of disappointment. She wanted it, even as her body resisted the effort, and still, my knot grew.

I sat up abruptly, bumping our chests together, wrapping one arm around Brigid's waist, holding her by the back of the neck with the other.

"Take my knot, Brigid," I rumbled, begged, whispered. "It's yours by right."

She whined, leaning back into my hold, and pressed down a little harder this time, a little longer, before rising up again, gasping for air. Her eyes met mine and I felt it between us, the way it always was, the way I could grab the very heart of her and hold it still, just for a moment, just with a look.

"I am yours, witch. Take me."

Her lashes fluttered, and her arms swung around my shoulders, our kiss clumsy. She bounced on me a few times, and I nearly rose up, forced her down, demanded what we both wanted. But with a delicious curl of her hips, her nose pressed to mine, our breath mingling, she swiveled her hips just so, seating herself with a sudden grace and ease.

She came with a cry, clenching around me, and a cannon went off in my body, rocketing through me, blacking my vision and denying me anything but the sudden boiling and pressured release that exploded through me. There was a roaring sound that matched the tired scratch in my throat, my own shout of release. On and on it went, heat and the throbbing pulse that started at my scalp and toes and grew unbearably dense at my core.

It didn't lessen, but I must've grown accustomed to it because eventually my vision cleared and the roaring subsided to a heavy, snarling purr. Brigid was on her back beneath me, mouth opened on a pleasured scream. Her body rolled to meet mine in the slow grind and press, her core still squeezing and milking my knot, keeping it hard, keeping us both riding that rough edge of ecstasy without end. She pulled my hair in her fists, squeaked out a strangled cry, and then drew my mouth down to hers, drowning sense from my mind again.

We were in the rut's grip now.

"TORION!"

My tongue swept through silky, swollen petals of flesh, and the nectar I found was a feast on my palate, sweet and rich and salty. I dug deeper, purring in approval as she nestled her hips into my face to offer more. She was so small now. No, it was the other way around. My dragon was swelling up inside of me, nearly bursting out through the taut stretch of my skin and the hard case of my rising scales.

Her soft little claws dug through my hair, and she cursed, called my name again. My name.

"Torion." A sweet little moan.

My omega. My woman. My...Brigid.

"Witch," I hissed, and lapped up a little flow of arousal once more as she strangled a cry and bucked against my mouth.

Mate. Yes, that was a better word. My *mate*. My match. The boon I'd claimed for myself and my dragon.

Her legs were trembling over my shoulders, my curls caught in her grip like reins as she arched toward her own release. Greedy little thing. I chuckled at the thought, and she shuddered and whined. Her crown of auburn flames had gone crooked after a day, and now the fire was spread over the sheets.

You should brush it, braid it. You have to take care of her, some sanity whispered to me.

"After," I mumbled, but the word was buried with my tongue inside of her, just another low sound to echo for her pleasure.

Her toes curled against my wing roots, and I groaned. She was close now. I could plunge inside her once more, knot her and fill her and breed her like she'd told me I must. I grinned, and some man's reason returned at the recollection of Brigid at my father's desk, sorting my supremacy as alpha out with lists and plans. She deserved this softness, this moment for herself.

And I deserved the taste of her on my tongue before I took her again.

But the taste of her was better than whisky, and stronger too. Her scent fogged my head and filled it only with hunger and lust. And the feel of her, wet and glossy, sweeter than water and more refreshing, cool and hot at the same time... I wanted it coating every inch of me.

"Oh, Torion, I—Ahh!"

I purred as she shattered, my mouth open wide and tongue stroking inside of her, her little legs quaking and spreading wider in an invitation my knot was eager to accept. And her pulse, it pounded against my cheek. I could hear the blood rushing inside of her, the very life of her, the way the pace of her heart matched mine precisely. The life I'd claimed, the one that belonged tied to mine. I rubbed my face against her thigh, mouthing my way to where it thrummed, calling to me.

I wanted to know everything about my witch, every flavor, every texture. She belonged to me, with me. My mate.

Her leg stretched long as I set my mouth over the pulse at the crease of her hip, sucking and kissing and nibbling till the blood was so close to the surface I could taste the way it changed her, made her sharper, a bitter salt to balance the sweet. I wanted—no, *needed* to taste it, to quench the dragon fire in my throat before it burned us both.

The feel of her thigh in my mouth was soft, so tender, so fragile.

"Mmm, Torion?"

Mine.

I bit without thinking, groaning and shuddering with the *rightness* of her in my jaws, the little cry and sigh of her voice, her fingers soothing down the back of my neck. For a moment, all the man's doubts faded away. It did not matter *why* my witch had come to me, nor why she stayed. She was here because she was mine and it was as it had to be. Mate.

Brigid was mine. The flavor of her, sharp and tart and as sweet as heather honey, was too perfect to not belong to me. The low ache in my wings that faded said as much. The hard pulse of my knot growing full again was further proof. The way she softened and hummed, as if some irritation had been stolen away and she was at ease again, was right.

I lapped at the wound, a careful one, not too deep. *Just enough*, a heavy voice in my mind reassured.

I rose up, and the little red beads of my work—just next to her pretty, swollen pink sex—filled me with a satisfaction that was deeper than sexual. This woman belonged in my marrow, and I in hers.

"Torion," Brigid called, one trembling hand reaching for me.

The blood I'd drawn out slicked between our hips as I made my home in her once more.

Chapter Eighteen

BRIGID

I wasn't meant to lose my mind this way. It had never happened before. Oh, a rut was fun, especially at the beginning, but exhausting too, and a bit of a chore by the end.

It had never been this...this *demanding*. This essential.

I couldn't stop kissing Torion. I was tired and my body was bruised, but the little strength I had only went to holding him closer, whispering pleas for more. I could barely keep my eyes open, but I held his face to mine, took his breaths for my own.

"Easy, now," he murmured as I whimpered, my legs too weak to hold his hips. He was massive now, almost twice as wide as before, too tall to stretch out against. His dragon was full in him. It was a wonder he managed to speak words at all. I sobbed as he pulled out of me, trying to scramble with useless limbs to draw him back.

"Your knot, I want—"

"I want it too, little witch," Torion rasped. Our voices were ragged.

I whined as he bundled me and then turned me to stretch out on the bed, tucking a few pillows beneath my hips.

"You'll have my knot, my seed. You'll have all of me, and more than you can stand."

I sighed, realizing his goal, and gave up the struggle, falling limp into the cushion of the bed, moaning my approval as he filled me once more. Every time he entered, I was shocked breathless by the fullness, by the completion, pinned in place and so perfectly satisfied to be trapped there.

Torion groaned, rolling into me, my legs caged between his, making me tighter, him harder and deeper and bigger—

"T-Torion!"

"That's it, rest now, just like this. I'll take care of you, I'll take care of us both. I'll fill you up, over and over like this while you catch your breath."

I wouldn't catch my breath, because every stroke inside of me stole it away again, but I would rest. Torion's hand held my head into the pillow as he thrust, and I shook as he settled his knot inside of me, delirious with how it pressed to every nerve, creating a sensation that rose and rose and rose and never fell.

CLAWS DRAGGED like fire down the back of my thigh, and I woke with a garbled shout, trying and failing to sit up as my stomach burned with the effort.

"You never stretch, do you? You're damn tight, witch. If I'd realized— Well, no, I didn't have the patience when it arrived, did I?"

I groped the bed, grabbed something soft in my fist—likely a pillow—and threw it at Torion in an attempt to shut him up. I deserved sleep. Another decade of it, at least.

His hands on the back of my thigh shifted, warm and

gentle, until they were forcing my knee toward my chest, the taut and tired muscles from thigh to ass and even back screaming in protest.

"Shh, just another moment. Try to breathe," Torion soothed as he tortured me.

I took a breath to scream at him, then realized I was too tired for that too, and released it. Some of the tension and tug in my body settled into something resembling more of a stretch, and less of a string about to snap apart.

"That's it," he said, and then his hands did something magical, stroking from the back of my knee down, pausing where I resisted the most to work his fingers over knots before continuing on. "We'll get through the worst of it and then you'll fall back asleep for the rest," he said, like a promise.

It was a tempting thought, whatever it meant, but it didn't make any sense. I frowned, wanting only to fall back asleep, but Torion was straightening my leg out, turning my foot in one hand to roll my ankle while the other massaged my calf.

"What are you doing?" I asked, managing to open my eyes enough to see his shadow in the bed. It was nighttime, but I could make him out well enough to know that his size had settled back some—still massive, likely more so than before the rut, but not as overwhelmingly huge as he'd been...a day ago? Or was it two? I'd lost track of time early in the rut and then time had ceased meaning anything at all.

"Taking care of you," Torion said, so easily.

I blamed my exhaustion on why the words made my eyes water.

"You're the alpha. That's what I'm meant to do for you," I murmured.

I tried so hard not to think of Malcolm constantly, to compare the two men, but it came up regardless. The way I'd dragged myself from nests on boneless, bruised legs to arrange baths and meals, to clean up after Malcolm's ruts, to ease his rest. And they hadn't been nearly so long or... vigorous as Torion's.

Faintly damp lips brushed against my ankle, and a little hazy recollection of Torion growling as he licked and kissed his way up every inch of each leg shivered through me, warming my limbs and core.

"I think you've more than done your part on that front, Brigid," Torion said softly. "I've never been so *well taken care of* in my life."

I snorted. "What about the brothel and the dozens of women you—" I grunted as he pinched the back of my thigh.

"Don't make me tell you how absolutely incomparable that experience was to this. It'll only make you frown and go shy and crabby," Torion said.

I blinked up at the shadow of the canopy over our heads, startled and exposed and embarrassed by my own temperament.

"See?" he said, lowering my leg, then shifting to my other hip to repeat the process.

I huffed. "You made a bad bargain for a crabby omega—"

Torion growled, and my heel thumped to the mattress as his hands braced on either side of my head. His heat was still rolling off his skin, and it covered me like a blanket as he brought his face nearly to mine, until our noses brushed.

"I didn't make a bargain. I claimed what was mine. And in exchange, you may have whatever you ask of me that's within my power to give, including my first heir I've no doubt we achieved recently. And because you don't ask for very much, I'll throw in a good stretch and some care for your well used body."

I swallowed hard, unable to think at all, let alone of anything to say in response. Torion's mouth settled over mine, hard and demanding, his tongue stroking my bruised lips and gaining the entry he sought. He still tasted of me, and I moaned, barely able to raise my arms to hold him close.

He gasped, stealing some of my breath for his own, and ducked his head away when I chased for another kiss.

"The rut's nearly over, enough that I can resist a bit. Let me take care of you tonight, and we'll burn through the last of it in the morning. Hold your enchantments at bay a little longer, witch."

I swallowed my whine as he pulled away and squeezed my eyes shut. Oh, how I hated him, this perfect, sweet man with words that made me feel as transparent as glass, words that cut me open and dug about in all my rotten places.

Please, I begged my heart, *please let this fire he stokes be hate.*

<hr>

TORION WOKE me with gentle kisses on my shoulders, then wrapped me up in a careful cradle of arms and legs, his chest against my back, and slid inside of me.

"Just relax," he murmured, barely moving inside of me, a soft and all too satisfying grind.

"I should be sick of this feeling by now," I blurted out, turning my face into a pillow to hide my panting breaths.

Torion laughed. "I'm sorry to tell you, but I'm quite sure I never will."

I grit my teeth against the claim, the way it lit a small match of happiness inside of me. He didn't have to mean it about me. He'd realize at some point any woman might do.

"I'll try not to burden you too much," Torion continued, playful and light, barely whispering, as if to keep the moment a secret even from the air around us.

He didn't mean it, didn't think yet how he might share "the burden" of our lovemaking with others. Logically, I knew that Torion wouldn't say such a thing. I was just too tired. I couldn't keep the shield around my heart up, couldn't keep the bitterness that had grown thorns in me at bay. We were too close now for me to withdraw. There was nowhere to go.

"Brigid?" he asked, holding still, tugging one shoulder to twist me enough for him to make out my crumpled expression. "Are you hurt? Too sore?"

I shook my head and tried to hide it, but he was already pulling out of me, drawing my sob out twofold at the aching memories and the loss of him. I rolled to follow him, scrambled and wrestled back his hands until I knelt over him, reaching between us to draw his still stiff length back inside of me, my sigh of relief obvious enough to give Torion pause.

"Don't stop," I said, my throat tight with tears, the words choking on the past.

He sat up as I started to ride him, a rickety, weak rhythm, but still, he felt so lovely inside of me, and I could see the way his breath hitched. In another moment, he'd forget my wavering and give in to the—

Torion's hands cupped my face, and my mouth wobbled, my eyes squeezing shut.

"Be here, with *me*," he pleaded, feathering his mouth back and forth over my cheeks, the bridge of my nose, down to sip at my flattened lips.

I took a deep breath, and together we rocked, just once. His hands petted over my back, up and down my shoulders where he'd worked his hands the night before. It wasn't his fault. He didn't know yet, didn't believe it of himself that his eyes would stray and then his heart and body too.

He's here now, I reminded myself. *Just now. Not forever. You don't have to give him forever. Just now.*

I breathed slowly, loosened my mouth, and kissed him softly. His thumbs stroked my jaw, then my temples. I opened my eyes and smiled when we both went cross-eyed, too close to look at one another properly. He dropped another kiss on my forehead, and together we moved, no thrusts, no surging, a soft back-and-forth, keeping close and quiet, right to the finish. Torion's knot throbbed between us, but he held my gaze, waiting and watching, until I pressed down, taking him in to the hilt. His eyes fell shut on a groan, and with gentle tugs I pulled him on top of me.

"I'm here with you," I promised, stroking his hair back from his face, wrapping my legs around his hips. "I'm here now."

Chapter Nineteen

BRIGID

Stab. Stab. Stab.

I dropped the trowel at my hip and grabbed up handfuls of compacted dirt, breaking it up between my fingers. The breeze was still cool, but the sun had risen to glow over my back, keeping me warm with my efforts. It'd been too long since I'd been elbows deep in dirt, and the keep had neglected its herb gardens in favor of the produce. I had work to do—work to keep my hands and mind busy. I'd started plants from seed before the selection ceremony, and they were ready to go into the ground now. Busy little sprouts that Maggie had tended for me while...

Glorious kisses that stole and gave breath. A body so thoroughly possessing my own, I became only an answering movement and echoing need. Husky groans and broken whimpers.

I shook myself and took a deep breath. I'd escaped the nest before Torion woke, before he might kiss me or soothe my tired body or circle me in his strong arms and say something so gently sweet, it brought tears to my eyes. I needed fresh air. I needed to keep my thighs together so I'd quit feeling so damned bowlegged, like I'd ridden a horse for days.

The comparison was a little too apt.

"Head's gone to rot," I snarled, forgoing planting a little seedling in favor of digging another hole. I needed to work until I was too tired to remember anything.

Dark green flashed out of the corner of my eye on my left and I stiffened, bracing myself, trying to stifle my temper.

"There you are!"

I supposed it made sense why Torion was so cheerful. He'd just experienced his first rut, and to my shock, it'd taken over two weeks to settle. He *would* be feeling quite pleased with himself.

Don't lie. You were more than pleased with him too, a warm and heavy voice hissed in my thoughts.

"The servants said you hadn't eaten, so I brought you a basket," Torion said, grinning widely as he raised the wicker in his hand. He set it on the ground to my right, bowing to kiss the crown of my head before throwing himself down to my left. "You've been busy."

"It's easier in the morning," I said, biting my lips to keep from scowling at the large man now helping himself to making a pillow of my lap. "You'll get dirt on your face."

Torion shrugged, and one of his wing hooks nudged my hip. "I don't mind dirt. Take a moment to eat. It's nearly luncheon, you know."

I gave my frown to the sky and winced as the sun blinded me in answer. I hadn't realized. I looked down at the bed I'd been working on and discovered I'd dug my way right to the end. And I was hungry.

"Did you just wake?" I asked.

"I woke as you snuck out," Torion said. The rotten man had the nerve to smile at me, to not be irritated with me for waking him. He probably even had the gall to understand why I might want to escape.

I huffed and bent over him, slanting my mouth over his at

an awkward angle but relishing the kiss all the same. Torion purred, reaching up to push the loose hair back from my face. I twisted above him slightly to ease the kiss, making it languid and thorough.

He was still smiling as I sat up once more, reaching for the basket.

"Have you eaten?"

"Earlier. I packed enough for both of us."

"*You* packed the basket?"

Torion just nodded and shrugged. "Easiest way not to make a great fuss over a picnic. And I don't think the keep has quite learned to treat me with the same deference as my father."

"Because you don't ask them to," I pointed out, pulling out a hand pie and stuffing it directly into my mouth. Now that Torion had pointed out the time, my hunger made itself known—loudly, I noted wryly, as my stomach growled.

"Should I, do you think?" Torion asked. He caught my free hand in both of his, resting it over his chest, fondling and tangling our fingers.

The feel of his heartbeat under my palm steadied my mood. I'd come out to the garden to do exactly that, to get away from that which unsettled me, and instead it was the man himself who seemed to make the nerves and worries and tempers subside.

I'd given Malcolm this power over me when I was young and hadn't known any better. I'd let him win it back after he'd broken my trust, wanting to believe what had existed between us once might be repaired, recovered.

It was madness to let another man do the same.

But feeling calm was such a relief, and the day was lovely, and Torion was still sweet, still earnest.

"Do you want the staff to treat you like a king?" If he did,

I might have to rise to the occasion, be more than the woman digging in the dirt in an old dress.

Torion's nose wrinkled, and I could've predicted his simple, "No."

"For what it's worth, they do respect you. But you grew up here, and many of them have known you your whole life, so they know you're the sort of man who packs his own picnic and doesn't want a procession of servants to wait upon him in the middle of an herb garden."

Torion lifted my hand to his mouth, kissed the back of it, and then turned it to kiss the palm too. "Well, when you put it like that..."

I smiled as he trailed off, settling my hand back to his chest, his gaze studying the clouds as I helped myself to more of the food he'd brought. It was peaceful, pleasant, but something more than that too. *Comfortable*.

My lips quirked at the thought. When I'd been a girl, "comfortable" had been the last thing I would've considered desirable in my future partner. Malcolm had made me giddy, nervous, and desperate. During our courtship, I had wept at night after dinners where he'd been less than constantly attentive and then awoken again in the morning, delighted by the depth of my obsession with the man. It had been torture and rapture and *never* comfortable.

Torion's heartbeat was steady beneath my palm, his breathing a reliable rhythm that I found myself matching. Crumbs fell from my fingers down to his forehead, and he laughed and grinned up at me. My heart flipped in my chest at the sight. I fed him the ripest of the strawberries, and he sucked the juice from my fingers, my body throbbing in want. And through it all, desire and affection and safety, I was comfortable here with this man.

This dreadfully dangerous man.

"Allow me to take that, Omega Feargus."

I blustered, but the pile of bedding was out of my arms before I could form a protest, and the maid hurried ahead of me.

"Do I look so useless?" I groused to Maggie at my side. The keep staff had done well cleaning and restoring the estate while Torion and I had been...occupied with one another.

"It's just deference. It's not just to be expected. It's what you're *owed*," Maggie said with a shrug.

I wrinkled my nose. "They weren't deferent when I arrived a month ago."

"You weren't likely to be carrying the alpha's heir a month ago."

I froze, staring down at the bustling keep, one hand hovering in front of my stomach. I clenched my fingers into a fist and forced my hand down to my side.

"That's the expectation," I said.

Maggie turned to me, eyebrows raised. She looked better than she had in years, as if the elevation of her position had brought some of her youth back to her. Now she didn't have to run from cellar to rafters all day, able to order others to do the running for her. She had a comfortable chair in a small but cozy office, and everyone seemed to like her even when she was correcting their work. I expected or at least hoped that it would be a long time before I had to find a replacement for her as our housekeeper.

"Of course it is." Her brow furrowed for a moment, and then her eyes widened slightly. She drew me back from the railing, away from where sound carried, and tucked her chin in close to whisper. "Should it not be?"

I shook my head. "They're exactly right. I just...hadn't given myself a moment to consider..."

I'd been avoiding the thought, in fact. There were too many risks. Early labor, the many lives of women lost in the delivery of a dragonkin son, and that was only if I managed to stay pregnant. I hadn't made it more than a few months last time before my body had failed the child.

And I hadn't told Torion that. I hadn't told anyone.

All at once, I felt sick, at the brink of tears, the hallway going dark at the corners of my eyes. What if I lost another child? Torion claimed indifference about producing an heir, but how would he feel when the idea became a reality? How would he feel if I stole the promise away from him, just when he'd realized how much he wanted it to arrive? I'd gone back to Malcolm's bed in want of a child, but I hadn't realized how much it would mean, how desperately I would love them as they grew inside of me.

I'd never imagined how devastating it would be to lose them, even so soon.

I might hate Torion if he didn't feel the love the same way, if the loss didn't break him as it would me. If I could even stand to go through that loss again.

"You're white as a ghost, poor love. It's too soon to worry yet, I should think," Maggie soothed.

I shook my head. It wasn't too soon. It was too late, if anything. I hadn't thought this through. I hadn't considered how horrible hope might feel after so long.

"You need to rest," Maggie continued.

"No," I whispered, shaking my head. I needed a distraction.

"Not to be indiscreet, milady, but the whole keep knows you haven't had a full night's sleep in weeks," Maggie said, dragging me toward the bedroom I shared with Torion. My face went hot, and my stomach turned. "We've finally got the place running as it should. Enjoy the victory, and take a moment to yourself."

She threw the door open, and I braced myself for the scent of rut, soiled sheets and desperate lovemaking. Instead, I caught a whiff of my own perfume and Torion's warmer scent, along with a breeze of fresh air. The servants had helped themselves to airing the room out. The nest was still up, but the curtains were parted to reveal a freshly made bed. I swayed woozily at the thought of what they'd dealt with while stripping the mattress, but Maggie was still towing me along and it was easier to follow than to fight.

"Have a little nap. I'll send something up for you to snack on when you wake," Maggie said, pushing me to the foot of the bed.

There was no getting rid of our scents now, mine and Torion's. It would take an entirely new mattress, perhaps even a new bedframe. And I hated how comforting it was to crawl over the soft cushions and into the cool sheets, for it to smell almost as if Torion was in the bed with me. I hated that Maggie was right, that my eyelids were heavy and I'd woken up too early and worked too hard in the garden and around the keep after a restless couple of weeks.

I hated that as Maggie left the room with a parting, "I'll let the alpha know you're here," it was an expectant kind of pleasure I felt at the thought that he might join me.

THE ROOM WAS warm and a little humid as I woke to the sound of water rushing from one container to another. I kept my eyes closed, my body heavy on the bed, one arm thrown over my head, the other covering my stomach. There was a whiff of dinner in the air, salt and meat and something promisingly tart. Soft footsteps paced over the rug to the fire and back to the tub, another kettle full of warm water pouring out. I opened one eye to golden, hazy candlelight.

The edge of the bed dipped, and a soft kiss landed on my shin, where my dress had hiked up to reveal skin. A hand landed by my hip, and then another on the opposite side, knees bracing on either side of my legs. Torion appeared, smiling gently, head bowing to rest between my breasts for a moment.

"It's your turn to be bathed," he murmured.

A scream tightened into a knot in my chest, but it came out as a sigh as I sat up. "You don't have to seduce me anymore, Torion."

He rolled his eyes—a rare sign of irritation with me that I found strangely attractive. Then he sat back on his heels. "Of course I do, but that's not what this is. Come on. Let me be gallant, or I'll pick you up and toss you in the water."

I wrapped my arms around his shoulders and he cradled me, carrying me over to the tub. "Maggie told you she had to put me down for a nap, I take it?" I asked.

He hummed for a moment, standing me at the foot of the tub and helping me out of my clothes. "Actually, I told Maggie to put you down for a nap. Not exactly with those words, but I suppose they suit."

I frowned as he lifted my dress and slip over my head. Since when did Maggie and Torion conspire to manage *me*?

"You looked cross when I sent the lads out to the garden with fertilizer and mulch."

"I could've done that myself," I protested, taking his hand to help myself step into the tub.

Torion scoffed. "With one wheelbarrow at a time for the rest of the day."

"I like to work," I muttered, and then let out a little groan of appreciation as I sank into the hot water. "You need one of these."

"I had mine while you were sleeping," Torion said, and then he smiled and kissed my pouting frown. "Don't be mad at me for sparing your back. Did you really want to smell sheep shit all over me?"

I humphed, and Torion laughed, taking one of my arms from the tub ledge and stroking it with a sudsy wet cloth. "You mean *you* didn't want me smelling like fertilizer," I muttered

Torion sighed. "If that's what settles the argument, then yes."

I stiffened. Were we arguing? It felt more like flirting.

There was a tug on my braid, and my head fell back. Yes, flirting. Torion's dark eyes were warm and happy, and he peppered kisses over my face as I relaxed into the water.

"Sooner or later, you'll do more than accept me taking care of you. You'll *expect* it," he said.

My heart thumped hard and stopped. Damn him, that was what I was afraid of. The day when I woke up and didn't wonder when he would turn away from me. The day when I trusted him completely. The day when I found myself happy and content and unafraid. The day when I woke up from the fantasy he invited me to believe in and remembered that he was just an imperfect man and I was just an imperfect woman whose heart loved too easily.

"We have some time to ourselves now," Torion murmured.

"Tonight?"

"Mm, the next week or so. Dragonkin will be busy resettling after the rut. No one will be hammering at the door with demands. What would you like to do?"

I closed my eyes as dozens of ideas floated to mind. Staying in bed with Torion was at the forefront. Flying along the coast. Maybe even a little trip to the city to shop. Strolling over brick roads with Torion's warm, heavy arm over my shoulders. Waking up early for the sunlight stretches I'd caught him at a few times.

It was all too sweet. It would be too tempting—an illusion that a part of me never stopped wanting to believe in.

I cleared my throat and leaned my head against Torion, his chin resting on my now damp shoulder. I found his hands with mine, braced over the ledge of the tub, and tangled our fingers together.

"I thought...I thought I might go back to the cottage," I said as gently as I could.

I was too cold with Torion sometimes. Whatever he might deserve in the future, I didn't have it in me to punish him now. Still, I felt him flinch, his hands tightening in refusal around mine and then going limp.

"The cottage?"

"Mm. Just for a little while. See to my usual patients and work on a new harvest. Different plants come up at...different times of the year," I said, realizing how stupidly obvious the claim was. Torion knew the Hills as well as I did. "I can come back whenever you need me, but it would be... It would be nice to be back there."

Torion was quiet, still surrounding me. He swallowed, his throat working against my shoulder. Steam rose up off the water, and the fire crackled.

But the room had gone chilly, stale. I'd dampened the magic of the evening until it died away to awkwardness. I mourned the loss even as I breathed a little easier.

"Very well," Torion said, his voice hoarse. "When will you leave?"

I held my lips between my teeth for a moment, blinked against the sting in my eyes. It was absurd, absolutely nonsensical that his easy acquiescence should hurt with a deep stab tucked up under my ribs. That didn't stop the knife from twisting as I answered.

"Tomorrow, I think." *Unless you refuse. Unless you drag me into the nest and chain me there with you.* The teasing words were on the tip of my tongue, and I knew they would be enough. If I gave Torion so much as a hint of opportunity, he would seize on my reluctance, make the decision for both of us. And the temptation was poisonous. I swallowed it down like necessary medicine.

Cool air breezed over my shoulders as my alpha pulled away, heavy wings whispering and stretching to cast shadows as he rose up from his crouch behind me. "I'll see that there's a wagon readied to take you," he said, the words flat.

I shivered in the warm bath and shut my eyes to seal the tears as the bedroom door shut behind him.

Chapter Twenty
TORION

I scowled down at the proposal in front of me, at the list of names I recognized, and the astonishing numbers alongside them. Acreage, miles of it. Beautiful land, forests and farmland, grazing hills and fishing streams, now listed on offer for potential sale. With a quick glance up, I caught the exchange between Francis Keane and Damian Worthington's aide, Mr. Dunkley—smug, knowing, Keane reassured the other man with a faint nod, as if my agreement was already settled. Behind them, in the shadowy corners of the room, the stormy beta and Worthington's bastard half-brother, Bennett Reeves, watched us all.

"You must admit the prices are fair, my lord," Mr. Dunkley said, drawing a pair of delicate spectacles from his nose and wiping them with a handkerchief.

"More than that, I'd say," Keane echoed, grinning at me and waggling his eyebrows, as if it were *we* getting away with something and not Skybern.

"Indeed," I said, scenting the triumph off the two men and resisting the urge to growl in answer. "In fact, such a high price per acre reeks of bribery."

In the corner, Bennett Reeve's head ducked, hiding what I almost thought might've been a smile. Mr. Dunkley, a human in a room of dragons, blustered nervously, twisting to look at Reeves before quickly correcting himself. "Sir, I assure—"

"So what if it is, Torion?" Keane asked, cutting the Skybern solicitor off. His smile remained silky, but I could tell he hadn't expected me to put up an argument and he was sharpening to the conversation now. "Our own lords struggle to make ends meet while the gentlemen of Skybern and even Bleake Isle prosper in trade. An exchange like this one—one in Grave Hills' favor—will provide wealth for generations."

"Is it in Grave Hills' favor?" I asked, sitting back in my seat, flexing my wings behind me briefly, ignoring the sharp ache of my muscles. I'd been flying too much, hieing off to every corner of the region, trying to keep myself busy. Trying to stay out of the empty nest my omega had abandoned.

The one you let her run from, my dragon grumbled irritably.

Keane's eyebrows raised. "You said yourself—"

I ignored him, turning back to Dunkley. "These Skybern lords looking to acquire our land, would they remain Alpha Worthington's subjects while living here under my rule? Would their sons? Would they be dragonkin gentlemen of Grave Hills or of Skybern?"

Keane's mouth snapped shut, his eyes narrowing on me. *You bastard*, I thought, refusing to look back at him. *You'd sell the Hills to the highest bidder.*

Dunkley shifted in his seat. "I'm sure... It might depend..."

"If they lived here, they should be gentlemen of the hills. But in whose interest would they vote, I wonder?" I continued, watching the poor ill-prepared man fuss with his papers and his glasses. I wasn't impressed. Worthington should've sent a dragon to speak to me. I eyed Reeves in the corner briefly, but he was idly studying the books on a shelf, only the hint of a curve lingering on his mouth.

"Or do they only seek idle sport here? We have good hunting in these forests," I mused. "Perhaps the Skybern gentlemen require our land for entertainment over brief visits. Who then will profit from the farms they buy? Who will steward them? To whom will they pay their taxes? If they commit a crime, who will they answer to? And—"

Suddenly, Reeves laughed, the sharp, loud sound clattering out from the corner and startling even Keane in his chair. "You've made your point, Feargus," Reeves said, cool and smiling as he stepped forward.

"Have I?"

"Sir," Keane said, barely turning to look at the younger beta, something snide in the wrinkle of his nose. He didn't think highly of Reeves, no matter how close Damian kept his brother at his side.

Reeves ignored him entirely, blank gray eyes holding my stare. "This was an overture, an initial offer. Your concerns are heard, Alpha, and will be relayed to our Lord Worthington."

Keane's fingers dug into the arms of the chair he sat in, and he leaned forward to catch my eyes. I ignored him too. Omega Cadogan had seen significant power in Bennett Reeves, and I was beginning to agree with her. I'd thought him a lapdog to Worthington, a pitied and scandalous by-blow of Worthington's father. But there was a slick bite in his words, as if he'd thought the offer was as outrageous as I did. I wondered if he'd known I'd refuse.

"Tell Damian not to waste my time with gestures like this one," I said, too blunt, too biting.

"Torion," Keane hissed.

"I am the *alpha*, Lord Keane," I snapped, my claws digging into the surface of my desk as I leaned forward to snarl back at the older man. "Just as Worthington is. But his domain is Skybern, *not* Grave Hills." Keane moved away stiffly, argument bubbling in his dark gaze, but I turned to Reeves once more. "If he wants some advantage from me, he should present something even he could not resist in return. Not make an obvious grab for power here in my hills."

Bennett bowed his head, and it *almost* looked respectful. "As you say, my lord."

I bristled at the deference but kept my mouth shut. It itched to be "my lorded," but it served the point I was making. The reality was simple—I was not at my best, not since Brigid had left four days ago. I slept poorly, my appetite was starving but never satisfied and everything tasted of ash, and I had the irrational urge to tear the keep apart stone by stone until all that was left was rubble. I was never going to be amenable to whatever scheme Keane and Worthington had concocted. Not in this condition. Not with my omega hiding away in her ramshackle cottage, preferring the company of cobwebs and field mice over my own.

I sighed and rose from my chair. Dunkley, who'd gone pale and silent, and Keane quickly followed. "Let's adjourn, then. I at least owe you a meal for the trouble of your journey," I said, trying for diplomacy and only managing to sound weary.

Still, they murmured their agreements, Keane all but boiling over to express his disappointment in me. He would have to wait. Perhaps I would drag out the dinner with Reeves until it might make it impossible.

I should've canceled the meeting, but I'd sworn I wouldn't be my father, controlled by my obsession with my omega, ignoring my responsibility to my people.

You could've sent for Brigid, a wicked, tempting voice whispered. And the voice was right. I *should've* called Brigid back yesterday. Or have persuaded her to stay another week. And then done my best to convince her not to leave at all. Part of me believed I'd let her flee because I wanted to prove to her that I was not Malcolm, that I was better than him. That she could have anything she desired from me, even if that desire was living separately.

The truth was more pathetic. I had some pride, and she had chipped at it by wanting to leave. Had she wanted me to beg her to stay? Or would it only have taken a little coaxing? If I'd played the tyrant, would it have been the excuse she needed to remain at my side, or would it have driven a wedge between us?

As if a twenty five mile distance wasn't enough of a wedge.

"Will Omega Feargus be joining us?"

I nearly tripped, finding myself halfway down the stairs to the main hall of the keep, with Bennett Reeves at my side. I existed in a fog of my own muddled, spiraling thoughts.

"Unfortunately not," I said, hoping to leave it at that.

"What an elusive woman she is proving to be," Reeves said, too light and smooth. He was an altogether irritatingly slick person, and it made me want to punch him in the face. A broken nose might not improve his sly appearance, but I thought it would lift my mood.

"She takes on many responsibilities outside of the keep," I said.

Reeves hummed, keeping pace with me even as I tried to hurry my steps. "If not for the...widely publicized commotion you caused with your new twist on the Choosing Ceremony, Worthington might enjoy the rumor that she doesn't exist at all."

For a moment, my mouth opened to explain that she must exist because I suffered every second of her absence, a taut, sluggish drag of an ache inside my chest that pulled toward her. That I knew perfectly what direction east was because every time I faced it, I felt that pull grow more insistent, that

I was almost certain it would serve as a true compass to the one place I wanted most to be.

Instead I shrugged and said, "Skybern puts too much stock in rumor."

Bennett Reeves only smiled. "Respectfully, my lord, you underestimate their value as a currency."

I ground my teeth in my jaw and swallowed down the warning.

Chapter Twenty-One
BRIGID

I caught myself sighing for the third time and pressed my lips together hard, sitting up straight at my stool and reaching for my tea. I grimaced as cold, bitter liquid touched my tongue and set the cup down.

"Wake up, you silly fool," I breathed, glaring down at yesterday's cup of tea, the leaves now atrociously steeped.

Glancing around the cottage, I found the kettle steaming over a weakly burning fire and shook myself. The sun was high in the sky, and I'd barely started my day. Not that it was easy to wake after tossing and turning on a lumpy, prickly mattress for half the night. More than half the night, really.

But this was my life—my *real* life. The one I'd set aside to be the alpha's omega.

It was a relief to return to it, to my normal patterns and the work that I loved.

Except my patterns weren't normal, because I wasn't sleeping and I couldn't focus. And my work was...

"Well, what did you expect? The whole Hills must know you're the omega by now. They'd hardly expect to find you here for healing," I groused to the empty room.

I slapped my own cheeks lightly and marched to the fireplace, determined that *today* would be the day that went well. I would make good progress harvesting herbs in the woods. I would take a tincture to the farm to the south and let the Murrays know I would be at the cottage if they needed anything. They would get the word out to other locals.

And if word reaches the local dragonkin too? What will they think of you abandoning the alpha?

"I didn't abandon him," I muttered. "He didn't put up even a whiff of an argument."

And he hadn't called me back. Even though I knew emissaries from Skybern had visited two days ago. *Maggie,* of all people, had been the one to let me know. She claimed my absence had been remarked on, but not by Torion.

Not to me, at least.

Huffing a sigh, I lifted the steaming kettle over a fresh cup and poured, then blinked down at the clear liquid. Damn. Tea required tea leaves. Setting the water aside, I pawed through the clutter of tins I'd left out on the work table until I found the one for tea and groaned as I found it empty. I'd forgotten yesterday to walk up to the village. And it wasn't just tea I'd run out of. My stores had been emptied out while I was away to keep mice and bugs from moving in and staking their claim. I'd been surviving on the few things I'd scavenged from the keep kitchens, but the apples and bread had run out yesterday evening as well.

I gazed balefully around the cottage that had once felt cozy and sacred, safe. Now it just looked *small* and decidedly bare. The quiet *had* been a relief when I'd arrived, a pleasant kind of solitude compared to the constant activity of the keep. But when night had settled in and I tried to find sleep in the loft, suddenly solitude had turned into being wholly alone.

I missed the days before I'd gone to the keep to speak to

the newly risen alpha, before I knew Torion and had made myself comfortable in his bed.

No, *he* had made me comfortable there. That bastard.

Shoving my hair back from my face and into a knot at the back of my neck, I scanned the room and made a list in my head. I needed food, provisions, *tea*. I needed to get out of the cottage and make my return to the area known again. Everything would be all right with a little time. This was just an adjustment after being away for so long.

And if there is no babe, I might never have to go back.

I stopped in place in the center of my cottage, my fist around the strap of my bags, and blinked at the stray thought. I could break my bargain with Torion. He would be...unhappy with me. I knew that much. But in another ten years, he could find a new omega, perhaps even sooner. I could be written out of his history.

He's mine, a defiant thought snarled, jolting me.

My throat tightened, and my stomach churned. My knees were wobbly, and my feet too heavy. I wanted to sink down to the floor and close my eyes and give up on this wretched day.

Except in the sudden silence, without all my huffs and sighs, the clattering sound of an approaching wagon reached my ears. I pressed my hand over my stomach, as if that might settle its sudden turmoil, and returned my bags to the hooks, crossing to the door. Perhaps word of my return had spread after all and I finally had a patient. At least that would give me some purpose.

But as I cracked open my door, bracing against the cold morning air, it was not a local farmer I saw turning off the road toward my cottage. I swallowed a yelp, one hand grabbing onto the doorframe to hold me up, as I caught sight of Torion's dark curls and broad wings, his face lifted to catch morning rays. I was wetting my lips without thinking when he found me watching him, and I waited for the smug and wicked smile, the anxious clench of my belly turning into one of hunger.

Though Torion smiled at me in greeting, it wasn't one of victory, of catching me staring at him in sudden desire. It was shy and... His chin ducked and his glances were brief, nervous. It seemed to take him hours to reach the cottage, and every look and breath was drawn out. I'd been waiting here in the cottage like a fool for him to come and drag me back to the keep. I'd wanted him to demand my presence at his side, so that I might hold onto a little anger with him.

But it wasn't Torion's way. The only demand he'd made of me was what we both wanted, and the moment I'd decided to balk and run away, he'd let me. And I'd tried to be angry with him for that instead.

"Is everything all right?" I asked as he rolled to a stop.

He nodded, staring at me, and it was no longer so hesitant or nervous, but shockingly thorough. Had I changed in the handful of days since we'd last seen each other? Had I changed in *his* eyes?

"Fine," he rasped out, jumping down from the bench of the wagon.

There was a yank inside of my chest, and I found myself stepping out of the doorway. He answered the movement, a kind of gravity in the air that only applied to us.

Torion straightened, blinking and looking behind him. "I thought you might need...provisions."

Tender aches raced through me. "You thought right."

His head whipped back to stare at me. "Have you been... Why didn't you send for—"

"Torion," I said, giving into the inevitable, into what every inch of me craved and the majority of my thoughts demanded, contrary and argumentative as they were. I crossed to him until I could savor that buzz of energy and excitement that sizzled between us.

He swallowed hard, and I realized his right hand was still fisted around the strings of the wagon. I reached for that hand, and the strings dropped, our fingers gripping tightly. "Hm?" he asked.

He was too damn tall, and even rising up to the tips of my toes—bare toes in the cold grass, but even they were sharply alive—didn't lift me high enough for what I wanted. His eyes widened as I reached my other hand up to the back of his neck, tugging him closer.

Torion groaned and fell upon me, our mouths slanting together, open and starving, tongues clashing for barely a moment before finding their natural rhythm together, stroking and twining and then sliding apart. Our hands remained clasped, but Torion's free arm circled my waist, lifting me up off the ground, my toes swaying as he marched us to the cottage, only making it as far as the door.

"Wait," I tried to say, but the word was buried in the kiss.

Torion yelped as his head collided with the low door-frame, my own just grazing beneath. He pulled away, blinked at the door, and then growled as if he might intimidate it into accommodating his huge frame. I started to giggle, to slide myself out of his arms, when his glare turned on me.

"Oh no, you don't," he snarled, his arm tightening around me until I was breathless. With a quick crouch, he ducked us into the darkness of the cottage, pinning me to the scant feet of bare wall just right of my door. His mouth was hot on mine, the taste of him beautifully familiar, a flavor I'd been craving for days without realizing.

My knees bent, legs wrapping around his waist, a soft cry rising up from my throat when his cock swelled between us, hunting through layers of fabric to press just under my belly.

"Brigid, I—"

I had no idea what he might say, but I couldn't take the chance that it might fracture the moment, that it might lead to him sliding out of my arms, back to the wagon and home to the keep.

"I need you inside of me," I gasped out, my hand on the back of his neck sliding up to anchor itself in his curls. I forced the next kiss, thrusting my tongue against his, and Torion moaned.

He shifted, pulling our hands apart, and I wanted to scratch at his chest, tear at his wings, until I realized he was doing his own urgent tearing, tugging and pulling the fabric between us up out of the way. The kiss broke as we both fumbled together, breaths panting and mingling. We'd barely touched aside from the kiss, but my breasts were aching, my core throbbing in anticipation. My skin had lit up, tingling and brightening, waiting for Torion's attention, but none more so than my suddenly ravenous core.

Wads of heavy plaid and coarse linen dug into my stomach, but nothing distracted from the brief tap of damp, swollen flesh. I gasped, and Torion grunted, our hands all but slapping together before I pushed his out of the way, finding his cock and taking it in a brutal grip. Torion groaned, head thrown back, knees buckling till they hit the wall. I guided the slick, pulsing head to my center and dove forward, taking Torion's beautiful, tan, flexing throat between my teeth.

He howled, and I buried my own scream into his flesh as he slammed home inside of me, the sudden stretch an explosion of heat, a sharp stinging edge that built and softened in equal measure as he held us frozen like that, my body not adjusting around him so much as relearning how to hold him better inside of me.

"More," I whispered, kissing the skin I'd bitten. "Harder. Deeper."

I tried to flex my hips forward but Torion had me trapped, my head against the doorjamb, spine perfectly straight down to the slightest tip of my hips to better bury himself inside of me. He pushed in until I lost my breath, held me in place with just the weight of his body, and pulled his arm from around my waist.

"Yes, my lovely witch," he whispered, and then he hooked one arm beneath my left thigh. I squeaked as he inched me up the wall with a rough thrust, then repeated the maneuver on my other leg until I was held up in his arms, helplessly pinned on his cock. Torion stood straight, his chest breathing roughly into my own, the pair of us still fully dressed with heaps of fabric shoved aside.

His eyes caught mine and I squirmed, whimpering, too stuffed to interpret the dark meaning of his stare.

"Is this what you want?" he asked, edging out of me, my mouth falling open with a pathetic sound of protest. My head thumped against the wall as he surged back in, his movement inside of me sudden and rough, our skin clapping together as an almost embarrassing amount of wetness eased the motion.

I couldn't speak as he fucked me, rough and fast, his grunts animal and the soft howl of relief that rose up out of me made of desperate vowels.

"Greedy omega, needing her alpha's cock," Torion snarled out, and I swore the cottage shook with his thrusts.

"T-Torion," I cried out. There was a kind of anger in his voice, in the heavy slap of his hips against mine, the brutal drum of his length inside of me. It thrilled me, as did the trap his body fashioned for mine, but his brow was furrowed, a determined scowl replacing the usual wonder on his face as he was inside of me.

My hand was still tangled in his hair, and I used it now to distract him, pulling until he shouted and then guiding his face to mine, nibbling at his mouth until the sneer there softened.

Torion wasn't Malcolm, I'd known that plenty early. But no matter what might come between us in the future, I didn't want to be Malcolm now either, dangling my affection just out of Torion's reach.

"I—Ah! Torion, I-I missed you," I forced out between his harsh pace. It faltered as I spoke, Torion's body shuddering against mine, his chest sinking into mine, crushing my breasts as his mouth claimed a kiss, gentler but no less hungry.

His hands squeezed at my ass, and his strokes inside of me sank deeper until he bottomed out, the swelling of his knot stretching me open before he eased out.

"I missed you," I repeated when he let me catch a breath.

"Missed you," he answered in a whisper, sucking on my bottom lip before licking back into my mouth, the kiss taking on the steady, thorough, deep pace of his lovemaking. "Is this... Fuck, Brigid, you feel so good."

I echoed his words, kissing across his cheeks, whining as his knot grew too thick to pull out of me. Torion stepped back, pulling my hips from the wall, and we gasped together as our bodies found a new rhythm, rolling and grinding, his knot throbbing in time with my whimpers.

I wrapped my arms around his shoulders, covered his mouth with mine, and howled into the kiss as I came, quaking in my alpha's arms. Torion swallowed my cries with his own groans, my clenching core milking at his knot until he burst inside of me. My back slid against the rough wall, but I only kissed and clutched at Torion. He would see us safely to the floor. And then I would whisper into his ear little filthy words until he fucked me there too. I would keep him inside of me until we were both too tired to do anything else.

Until there was no chance of him getting back in the wagon and leaving me. Not today, at least.

Chapter Twenty-Two
TORION

Brigid's face was peeking over the edge of the loft as I carried in the last basket of food from the keep Maggie had sent with me. I'd been ashamed to realize that I'd been too bothered by Brigid's abandoning me to wonder how she would manage here at the cottage. And given the ecstatic expression on my omega's face when I'd mentioned there was a bag of tea in the cart, Maggie had been right to worry about her mistress.

I set the basket down and tried not to let *all* the hope I was feeling rise up into my expression as I looked back at Brigid. I had expected a prickly, cautious, stubborn Brigid upon arrival, was perversely looking forward to teasing and poking at her until she relented and offered me another half smile or a roll of her eyes. The hunger my omega met me with—a rival to my own for her in the dark nights and dragging days that had passed—had shocked me nearly to my knees.

Anger had followed. Anger that she'd even thought to deny us one another, that she'd stayed away when I couldn't stand to, that I would forgive her the neglect if she would only kiss me again.

I missed you.

"Torion?"

I blinked and focused on the Brigid above me, not the aching memory from less than an hour ago.

"Will you stay here tonight?" she asked softly, shyly.

I swallowed hard and locked my knees to keep from crumbling to the floor in a pathetic display of gratitude.

"I know I shouldn't ask," Brigid continued, wincing slightly, interrupting me before I might blurt out the cry of *yes* that rested on the tip of my tongue.

"Why shouldn't you?" I asked instead, turning to the basket and pulling out the bag of tea. There was a kettle hanging near the fire, and with a nudge, I could hear the slosh of water inside.

"You're meant to be at the keep," Brigid murmured. Out of the corner of my eye, a lock of auburn hair slipped over the edge of the loft, and I busied myself making tea to keep from twining it around my fingers.

"I've kept busy this week" —*distracting myself from your absence*— "enough so that there's nothing that really requires me for the next day or so."

"Really?"

If she hadn't sounded so pleased, I might've had the sense to guard myself, to offer her the night but leave in the morning. With a single word and a hint of hope, my will crumbled.

No, that wasn't true. My *will* wanted to be wherever Brigid was. It was the voices of betas like Francis Keane and even Ned MacIntyre in my head, hissing that it shouldn't be the alpha chasing down his omega but the other way around. My father had deferred to my mother's whims at the expense of his reputation, if not also his duty.

Brigid doesn't have whims, she has worries, I reminded myself. Worries I wanted to erase.

"Really," I answered.

Her arms folded in front of her, and I suspected she hid a smile in them. "Are you making me tea? I can do that—"

"No, stay up there and rest," I said, a weight lifting off my shoulders as the matter was settled. I would stay at the cottage "for a day or so," as I'd said. I would observe Brigid here in this place that she felt safest, and try and do my best to find ways to make the keep such a place for her as well.

"Very well. Catch me up on the keep," Brigid said, rolling back from the edge of the loft. I wanted to call her back just to savor little hints of her as I puttered around her cottage, but I bit my tongue and took the opportunity to study the space unobserved.

"For the most part, it's been uneventful, but Alpha Worthington and Francis Keane brought me a scheme," I said.

"A good scheme?"

I huffed. "For them, if I fell for it."

"Tell me," she bossed, sitting up slightly, her frown just visible.

I ducked my head to hide my smile, and filled my omega in on all of the news.

***

"Is it too late, then?"

I paused before reaching the cottage window, the quavering, feminine voice startling me out of my thoughts. Brigid had sent me to bathe out by the river while she organized all the goods I'd brought into their proper places, saying she would join me. I'd floated aimlessly until my curiosity—and my desire to be back in Brigid's company—had made me too impatient to wait.

She'd received a patient, apparently. I knew I shouldn't snoop, but I also didn't want to interrupt them. Preparing to turn back to the water, I caught Brigid's answer.

"It would've been better if you'd come to me *before* the rut, you know," Brigid said, the words softened by a gentle tone.

"I could hardly arrive at the alpha's keep asking for the preventative! And it's not as if anyone expected *you* to be claimed, you must admit."

I bristled on behalf of my omega, my mind racing to catch up to the conversation. Brigid's sigh carried out of the cottage windows to my ears.

"Fair enough."

"P-please, say you can help. I won't survive another son. I'll drink the tea everyday—"

"The tea only helps before," Brigid said, and the other woman sobbed before my omega interrupted her once more. "But there are other herbs. Their effectiveness is less reliable, but it's what I can offer."

I crept back slowly, careful not to be seen or heard, mulling over their conversation. Preventing a pregnancy, especially during a rut, was illegal for dragonkin women. If Brigid had ever offered such services to women before, and that information got back to the betas of the territory, it would be expected that I would punish her at the very least, if not imprison her. Of course, one of the women she helped would have to admit to such an act and receive the same judgment.

Fang's fire, I hoped it would never come to that. If it did, I would burn every last remaining splinter of a bridge left between myself and the betas by refusing to act against Brigid. My head spun, racing to consider new options, ways I might adjust the law before Brigid could be exposed. As long as anyone knew what she'd done, both she and I were in danger of retaliation, if not simple blackmail.

The sound of carriage wheels churning over gravel was muted under my thoughts where I waited by the gate, watching the sunset, but the soft slip of footsteps on the ground roused me. I turned toward Brigid as she approached, her face stony and guarded. I stretched my hand out in her direction and the shield fell away, her eyes widening and welling slightly.

"I didn't mean to overhear," I said.

"Torion, I swear to you, I did not break my promise—"

I caught her hand and tugged her to me, stopping the worried words with a soft kiss, wrapping my free arm around her trembling frame until she sighed and sagged against me.

"I know that," I mumbled against her lips, claiming another, firmer kiss before adding, "I wouldn't care if you had." Brigid winced and jerked at that, and I hurried to recover. "Well, I would, but only because all your talk of our parcel of children has me excited to have them running wild about us. But I wouldn't begrudge you the choice, and it wouldn't change my resolve to keep you at my side as my omega."

Brigid was burrowing into my chest before I'd fumbled my way through the speech, her ragged breaths puffing against my skin at my open collar. One of her hands slid up my chest to find my jaw, rubbing there, before she leaned back, arching in our embrace. "Torion. You are intolerably good," she said, voice weak and eyes wet.

I frowned, unsure if her words were meant to be praise. I caught one of her tears with my thumb and wiped it away. "As long as I am good to *you*." The words fell out of my lips without thought, precisely the sort of sentiment a council of advisors would warn me against. My duty was to the Hills, not to my omega.

But I hadn't taken a true council yet, and if I did, the first person I would call to my side would be Brigid.

She let out a choked cry and rose up on her toes, shaking hands clasping my head, fingers tangling in my hair, drawing me down to fuse our mouths together in hunger and succor.

———

THE COTTAGE WAS BARELY big enough to accommodate us together, so when a small family arrived to consult Brigid on their daughter's cough, I kept myself out of the way outside, brushing down and watering the horse that had pulled them in on a cart. I could hear them speak, Brigid's gentle and precise questions, the way she sweetly teased the nervous little girl until they were giggling together. I watched her through her windows, quick and competent as she grabbed jars from shelves, filled a small cloth bag with herbs, and instructed the family on the preparation of baths and teas.

"If I write out my instructions and the herbs I've given you, will that help?" Brigid asked.

"Aye, miss," the mother said, studying Brigid's scribbles over her shoulder with quick nods. "We can find those easy enough."

I ducked out of view again, rounding the back of the cottage and listening as my omega made her farewells to the family. I slipped back inside as their cart rolled out of view of the cottage and watched Brigid carefully arrange the jars she'd pulled back onto shelves and in cupboards.

"Why are only some of them labeled?" I asked, finding my usual spot out of her way in the rocking chair by the fireplace.

"Most I recognize by sight or smell, but some can be easily confused with one another, so I make sure to paint the name on the jar," she said.

"And do you gather every herb yourself?"

She shook her head. "There are merchants who travel the Hills. Mine brings herbs from farther south or north that I don't find here, and I trade him for those which only grow by water beds or in these particular woods."

I hummed as she continued her work, tidying everything away. I considered my own careless habit of leaving things out wherever I finished with them, knowing some maid or other servant would come along and put things to right again in my wake.

"Is this just how you would keep things organized in any space, or do you have it this way to suit this cottage's size specifically?"

Brigid flashed me a narrow-eyed look over her shoulder, and I was a little embarrassed at the pang of desire that sharp look conjured in my loins. "Why are you asking so many questions?"

I shrugged. "I like to watch you."

Her lips pursed. "It's just...it's just how things were organized when I came here. I suppose it's this way just because that's how it can be in such a small space. I don't know how I would change it, now that it is what I'm used to."

"It was your mother's cottage?"

Brigid nodded. "My mother left my father's house so he could take another omega, and came here where her own mother, my grandmother, was still living. She was lucky in that way, that she didn't inherit the property until after my father had dismissed her."

"How old were you?"

"Four," Brigid said softly. "They had me between ruts. And then when another rut passed without my mother bearing a son, their union was dissolved."

"Did you see her often?" I asked, frowning.

Brigid shook her head. "Rarely, in truth. And she was

so..." Brigid paused in her path through the cottage, blinking into a mirror and then laughing ruefully before turning back to me. "Well, I suppose she was what I have become—a bit roughened and countrified. At the time she seemed rather wild to me, and raggedy. I didn't mind my father's new omega, Janet. She was young and sweet and treated me like a little doll. It wasn't until after my union with Malcolm that I saw more of my mother."

Brigid helped herself to my lap, and I tried not to preen as her arms looped around my shoulders, her legs folding around my own. I wasn't sure if I was imagining that her ease was greater with me here in the cottage, but I was certainly relishing the change.

"If I'm honest, she terrified me," Brigid said softly, tucking her head down beneath my chin. "I thought if I wasn't careful with Malcolm, I would end up in her position. I..." She sighed. "Well, needless to say, after she passed, after I had enough of the life I'd chosen, I came here. It was a punishment for myself at first, until I realized what independence she had. I wish I'd had the same accord with her while she was alive."

I planted my feet firmly on the floorboards, rocking the chair beneath us, cradling my omega. Any inclination I'd had to order Brigid back to the keep with me vanished. This place was her sanctuary. She would return to the keep when she was sure it was safe, and as long as she did not bar the doors, I would meet her here where she was comfortable.

Chapter Twenty-Three
BRIGID

orion's breaths were rough against my cheek, a contrast to the sleek roll of his hips, the fluid stroke of his fingers between my legs as I trembled in the cradle of his body. The loft was too high for Torion to lay between my thighs without scraping his wings against the beams of the ceiling, so at night we found each other on our sides, my leg over his hip as we kissed, or like this with him curled around my back. It forced us to be slow and patient with our pleasure, made urgent need turn tender and gentle.

Torion's pinky finger stroked against the scar on my inner thigh, and my breath hitched at the strange response, the way the small touch pulsed like fire in my blood. I shook, nearing the edge, clawing at Torion's hand as he slowed his rocking.

"*Please*." My voice was harsh, but I melted as his mouth found the pulse of my throat, kissing and sucking softly.

"I can't believe I bit you," he said, chuckling, fingers abandoning their post on my throbbing sex to walk over to the mark he'd left on me during the rut. "Well, I suppose I can. I am always ravenous for you."

He had stopped moving, his hard cock resting peacefully

inside of me, and he was only tracing circles around the bite mark. There was no earthly reason why such a simple touch ought to drive me so mad, make me so feverish, so—

I cried out as he pressed into the scar, my core clamping down in a sudden and shocking orgasm. I covered my face with one hand, squeezed my fingers over his until he was digging into the scar, and came with a release that seemed to go on and on in waves of heat and sweetness. By the time I settled, Torion's arm was wrapped around me and he was thrusting, sheathing himself deeply, purring and growling into my ear.

"Witch," he rasped, and I shuddered once more, gentling my grip on his hand and moving it away from the baffling scar and back to my swollen lips and pulsing clit. "Yes, that's it. Again for me, darling Brigid."

I whined and twisted, and Torion read my mind as he always seemed to in these moments, his mouth slanting over mine, tongue thrusting in time with his cock, quick to swallow my whimpers and cries.

We'd already reached for one another twice in this night, although the first time I'd pushed him down to the rug by the fire and taken him with a rough quickness that left us both winded.

He would have to return to the keep in the morning.

We'd spent the day flying to the nearest village and shopping together. I'd greeted familiar faces not as the local woods witch or healer, whatever they called me, but as the alpha's omega. Still, I'd given my instructions to find me at the cottage, or the keep if I was not at home, ignoring the puzzled expressions I'd received in response. It had felt like a kind of defiance, although the effect was lessened by Torion's easy manner at my side.

"I want you back at the keep," he'd said as we'd walked

slowly back to the cottage, shrugging and meeting my gaze. "But if you want to be here, I will make time to come to you."

In an absolutely contrary fashion, it had been on the tip of my tongue to declare that I would return to the keep with him. I'd swallowed the impulse, stubbornly clinging to the cottage, to my solitude, to bitterness.

"Brigid," Torion gasped, mouth gaping over mine as he panted. "Oh, come with me. Come with me again."

The words would've been an empty plea if not for how well Torion knew my body. He claimed my breast in his hand, molding and gripping and pinching, orchestrating my climbing pleasure, a finger tucking inside my body to stretch me for his knot as two others rubbed urgently over my clit. He planted himself inside me as I came with a wail and a brief thrash of my body, arching my breast into his rough grip and trying to skirt my hips away from the touch that tortured and teased me so effectively.

Torion released me, circling me in his arms, lodging his knot deep and rubbing it inside of me to extend my ecstasy for endless divine minutes until we were both wrung dry and limp, too tired to sway and work our bodies against the pleasure. It pulsed as we caught our breath, shuddering in time with gasps and sighs until we settled, joined and sweaty and wonderfully weary.

I opened my mouth to speak, something silly and meaningless, just a word or two that he might answer so I could hear his voice again, but he beat me to the impulse.

"Rest for now," he whispered, brushing kisses over my ear and temple and jaw, against the corner of my mouth. "I already know I will need you again tonight."

I snorted, sleepy and pleased at the promise. "You can't be in rut again."

"It doesn't take an alpha's rut to make me want you,

witch," Torion answered darkly. "I have to sustain myself to leave on the morrow."

My breath hitched, and I turned my face into my pillow to keep myself from pleading for him to stay.

THE DAYS DRAGGED by after Torion's departure. My regular visitors returned, but the hours seemed to triple in length whether I was alone or working. Still, I stubbornly refused to face the solution. I had lived in this cottage for five years, taken on the mantle of the wise woman in the woods. Surrendering the title felt as if I was pretending those years had never had any value, when they had made me a truer version of myself. Gone was the girl who sought only to please the prominent man in her life, first her father and then her beta.

It's Torion who seeks to please you, a sly voice murmured in my thoughts as I returned to the cottage carrying a train of willow reeds to make a new basket. The words slithered through my head, a restless body turning and resettling, waiting.

"For now," I muttered to myself, rounding the corner and stopping in place at the sight of the carriage waiting in front of my cottage, recognizing the crest on the door as the strong Feargus oak.

My heart leapt into my throat, a smile growing on my face at the thought that Torion had returned so soon, until I noticed the driver still waiting atop the carriage bench. Perhaps I was being called back to the keep? Even that wasn't so much a disappointment, for reasons I didn't care to examine in the moment.

A soft murmur of feminine voices reached my ear from inside the cottage, and I paused for a moment, trying to catch words or tone, before placing my willow reeds aside. I brushed the debris from my skirts and headed for the door. The driver, a man I recognized from visiting Torion at the keep stables, spotted me and offered a respectful half bow from his seat.

"Ah, there you are, milady," Maggie offered me in an uncharacteristically formal tone.

It took me a moment of squinting to make out her company, and when I did, I wished I'd spent a little longer righting my appearance. The other woman was impeccably dressed and appeared to be of middle age. She was tall enough that she would have to duck to avoid hitting the low beams that held up my loft.

"May I introduce Mistress Baird. She's the best dressmaker in Cambelton," Maggie continued. "Omega Feargus."

Mistress Baird made a point to give the general surroundings of the cottage a derisive sweep of her gaze before landing on me and delivering an appropriate curtsey. "Omega Feargus. What a...rustic hideaway you have for yourself."

I took a moment to swallow all my stammering confusion, drawing myself up a little straighter. "It suits my purposes when I am alone. I apologize if you've been waiting. I was unaware of any appointment."

Maggie blushed slightly, but she too seemed to be doing her best to appear dignified and composed in front of Mistress Baird. The woman had more of the air of a stern school marm than solicitous dressmaker.

"I took the liberty of arranging it for you, milady," Maggie murmured. "As you were kept so busy before taking your retreat."

I wanted to take Maggie aside and quiz her on what precisely she thought she was doing, arranging me appointments for new clothing, but Mistress Baird's presence was both oppressive and impatient. Better to get the thing done.

"Industrious of you, Maggie. Very well, how should we begin?" I asked the dressmaker.

Mistress Baird perked up at that, snapping a tape measurer between her hands, and the next hour was spent with simple, efficient questions. What fabrics did I like? What cut of collars did I prefer, high or low? No, she would make the best choices of colors for me now that she'd seen me. Simple or adorned?

She would never have said so, but I thought perhaps our estimation of each other was repaired by the end of the appointment. I appreciated her directness and what choices she was willing to afford, and I suspected she appreciated that I had quick and ready opinions for each of her questions.

"There will need to be final fittings. Am I to return here, or will I be attending you at the alpha's keep?" Mistress Baird asked.

It only stung a little that she'd referred to it as the alpha's and not mine as well.

"The keep," Maggie was quick to answer, and I did not feel remotely inclined to correct her.

Mistress Baird seemed pleased by this too. No doubt when Maggie had secured her for the work, she'd expected better than to be transported to my little ramshackle cottage.

"I'll await you in the carriage," the dressmaker said, before offering me a deeper curtsey than before and taking her leave.

Maggie and I both waited for my door to swing shut before releasing long sighs.

I slanted her a glare out of the corner of my eye. "What on earth was that for, Mags?"

She crossed her bony arms over her chest and jutted her chin out at me, and I had to stifle the urge to smile. I'd missed Maggie over the past week and a half. "Did you think you'd just carry on being the alpha's omega while dressed in pauper's rags?" Maggie asked, sharp tongued and red cheeked.

My eyes widened. "I didn't realize you had such an opinion."

"I didn't. Not at first, at least. But you had plenty of time to do better, and you never did, and then you took haring off back to this—this—"

"Hideaway?" I suggested, liking the term Mistress Baird had used, even if it did make me sound like a coward.

"Humph," Maggie replied.

"You're right, of course," I said, and smiled at Maggie's flustered huff. "Were the staff gossiping about me?"

Maggie looked down at the floor, her arms dropping so her fingers could tangle and twist. "A bit," she said softly, in such a way as to make it clear that the staff certainly was, and it wasn't just them.

"I see," I said, trying to ignore the nervous flutter in my belly, the warning ring in my ears that I was making some kind of mistake.

Maggie looked up, her lips pressed grimly together for a moment before she took a breath and spoke. "You're going to have to buck up your courage, milady. He'll need you soon enough, and I *know* no matter what else, you won't want to let him down."

My face flushed with heat as Maggie reached out and caught my limp hands and squeezed them once before releasing me and heading for my door.

"Thank you, Maggie. I appreciate your candor," I managed, and she offered me a grim smile before taking her leave.

She's right, I thought, but it didn't sound quite like my own voice. And it felt a bit like a stranger had just called me a coward.

Chapter Twenty-Four
TORION

T he crackle of wheels on the brick was faint but sent me running out of the front door of the keep, nearly barreling into a young boy.

"Milord, they're coming—"

"It's clear enough he knows that, Freddy, now get out of his lordship's way!" a maid called from inside.

I paid them no mind, my eyes tracking the carriage slowly approaching the keep, my feet nearly stumbling in my haste to get down the steps. It had been nearly a month since Brigid left the keep for her cottage, and even though I'd seen her there only a few days ago—the most recent of several regular visits—I was plenty eager to have her back here, even if it was only temporary.

Unless you can convince her to stay.

I shushed the thought, not wanting to raise my own hopes too high. Brigid was returning now out of a less than pleasant duty for us both, and the setting and company weren't likely to endear her to my goals of placing her back under my roof.

The carriage came to a rocking halt, and I shot a glare at the young porter, hurrying to beat him to opening the door.

My poor staff had seen the worst of me over the past few weeks, my moods cycling through a morose sulk after my returns from the cottage, a sour temper midway through the week, and an impatient fervor in the day or so leading up to when I might leave again.

None of those moods were present as I opened the carriage door to find Brigid's face flushed and wearing a slightly harried expression as she eagerly leapt out and into my arms.

"I'm sorry I wasn't able to come myself," I said first.

"You'd only have been stuck with pins too," Brigid said, rising up on her toes. I held her too close, and her body pressed temptingly against mine, an unnecessary reminder that I'd spent three days without her touch. As if I wasn't counting the minutes.

"Pins?" I asked, head spinning from my omega's proximity. It was like being able to breathe again, I only smelled the clean air of the hills I loved when Brigid was close, her clear perfume turning the heady senses of the world back on for me.

"A carriage is not an ideal place for a final fitting, Alpha Feargus," a stern voice called from the carriage.

My arm tightened around Brigid's waist as she tried to pull away from me, but she pushed me back to the open door and I recalled my manners, offering my hand for the older woman. She waved me away, only leaning out and pinning Brigid with a direct stare.

"I must hurry on to my shop to complete the rest of the order now. I'll send it on when complete, and you'll let me know if anything needs...adjusted later on?"

Brigid nodded, her smile wobbling in a way that made me tense. "Thank you, Mistress Baird."

I opened my own mouth to echo Brigid, but the door

snapped shut and a rap was heard from inside, the driver hurrying to obey.

"She seems like a formidable woman," I noted, and Brigid sighed and leaned into me as the carriage circled the drive. "How are you?"

"Feeling a bit like a pincushion, but I'll recover now," Brigid said. She slipped out of reach before I could enclose her in my arms again, stepping back in front of me and holding out her arms. "But how do I look?"

My one track mind—a track whose only goal was being near Brigid again—took too long to put the pieces together, and Brigid started to fidget, smoothing her hands over her dress and plucking at the skirts.

"One of the maids will have to manage my hair, of course," she said, eyes darting over my shoulder.

Pins in the carriage, a school marm woman talking about fittings and—

I shook myself. The dress! She was wearing a new dress, one that'd been finished as recently as the carriage ride.

"You look magnificent," I said, hurrying to cover my blunder. Brigid huffed and rolled her eyes. "You do! Regal."

Her cheeks pinked, and I guessed I was on the right track. I took a step closer to her, catching her chin in a gentle grip. The words weren't lies, even if it didn't matter a whit to me what Brigid wore as long as she was within reach. But the rust red dress was fitted perfectly—my compliments to Mistress Baird—and draped over her shoulders and around her waist, adding to curves I already loved so much, were two of the Feargus tartans, one new and in our hunting colors of brown and green with thin stripes of red and blue, and the other my mother's embellished dress tartan.

"You represent me well, Omega Feargus," I said, because I liked the way it felt to put my family name on her.

Brigid sighed at that and offered me a real smile, although there was something still skittish in her gaze that worried me.

"How long do we have?" Brigid asked, glancing over her shoulder to the road that lead to the keep.

"A handful of hours, and that's if no one arrives early," I said, recalling why I'd brought Brigid back to the keep.

"They will, no doubt," she said drily, catching my arm to slip hers through, turning and guiding me back inside.

"No doubt," I agreed, swallowing hard as Brigid nodded and smiled to the keep staff as she directed us both toward the stairs.

Brigid leaned more solidly into my side, tipping her head to my shoulder and lowering her voice. "Still. That might be enough time for us to—Torion!"

I laughed as she screeched, my arms scooping beneath her legs, my own carrying us up the stairs two at a time. "Oh plenty of time for..." I trailed off meaningfully and waggled my eyebrows.

"I was being *subtle*," Brigid hissed.

"There's nothing subtle about it when I'll have you screaming my name in under ten minutes," I answered, rushing for the bedroom. It was about damn time I had my omega back in our bed. Any betas who arrived early would just have to *wait*.

"RESPECTFULLY, Alpha Feargus, you don't seem to be taking this meeting very seriously," Francis Keane bit out.

Considering I caught myself smiling lazily for no reason at all, I couldn't exactly *blame* Keane for calling me out, even I questioned his motives. Stifling my expression once mor and attempting to shake off some of the drowsy satisfaction still lingering in my body after my reunion with Brigid, I narrowed my eyes on Keane before slowly circling them around the table at the other betas. We were holding our assembly in the library, a room that had been closed for a number of years, neglected by my parents disinterest. There'd been some damage from a cracked window, but Brigid had arranged for the repairs before the rut. With the work complete, the room was restored to its former grandeur, ceiling beams elaborately carved, windows paned with stained glass, a fireplace roaring at the far end. Rather than refurnish it with sofas and work tables, Brigid had instructed the staff to bring out one of the grand tables and turn the space into a meeting room for me. Clever witch.

I opened my mouth to respond to Keane, when I was swiftly interrupted.

"Respectfully, Beta Keane, some of the gentlemen here have brought rather pathetic complaints to our alpha."

I stirred in my seat, startled by the speech of support. There were new faces here for the first time in decades—younger dragons who'd climbed in stature since my untraditional twist on the selection ceremony. Samuel Cameron sat bristling at the far end of the table, his young face red with either temper or embarrassment or both, his eyes shooting daggers at many of the older betas. Cameron was the beta chosen by the wealthy omega Emily Anderson, and it hadn't taken long for the young man's transformation to take place, from a rough and unfinished lad to a gentleman of consequence. While I'd had some part in that transformation—namely, making sure the farm he'd inherited from his uncle got as much support and staff as it needed for repairs—I hadn't expected a show of loyalty.

"Pathetic?!" Lord McKinney squawked, hands slapping against the table.

"Tenancies that have gone all but fallow in the past two decades are now already restored and on schedule for harvesting," Cameron said, bucking his chin at the older man. "Local merchants are happy. One man I know even called his son home from Skybern in expectation of better trade and needing help. All in a few months of our alpha's reign. And yet you speak to him of poor weather, felled trees, and a missing sheep or two, as if these are things any man might control."

A few men shifted in their seats, perhaps chastised, but one halfway down the table turned his face to the back of the room and muttered under his breath. I only made out the words "his witch" and "omega," but the men around him froze with nerves. I took a moment to recall the man's name as the ripple seemed to circle around the table of betas.

"My omega is a healer, not a witch. Although I tease her often enough about her enchanting nature," I said, clearly and steadily. Superstitions were for old women and children, in my opinion, but even those who didn't believe might take up a rumor for the sake of ugliness.

"She may be nothing more than an omega, my lord, but you allow her to set a poor example for our daughters," Ben Danielson said. He was not a beta I knew well, but he was also not a recent thorn in my side, so I met his gaze and braced myself.

"In what way?" I asked, afraid I already knew the answer.

"Her leash is a little long, don't you think?" Francis Keane asked, eyebrows raising and turning to look around the table. "Out there alone in that ramshackle cottage, acting like some kind of changeling creature?"

In spite of the concerning turn of the conversation, I found my lips quirking at that depiction of Brigid. "Omega Feargus is, as you all saw today, here at the keep. She is also the most practical person I have ever met in my life, and as such, takes her responsibilities to both me, and her former community while she lived independently, with the utmost seriousness. She has her own property to care for, but she by no means neglects her role at my side."

Except for in the most personal ways, but I have the good sense not to force the issue, I added to myself.

The speech was as measured as I'd ever been in my life, and it seemed to appease some around the table, but I didn't miss the way many eyes slid in Malcolm Barr's direction where he sat stewing in the corner. I wanted to shout that Barr had certainly abandoned Brigid in far more reprehensible ways than she had by retreating to her cottage, but there would be no point. I'd said my piece. It was up to the men around the table to see reason, and in my experience that only happened if a man was already inclined to do so.

"As Beta Cameron has pointed out, I cannot control the weather, but I will be sure to send out men to your estate, Lord McKinney, to help with cleaning up the trees. And to yours, Danielson, to repair fences. We've had a record number of kids born this spring, and if your sheep can't be recovered, they can at least be replaced with my compliments." It was a more magnanimous offer than the fools deserved, and they seemed to realize as much because mouths remained shut this time. "With these matters settled, may I recommend we retire for the day and enjoy the feast my omega has planned for you all."

I rose from my seat and made eye contact with the men who opened their mouths from the corners to mutter to one another, until one by one, the betas filed from the room. Samuel Cameron was at the back of the pack, and I stepped to his side to make my exit with him.

"Thank you for speaking some sense," I said.

He looked more nervous now than he had telling off the whole room, and he glanced behind us. "I don't know what good it will have done. They don't take me seriously."

"All these men have money, loud opinions, and reputation. Keep using the first two now that you have them, and the third will come soon enough," I said, clapping the young man on the shoulder.

He snorted at that, and we slipped apart as we broke out of the hallway and into the great room, alive with candlelight and musicians, a number of staff ready to serve from jugs of mead and ale. The tenor of our group brightened considerably at the sight, and I chewed at my own scowl as I caught sight of Brigid escorting McKinney and Danielson to a table, all their ire and skepticism vanished in the face of her beauty and smiles.

Fire burned proud in my chest. I'd never imagined what my omega might be. My mother had been a flower at my father's side, adored by him and admired by other men, but she'd never been an active force in the keep. Brigid was exquisite, precious, and an asset to me as alpha. It didn't seem to matter what the men *wanted* to think of her. When she turned in their direction, they flirted and blushed and let her guide them like lovestruck boys to their table.

An absurd grin spread over my face as I watched my prickly, defensive, skittish omega charm and cajole the men in the room, knowing she would never bother to sweet talk me in such a way. No, she would roll her eyes and boss me to my seat under her breath before turning a smile onto another man.

And I would carry on loving her as I had almost from the start.

Chapter Twenty-Five

BRIGID

Less than ten years ago, I'd considered myself a weak woman. I'd blamed myself for Malcolm's interest in others, hated myself for accepting his disloyalty and remaining with him, resented my lifetime of going along with my father and Malcolm's orders.

But I couldn't be a weak woman, not with the way I kept my spine straight and my smile fastened on for the betas and for Torion too. When my hands shook at dinner, I hid them under my napkin until I could gain control of them again. When I thought I wouldn't be able to take another breath, I ducked my chin and pretended to listen to whatever someone was saying to me as I counted slowly in my mind and nodded to the rhythm of their words.

When the evening finally wound to a close, the meal taken away and the requests for drink slowing, I wondered if I was relieved or terrified to be retiring to bed with Torion. I'd managed a full day of keeping my panic at bay, or at least hidden from others, but I wasn't sure I could hide it from him if we were alone again.

Torion, as usual, didn't give me the chance to brace.

"Do you know how proud you make me?"

We'd barely made it through the door of our bedroom when he spoke, low and earnest, voice rough with feeling and gaze hot with desire. I tried to catch my breath, to slip away, but I was too weary and the air hiccuped in my throat as Torion's arms circled my waist. It was as if he'd tailored the words to strike me perfectly, to shatter the lock on the fragile cage where I'd stuffed my worries away. When I tried to step closer to hide my face against his chest, his thumbs curled around my ribs, holding me just far enough away to look down at me, eyes glittering warmly, smile soft. And then a tense V formed between his eyes, and I knew my mask was slipping.

"Please, Torion, let me—" I gasped out, the words faltering for air.

His shoulders fell in disappointment, gaze shuttering, and something soft in my chest tore as he sighed.

"Brigid—"

Was it worse to drown in guilt as I basked in Torion's sweetness, or face the reality of him pulling away and knowing it was my fault? For the first time, I refused both options, reaching out to cling to his shirt.

"I'm so—I'm sor—" I couldn't catch my breath, and my vision was blurring, hot tracks rolling down my cheeks until salt pooled in the corners of my mouth.

"Brigid?" I couldn't make out Torion's features, but I swallowed down lungfuls of his scent as he enclosed me into his chest and then surrounded us with his wings. "Brigid, love, what is it? What's wrong? Did someone say something?"

My spine bowed at the word 'love,' and the shaking in my hands spread upward into my arms and shoulders and all through my body, unraveling all of my control once and for all.

I was babbling a nonsensical apology, tears flavoring the

panicked words. Sorry for pulling away, for pushing him back, for not being *able* to trust him when I was realizing Torion was a man a woman *could* trust.

Torion's hands cupped my elbows, pushing my arms around his neck. I tightened them on my own as my feet left the floor, squeezed him tight until I thought I might be strangling him. His hands cradled me gently, my feet swaying, and I wasn't sure how he managed it, but I felt the softness of the bed beneath me without him ever pulling me off his chest.

"There now, let me hold you. I have you, love."

His voice was low and slow, spilling out comforting words without ever hushing me. His heartbeat drummed steadily under my ear, counting the seconds and minutes as my speech fell apart into simple wounded sounds. I'd never been held like this, not since I was a little girl, and that only made me sob harder until there was no breath for sound at all, just a lifetime's worth of weeping as Torion stroked my back and let me soak his shirt.

When my breaths grew uneven and sparse, he rolled me to my back, leaning back just enough to press his hand over my chest in a slow rhythm, coaxing my lungs back into the right pattern.

"I'm here, love," he whispered, the words landing softly as he kissed away tears on my cheeks.

He didn't offer false promises, I realized. Didn't tell me it would be all right. Dragon's fire, he didn't even know what was wrong, poor man.

A hysterical laugh came out with a sob, and my eyes were sore as I opened them to gaze up at him. The furrow in his brow had grown deeper, and his own eyes were wet, like he'd been crying *for* me, with me. The sight untied my tongue at last.

"I-I th-think I'm p-pregnant," I said, the words thick with

tears, almost unintelligible with how hard I had to work to force them out.

But Torion stilled and searched my face, eyes widening with confusion.

"It's not—not the first time," I said, covering his hand on my chest, pressing there to anchor us both, to stamp down the hope that tried to fly out of me every time I thought about the queasiness I'd been suffering in the morning or how long it had been since I'd had my courses.

"Not the first time?" he echoed.

For a moment, I thought I might get up from the bed, run from the room, the keep, back to the cottage, rather than tell Torion the story. But then I met his dark eyes and knew that this time, he would follow me. He might let me run if he thought it was what I needed, but not after I'd been sobbing in his arms. I was grateful for the space he'd given me, and I would be grateful if he chased me down and held me close. It was time to start letting this man in.

"The last rut. With Malcolm. I wasn't...I wasn't even showing yet when—when I—lost—"

Tears welled up in my eyes once more, all the traps and walls I'd built to keep them back now broken, Torion's shelter too tempting to resist.

"No," Torion murmured as a strangled wail choked and remained locked in my throat. "Oh, Brigid. No. I'm so sorry."

My sobs were softer now, tired, and Torion bundled me close, lifting me and moving me to his lap to rock us back and forth on the bed, a kind of comfort I'd never been offered, so patient, as if he'd hold me like this forever. I would let him. The idea sounded wonderful. I was too tired to lie to myself about how much I wanted Torion's affection now.

It could've been hours that passed. The candlelight grew dimmer in the room, or my eyes were simply too tired, lids swollen. When I settled once more, my breaths coming deeper and steadier, Torion still kept me to his chest, his hand at the back of my head cradling me gently.

"Barr doesn't know," Torion said eventually.

I had to clear my throat twice to speak, and my voice was hoarse. "No. I don't want him to. The babe is mine to mourn."

Torion brushed his mouth to the crown of my head, breathed there against me, and I realized that he had joined me in my mourning. I opened my fist to feel his heartbeat against my palm.

"I'm so scared," I whispered.

Torion nodded, the bristles of his cheek scratching through my hair. "You want this child."

"More than anything," I managed through new tears and thin breaths. One large hand slid to rest over mine on my belly, warm and strong.

"Share with me," he murmured.

I tipped my head back, frowning. I had shared more tonight than I had with any other person in my life.

"Share this fear with me. And your joy. Don't carry this alone, Brigid. Not when I'm here and all I want is to help you bear it." His eyes searched my face, waited for me to accept what he offered.

"You're the alpha, Torion, you have a duty—"

He shook his head, and his tear wet lashes were thick and spiky. "I'm *your* alpha, Brigid. I'm yours. Please. Let me help. Let me care for you and for our child."

He's so serious, I thought numbly. I forgot sometimes, in all of Torion's playfulness, how big and earnest his heart really was. He kept showing me the proof, and here it was again. His hand was warm over mine. His heart beneath my other hand was steady, beating against my palm. Torion was the alpha, and while he made vows easily—offering me the position as omega, promising to keep me in his house, promising me children and respect—he didn't make vows *lightly*. What he offered, he meant to stand by.

He sighed, softening around me, cuddling me gently into his side, shifting down the bed. "Let me try," he said, and I found myself nodding.

"I'll try too," I said, wondering at myself, wondering at Torion's tired smile. "Aren't you afraid that I might fail again?"

"Fail?"

"To carry the child to term."

His smile turned to a scowl fast as lightning. "It's not failing, Brigid. Don't speak that way."

"But—"

"Any worries I have are for your sake now," he said firmly. And then he was quiet for a moment, a frown slowly deepening and taking over his face. "That's not true. I want this child too. I don't want to lose them, and I don't want to lose you. I'm scared too."

It shouldn't have been comforting, but it was. I stretched and kissed Torion's brow.

"Tell me more," he said, settling us deeper into the bed, one of my legs remaining draped over his, the both of us fully dressed, our hands joined over my stomach.

I told him about the evidence of the pregnancy so far, answered his questions about how I was managing my morning sickness, how I made meals out of the porridge I suddenly found myself craving too often, and the pickled wild ramps I snacked on.

I paused as I started to describe my first pregnancy, but Torion held my gaze, my hand, and I found my tongue growing loose and eager. I told him about discovering Malcolm with another woman just after I'd started to suspect I was with child, the depression that had followed, how much I'd loathed myself for accepting Malcolm back in my bed.

And I told him the very worst of the truth.

"There were days I regretted getting pregnant. Where I was frightened that a child would force me to remain with a man who didn't love or respect me. Some days I was ecstatic, and some days I thought the child would transform Malcolm into the man I wanted him to be, and some days I wished I wasn't pregnant at all. So when—"

Torion cut the words off with a swift, hard kiss and a simple, "No."

I blinked, the tears that had been gathering slipping away. "But—"

"You're not at fault, Brigid. Don't argue," he said, lifting his hand from mine just long enough to pinch my lips shut before I could speak. "Every time that thought rises, I want you to throw it out. It's not true. If women could control their own pregnancies simply by wishing they weren't pregnant, we would have significantly fewer dragons. So don't take that route, my love."

My love. He kept saying those words. It terrified me how much I liked to hear them, but the terror was muffled tonight. I was far too exhausted now to give it any energy to grow. I poured out every secret and every fear I possessed into the lap of this man I'd known just a few months. And he'd taken them into his care, just as he had me.

As we settled, clinging to one another, I slipped my hand on my belly out from under his to reach up and stroke his face, the rough stubble over his strong jaw tickling my fingers. His palm rested over my stomach, warm and weighty, promising protection. For the night, for a few hours, just to help me fall asleep, I would believe the promise.

Chapter Twenty-Six
TORION

My world had been shifting for months now. First, with my father's death, then again with Brigid's arrival at the keep, and once more during the days and nights of our rut.

Now I was realizing these weren't separate disruptive events, but simply that my life's axis had changed, tilting and sending me sliding down into the arms of the woman asleep beside me.

How could someone take such a firm and unyielding grasp on my heart, while breaking it at the same time?

It was barely dawn, the room cast in gray light, and Brigid's eyes were still swollen from crying the night before. I'd managed to unwrap her from my family plaids while she slept, but I hadn't wanted to disturb her any further, and the red of her gown made her cheeks look especially pale, her freckles faded.

There was no outward sign of her pregnancy yet, but I had already begun picturing how it might go—a subtle swell at first, a rounding where now she dipped in, and then slow growth till she was swollen and irritable and burdened with our child in the most beautiful way. It filled me with pride and terror and hunger, made my head spin. Brigid was constantly in motion, at work. How would I contrive to make her rest, or would being pregnant manage that for me?

How would she take it if I followed her back to the cottage? There was no question in my mind now that wherever Brigid went, I would be, and if that meant I had to abandon the keep to crowd her in her little home, so be it. If she made me sleep outside the door, I would.

Bellfry's ballocks, I was going to be a father the same year I'd risen as alpha. This was some combination of madness and uncanny luck.

Brigid stirred with the soft and familiar grunt of her rousing, and everything but my omega slipped out of focus once more. She came before all else now. She had to. Ned might say I was making the same error as my father, but Brigid was not the same woman as my mother. She took her duty as omega to the Hills seriously and would remind me of mine, but no one had ever honored their responsibility to *her*. That was my right now.

"Don't tell me you've been guarding me all night like that," Brigid rasped, one barely slitted eye offering me a glare, her face mostly buried in the pillow.

I had been, and I wouldn't apologize for it.

"I've been thinking about how to get the betas to leave this morning," I admitted instead.

Brigid sat up, rumpled and dreadful looking and grumpy... and so stunning, it struck me dumb. "Torion, you know you can't."

I was wearing a fool's smile as I gazed down at her. "I can."

Her eyes narrowed in answer. "Then you know it would be unwise. I'll be all right today, I promise."

Seeing a win waiting directly in front me, I seized it

before she could realize what she offered as a bargain. "You will. You'll stay here this morning. Have a long soak, and let Maggie bring you breakfast and all the gossip she gathered from the visiting servants."

Brigid huffed. "Torion—"

I brushed my mouth over hers and savored the startled blink of her eyes. "If you insist I tolerate the betas..."

"I do," Brigid said, frowning.

"Then I insist you relax this morning and simply join us for the evening meal. These men are here to gain favors from me. I don't have to let them ogle my omega while they do it."

Brigid snorted, but her expression smoothed at last. I would instruct Maggie to bring her a cool compress for her eyes too.

"Fine," she sighed. She turned, and I held my breath as she snuggled into my chest. Had she ever done that before? Probably, but I couldn't think straight with her so close. Everything was different this morning. "Let's go back to sleep. No one will be up so early."

"No..." I agreed, wondering if I could push my luck this morning as I added, "But I do have something to show you."

I'd planned on waiting until the betas had left, but perhaps after last night's confessions, it might be best to give her some time to think over my offers before she'd already made her arrangements to leave the keep again.

"Mm, is it important?" she mumbled, her lips brushing against the bare skin of my chest.

Was it important? I couldn't remember. Probably not. It probably wouldn't do any good. I would be more likely to make her relent and return to the keep by annoying her and getting in her way at the cottage with an extended stay. I didn't want to annoy her. I wanted to show her that I under-stood her, that I could take care of her in a way I suspected no one had tried before.

Brigid sighed and leaned back. "Oh, very well. Show me."

I glanced toward the window once more. It was too early for our guests to be waking. Then again, it was too early to warrant dragging Brigid from the bed after a difficult night. "It's not very—"

"No, you've made me curious now and I won't be able to rest while I'm wondering," she huffed, twisting away from me, but not before I caught the hint of a smile at the corner of her mouth.

"You look as though you expect to be pleased," I said, following after her, watching with greedy eyes as she shucked off yesterday's gown. There was just enough light through the window to tease me with her silhouette through her new thin chemise. It had pretty lace along the hem, which meant I probably shouldn't tear it off of her any time soon.

Brigid paused, half turned toward me, head tipping thoughtfully. "I suppose I can't imagine you wanting to show me something that would displease me."

With my throat strangely choked, I stumbled to her side, wrapping an arm around her waist and drawing her in to kiss her temple. "Fair enough," I rasped out.

Afraid of popping this tenuous bubble between us, formed of something like ease and something like harmony and something infinitely more fragile, I hurried to dress. Brigid was learning to trust me, even if she didn't always realize how much that trust had grown. My patience continued to be fruitful, which made my path forward easy enough to follow. The mistakes a man like Malcolm had made were ones I wanted nothing to do with. Brigid was my omega, and whether she was here at my side, sliding into a simple day dress, or alone at the cottage while I suffered without her, I wanted no other woman. I would not leave her coping with her stress alone, not as long as she was willing to share her concerns with me...or I could ferret them out on my own.

I finished dressing and returned to Brigid as she struggled braiding her hair, taking it and completing it for her.

"Can we sneak by the kitchens on the way to whatever it is you have to show me? Maggie will have my ginger tea brewing by now," Brigid said.

"For your morning sickness?" I asked, wrapping an arm around her waist.

"It isn't very severe, although it's still a little early yet," Brigid explained as I led her out into the hall. Her voice lowered. "Most days, it's nothing more than a queasy kind of feeling that pops up, morning or otherwise. The tea manages that easily enough." She was quiet until we reached the stairs, then leaned against me briefly before adding, "Some days, I think the feeling has more to do with nerves about the pregnancy than the pregnancy itself."

I took Brigid's free hand and lifted it to my lips as I tucked away the information. Brigid would need ginger tea at her side until she declared otherwise. Perhaps ginger biscuits too, just in case.

The tea was ready when we reached the kitchen, steaming in a large ceramic pint mug instead of the fine china, and Brigid took it gratefully, warming her hands around the base as she took small sips. The keep was chilly in the morning, especially downstairs, where doors to the outside were being opened as the staff busied and prepared for the day. Perhaps I could find some nice woolen gloves or a thicker shawl for Brigid as well.

"You're staring," she said to me. "Aren't we meant to be going somewhere?"

Caught, I thought, and I wrapped Brigid closer to my side with an arm and spread my wing at her back to block any drafts as we continued on our way.

The office I'd arranged for Brigid had been previously used as a ladies' sitting room, although my mother had found it too small and tucked away, the last door in the left lower hallway. Still, it was twice the size of Brigid's cottage interior, and had a large—and newly repaired—window that over-looked the small loch to the south of the keep. It also had a secret door that opened to a stairway down to the herb garden, making it easy for Brigid to gather and store her wares.

"If you don't like it, or just parts of it—" I started before opening the door.

"Torion," Brigid said with a little huff of impatience.

"Anything can be changed," I said, knowing full well that the men I'd had laboring to set this room to rights might have something to say, or at least think about that.

Brigid just stared at me with dry expectation. It struck me suddenly—the contrast of the woman I'd met who'd told me how our union would be, who stood in front of me now, and the woman I'd held as she fell apart in my arms the night before. I stepped forward and pressed my lips to hers, my blood rushing as she rose to her toes to lean into the kiss.

She was mine.

I hadn't been sure until now. She still might not be, but I told myself we would get there, in time.

I stepped back and then pushed open the door, turning immediately so I could catch her reaction. Brigid's eyes widened immediately, breath catching and lips parting. The room was fragrant with hanging herbs tied to racks that lined the high ceiling, carefully curated to match what I had cata-loged from her cottage, and lined with freshly built shelves I'd designed with a thin brass bar across to better secure the glass jars that waited to be filled. A cozy fireplace took up a large part of the right hand wall, and I was grateful to what-ever maid had thought to set alight the fire this morning, now crackling and making the room warmly pleasant.

"Torion," Brigid breathed, stepping inside and stopping at

the large counter that ran along the left wall, lit by three oil lamp sconces above. Below the counter were drawers filled with paper and ink, bandages, pouches waiting to be filled, and instruments for mixing concoctions.

"There is no reason why you may not continue your work here...when you are in residence," I said, trying not to sound too hopeful, too obvious in my goal. "If it pleases you."

A plush couch and two armchairs surrounded the large window opposite us, and a high bench waited near the counter for patients. And still, there was plenty of room for Brigid to maneuver, for her to fill the space with more furniture or tables if she chose.

"You did all this?" Brigid asked as I joined her at the center of the room. She turned slowly, her mug of tea still cupped in her hands.

"Anything you need—anything you *want* is yours, if it's in my power to offer it," I said simply. I'd said it before, but Brigid often needed to be reminded of my promises.

Brigid turned to me. She was still pale, the rim of her eyes still red, but now her gaze was filled with an open wonder, startled but not unhappy.

"If there are changes—"

"Don't you dare," she said quickly before pressing her lips flat and gazing once more around the room. Her expression eased as she looked her fill. "It's perfect."

I shrugged, ignoring the rush of pride bursting through me. "I'm sure you'll know what you prefer as you work in it. There is a—"

The secret door would have to wait. Brigid moved swiftly, setting down the tea and then catching my face in her warm hands and drawing me down for her kiss. Her mouth covered mine, firm and earnest, and offered a long, simple press that for some reason left me blushing as she pulled away.

"Thank you," she said, holding my stare for a long moment.

"You're welcome."

I'd barely answered when she wrapped her arms around my waist, pressing her cheek over my pounding heart.

This is enough, I thought. But Brigid wasn't done twisting my heart into happy little knots.

"I'm sorry I ran," she whispered.

My arms circled her, and then my wings too for good measure. I lowered my head and murmured into the soft silk of her hair, "I'm sorry for all the reasons you felt you had to."

Brigid sighed out, ragged and weary, and perhaps relaxed too. She spoke again, barely audible except for the fact that we were cocooned and there was nowhere else for the words to go but in my waiting ear. "Would you send someone to collect my things from the cottage?"

I closed my eyes and took in a deep breath of her, my scent of home. "Yes, witch. If it's what you want."

Brigid nodded, nuzzling into the open collar of my shirt, swallowing her own greedy breath. "It's what I want. And what I need too."

Chapter Twenty-Seven
BRIGID

❧

"I ought to delegate the trip to someone else," Torion muttered, scowling behind the large desk he used so rarely.

"You don't trust anyone well enough," I said, smiling at his resulting pout. "I thought you said you'd be back the same evening?"

"I will," he said roughly. "Seamus won't drag the business out. I could send for him to come here instead. He'd understand if—"

"I'm not ready for others to know, Torion," I said gently, rounding his desk and trying to contain my laugh as he snatched me up and put me in his lap like he was getting away with something. Being nestled against him was precisely my aim in walking over, silly man.

Torion grunted. "Much as I'd like to crow the news from the rooftops, I feel the same. But I don't like leaving you on your own."

"Hardly on my own, unless you plan on taking everyone in the keep with you," I said easily. Torion didn't spare my teasing a thought, his frown still firmly fixed in place. "Tell me what has you so disturbed. It's only a few hours."

His gaze skittered away in an intriguing display of wariness or shame, and I caught his chin in my hand, stroking the bristle along his jaw with my thumb.

"I don't want you to take this as a slight to your competence or...independence," he said slowly. My eyebrows rose in interest, and perhaps a little expectant offense. "I recently swore to myself that I'd be firmly attached to your hip and not leave you for so much as a moment."

I snorted at that. "How could you have managed that if I went back to the cottage?" His eyes lifted to my face finally, expression dry, and I froze. "Were you planning on coming with me? You barely fit in the cottage! It would've driven me mad in a week, and we'd have to come right back—"

My tongue stilled as Torion's cheeks warmed with color.

"Very clever," I admitted, pardoning his schemes by stroking my fingers into the tangled curls at the back of his neck.

"I know you fend for yourself very well. I just despise the causes of that necessity," Torion said.

It had been a scant week since I'd unburdened myself, spilling out my fears and hopes and secrets to Torion. He hadn't changed in that time, although it took me a day or so to realize that this version of Torion—devotedly attentive, a stable figure for me to prop myself up against—had been the man he'd offered me from the very beginning. I was only just now learning how it felt to *allow* him to provide that to me.

It was wonderful.

Terrifying, a shrinking part of me corrected but was promptly swatted away.

I was learning how to put away the frightened part of myself. I might not trust Torion completely yet, but I was endeavoring to stop myself from actively *distrusting* him. Perhaps they were one in the same.

"You know I'll be all right for the day," I said gently, my fingers picking through the tangles I found.

"I do," Torion admitted with a sigh.

"You're not breaking your vow to yourself or to me," I continued.

"I knew you would be like this," Torion said, smiling slightly.

"Like what?"

"Eminently reasonable. You are the better part of me, little witch."

I rewarded that compliment—and the bubbling warmth it conjured in my chest—with a sipping kiss. "You should take someone with you."

"Worried for my safety?" Torion asked, looking absurdly pleased.

"Not particularly," I admitted, grinning. I was teasing him, but it was true. I had a difficult time imagining Torion coming into any danger. He was too commanding and strong in my eyes. "But I think you should start to curry favor with men you like."

"As a matter of fact, I did invite Cameron. He and Emily Anderson are expanding her shipping interests, and I think Seamus will like him."

I nodded. "He's a good choice. Although I recommend in the next instance you consider a gentleman who's been established longer, but on the fringes of the usual cohort."

Torion nodded at that, his head tipping into my fingers that rubbed at the back of his skull. "Tell me who you'd recommend."

"Ben Danielson might do," I said.

"He's fairly mild mannered. I've rarely had cause to meet

with him. Gave me some trouble at the meeting, but I feel as though Keane put a bug in his ear," Torion mused.

"Danielson had a daughter that chose her beta this past ceremony, and he settled a good sum on the couple, so we know he's not as obstinate as some. He keeps his estates and the near village in good order. He might be resistant to politicking, but if you ever wanted counsel, I think he would take it as an honor."

Torion was smiling at me, gaze heavy lidded and warm. "I'll make a point to approach him soon. Thank you, Brigid."

My head spun. No man I'd ever known in my life—intimately or on bare acquaintance—would ever have been lenient enough to even let me voice my opinion on such a topic, let alone be *pleased* with me for doing so. And I'd been comparing Torion to them this entire time, waiting for him to transform into what I expected to find.

I owe you an apology, I thought. But instead of saying so, I kissed him, lingering this time, delighted as he seemed content to do the same.

I pulled away to suggest we take ourselves to the bedroom, or at least make new use of his desk, but Torion spoke first.

"I think if I had no other counsel but yours, I would be as well off as I could be. But since there is strength in numbers, who else do you recommend I court?"

I grinned, settling myself more comfortably in my alpha's lap, and shared my observations without reserve.

TORION LEFT before dawn the next morning, and I had a hazy memory of his lips kissing almost chastely up my spine before whispering his goodbye in my ear. I woke with sunlight streaming over my bare back and a smile on my lips.

I opened my eyes to the sight of my tea steaming, little dust motes sparkling in the air, the scent of lemon and ginger a fresh greeting to the morning.

I caught Torion's pillow, the indentation from his head still in place, and drew it to me, breathing his cinnamon ash scent in as deeply as I could. I knew what was happening, the way my chest felt effervescent and light enough to float away, even as it grew dense and full and heavy. The nervous expectation was icy with fear, and yet exhilarating too.

I groaned into Torion's pillow and tried to find a calming center once more. I would work in my office today, the beautiful space Torion had built for me, and it would help settle some of the flurry of feeling. I had made a vow to myself not to push those feelings away, but dwelling in them too much made anxieties stack just as high as hopes.

I sat up in the bed, shoving my many gathered pillows and blankets aside, scooting back and preparing to throw myself out of the nest and into the day, when the sight of a few marks of dull reddish brown on the white sheets froze me in place. A small cry quaked out from my barely parted lips, and my eyes shut on the sight as I tried to find my breath.

The old nurse in the village near Malcolm's estate had assured me it was a common symptom for early pregnancy, that it was as likely to amount to nothing as it might signal any concerns. My mother's notes had said much the same, offering some recommendations of rest and certain teas if there were any other hints of trouble, like a pinching cramp. I'd hid my worry and my old sorrow and offered the women who'd come to me with their own worries over blood spotting false words of comfort and patience.

But I'd spotted with my first pregnancy, and that spotting had turned to cramping and bleeding and a day spent in bed weeping as I suffered through the physical loss of a gift I'd barely been able to cherish.

Torion's name was on the tip of my tongue, a ready plea for him that horrified me. I wanted his hand in mine, wanted to feed him the same words of comfort I'd given others, so that he might return them to me with all his ready confidence.

My fingers reached down to the spots of blood but stopped short, settling instead on the shining white scar at my inner thigh—the absurd bite mark Torion had left on me in a downright scandalous moment of lust and possession. I'd never properly given him a scolding for biting me. I couldn't. There was something about the mark that I...liked. Cherished. I should've thought of it as violent, but it felt more like a promise. My lips quirked and wobbled. He would be so upset when he returned and discovered my distress.

The thought comforted me, as did touching his mark on me.

A knock sounded on the door, and I jerked, throwing the blankets back over me, trying to wipe terror from my face. It was Maggie rather than my usual maid who entered.

"Beg pardon, milady, I have just a few questions for you regarding—Oh my, you're pale, lovey! What's the matter?"

Maggie tucked her little notebook into an apron pocket and marched toward the bed, and I made a subtle fuss to be sure there were no signs of my distress or its cause visible. Maggie's slightly gnarled hand rose to my forehead as she tutted.

"Not feverish," she said, and for some reason the declaration soothed me.

"Just tired and still awaking," I said, swallowing hard around my tremulous voice and twisting away from Maggie's touch to take up my tea.

Maggie hummed and stepped back, looking me over. "Well, if that's all..." she said slowly, but when I managed a closed lip smile she rattled off her queries, mainly about meals and if she could hire a new boy for the kitchens and what room I would like the renovations to focus on next.

"All of that sounds very good," I said, after deferring to Maggie's first choices. Her eyes narrowed and I hurried on, not thinking, just not wanting Maggie to examine my mood too closely. "Could you have my breakfast sent up on a tray? And a bath and...bring me my notebook from my workroom and maybe a book to read?"

Maggie blinked at this. "I certainly can. You're *not* feeling well, are you?"

"I'm not poorly, I promise. But with the alpha gone for the day and you in charge, I feel safe in taking the time to rest. Even to...be a bit lazy."

Maggie's lips pursed, and then she smiled, and it was too kind and tender. She rested a hand over my bent knee and rubbed there through the blankets. Maggie had a number of sons and grandchildren, and I knew in that moment that she saw right through me.

"Of course, milady. And don't you deserve a laze. I'll have all that sent up straight away."

"Thank you, Maggie," I rasped out, staring down into my lap to hide my watery eyes.

And truth be told, Maggie was likely right, because the morning spent in bed seemed to restore some of my equilibrium. There was no more spotting of blood, and no cramping, and I spent a couple hours untangling a collection of notes about the uses for juniper, while the background of my thoughts ran on one stern refrain.

I was not going to lose this child. If it took every tea and every tonic in my mother's and my arsenals, every old wives' tale and superstition, and every doctor from here to Skybern, I would hold tight to this life Torion and I had created. I would dig out the old temples for the ancient dragons and fill them to the rafters with precious stones and gold and any manner of tokens of plea.

Well...perhaps that was going a little far. Digging was probably not wise under the current circumstances.

But if that was what it took, by Tylane's tail, I would do it.

It was after luncheon when I realized that sitting in one place all day doing as little as possible didn't really suit my nature. And since I felt well enough, and a little silly for my initial panic, I roused myself from bed and dressed, just in time to hear a flurry of activity from the great hall. I made it as far as the inner balcony, seeing only the back of a dragon's wings that I thought *might've* been Samuel Cameron's, when a young boy ran to me.

"What's happened?"

"A challenge on Bleake Isle, milady. The alpha's gone to give them support," the boy said in a breathless rush.

I stood straighter, throwing myself to the edge of the balcony. "Beta Cameron!" I cried out, relieved when the young man who'd nearly reached the door turned and met my gaze. "Is Alpha de Roche with Torion?"

Cameron nodded. "Yes, Omega Feargus. And I mean to go join them. I would've from the start, but Alpha Feargus insisted I give you word, in case matters kept him longer than predicted."

A pang in my chest burned sweetly. "Thank you." I bit my lip as Cameron turned back to the door, and I found myself calling out. "Tell Torion to be quick about it. And safe," I added, my voice cracking out at the end.

"I think he means to be, ma'am," Cameron said.

I swallowed hard and folded my arms over my chest, my feet demanding to pace the length of the hall. But I forced them back to the bedroom, knowing there would be no peace now, no patience. I was left alone with worry and waiting until Torion returned.

Chapter Twenty-Eight
BRIGID

'd forgotten how tired pregnancy made me, but on that day, it was a small blessing. If a nap was what my body wanted, it would help itself to one. I slept fitfully that night, but at least I did sleep.

Still, when the front door of the keep opened with a creak and groan, then voices called out, I was sitting up from the bed before I'd finished waking. It only took a drowsy moment of blinking into darkness for the low tenor of Torion's voice to reach me, and then I was in motion. I stumbled through the bedroom long enough to grab a robe and only managed to get the damn thing on and tied around my waist by the time I reached the stairs down to the main hall.

"Brigid."

I stopped on the top step, bleary eyes blinking in pleasure to see Torion taking the stairs up two at a time.

"Are you all right?" I asked, reaching out, my hands eager to grab hold of him.

"The challenge failed before I'd even made it to the Isle," Torion said. "Everyone is fine."

I scowled at him as he reached me, my fingers fisting in his shirt. "Are *you* hurt?"

He smelled wonderful, like sea air and musky sweat, and when I swayed into him, his arms wrapped around my waist to hold me still. "I'm fine," he laughed. "Didn't even get to enjoy a moment of fighting."

He bent and pressed his lips to my forehead, quieting the storm in my thoughts that had been plaguing me since Samuel Cameron had given me word of the challenge in Bleake Isle. I sighed, settling against Torion's chest, and finally heard the raised voices below. Torion's hands held my shoulders in place against him, preventing me from twisting to see what was taking place.

"I told Ronson we'd stash some of the troublemakers here in the keep cells," Torion said. "De Roche leant us black irons for the cause."

"Is it safe to have them here?"

"The cells are the one part of the keep it seems my father kept in the best repair. There's no danger to us, and they'll have their trial soon enough. Brigid, there's something I must tell you."

I frowned and leaned back, suddenly able to see the fervent excitement, even shock, making Torion's features vivid and wild.

"What is it?"

"Not here," he whispered. He called instructions down to the men below and then guided me back to the bedroom. "The most astonishing thing took place today."

Aside from the challenge? I wondered, but my thoughts were slower than Torion's intense energy, and he placed me back on the edge of the bed, taking his seat beside me and clasping his hands in mine. His dark eyes were wide, an absent smile on his lips.

"Mairwen is a *dragon*."

I blinked. "Aren't we...all?"

Torion huffed and shook his head. "She transformed, Brigid. She was one of the most ferocious dragons I'd ever seen!"

Mairwen? Quiet, sweet Mairwen? My mind remained blank at the suggestion.

"Torion, do you mean she...flew?"

Torion laughed at my own bafflement, apparently a match for his own. "Flew. Breathed fire. Fought off the dragons attacking Cadogan! I wouldn't have believed it was her, not even with Cadogan bellowing at us all not to hurt her, but she shifted back in front of my very own eyes."

For a moment, I only stared at Torion. He was telling me a fairy story, one I'd never even heard the likes of. But he wasn't joking, and he looked as startled by the tale as I felt hearing it. "But...but *how*?"

Torion shook his head, grinning now. "I've no idea! But I think they might know, and Niall said Ronson and Mairwen would come here soon and explain it all. She has *wings*, Brigid!"

"Where on earth did they come from?" I asked, sitting up, racking my own memory, as if I might suddenly recall seeing the woman with wings during her visit. As if such an unheard of sight might've somehow slipped my notice.

Torion shrugged, laughing again. "I can't blame Ronson for carrying her off once he had her back out of her dragon's shape. I'd have done the same with you if you'd flown into battle for me. But I'm... My head is reeling. It won't settle until they come and tell us what happened, I think."

"A dragon?" I repeated stupidly, just in case his answer might change to something sensible.

Torion rose from the bed and proceeded to pace, describing Mairwen's dragon—Mairwen's *dragon*—in detail. To imagine the gentle woman as a dragon at all was a challenge, but the vision Torion painted, in brilliant shades of copper and rust and turquoise, not to mention the size of her talons and spikes measured in a wide span of Torion's hands, made the whole story even more impossible to believe.

As I sat watching him, I realized I hadn't yet mentioned my spotting or how scared I'd been. I didn't know if it was that weight in my mind, or the fact that it was some hour of the night or pre-dawn and I was still groggy with sleep, but I couldn't grasp at Torion's excitement in the wake of this news. A female dragon was certainly some kind of marvel, but I wasn't sure how it would be accepted widely.

"Would you like to fly?" Torion asked, slightly breathless at the conclusion of his story.

"Now?" I glanced out the window into the dark, frowning slightly.

Torion grinned and threw himself back down onto the bed on his side. "No, I mean if it was possible for you to be a dragon like Mairwen, would you like that? To be able to fly?"

"No."

Torion's eyes widened, and I pressed my lips flat. He propped his head up on his hands. "Really? I thought you liked flying."

"I—" I shook my head and fell back to the bed, rolling to face him on my side. "I do like flying. And if my suddenly being able to transform into a dragon was only a simple matter of doing just that, I would enjoy flying on my own. But, Torion, this is going to...create a rather large commotion for Bleake Isle. At the very least. Possibly for *all* of dragonkin."

I expected that Torion might be struck by the words, grow thoughtful. I almost felt bad for poking a hole into his balloon of excitement. Instead, he just smiled softly.

"You take on such worries, little witch," he said, reaching for me, pressing a kiss into my forehead.

"You don't think it's true?" I asked, a little tartly.

"I know it's true. You're always right. If it's possible for our women to have their own dragons, the betas are sure to resist the change. I just can't help but consider the ways it might improve matters for omegas, after that resistance has been dealt with." Torion brushed my hair back and looked me over, smile stretching wide again. "I think wings would suit you."

The only response I could think of was a kiss, and with Torion returned to me, it was far too easy to fall back asleep.

<hr>

THERE WAS MORE SPOTTING the next day, and if I found Torion's resulting panic somewhat gratifying, no one but I needed to know. If there was also a brief, half-hearted wrestling match to keep him charging out of the bedroom in search of a doctor—he was too concerned for me to really fight back—that was our business too. In the end, we made our bargain.

He would go fetch a doctor *discreetly*, whom I would meet with in my office. We wouldn't be able to keep the secret of my pregnancy for very long in the keep. Servants were far cannier than most dragonkin gave them credit for. But I wanted to wait at least until my quickening, when I was first able to feel the flutters of life, before we made any official announcement. I hadn't gotten to experience that my first time, and it seemed as if it might be a marker, a moment where I could start to enjoy the idea of being pregnant, instead of only clinging nervously to the hope it presented.

"I'm less concerned with the little bit of blood than I am your age, Madame," Doctor Thistlethwaite said, glancing down at his watch rather than meeting my eye.

I pursed my lips, already prepared to hear as much, but

Torion let out a brief snarl. "She's not yet thirty-five. She's hardly in her dotage." His hands rested on my shoulder, standing behind me as I sat on the bench in my new office, mulling over the irony of being its first patient.

"And yet most women come to their first rut more than a decade prior to her. Young women's bodies are more...flexible, able to bear the growth and change that comes with a dragon brewing inside of their bodies. The more they age, the more their body fixes itself into position."

I stiffened in my seat, offended and worried over the words, but Torion scoffed loudly.

"That's absolute rot," Torion said.

"Torion," I murmured, worried he might go too far in speaking against the doctor.

I wasn't sure I was convinced by Thistlethwaite's claim either, but I knew better than to offend the man who might become responsible for my care.

"I understand your disappointment, my lord, but it would be best for us to begin planning to preserve the heir's life now, in case of any...later concerns," Thistlethwaite said.

My eyes closed and I took a shuddering breath, my hand rising from its limp resting place on my lap to cover my lower stomach in reflex. It would be a cruel fate to bring a child into the world I never got the chance to meet, but I already felt those stirrings of love, found the clock hands spinning too fast as I spent an hour dreaming of the child.

Torion's hands tightened briefly on my shoulders before releasing me, and he moved around the bench, catching the doctor by the shoulder and drawing him quickly away from me.

"Come speak to me in the hall a moment," Torion said, his voice thick with what I suspected was a barely restrained growl.

I started to rise, to speak my alpha's name, but as if he

could read my mind, he shot me a quelling look and I sank into my seat. I knew what Torion would do next, knew that he wouldn't stand for the doctor's claims or any plan that might sacrifice me in exchange for an heir. And while I wasn't sure if my own desires matched his, there was a small warmth in my chest at understanding that *I* was Torion's priority.

The voices outside of the door were muffled, although the doctor's began to rise with irritation, and Torion's interruptions were quick and heavy. Footsteps receded, and I could hear only my own heartbeat in my ears and the slow inhale and exhale of my breath for a moment. Then the door opened again, and the ambient noise of the keep outside my office bubbled the world back to life.

Torion's head was shaking before I could so much as open my mouth. "I'm not having a doctor attend you when his practice leans more towards butchery than healing. Catherine Eames gave birth to *four* sons. And those sons' omegas have all successfully given birth to more sons. I bet you anything she'll know more about the matter than that doctor knows about his own balls."

My lips twitched, and my heart ached. "Come sit with me," I said.

Torion's eyes narrowed. "Not if you're going to try and convince me that the doctor was in any way right."

I shrugged and tried to sound playful. "You must admit even you said my muscles were stiff." Torion scowled at me, and I sighed. "Torion, even if I make it to the birthing—"

"Brigid, please," he said, the hard stone of his voice starting to crack.

"Dragon births are dangerous. You may have to make a choice—"

"I have already made it, but I'm not sure you're prepared to hear it," Torion bit out, crossing the stone floor and hitting the bench hard, wrapping his arms around me.

"—or the worst may happen and we get no choice at all," I continued, closing my eyes and pressing my face to his chest.

"I...I can't let that happen, little witch," Torion whispered, his head bowing over mine and lips brushing over my hair. "Damn it, I never should've brought that man here."

I knew these were realities we might have to face eventually, and only if I'd managed to *keep* the babe alive longer than I had before. But I found my arms wrapping around Torion's chest, found myself clinging to him like he was my anchor, and that reliance didn't scare me for once. I had greater battles to fight than my feelings for Torion now.

Chapter Twenty-Nine
TORION

"Is that..." Brigid trailed off, her finger pointed skyward as a flash of light bounced off the scales of a brilliant amber and fire dragon.

"Yes," I said, grinning. "Yes, that's them now. And that is Omega Cadogan."

I turned my head to watch Brigid's jaw part, eyes wide in disbelief as the dragons grew in their approaching flight, the sea green of Mairwen's colors clearing from the sky, wings beating in slow strokes to keep pace with her smaller mate.

It'd been almost two weeks since I left Ronson and his omega cleaning up after the challenge issued against Ronson. The prisoners I'd kept for him had remained sullen and resigned to their fate, which relieved me. I'd almost sent them back to Ronson after returning to the keep and facing the perilous reality of Brigid's pregnancy once more.

It didn't seem right that my omega spent her time soothing me, rather than the other way around. Brigid's almost martyr-like calm made me slightly ill, as if I were experiencing her nausea in sympathy. I wanted to see her fight for herself, not stoically accept the risk of her fate, but it was my role to be her warrior now. If only I knew how these battles might be won. Brigid had begged me to wait a little longer to call for Omega Eames, and I'd relented. We were not yet three months into her pregnancy. There was time yet.

And there was the mystery of Mairwen Cadogan's new status as a dragon to unravel now too. I hoped my friends came with answers, and I prayed to the old dragons that some of those answers might help Brigid.

"Incredible," Brigid gasped as the ground rumbled with the dragons' landing.

Their transformations made the air rush forward, and I shielded Brigid from the wind with my wing as the magnificent bright beast shrunk down into the statuesque but comparatively tiny woman with amber gold wings. Mairwen patted her hair and dress, then turned and said something to Ronson that had him throwing his head back and laughing loudly. It was almost as shocking to see the somber and serious alpha smile as it was to see a woman with wings. Well, no, not really, but it was still surprising to see my old friend so merry, smile at the ready and eyes on his omega.

The pair approached us, and Brigid's hand squeezed around mine as the hooks of their wings that brushed one another linked together.

"You've been busy, I see," Brigid greeted the pair, her smile wide but still wobbly with shock.

Mairwen's answering smile was sheepish, but I thought she stood proudly with her wings at her back and her alpha at her side.

"How has the Isle been taking the news?" I asked. I'd had a missive from Seamus about the initial announcement going as well as could be expected, even with Ronson tossing aside the old choosing ceremony tradition.

"Surprisingly well," Ronson said, and Mairwen winced. "We know there's resistance at the very least, but we've had no outright defiance yet. I think it helps that Mairwen's dragon is absolutely terrifying to the betas."

"We might be more in danger of some of the young women demanding their own wings," Mairwen said, and she looked a bit proud of that announcement.

My eyebrows rose. "So you know the cause then?"

The couple glanced at one another and then our surroundings. It was busy outside of the keep, and I'd given my staff warning of what they might expect to see upon Mairwen's arrival, but many were certainly staring, slowing their progress across the yard to have a better look.

"Why don't we go inside and have some tea while we discuss everything?" Brigid offered, stepping back. She moved to pull her hand free of mine, and I tightened my grip just a little, pleased when she instead moved into my side and let me wrap an arm about her.

Would our wings tangle together if she underwent the same transformation as Mairwen? I wanted to see my brave, bossy omega as a dragon. Would she be huge and beautiful, sleek and powerful? Bright like a blade of grass or silver as stone?

If she was a dragon, would it keep her safe? Keep our child safe? Or was it just another risk to the woman who reluctantly held my heart?

***

"A BITE?" I repeated, dumbfounded, staring at Ronson as he sat holding his omega's hand, the pair nestled close on the small settee designed for wings. Two pairs of wings.

The teapot Brigid held rattled in her hands and I jumped up, catching it before she could drop it to the floor. She swayed into my arms, her face pale.

"Yes, from alpha to omega. One that breaks the skin,"

Ronson said, his words slowing as I eased Brigid down into her own chair. I rested the pot back on the tray before kneeling before her and taking her hands in mine, rubbing them to warm her chilly fingers.

Brigid was looking down at where I clasped her hands, eyes wide and blank.

"And that's all?" I asked, a strange triumphant thrumming growing in my chest, a low purr rattling at the back of my throat.

"My dragon was very...present when I claimed Mairwen. We think that's part of it," Ronson said.

I could tell my friends were watching Brigid and I carefully. It hadn't taken very long since we'd seated in the old library by the fireplace for a sharp understanding to begin to burrow through me, but that knowing had been sealed with the words *"the mating bond is manifested in a bite."*

"You..." Brigid breathed out, finally looking up at me with a question in her whisky brown eyes.

I nodded and then sat back on my heels, looking at last back at Mairwen and Ronson. "I bit Brigid during the rut. I didn't know about the bond, but my dragon certainly knew what we were doing. I claimed her."

Mairwen looked shocked, but Ronson's eyes narrowed and his lips twitched as if he might laugh.

"Did your rut settle not long afterwards?" Ronson asked me, and I nodded. He turned to Mairwen then and smiled. "See? All that aftermath was just because I didn't bite you at the first impulse."

"You're sure you—" Mairwen started to ask me, ignoring her alpha—no, her *mate*.

"I was calling her 'mate' in my head. I think of her—" I cleared my throat and turned to Brigid, not liking that she was still in shock, left out of the conversation. I lowered my voice slightly. "I think of you as mine, like a part of me."

"Torion," she murmured, reaching a hand up and soothing it over my cheek, like she thought she had to comfort me. "They said it's permanent."

I could bear it no longer. A grin broke out on my face, so wide and full it almost hurt. But nothing hurt at this moment. "I know, little witch. That's the best part."

Brigid's eyes widened a little further, and pink bloomed in her cheeks. I wished we were alone, so that I might say more, tell her that all I wanted for the rest of my life was to be the dragon responsible for making her feel loved and wanted, to enjoy the sweeter air I breathed at her side, the greater purpose I woke to each day. It wasn't Ronson and Mairwen's presence that held my tongue. I didn't care if they heard, but only that I knew my omega well enough now to see she was already overwhelmed and that she hated to be vulnerable in front of those she wasn't comfortable with.

"It's not just permanent to your current lifetime," Mairwen said, her voice low and gentle. "It extends an omega's life to match that of a beta or alpha. If you have any historic records from a few centuries ago, I might be able to confirm the same was true in the Hills. It seems to undo what prohibits omegas' conception of male heirs outside of a rut as well. And most gratifyingly, from what I've found, significantly decreases the danger of those births."

My eyes were on Brigid as Mairwen spoke, so I saw the moment the words struck her, made her blink and stiffen, her own gaze flickering to mine with a combination of hope and terror. My poor omega—*my mate*, I thought with dark relish—was so afraid of her own hopefulness, and it crushed me gently.

"What do you mean? What do you mean it decreases the danger? For the omega or—" Brigid was leaning forward, her hands squeezing hard around mine.

"For the omega and the baby, from what I can tell. The

Bleake Isle records had enough information to assume that mated omegas were surviving their sons births, while the unmated omegas seemed to be struggling at the same rate we still are," Mairwen said. "The birth rate was higher too, for sons and daughters."

I might've toppled backward onto the floor at the sudden weight that seemed to fly off my shoulders, if not for how desperate a grip on me Brigid still held. There was a victorious roar trapped in my chest, a sound of relief and joy, but I swallowed it down and watched Brigid's expression still.

"Oh," she said softly.

I held my breath. Was she thinking of the baby she'd lost? Thinking of the beta who hadn't been true to her? Was she wondering, *wishing* for a life where Malcolm had mated her and their child had been born?

Her eyes grew glassy with tears and she blinked slowly. "Ohhh," she breathed out, and I sat up straighter, a welling in my own chest rising higher, a profound exhalation. It was an echo of her own feelings, I thought, some calling from a bond we hadn't even realized we'd created. A bond I savored and relished, but not one Brigid had chosen for herself.

Then her breath hiccuped and the tears spilled over, and Brigid was wilting, falling into me as I rose up from my kneeling to catch her. She let out a small sound, something like a sob, and her arms circled my shoulders, fastening firmly to me.

This wasn't sorrow, but the sudden snapping of a string pulled taut, suspended worries that she'd turned into a brick wall around her thoughts now crumbling, releasing down into harmless pebbles.

"It's all right," I said, scooping her up into my arms, cocooning us in my wings. "It'll be all right now, love."

I'd been afraid to say the words, afraid to lie to Brigid, to make a promise I couldn't keep. She nodded against my throat as she cried, and the little brush of her forehead against my skin was wonderful—all the confirmation I needed to assure me this wasn't a *rejection* of the news we'd received.

"Excuse us," I said over my shoulder. "The Grave Hills records are in that corner by the window, but I don't know what you'll find."

Mairwen and Ronson had both risen, looking startled but aware. Ronson nodded gravely to me and pulled his mate closer. "Take your time. Mairwen can spend days in a library, and I am happy to help her search.

"I'm so s-sor—" Brigid started, but I hushed her gently and carried her from the room. "No, the servants. I should—"

"Tuck your face to me, and they'll think I'm carrying you off for a tryst," I said. Brigid snorted against me, and my answering grin probably sold the lie easily enough as I held my mate close.

Chapter Thirty

BRIGID

I took a breath and ignored my shiver as cool water dribbled down my neck. "We should return. I didn't mean to—"

"Not yet," Torion said.

He'd remained close as we made it up to the bedroom, but it hadn't taken long for me to recover from the shock of the announcement.

No, that was a lie. I hadn't recovered from the shock. I could barely think the words that had been spoken, let alone feel the reality of them. But I'd stopped crying fairly quickly, although something inside of my chest still felt tender. If Mairwen had anything else to tell me, perhaps it was better if I waited until I'd gotten my equilibrium back to hear it.

Torion sat down on the bed, just visible out of the corner of my eye, and I stood frozen at the washbasin, suddenly terrified to turn and look at him. He had mated me in the frenzy of the rut, created some sort of fantastical bond between our lives, one that couldn't be broken—all with a bite.

"I don't regret mating you, even if it was without my full understanding of the action," he said, voice clear and steady.

And so hypnotically direct. I was looking back at him before I'd given myself permission to do so, drinking him in as he sat on the edge of the bed, smiling gently at me, his wings bracing him up and his hands resting open on his lap.

"But, Brigid, do you wish I hadn't?"

It was shocking how ready my answer was, how it was on my tongue like a reflex before I'd even fully heard Torion's question. I pressed my lips together hard to keep from speaking it too quickly. I took the towel from beside the bowl of water and patted my damp face and neck gently before placing it back and crossing to Torion.

"I'm glad you did," I said, a light flutter of joy twirling in my chest as I helped myself to his lap and he beamed at me, that brilliant easy smile of his, as his arms circled my waist. "I'm *grateful*. I'm so scared to believe what they've told us, but Torion...if it's true..."

"I know," Torion said when my voice started to break. One hand rose to the back of my head, and he drew me in, pressing a long, soft kiss to my forehead. "You and our child will be safe. I believe that."

I *needed* to believe that, I realized. I had to, or my fear might destroy me.

"It's not just that. Although, yes, that's...enormous to me," I said, and I rested my temple on Torion's shoulder. It was often still easier to speak like this—close, but not with his beautiful warm eyes begging me to throw myself open to him. "A long life. With...with as many children as I might dream of."

"I thought I might give you a good handful of daughters, but I suppose now we won't know if they'll be boys or girls after this," Torion mused.

I might've balked at the claim of "a good handful" of any

sort of children, except my head was busy conjuring the picture of a little girl with thick black curls and big dark eyes and *lots* of freckles. More freckles than I could kiss on a sunny afternoon.

A small, happy sob rose up in my throat, and I turned deeper into Torion to stifle the sound against the soft lawn of his shirt. His hands soothed up and down my back, cupping my shoulder blades and touching there. It took me a moment to realize he was searching for any hint of wings.

"Will you be disappointed if I don't have a dragon like Mairwen's?" I asked, the words mumbled against Torion.

"No," Torion said, just a little too quickly. I leaned back and narrowed my eyes as color warmed his cheeks. "Not disappointed with you, but perhaps a little *for* you. And for me, because I would like to see you as a dragon. To know that, no matter what, you could defend yourself as a dragon."

"It would start a riot here in the Hills. Even before this, Bleake Isle was much more relaxed in their traditions than here," I said.

Torion nodded and grinned. "I know. And I've already shocked dragonkin once."

Likely at least twice, I thought, *considering they think you claimed me out from under Malcolm.*

"You have enough to worry over without another transformation," Torion murmured, bowing his head and kissing the bridge of my nose.

My hand rose, fingers resting lightly against Torion's smooth jaw, and his gaze grew heavy lidded, content with such a small touch. "You really don't mind that you claimed me, tied me to you permanently, without even realizing?" I asked. The words felt too large to be real, something that could be said but not believed.

"It was what I wanted. In that moment, and in all the moments after, and many of the moments before too." Torion's eyes searched mine for a long pause, and his tongue wet his lips. He was debating on saying something else and rather than afraid of the words, I found myself waiting patiently for them. "You are *right* for me, Brigid. You're the woman that I need at my side, not just to be a good alpha but to be a good man. I love you. I love how serious you are, and how you light up as you laugh. I love that you tell me precisely what to do and how it should be done, and I love how you give yourself over to me when you feel safe. I only want to do everything in my power for you to feel that safety with me everyday, to be the man you feel is *right* for you."

I wanted to let out a moan, to melt in Torion's arms and then slide free of him, slip away from the beautiful words and how absolutely I knew he meant them. But his gaze held me fixed in place, and his confession—a confession that hadn't even been a secret, because Torion had always shown me as much with each of his actions—was too earnest to deny. I would hurt him terribly if I turned away, and whatever I felt for Torion, I didn't want to hurt him.

"I...I don't know if I can give myself to-to *anyone* so wholeheartedly again," I whispered, wincing as I spoke. But Torion didn't look surprised, and he didn't flinch with me, just leaned his head into the hand that still cupped his jaw. "I spilled myself out before, gave everything I could spare and then some, and it was all just...washed away. Wasted. I'm not sure what's left."

Torion's smile was sore, and he turned it into my palm, kissing there. "I don't want you to spill yourself out for me, Brigid. I like you as you are. I just want to be the man at your side, for you to let me in when you're able."

How did Torion find a way to love me without carving out space in himself? If I could learn to love that way, without sacrifice, it might be easy.

"I can try," I whispered, and he kissed my palm again, as if in thanks. "I do *want* to."

His smile was wider when he turned back to me. "We have the bond. We have as long as we need. If you're willing to share this life, that's enough for me."

He meant the words, or lied spectacularly. I just wasn't sure if I imagined the sliver of hurt at the corner of his eyes.

***

ALPHA CADOGAN HADN'T BEEN JOKING when he said his mate could happily spend a day in a library. I found Mairwen flying halfway up the tall shelves, filling her arms with dusty books, stirring motes into the air with her wings. Torion had taken Ronson to his office, and I wasn't sure if it was his intention to leave me with the other omega, but it seemed appropriate of me to offer to keep her company.

She barely noticed my presence at first, muttering a hello over her shoulder as she skimmed a finger over the leather spines lined on the highest shelf.

"I apologize for my...earlier outburst," I said, not quite sure what to call collapsing into tears at the revelations of being *mated*.

"Oh!" Mairwen bobbed in the air. "I'm so sorry, I was distracted by the collection here."

I realized the drape of her gown was actually something like a riding habit, with tightly fitted trousers under the skirt, which could part like a curtain. I'd worn something similar when Torion had flown us around Grave Hills, but it had been old and belonged to his mother. This was a slightly new and more fashionable interpretation of the functional gown, and I wondered if it was liberating to wear trousers beneath a dress, or just hot.

She flew back down to the floor, and I realized this library hadn't contained a ladder, because the former alphas hadn't intended for the women of the keep to read the contents.

"It looks like you found quite a haul," I said, noting the two other large stacks on the table, as well as the one she brought with her now.

"I'm not sure how much will be of use exactly, but records as old as millenia are here," she said, gesturing to a pile of fairly mildewy looking pages. "Which would certainly be far enough back to give us an indication of what it was like here. At that time, bonding was common practice on the isle."

I nodded, although my head still spun every time I remembered that Torion had bit me in what I vaguely recalled as a fugue of passion, and that it meant that I was now closer to a dragon than I'd ever been before, that I would live as long as him, and possibly that I would have an easier pregnancy. None of which really made sense to me yet.

"I also... I found this old book about birthing practices for dragonkin women. It's certainly not the archaic practices of modern doctors," Mairwen said.

I sat abruptly. "May I see it?"

Mairwen nodded and let out a breath, sorting through the books she'd collected and passing me a large old text with a cherry red binding. "Ronson says we can't stay long enough for me to do all the research I might like, but I'd like to organize what I've found so far. And I should be able to convince him to bring me back. I...I elected not to get with child yet, but I'm very interested in how to offer safer solutions to the women on the isle. Everywhere, really."

I'd always preferred to learn through practice, my mind often skipping away when I sat down to read something for pleasure or purpose. Going through my mother's notes had been a process of interpreting both her scribbled hand-writing as well as how my own mind understood her direc-tions. But I would seat myself in this room and read every text we had if I thought it might mean I would deliver my child safely into the world. If I could be there to meet them too.

"Thank you, Mairwen," I said, reaching out a hand even as I cracked open the red book with a satisfying creak of leather pages.

Mairwen reached back, squeezing my fingers firmly. "I had some symptoms before my dragon emerged. A heat in my chest. Some dizziness. Nausea. Have you—"

I laughed. "I'm afraid those are all fairly common in pregnancy. So yes, I've experienced those lately."

It was the first time I'd really said to anyone other than Torion that I was expecting, and there was such a lightness in telling Mairwen, who was sweet and a little shy and so obviously compassionate.

"Oh!" She laughed and sat down around the corner from me at the table. "I see, then. Well, have you... Sometimes, she speaks to me, my dragon. Like a rougher, more direct version of myself. She's proud and certain and..."

Mairwen looked at me, eyebrows raising slightly, waiting.

I shook my head, smiling. "It would be hard to know. My mind never seems to quiet these days," I said. Mairwen hummed, and her gaze trailed over the arrangement of books, until she settled on the old sheaths of records. "You said that the mate bonds that are...chosen, seemed to be the more specific ones? And it wasn't just Alpha Cadogan that chose *you*," I guessed.

Mairwen smiled. "No. I definitely chose him too."

I nodded. Perhaps that was where I'd gone wrong. Torion loved me, chose me, but I was fractured still, uncertain I could ever do the same in return. But what if with time, with all the promises Torion had given me, the ones I believed were true or at least sincerely meant, I did learn to share my heart again?

"Would it be dangerous for the baby if I did discover my own dragon?" I asked.

Mairwen's nose wrinkled, and she set the papers aside. "I doubt it. I've really only found *advantages* to omegas being dragons too. But let's see if I can find any more information."

She gamely went to work, reading titles, checking contents, studious and entertained by all the information before her. I did my best to do my own focusing, but my thoughts were full and they kept drifting away from me, wondering where Torion was and when he would be near again. The world and my thoughts only seemed to settle when he was near.

I'd been waging a war with my heart for months, and now I wondered if I would know how to lay down the sword.

Perhaps I've already lost, I thought, and the idea felt hopeful.

Chapter Thirty-One
BRIGID

I sucked in a deep breath as I leaned against the large mossy boulder. Ned MacIntyre, my escort for the afternoon while Torion met some of the betas he'd taken into his confidence, leaned into his cane. I'd thought the older man a match for my exercise, likely more interested in a slower pace through the winding and climbing paths, but I realized he was more spry than he let on.

The wind rushed against me, sculpting my dress around my body, and I rested an arm over my stomach, as if it might disguise the distinct low rounding that was increasing there.

Time was passing too quickly. I was almost four months along. Some of the staff at the keep had been informed of my pregnancy, which meant all of the staff was likely now aware, and I was further along than I had been...

Before.

It still didn't quite feel real, more like a terrifyingly beautiful dream, or just a very sweet and gentle nightmare. Like I might wake up and my stomach would be hollow and flat, and there would be no reassuring scar on the inside of my thigh that spoke of accidental but earnest devotion, and Torion would not smile that very particular smile he wore when he first laid eyes on me each day.

"I'm slowing you down, I'm afraid," I said to Ned. I thought he was something between an advisor and a grandfather to Torion, and while he teased me politely and bowed gallantly, I wasn't yet certain he really liked me.

"Nonsense. We are well matched. Now, your young buck made me swear to thrust water and food upon you every time you paused to take a rest, and I'm sure he'll check the bag when we get back. I am too old for a young alpha's punishments, madame, so we will have to obey."

I snorted, but it wasn't hard to follow Torion's rules. My last bout of nausea had probably been over a week ago, and I was now constantly somewhere between peckish and starving. At the moment, that gauge was slightly above peckish. I accepted the tin from Ned and smiled at the collection inside. Torion and Maggie now regularly conspired together on a number of things, starting with how to coax me into resting and ending with how much they might manage to feed me.

"I take it Torion is waiting for the accounting feast to announce?" Ned asked.

I stiffened, my hand holding the tin of treats moving closer so that my arm might cover my waist. Which was as much an admission of Ned's guess as it was an attempt to hide what he might see there. I forced myself to relax and nibbled on a dried strawberry.

"That was my preference," I said, just loud enough for the old man to hear me on the windy hillside. The accounting feast was a grand event that took place roughly five months after the alpha's rut and allowed all those betas and omegas who'd been blessed with a pregnancy to announce their impending sons. Malcolm had attended them while we'd been together, but he'd never taken me—a punishment for my failure to get with child.

Ned MacIntyre nodded. "Smart of you. It will take the wind out of the sails of the men who thought Torion was a fool for claiming you."

I smiled at that and turned my eyes back down to my snacks. "You mean men like yourself?"

Ned laughed, and it was a charmingly rickety sound, without any malice. "Like me, indeed. Like your former beta, who has no issue to announce but will come anyway because he thinks he'll get to gloat."

Spite and curiosity swirled in my head, itched on my tongue. So Malcolm still had no son. So he thought he would get to witness Torion's disappointment in me as an omega. I breathed the petty feelings out.

Malcolm was no longer my concern. Only my child and Torion mattered.

"I hope I live up to your expectations for him," I said, touching Ned gently on the arm.

For a moment, Ned looked stricken by my comment, then his brow furrowed and his smile gentled. He lifted my hand from his arm and brought it to his lips with gentlemanly flair.

"I apologize if I've left you with any impression but that you exceed my expectations, Omega Feargus," Ned said. He took the tin when I passed it to him and turned us toward the path that would lead us back to the keep. We walked in quiet for a moment before Ned cleared his throat. "There are men who have a weakness for women. Your former beta was one, I believe."

I swallowed hard but didn't answer, and Ned offered me a wry curve of his lips, a gleam of approval in his gaze for me. This man was traditional, and I knew perfectly well that a dignified silence would impress him more than a gossipy unloading of woes from my time with Malcolm.

"Then there are men like Torion's father, and I suspect Torion himself, who possess a weakness for *a* woman," Ned said slowly, keeping us in gentle motion, not meeting my eyes for a moment until he turned his head with a smile. "For your sake, at least, I am pleased."

I returned his smile, but I knew what his words weren't saying. Ned thought Torion's loyalty to me would affect his care for Grave Hills, as if our alpha might only have enough room in his heart to do his duty in part, not in whole.

"You underestimate him," I said softly, because I couldn't help myself. Ned glanced at me, but I kept my eyes forward and wet my lips. "You underestimate not how much he cares, but how seriously he takes the responsibility of caring. Even if he only loved this place a little, he would never offer less of himself, and we both know his love for the Hills is a far sight more than a little."

Ned hummed in acknowledgement, but I caught the hint of a hidden smile twitching at his cheeks.

I GLANCED up from my notes at the knock on my office door, my brow furrowing. "Come in?" My frown smoothed as Torion appeared, darting through the door and shutting it quickly behind him. I'd only made it as far as rising from my seat before Torion had crossed the room and wrapped his arms around me, head bowing and mouth covering my hello.

He groaned into the kiss and I sighed, my arms lifting to circle his shoulders, taking hold of his wing roots to keep him close. Not that he seemed inclined to move away, as he crowded closer until I bumped into my desk. His tongue stroked against mine, his hands sliding down and molding around my ass, squeezing gently, trying to fuse our hips together.

Desire breezed through my veins, warm and languid. I moaned into the kiss, melted in Torion's arms. I was embarrassingly responsive in the past few weeks, although I wasn't certain Torion had noticed yet, given his need for me had always been...so much. Tylane's tail, this man enjoyed kissing me. When it went no further than that, he still walked away from me with a grin on his face and a swagger in his step. But lately...

"Don't you dare walk out of this room," I gasped out when Torion started to pull away. I was clinging to him, my body throbbing with need.

Torion looked down with fire in his bright eyes, his cheeks warm with color and lips damp and shining from my kisses. "I don't have long."

I blinked at him, dazed for a moment, and then recalled that Torion was meeting with Alpha Worthington from Skybern. Damn.

He cleared his throat and then added with a low rasp, "So I won't be able to knot you."

I grinned and nodded. "A compromise, good." Then I turned in his arms, bracing one hand on my open notebook and using the other to hike my skirts.

Torion groaned loudly behind me before falling eagerly into my back, helping me lift fabric out of the air, his hand sliding up to cover the mound of my belly, the other circling above and sliding down into the collar of my dress to fondle my breasts.

"H-how is the meeting going?" I asked as some distant part of my head rose up in the urgency of the moment, demanding I express interest in Torion's duty.

"Brigid!" He laughed, his breath on my neck creating gooseflesh. His fingers found a nipple to play with at the same moment he guided himself to my entrance, and we both exhaled with rushing moans. "Fuck. You're so wet already. Have you been thinking of me?"

Truthfully, I hadn't been thinking of Torion at all. I'd been focused on my work with perfect attention until he'd stepped through the door. But for a month now, it was as if the second I set eyes on him, my body prepared itself for pleasure. I'd taken to avoiding meeting him throughout the day, if only so I wouldn't interrupt us both with my desire.

"P-please," I hiccuped.

Torion sank into me with one endless, smooth stroke, and my entire body bloomed at the union. I collapsed down to my elbows, arching my back to take him deeper, carelessly wanton and so perfectly empty headed.

"Damn, now all I can think about is knotting you," Torion said, breathless as he covered my back with his warmth, staying deep inside of me and cuddling me as I bent over the desk. He moved in deep nudges, the hand on my stomach sliding down to touch me between my trembling legs. "As soon as Worthington leaves, I'm taking you back to bed."

I whined, trying to pin my lips together to keep the words inside of me. Except when had a secret from Torion ever served me? He took every confession I offered and protected it, protected me. And this one was hardly likely to disappoint him.

"I wish you were in rut again," I gasped out, and Torion bucked in surprise over my back. "Every time I'm near you, I just want you to drag me to bed and keep me there for days until I'm too weak to move again."

Torion let out a long, low curse and began to move, rough and deep, never pulling more than halfway out of me.

"We have four days until the accounting feast," Torion gritted out, nuzzling against my ear as I opened my mouth and whined down into my desk. "And you're going to get your wish if it kills me. Now cover your mouth so no one hears you screaming, because I know what it means when you get tense like this."

I rested my forehead to the cool, dry pages of my open notebook and held my hands tightly over my mouth as Torion drove me to oblivion.

Perhaps Ned MacIntyre was a little right to worry about Torion and his responsibility to Grave Hills, because after carrying me up to nap in bed, it only took him another two hours with Alpha Worthington and his men before he returned to me to make good on his promise.

IF I WAS WALKING funny at the accounting feast, I hoped the attendees would blame my now apparent pregnancy and not notice Torion's incredibly languid and smug expression. We'd barely made it out of bed in time to get ready this morning. There'd been as much quiet conversation—whispered dreams and worries, gentle reassurances and teary eyed hopes—as bright cries of ecstasy in the past few days. I found myself smiling shyly every time I looked at Torion and was just satiated enough to manage the public event.

"Have I mentioned how beautiful you look tonight?" Torion asked, bowing his head to murmur the words in my ear.

I flushed as he lifted my hand and pressed a long kiss to my knuckles, holding my gaze and letting the whisky heat in his eyes warm me throughout. "You have," I said, pulling my hand free when I realized he had no intention of releasing it. But I found myself smoothing a few stray curls away from his face.

"It bears repeating," he said with a shrug.

I glanced around the full great hall at the many couples gathered—so many young betas grinning madly at one another, women in small groups huddled with heads bowed and more subdued smiles. My eyes landed on Emily Anderson leaning against Samuel, her beta, and caught the moment his head bowed and his mouth landed on the exposed skin at the edge of collar, before sliding up her throat to whisper something in her ear. She flushed and glanced around, checking to see if they were observed, but I smiled as her head jerked in a brief nod, face sharpening with a familiar expectation. Then the couple stepped back away from the crowd and moved to the shadows of the departing hallway.

Years ago, I'd never imagined myself having a pleasant conversation with the woman, but earlier this evening, I'd laughed at her dry humor and sharp wit.

"Young dragons are so exhausting," she'd said, her gaze traveling across the room, where Samuel shoved at a friend of his and laughed loudly. And then she'd looked at me, eyes glittering warmly, and we'd shared a conspiratorial smile.

"I do find myself sleeping heavily," I allowed, smirking.

"When he lets you sleep," she added, grinning.

They had no pregnancy to announce—Emily was a slim woman, and the waistband of her dress made no attempt to disguise that fact tonight—but I predicted they'd have a daughter soon enough, if they wanted one.

"Will we start the announcements?" I asked Torion, leaning against his shoulder.

He shook his head, and his arm lifted to tug me closer to his side. "We'll finish them. Are you still eating?"

"I'm a little too nervous," I admitted.

Torion rubbed my shoulder. "I'll make sure there's a tray in our room when this is over. We can take our leave before the betas get too deep in their celebrations. Are you ready?"

Nerves spiked, little bolts of ice that shot up my spine, urging me to retreat. But Torion's arm was heavy and warm over my shoulders, and by the time they reached the nape of my neck, his steady presence melted them away. I nodded once, and he smiled before his gaze flicked over my shoulder, sharing a look with one of the men at the far right of the hall.

A bench squeaked as the man rose, and the large rustle of conversation fell away easily, as if everyone had only been biding their time until this moment.

"Grave Hills will welcome a son by harvest," Lord McKinney called out loudly. He hadn't brought his omega with him, but he beamed and clasped a hand over his heart.

As the whole room held its breath, another man rose from his seat, this time holding a young, blushing woman's hand in his. "Grave Hills will welcome two sons by harvest."

One by one, the men stood from their seats, adding to the tally. Three sons, four sons, five, and on and on it went. I hadn't attended the last accounting feast, but I'd heard the number murmured through the village—eight sons. Only eight, and if I hadn't lost my child, it might've been nine. But by the end of the nine months, only six of those sons took their first breath in the world, and only five of the eight mothers survived.

Torion lifted my hand to his lips, grazing a kiss back and forth over my white knuckles, his gaze holding mine until I realized I hadn't breathed properly as the tally rose higher and higher. I tried to release my viselike grip on his hand, but he covered it with his free one, understanding and flickers of worry in his gaze. How could any person understand another so well without a word between them? I sighed, and Torion's lips curved gently in unison with my own.

"Grave Hills will welcome fourteen sons by harvest."

There was a pause of quiet, a hush of expectation, as the room held its breath and waited. Still, Torion held my gaze. Gentler now, I squeezed his hand in mine, nodding slightly. His eyes never left mine as he leaned forward, pressing his chair back from the table, rising up. His hand tugged at mine, held tight, and I found myself rising from my seat as well, staring up at him in a daze, forgetting the room and the crowd and anyone but my alpha in front of me.

"Grave Hills will welcome—"

The door to the keep banged open with a crash, and I caught the barest glimpse of a familiar dark head storming out—Malcolm. I didn't enjoy his anger, and I didn't mourn it either. All thoughts of my former beta were brushed away by the sounds of chairs scraping over the floor and cheers rising up from around the room. Any words Torion said that followed were lost beneath the rousing cries of celebration, although it hardly mattered. We all knew what would be said.

And of course, privately and quietly, we all knew the words would be a lie. Sons would be lost before harvest. Women too.

Chapter Thirty-Two
BRIGID

I woke frowning, squinting at the bright light glaring down at me for a moment, groaning as I tried to move from the hard ground, and then paused as I recalled where I was and why.

Outside, napping in the sunshine underneath an umbrella for shade. I closed my eyes once more, lifting my chin and letting the light summer breeze coast down the hill and over where I lay. Torion had been the one to insist that even if I were set on working outside in the garden, there was always somewhere for me to take my rest if I wanted it. I'd stubbornly insisted the idea was foolish and then cheerfully enjoyed the accommodations every day since.

I propped myself up on one hand, the other falling to my stomach unconsciously as a funny fluttering and popping sensation simmered there. My brow furrowed, eyes skipping over to the basket of fruit preserves and bread I'd brought out with me. It was well past the time I should've experienced nausea, but this was different, not unpleasant but foreign, and—

Heat bloomed in my chest, and a soothing brush blanked my thoughts as it struck me.

The quickening—the movement of life inside of me.

My *child*.

My eyes fell closed as tears welled there, my throat tightening. Fire burned in my chest, but it was a soothing warmth, rushing through my veins, protective even. My dragon and my child. I didn't care if I never had wings, and I didn't want to transform into a dragon at this moment, but I was grateful for the reassurance, the gentle blanket that swooped over me as the growing babe announced itself with faint taps and bubbles.

Sun shone red through my eyelids, and dragon fire shimmered in my heart. The activity of the keep was a gentle murmur around me, familiar voices calling to one another. I was here in the safety of this place, alone with my child. And my dragon, quiet and watchful as she seemed to be, hidden away inside of me, would assure that I would survive, and the babe would survive.

On a sunny hill in an herb garden, tucked under an umbrella, I knew for the first time in years that I was safe.

"Brigid? You're crying."

I opened my eyes, and my smile beamed up at Torion. I wondered if maybe our bond had drawn him to me when I'd felt the first movement, or if he was just following the magnet that always seemed to draw us together.

"I felt the baby move," I said, grinning.

Torion's eyes widened, and he fell to my side on the blanket, one hand automatically reaching out and then pausing to hover over my waist. I took it and pressed it over where I'd felt movement.

"You won't be able to feel anything yet," I said, leaning into his side.

"I know...I know, I just..." Torion shifted closer and then

wrapped his other arm around me, pulling me to rest against his chest. "I didn't realize how much joy I could feel."

I stretched up, and his head bowed to meet mine, our lips joining softly, holding the kiss for long breaths.

I didn't realize how easy you would make it to feel safe with you. To trust you, I thought, but didn't say. Instead, I rested there, held and loved by my alpha.

I'D WRITTEN to Catherine Eames after the accounting feast, plain words seeking advice on childbearing, and she'd agreed to visit readily enough.

Upon first glance, the older woman was exactly what I'd been led to believe a grandmother ought to look like. My own personal experience of a grandmother had been my father's mother, a nervous woman who'd never seemed very comfortable with me in her home, but I'd read fairy tales and seen the gentle village women who gathered together to knit under the shade of a tree in the park. Widow Eames, at first glance, matched those women who'd always had gingerbread wrapped in wax sheets in their bags and spared smiles to little girls who passed them on the street. She was petite, her round cheeks doing favors to her age, and her fashion seemed to favor a ruffle, even down to the little frills around her wrists.

But appearances could be deceiving.

"Well, you've certainly grown yourself in consequence, my dear," Catherine Eames declared upon seating herself in my office at the keep.

"I...thank you," I said, and tried not to let it sound like a question.

"I wouldn't have said you were wasted on Barr. You seemed just his type. And plenty of women seem to stagnate after their youth. But the best of us grow sharper and stronger with age," she said, nodding once.

I took in a breath and decided that was a fair assessment of me. I knew plenty of omegas whose betas strayed from their beds, and either they were oblivious or they chose to be oblivious. I'd borne a grudge. I couldn't say whether or not it had done me many favors, but it had gotten me out of Malcolm's house.

And then I'd found my way here.

I cleared my throat and scooted to the edge of my chair, reaching for the tea.

"Are you drinking raspberry leaf?" Catherine asked, voice still sharp, those eyes I'd thought twinkled now hawkishly observant.

"I am," I said, nodding.

"Good girl. You're securing your place here with the alpha well enough, I see."

I smiled at that. "Torion was set on keeping me, regardless of the outcome of the rut. But I do want any wisdom you can offer, for my own sake. And for the child's."

"Who is your doctor?"

I frowned. "We've spoken to Thistlethwaite."

"An absolute idiot of a physician," Catherine Eames said without hesitation or any gentling of the insult.

I snorted in spite of myself and passed her a cup of tea. I brought my own cup to my lips and paused, the rim heating my flesh as I considered how to broach my questions.

I found myself saying something else entirely. "Thistlethwaite considers me too old to bear the child safely. He wants Torion to consider a plan for extracting the child."

"More omegas die in childbirth as a result of extractions than the challenge of labor," Catherine Eames said with a dark scowl before turning to study me speculatively. "You're young enough yet to give the alpha an heir and a few daughters to boot, I'd guess."

I hummed, thinking of what Mairwen had told me. If my lifetime were to match Torion's because of our mating, I might be young enough to give him several sons and daughters. The thought warmed me and I fought my smile, not wanting to explain it to the other omega. Mairwen might think that the bite Torion had left on my thigh would assure an easier pregnancy or a safer labor, but I wanted every advantage. My future was precious to me now, and I would take no chances.

"Your family is known for healthy children, safer deliveries," I said, holding the woman's gaze.

Her lips quirked and her head tipped, one thick white curl bouncing free of its pin. "Don't be coy, dear."

I sucked in a breath and nodded, setting my cup back to its saucer. "Do you have any wisdom, any advice to impart that might help me see this child safely into the world, preferably without sacrificing my own life?"

Catherine Eames sighed and sank back into her chair, almost nestling into the cushions and resting the saucer and tea on her belly.

"For starters, my dear, keep Thistlethwaite out of the picture. Rest when you are tired, move when you are not. Don't let them put you to bedrest if nothing troubles you. Is your alpha indulgent?"

I smiled at that. "Indulgent, protective, a little overbearing."

"Let him be. Take every moment of simple enjoyment you can find in these next few months," she said, then took a sip of her tea, considering. With a slight nod of her head, decision made, she lowered the teacup once more. "As for the birth, you should bind the wings."

My eyes widened. Wing binding was highly frowned upon

by doctors, who claimed it risked the integrity of the dragon's flight later in life.

"Both my sons had their wings bound during delivery, and one has a dragon and one does not. Of all the gentlemen of local dragonkin who no doubt were left with their wings unbound, the odds are as ill in their favor as my boys. If my sons are any indication, a dragon is a matter of character, rather than anything to do with the manner of birth."

I mulled her words over and nodded slowly. "Then how does one bind the wings before the babe is out of the mother?"

Catherine smiled approvingly at me and nodded, continuing with perfect authority, explaining the method. "If the alpha will object—"

I shook my head. "Torion mentioned the method himself."

"Excellent. My daughter and I will attend you at the birth. And there is a young woman from Skybern we will call here. Her father was my own doctor, and he taught her all his methods. I trust her far more than any of the physicians here in the Hills, who use the methods written for them by men without a care for women's lives."

"The Omega of Bleake Isle is very interested in progressive delivery methods. Have you heard of a water birth?" I asked.

Catherine Eames sat up straighter and extended her cup toward me for a refill. "I haven't heard of the method, but I have heard of *her.* They say she has wings!"

I hoped my friend didn't mind me gossiping about her to Widow Eames, but the woman's excitement raised my own. I'd been focused on my own well being for so long, surviving and hiding from dragonkin, I'd forgotten to care about others.

Feeling bitterly selfish, I realized that just because I

wasn't very interested in being a dragon didn't mean it wouldn't be enormously powerful to other women. And if I had my own dragon before Torion, not because of Malcolm, where might I be in life?

Where you are now, a warm voice answered in my thoughts. *The alpha would've taken one look at your dragon and begged to claim you.*

Perhaps I might've claimed him first.

I TOOK my daily constitutional walk with two escorts now that we'd made the news public that I was pregnant. The walks grew shorter as my belly bloomed forward, but the warmer weather delivered refreshing breezes and heady fresh air. Torion had constructed a sheltered hammock in the gardens for me to return to and rest in, and he usually met me there for luncheon.

Today, my return to the keep was marked by noisy activity near the barns, and it didn't take me long of searching the crowd to find the tallest, broadest figure with dark ash green wings.

"Torion?" I called out, my heart sinking as he spun around with thunderous worry and anger tangling his handsome features.

The escorts peeled away, moving toward the crowd of workers as Torion marched in my direction.

"What's wrong? What's happened?" I asked, my hands reaching for him, clasping his arms as he neared and steadying us both. Torion usually wore that expression on my behalf, but I was well and they were readying riders onto horses.

His breath was short as he answered, wings spread wide like a shield. "We just got word. There's a fire at your cottage. I don't know the damage yet."

"The cottage?" I gaped. "Was anyone..." But who would've been at the cottage? It was a wonder we even received word, and I doubted if by now there would be time to salvage anything, even with the river so close at hand.

"Stay here. I'll do everything in my power to save it for you," Torion said, brow tightly furrowed and jaw clenched as he bent toward me.

"It's likely already lost, Torion," I said as his lips landed firmly on my cheek.

"I'll fix it, I promise, love."

"T-Torion—" He was slipping free of my hands, and at first, I couldn't understand the panging ache in my heart. Was it for the cottage? For the last remnants of the mother I hadn't known well enough to value while she was alive?

A little, yes. But as I watched Torion bark orders to the men mounting horses before leaping into flight, I knew that the cottage was a loss I could easily bear. I didn't intend on running away again. I wouldn't *need* to. I was safe here. I was loved.

"Be careful," I called, my hands cupped around my mouth, then falling to rest on my hips, my nails biting into my waist.

A warning—one most likely not even heard—was not enough. Torion would throw himself into rescuing the cottage. And if he was hurt in the process?

I heaved a sigh and marched forward, catching a young human lad by the arm. "Ready my carriage."

"But, Omega—"

"Now," I growled.

Chapter Thirty-Three

TORION

"Alpha Feargus!"

My lungs were tight, and cold water sloshed over the lips of the buckets I hauled, shocking my burning arms. I didn't know if the heat scorching me from head to toe was a result of the effort of a half hour of hauling water, or the ash and sparks still floating through the air, hiding in billows of smoke to kiss and sting against my cheeks and sizzle at my hair.

"Alpha!"

I ignored the lad calling for me. Anyone not working to douse the last of the flames would have to wait for my attention when it could be spared. There was nowhere for a dragon to land near Brigid's cottage, so we were left hauling water by hand. It was slower, grueling work, and we were already too late.

"Omega Feargus demands I bring you to—"

I let out a snarl of effort as I tossed the bucket of water onto the unrecognizable blackened skeleton of Brigid's cottage. My arms went immediately limp, the wooden bucket knocking uselessly against my knee as I spun, eyes burning as I searched for the voice.

"Reassure her that I'll come back to the keep when this is done. There's no danger now."

"But she's here, my lord."

The bucket dropped and hit my toe, another tally of pain that I ignored, cursing and striding toward where I thought the voice was coming from. "What do you mean she's—"

"Torion!" Her voice was distant, a spirit in the woods meant to tempt me away from my duty. I followed it immediately.

I tried to call out Brigid's name, but all that came out was a rough cough. I raised my hand over my mouth, only to find it tasted even more bitterly of ash than the air.

"This way, my lord." Suddenly, a young man appeared at my left, catching my elbow and guiding me out of the smoke. I'd turned myself around in the smoke, a thick cloud which felt endless from near the cottage but dissipated near the road. A carriage waited there, and in front of its door stood my omega, her arms crossed atop her rounded belly and her scowl fierce.

"You shouldn't be here," I croaked out.

Brigid's arms unwound, her head shaking, and she twisted toward the open door of the carriage, pulling a sodden cloth from a bowl of clean water. "Come here. Look at what a mess you are. Thank you, George. Tell the men to get back from the smoke. We only need to be sure the fire doesn't spread now."

I was stumbling closer. My arms were useless at my sides, and my feet were barely more helpful than lead blocks at the end of my legs, but I managed to stay upright. "We aren't done—I need to—"

"The others will manage," Brigid said, snatching my hand

with the cool cloth. I hissed and then groaned in relief, my eyelids slowly closing over what felt like gritty rocks.

"There's only a few of us," I said, but it was a token protest. Now that my omega had me in her clutches, I was sure I was too weak to escape.

"Nonsense. There are dozens. I brought five myself," Brigid said, and even her voice was refreshing to my fevered mind. She finished wiping clean my hand and huffed, holding it in her own smooth grip for a moment before replacing her touch with cold, hard glass. "Drink."

The water was sweet with honey and mint, and I gulped it down greedily, wasting some that ran from the corners of my mouth and down my throat. "I'm sorry," I gasped out when I finished the glass. "I wanted to save it for you."

Brigid's smile was half-hearted. "I know you did. Take that filthy shirt off and let me see the worst of it. Are you burnt anywhere?"

I started to strip the shirt, but my arms had lost all their strength. Brigid huffed, batting my hands away and unfastening the shoulders so the fabric fell from my wings easily enough. "I should dip into the river," I said.

"It would be expedient, but let me look you over first."

"We'll find who did this," I assured her.

Brigid hummed and frowned, circling me. I was relieved to note that the breeze was carrying smoke in the opposite direction from where we stood. When I looked back at the cottage, I realized Brigid was right—many more men had arrived to help while I'd been focused on the repetitive path from stream to cottage and back again.

"You're right, I suppose. We shouldn't let it go without investigation," she mumbled, lifting one arm and giving it a cursory wash before moving to the other. "Your wings look dirty but uninjured. You'll sound like a frog in your meeting this week."

I wasn't sure if the smoke had addled me, but I was beginning to feel like my mate and I were holding two separate conversations. "I'll rebuild you the cottage. I promise."

Brigid stepped back and her gaze lifted to mine, her smile gentling. "I have a towel for you. Go wash properly. Make sure to go upstream. Then join me in the carriage, and we'll ride back to the keep together."

"I could fly and meet—"

"No. We're taking the carriage," Brigid said, her eyes narrowed with something like a warning.

Fighting the oddest smile on my mouth, I took the towel, careful not to dirty it against me, and hurried to obey. The men were dispersing, and the smoke was starting to thin now that water wasn't being added. There were still coals smoldering on some of the larger beams of the cottage that had come down, and it was more apparent now that there was nothing but charcoal to salvage from the mess. I'd expected Brigid to be rigid with shock or inconsolable, wide-eyed and skittish.

As usual, I'd been wrong. I washed quickly, savoring the feeling of splashing cold water against my face, cleaning out my swollen, stinging eyes, and helping myself to a few gulps. When I returned to the carriage, wrapped in the clean cloth, Brigid was sitting in the opening, and she eyed me speculatively, as a healer. Even that stare made my blood feel warmer.

"You have a few burns, but they don't look too bad. I'll put salve on them in the carriage. Come."

Sheepish for some reason, as if I were a boy who'd been caught mucking in puddles and was about to enter the house with muddy footprints, I climbed into the carriage after my omega.

"Here on the bench with me," she instructed, patting the cushion.

I took my seat and shut the carriage door behind us as Brigid knocked on the roof and the driver set us in motion. All at once, my mate seemed to deflate. Lifting my arm at her side and throwing it around her shoulder, she fell into me, scooting until we were hip to hip on the bench and nuzzling her face into my chest.

"Don't run off like that without me," she grumbled.

However tired my arms had been a moment ago, they found the strength to wrap around Brigid without a second thought.

"I didn't want you to lose the cottage. It means too much to you. You don't have to pretend it's all right."

Brigid sighed, and her warm breath soothed over my skin, her cheek so soft against me. "Of course it isn't all right that the cottage burnt down. I am sad about that. But, Torion..." She leaned back, and there was enough light from the carriage windows to make her easy expression perfectly clear. "I don't need the cottage."

I blinked at that. Brigid hadn't been back to the cottage for more than a quick visit to check on the property or collect things since she'd told me about her pregnancy. I hadn't been sure how we would handle it in the future. I wouldn't have wanted her to leave the keep with our child, not without me at their side, but I had assumed the discussion might arise if she grew overwhelmed one day, if she discovered a need for space. I was fairly sure I could coax her back to the keep again, or even that I would be welcome at the cottage, but I didn't plan on restricting her.

Brigid's hand rose and soothed over my cheek, nails scratching over the faint bristle of prickling hair from the day. "When we rebuild, we should do so intending to make a property for one of our children to inherit," she said softly, smiling up at me.

Heat flared and tightened in my groin, and I forced myself to remember that Brigid was still currently pregnant with our *first* child and I was not about to go and get her with child a second time already. Still, practice never hurt anyone.

"I already have everything I need at the keep—of my mother's and of my own. Most importantly...I have you," she said, almost whispering the words. Her eyes were growing glassy and glittering, and she blinked quickly for a moment, throat flexing with a swallow, tongue flicking out to wet her bottom lip. "I do love you, Torion."

I held my breath for a moment, part of me expecting to be woken from a dream. Perhaps I'd been so overcome by the smoke that I'd collapsed? But no, in my dreams Brigid welcomed me with glowing eyes and open arms and a sharp wide smile. Here, Brigid was near tears, looking terrified and determined. This was *my* omega, in all her reserve and all her fears.

I lowered my head slowly and pressed my lips to her forehead, her sigh sliding down my throat. I knew why the words challenged her. I knew that for her to admit as much against her own forged resistances meant the feelings ran even deeper than she was ready to say. But she'd said it aloud for me, and even more importantly, more readily, she'd promised in her own way not to run away from me again. The confession, the *declaration*, was the most precious gift I'd ever received, and she was the only one capable of giving it.

"I love you, mate," I rasped, my voice ragged with feeling more than smoke.

Brigid shuddered and climbed into my lap, and I bit off my hiss as she accidentally brushed her hand over a sore spot on my upper arm. Salve could wait. Holding my mate close was all the healing I needed for the moment.

I SAT BACK on my heels, gaping down at the beautiful feast before me, a buffet of pleasure—one I'd just partaken of, but could be easily persuaded to do so again. Brigid, with her thighs splayed open over my lap, her nipples red from being nibbled and sucked, and her hair a riotous mess over the pillows, groaned and swatted a hand through the air between us.

"Don't," she growled, kittenish and weak, hand falling to rest over her rounded belly, drawing my eyes there.

"Don't?" I repeated, my own voice throaty with a purr.

"I *can't*," she moaned, trying to wiggle back from me but finding the headboard keeping her trapped.

I laughed and relented, bending over to drop simple kisses between her breasts and over the rise of her stomach to its highest point, withdrawing from her with a groan of relief and protest in equal measure. Her legs closed and turned away from me as I moved to curl up against her back. Not that I couldn't take her this way too. I would remind her of as much in a few hours when she started to squirm against me in her sleep.

"I've been thinking," Brigid murmured, taking one of my hands to wrap my arm around her chest. She brought my knuckles to her lips, and I let my face relax into an absurd smile, hiding it against Brigid's hair.

"We need to tell the local dragonkin about our bonding," she continued.

My eyes widened, and I tried not to yelp out my enthusiasm. "You think your dragon is coming?"

Brigid shook her head and then squirmed backward, nestling tighter against me. "Not really, but I think it would be better to be clear about what the bonding might mean. They might not notice I wasn't aging so soon, but if I bore you another son in a few years, that would certainly shock the kin."

My purr could not be restrained, not just at the thought of Brigid and a parcel of children to match us, but that my reserved omega was discussing our bond. She'd danced around the topic for months, shrugging when I asked her questions about her dragon or the future.

"You're right, of course, mate," I said, my voice growling in satisfaction around the word *mate*. And in my arms, she melted just enough for me to notice. "Do you like when I call you that?"

Brigid was quiet for a minute and I tried not to sigh in disappointment, assuming I'd pushed her just that tiny measure too far. "I do," she whispered instead.

I could do nothing but purr in answer for an even longer pause, one of my legs rising to cover hers, to tangle her firmly against me, trying to force down the persistent craving I always had for this woman. "I'm sure I would feel the same if I heard you say it," I said, trying to sound reassuring, but there was too much need, a hint of a whine exposing the plea I hid in the statement.

Brigid wiggled in my arms, huffing impatiently, but when I eased my hold she simply turned to face me. One of her hands rose and stroked over my cheek, a long leg sliding between mine, her smooth, bare thigh caressing like silk against my own.

"Thank you for taking such care with me, *mate*," Brigid said, and the corners of her mouth hooked as I shuddered and restrained a groan of pleasure. She leaned in and kissed my chin, as close as she could reach with her firm, round stomach trapped between us. I loved the feel of her pressing hard against me. I would not trade a moment of these months with her, but I also knew I would relish our union again after the pregnancy and her healing, when I could cover her head to toe, every inch of her body against mine at once.

My hands stroked her sides, and I wondered if she was terribly tired or if I was slow, gentle, patient, I might coax her into another roll in our sheets. And then, before I could start to peck kisses at her lips—brief, light ones that would irritate her into grabbing me and fusing our lips properly—there was a whisper light nudge against my stomach, directly from hers.

We both froze, breaths stolen. Brigid's eyes crinkled at the corners with laughter, my own wide and stupefied.

"Is that—?" I started, then hiccuped as another firmer touch prodded against me.

"Oof." Brigid laughed and leaned back, her hand falling from my cheek to cover the spot on her belly. "Seems someone is awake."

I gaped at her, then down at her hand. She pulled it aside, and it was too dark in our room for me to make anything out, if there was anything to see.

"Here," Brigid said, catching my hand and drawing it to her belly, laying it where hers had been and then nudging slightly upward. "Ah, on the move, I see."

I waited, breathless, for several beats of time until a gentle touch, like a finger muffled through woolen layers and Brigid's silken skin—and not like that at all—pushed against me just enough for me to know, to *know* that our child was there with us.

"That was a wing, I think. They tickle," Brigid said, smiling at me.

I didn't know what my own face was doing. All of my attention, all of my senses, were wholly stolen by the slight back and forth pressure against my palm.

"It's wonderful," Brigid said, sighing, eyes falling shut. Then her brow furrowed a little. "Put a pillow at my back."

I switched hands and hurried to obey, settling my mate inside a nest made of pillows and my embrace as our child waved a wing in greeting to me. Our first hello, our first touch.

There had been a fire today, I thought distantly. My throat was tired, and my hair—in spite of a good washing—still faintly stank of smoke. But it was a perfect night, I decided. One of many more to come.

Chapter Thirty-Four

BRIGID

"I might not have recommended guests at this time, but at least the visiting alphas got your man out of your hair for a bit," Catherine Eames muttered to me.

I answered with a half smile but didn't glance at the older woman, keeping my careful, steady pace over the stone floor of the large room claimed for the purpose of giving birth. My bottom lip was sore, and I winced even as I continued to gnaw at it ruthlessly. Widow Eames was right—Torion had been hovering for weeks as I approached my lying in. I couldn't so much as blink without him checking on me, seeing if I was experiencing cramps or contractions. He sent daily notes to Widow Eames herself, asking questions as if it were him who was going to be delivering the baby.

He was driving me mad, and if I could've run in my state —a waddle, only—I would've taken off into the hills. And yet part of me wanted to go out the door and call for him. He'd always borne so many burdens for me, and I had no doubt that if he could, he might do the same now.

To both our consternation, what came next would be strictly the responsibility of my body and my will.

A gentle hand soothed over my arm, and I glanced at the woman escorting me in my slow pace, back and forth in the hollow room. "They'll be back soon," Mairwen said, as if reading my mind. She smiled, and for some reason her softness reminded me to breathe.

I'd thought the labor would take place in our bedroom, but Widow Eames had smirked at the suggestion. She'd gone along with me there, with her two daughters and Mairwen in procession. We'd barely taken a foot over the threshold before the scents of other omegas near my nest had me releasing an unfamiliar growl. A guest room was quickly prepared. It felt wrong somehow not to be in my nest, but the idea of anyone but Torion following me there was impossible. Widow Eames said it was a normal instinct, but that women had been managing in doctor's beds and guest rooms for centuries and I would as well.

My reverie was interrupted by a sudden shock of lightning low in my groin that stole my breath and weakened my knees. I made a garbled cry and Mairwen shored me up, holding me above the floor with surprising strength as the other women in the room held still and watched, waiting. The pain was sharp and sizzling, but it passed quickly. I shuddered and leaned into Mairwen for a moment before straightening and letting her guide me back to the bench waiting at the end of the bed.

"You said we could be at this for hours before labor starts," I said, trying not to whine as I looked to Catherine. She'd brought two of her daughters with her, but I'd already forgotten their names. Hopefully, someone would say one again to remind me. Or perhaps none of that would matter in the upcoming efforts.

"Hours. A day, even." Catherine's smile was wry as I groaned, my arms barely fitting around my massive belly as I rocked a little. "It's not likely that long, dear."

"Your belly's dropped, and you've got the shocks. The lad is getting ready to arrive," one of the daughters assured me.

I tried to smile, but it was sure to be more of a grimace. The babe was having a restless hour, but not long ago it had been so still I'd grown terrified. Nothing would feel right until they had arrived, until I'd seen them with my own eyes, held them in my arms.

My belly had indeed dropped early in the week, and I'd been a groaning, waddling, aimless, and impatient monster ever since. Mairwen and Ronson had been summoned days ago, and Catherine Eames had finally come with her daughters, and there was a doctor...somewhere, ready and waiting.

Waiting. So much waiting.

And when I grew sick and scared and bored of waiting, all I could do was—

"Walk," I growled out, and Mairwen helped heave me up to pace once more around the room.

THE MOMENT of arrival was in a quiet spell, Eames and her daughters napping in armchairs as Mairwen read by candlelight. I braced my hands against the cold stone of the windowsill, watching the sun lower toward the horizon. Ronson and Torion had returned, only to drive us all mad and be sent to the kitchens to brew tea.

There was a strange, gentle shift inside of me, and then a not so gentle trickle of fluid down my thighs. Mairwen looked up at my gasp or the sound of the water dripping to the stone floor, and we shared the shock and understanding of two women who had never given birth before but were somehow made for the experience, designed in nature but novices all the same.

Her book snapped shut, waking one of the Eames daughters, who took one look at our pale faces and stood up.

"Very well. Let's see if we're ready to start."

But I'm not *ready*, I thought, even as fiery hope bubbled up alongside the fear and eager excitement.

You are, a bright voice answered my thought, foreign and familiar at the same time. *We are ready.*

"I'VE GOT YOU. I'm here, my love. Deep breath."

"We'll bind the wings now, my lady."

"Do it."

My mind was on fire. The rest of me was possessed by pulsing thorns, digging in and tearing me apart. I was exposed and everything was *wrong*. It was too bright and too open and there were too many scents, and I might be sick or faint, except that there was too much pain. Words rumbled through my back, and the contact of another body against me was madness and horrible, but familiar too, safe. My hands gripped tightly around broad fingers and callouses and the steady, reassuring presence of...

Mate.

Torion was here with me. In spite of the older woman's claims that I wouldn't be able to stand the sight of him, I was grateful for his presence. I grabbed onto him and focused on the scent of cinnamon and ash, on his warmth. He was right. He was meant to be here with me. It should've been just us but—

"May I watch?"

I snarled at the question, at the reminder of the others who were close—other omegas.

"Don't ask her, lovey, she can't be spared to answer. Come

and see if you must, but don't faint. You'll be too underfoot on the floor."

I was both insensible and too aware of what went on in the room, and I shut my eyes against the view of bustling bodies and the sunset colors washing the room and bright candlelight and heavy shadows and three feminine faces peering down between my spread legs, like a gathering of the fates. One maiden, one mother, one crone.

I giggled, but it came out like a sob.

"I have you, and you have the child. Deep breath, my love," my mate murmured, and then he purred for me, and the sound filled my body and my ears, softening the edges of the world.

I breathed as deeply as my body would let me while in the throes of nature's most insane plan.

"Done. Now step back. Do we mean to get her in the water?"

"Just *do* it," I found myself howling, my body gathering strange strength to bear down on itself, to shrink and condense into a blinding point of effort.

"Here, then," someone said.

Here, indeed. I was here, and my child was coming. My child was coming.

I wept and tried to break the fingers that held mine.

THE WORLD WAS TOO QUIET, strange and wrong after so much blaze and bellowing screams. An uncanny, terrifying, peaceful moment of silence, like the whole of Grave Hills was holding its breath.

A crackling, glorious, gusty cry sounded, and my lips found the strength to curve.

"Dragon's breath," Catherine Eames murmured, staring

into her own arms, eyes fixed onto the delicate, powerful, reddened little being she held.

"Is that—"

"Widow Eames?" Torion rasped, still holding me.

"It's—it's—"

Alarm was dull in my body, but what could possibly be wrong when another sweet scream was released, a small fist raised in defiance?

"She's perfect."

It was Mairwen who spoke, peering over the widow's shoulder, rousing the woman from her stupor. The young, winged omega smiled at me, canny and sweet and a bit dazed too.

"She's perfect," Mairwen repeated.

Catherine Eames looked to Mairwen, blinked, and then nodded. "Healthy. Healthy little...girl you have. H-here you are."

It wasn't until she was in my arms, laid down on the softest linen, wings still gently bound at blunt tips and hooks, that all the pieces fit back together. A baby girl, my *daughter*.

With *wings*.

"Perfect."

The word stroked over my shoulder before terror or shock could rise up in me. Torion's hand—which looked a little bruised from my grip—reached down, one finger extended to hover near her foot until she kicked and nudged at him. Her cry hiccuped, gentler now.

My eyes watered, and it wasn't fair. It wasn't fair that anything, any emotion, no matter how beautiful, how strong, might interrupt this moment, my sight of her. My daughter. My child. We'd made it into the world together after all. She'd made it into my arms.

And she was perfect. And suddenly, that was all I'd ever truly known in my life.

I have a daughter. And she is perfect.

"So soon?" Torion asked, and I blinked, but I didn't look away from the little bundle nestled against my chest. She had black hair, and the red of her skin had settled to a softer, pale sandy brown.

"Mm?"

"You're frowning already. I thought it would take longer," Torion said.

I ran my tongue around the inside of my mouth and grimaced at the stale flavor, then let out a sigh and tried to ease the muscles of my face. "Is there tea?"

I was trying not to pay too much attention to how my body felt in the aftermath of the birth. The little baby girl in my arms was a strong distraction, but my throat did hurt from shouting. Tea would be welcome. They'd moved me and the babe at some point when weariness hit too hard for me to keep my eyes open, and now Torion and I were alone in the nest, in our chambers, with our *daughter*.

Torion ran his hand down my arm and then brushed a fingertip against the back of our daughter's head, through the fine, dark hair, before rising from the bed. With his back turned, I finally lifted my gaze and watched him. He moved smoothly, relaxed, not edged with the tense energy he sometimes got when he was worried for me.

"We don't have a name for her," I said.

We'd had a small collection of boys' names—Torion's father's, my own father's, and then our preferred choice of Lachlan. Torion's head turned, and he smiled. "We don't. Our little surprise."

"Will you hold her?" I asked, forcing the words out. He'd

been so patient, settling for little touches, briefly bowing over me to kiss the back of her head.

He grinned now and almost tripped over the rug in his haste to return to the bed, but he didn't spill a drop of the tea and he moved oh so gently back onto the mattress at my side.

"You know why I was frowning," I said in a whisper, my hands fisting into the sheets as Torion lifted our baby from my chest and then eased himself down into the same reclined position I'd been in.

"You're worrying," Torion said, his voice equally hushed, barely audible under her fussing. I clenched my hands tighter to keep from stealing her back until they both settled together. "But that's okay."

I snorted and buried my groans as I attempted to get myself into something resembling sitting up so I could drink. "It's okay?" I repeated.

Torion nodded. "Because when you worry, you always plan."

I sipped the tea. It was still warm and minty, and it soothed my hoarse throat and was fresh on my tongue. "We should make the announcement as soon as possible. Word might be traveling already if the servants talk. But if we have any chance of dragonkin not rejecting the idea of a...a girl with..."

Torion frowned at me as I stumbled over the words. "It disturbs you?"

I shook my head quickly and then hesitated. "The idea of there being some sort of communal rejection of her disturbs me. At the moment, I am only... Is she an omega? A beta because she has wings? If we don't understand, how can we make others?"

"I'm not sure this is something that needs understood. More is possible than we'd known before, that's all," Torion said, smiling down at a whip curl of black hair.

I stared at him and wondered what it might feel like to be so assured, so self-confident. It wasn't naivety. Torion was simply open minded, flexible, able to embrace change in a way I'd never managed.

"They'll want something, some kind of reason that gives an explanation for how she exists. And that's...the best of what will come," I said.

"The mating," Torion said, smiling. "Rumors about Bleake Isle, about Mairwen, have spread far enough now. Mating allows for women with wings, even daughters. She's an omega or a beta. Who knows now? She's just a baby. She's a perfect little baby with wings."

He was grinning now, and I didn't know if it was his joy or my own or the picture of Torion laid back on the bed with our daughter bundled against his bare chest, smacking her lips in sleepy mouthings, but I was smiling too.

"She needs a name," I whispered, taking another sip of the tea before falling back into the pillows, giving up on effort and worry, probably because my body simply lacked the strength to bore on with them any longer.

"Mmm, I suppose we'd better keep it traditional. The best we can do for her against the stodgy old dragons, hm?"

I smiled. He was mumbling now, eyelids heavy, speaking to her rather than me.

"Name her after your mother? Name her after you?" he continued, one huge palm almost entirely covering her.

"Give her her own name," I protested, rolling toward them as much as my exhausted body would allow me. Someone would be in soon to check on us all, to put her in the little bassinet next to me.

"She's a dragon," Torion whispered, turning to beam at me. "Let's give her a name they can't refute. One we were raised to respect."

"What are you suggesting?" I asked, brow furrowed.

Torion's sleepy eyes lit up. "Name her after one of the old dragons. Tylane of Dagger Hill."

I chewed on my lip as a stared at my daughter. She was so small, so beautiful. There was a sense of foreboding in giving her a name that had belonged to a warrior dragon. But if it gave her strength for the fight ahead, one that might last longer than I could wage it for her, then that was for the best.

"Tylane," I whispered, stroking her soft cheek.

Chapter Thirty-Five
TORION

"How did it go?"

I stopped in my tired tracks and found my body lightening, my weary bones regaining energy, my scowling lips turning up once more. Brigid stood just inside the keep doors, her braid unraveling, dark circles under her eyes, and a wailing little beast of a beauty bouncing gently in her arms.

Tylane. My little sun, and unfortunately, the reason the local betas were causing me so much strife at present. Grave Hills had welcomed eleven sons by harvest. Eleven sons, and one daughter.

"Let me hold my girls," I rasped out, spreading my arms wide.

Brigid huffed, but she tucked herself and Tylane into my embrace. Within moments, Tylane's cries settled into little grunts of appeasement.

"She prefers you," Brigid muttered.

I laughed, and Brigid softened and rested her head to my shoulder. "She prefers when her mother is calm and content," I corrected, trying not to sound smug.

Brigid let me get away with it, making a similar little grunt as our daughter, which I took as some acknowledgement of the truth.

"Tell me how it went. Honestly," Brigid said.

I sighed, walking our little huddle away from the door and over to the fireplace, to the armchair where I'd first seen my mate. I drew them down to sit in my lap, taking turns kissing each of them on the temple, rewarded with two sighs.

"They asked a lot of questions I don't have the answers to. She's only a baby, she won't present a scent for years yet, if she is an omega. And we don't know her lifespan. That sort of thing."

"Why should they need to know her lifespan?!" Brigid cried out, and Tylane joined her in a quick yelp that we both hurried to soothe.

"They don't. Perhaps they just think it will help to define her in their mind. You understand why they're shocked," I reminded her.

She was quiet for a moment, eyes fixed with wonder and worry on Tylane, who'd seemed to take the opportunity of the warmth of the fire and our lowered voices to settle back into sleep. She was already almost a month old. It had been a month without sleep, a month of wonder, of scrambling for answers to questions we hadn't anticipated. A month of a love that left me breathless with a little daughter who'd grown and stretched and screamed and had left her mark in a number of ways on my heart...and my plaid. A family plaid was not a good choice for a baby's blanket.

"I understand their shock enough to fear it," Brigid said softly, searching my face.

"I don't think you need to fear yet," I assured her, rocking my girls in my arms slightly. "Mairwen and Ronson did seem to help, as did making sure the omegas were in attendance. The young couples looked pleased with the idea of mating."

Brigid smiled at that. "The ladies want wings. They want to fly too."

"And the young men in love want their omegas to remain at their sides for a lifetime," I said.

Brigid looked up at that, and there was all the warmth I could hope for in her gaze.

My father had met my mother quite late in life. Perhaps that was part of why he'd been so grateful for her, so determined to enjoy every moment. I'd been outrageously lucky to find Brigid so young. We'd have decade after decade together. We'd have as many children as Brigid might wish for. If our children were as lucky as us, we'd meet grandchildren and great-grandchildren for years to come.

"I didn't change all their minds in one day," I admitted.

"You couldn't have," Brigid said easily, and her eyes blinked slowly. She was tired. Tylane was sleeping now, but it wouldn't last long. I ought to get them both up to bed.

"There's something else," I said instead, and winced. Now wasn't the time. Brigid slipped a hand out from under Tylane and hummed in question, stroking curls back out of my eyes. "The men investigating think the cottage fire wasn't an accident."

"Local boys, I've guessed," Brigid murmured. "Using the cottage for mischief or some like."

"They found oil on some of the high beams that didn't catch."

Brigid's eyes widened slightly, her stroking palm pausing against my cheek. "Oh. Then it was...very intentional."

I frowned, immediately regretting bringing this news up. "I've spoken to all the surrounding local farms, and they're more concerned about you and your property. I don't think you've any resentments from them to worry over. And the men investigating are putting together a record of everyone who was seen passing remotely near the cottage."

Brigid sighed and curled into me, and I stamped down the irrational triumph blazing in my chest.

"I almost hope we don't discover who's responsible," Brigid said.

I frowned. "Why not?"

"Things are tense enough as it is. If a beta is responsible, we can't overlook the defiance. It'll have to be answered with punishment, but retaliation may just burn resentments hotter."

I might've been inclined to agree with Brigid. It would at least allow for a false peace if we could ignore the crime. But I had my suspicions already as to the culprit, and if I was right, there was no question of a pardon.

"One day at a time," I said, staring down into our daughter's beautiful face, smiling as it scrunched and relaxed.

The truth was, if things in Grave Hills grew dire, if dragonkin couldn't accept Tylane, then Brigid and I would leave. Seamus would help us, and if Mairwen and Ronson continued to win over Bleake Isle, we'd have somewhere to go. But a divide in dragonkin, one that crossed territories, would foster even more strife in the long run. Bleake Isle might offer somewhere for women to go to, but the other territories would resent the loss of their omegas if it came to it. We needed to be united if we were going to successfully move forward.

I wanted to serve my people. I wanted to draw dragonkin forward into the future, a future where our women didn't flee, but I would never risk my family.

"Are you very tired?" Brigid asked, her voice turning soft and syrupy slow.

"No more than you, I'm certain."

"Do you think you can manage it?" she asked, and I looked down to find her eyelids drooping. "Carrying us both up to bed?"

I snorted at that and shifted my mate in my arms. Tylane was a feather of an addition, and it troubled me not at all to hold Brigid, even when she was just to the point of giving birth. I proved as much by rising with them cradled, babe atop mother, and carried them with the utmost gentleness up the stairs to our room. Brigid was fast asleep before I reached the bed.

"THE BENEFITS SKYBERN OFFERS US, offers the betas *you're* responsible for—"

"I am responsible for the Hills, for our dragonkin, yes. I am not responsible for Danielson's gambling debts, or McKinney's mismanagement of his own fields. Honestly, Keane, you *know* this as well as I do. You also know what we risk by giving Skybern this grip in our territory." The sun was low in the sky, and I was exhausted, and this damn meeting was going nowhere. I never should've agreed to hear Keane out again, but I hadn't expected an exact rehashing of issues we'd presumably put to bed several times over already.

"What I know, what every dragon I speak to agrees, is that your priorities lie in the wrong place now, my lord. As evidenced by—"

Sam Cameron cleared his throat at my side, his eyes narrowed on the older dragon. "Be careful what you say next. As for the alpha's priorities, it's clear you're speaking to your own circle and not the majority of the Hills' betas."

I couldn't let myself release an outright sigh, but I took the brief reprieve from the council's focus to breathe out my nose, trying to force some of my tension out as well.

Keane's feathers were ruffled, and he shifted in his seat, staring down his narrow nose at the younger man. "While you might be very grateful to the alpha for your recent elevation—"

"Are you saying there's some superiority between us outside of he who rises as alpha? Can you point to it, sir, so I might recognize it too?" Sam bit out.

I raised my hand and Sam settled back into his chair, glaring daggers at Francis Keane. On Sam's other side, another of the younger betas clapped my friend on the shoulder. The council had grown contentious as of late, I admitted, but there was a balance in the arguments. Unlike my father, who had surrounded himself with the same men all his life, I was hearing *all* of the betas' differing opinions, not just those of my own generation. That didn't stop me from having a preference as to the opinions expressed.

"MacIntyre, you tell him. You're the only one he listens to," Keane bit out, narrowed eyes turning to my old friend, the closest figure I had left to my father.

It was a punch to the gut to think he might've been won over by the likes of Keane—Keane, who wanted to sell us, our land and dignity, to the highest bidder.

"You think we should sell?" I asked, baffled. Had Ned fallen on hard times without me realizing? If so, it was true he was the kind of man who would be too proud to say so directly.

"It's not that," Ned said with a quick roll of his eyes in Keane's direction. "But I..." He scowled and looked around the table, shooting me an indecipherable look. Ned had always given me his truest opinion in private. He rarely attended council meetings like this, and he'd once referred to these settings as packs of wild dogs waiting to snatch food from each other's mouths.

"Go on, Ned," I said, voice low but without growl or censure.

He sighed. "You know I've concern for where your first interests lie. You...you push dragonkin to your liking, lad."

"I push you forward, you mean," I said.

He shrugged. "'Forward' is only defined by the man holding the map. You can't herd men like sheep, la—I mean, milord. My concerns are what happens when you let too many slip through your grip." His eyes slid toward Keane for a moment. His words were meant to be a warning to me, the advice of a friend, not just a reprimand.

But the advice was to keep the status quo rather than challenge my people to grow. Ned was more afraid of giving offense than of what would happen by risking our women's lives and happiness. More afraid of refusing men like Keane than of what happened when those men finally died and there was no one in a position to carry their place to be a new leader.

I took a deep breath and circled my gaze around the table, bracing myself for the blow as much as the men who had the guts to raise their eyes to meet mine. "I will not coddle the fears of men who seek to keep us in the dark ages. We can grow, if we are wise enough to do so. We can protect our people, if we are brave enough to do so. And we can meet the changes ahead of us, if we have the sense not to hide in the past.

"I refuse to allow Grave Hills to be bought out from under its own people," I continued, pulling my gaze from Ned and turning onto Keane, who no longer bothered to hide his malice. This argument wasn't over between us. He'd found his way into Damian Worthington's pocket without my realizing. They'd made up their mind to give Skybern a grip in Grave Hills, and my refusal wouldn't stop their scheming.

I'd never wanted to be the kind of alpha who planted spies in other dragonkin territories, but I might need to call in comfortable favors now. Worthington wouldn't show his hand until too late, and if it held any serious force, I needed to be ready.

Chapter Thirty-Six
BRIGID

I paused in the door of Torion's office, my hand raising to rest over my racing heartbeat as I caught sight of the pair of them. Torion's arm curled toward his chest, cradling Tylane there even as she squirmed and kicked impatiently, small grunts of sound from her precious bow lips entertaining them both.

"I thought it might be feeding time," Torion said, glancing up at me with a soft smile. "She gets bossy, like you, when she's hungry."

Tylane's face turned into Torion's shirt, likely leaving a wet mark from her open mouth there. She slapped a small red fist to his heart, and the grip of her perfect possession squeezed in my own chest. This tiny child owned us absolutely with the blink of her eyes.

"Did it startle you when she wasn't with the nurses?"

I shook my head and entered the room. "I knew she'd be with you. They said as much."

"Did you get some sleep?"

I laughed. "After last night, I was so tired it was impossible not to. Have you, yet?"

Torion turned his face back down to gaze at Tylane, and even as the lines of tension eased, they didn't vanish completely. His head shook slightly.

"But not because of our little terror," I said, crossing to the desk.

"Noo," he cooed, lips quirking up. "Not because of this little fire queen. Let me hold you both while you nurse her?"

That sounded like an unnecessarily complicated production, but his office chair was comfortable. Torion and I hadn't really had very much time for *each other* in the past month, for all the time we did spend together. I accepted Tylane from his hands and waited for him to push the chair back from his desk.

On second thought, Torion had an extremely accommodating lap, and his arms were wonderfully warm and strong. It wouldn't matter what position it left him in as I settled down to take my seat, he would hold us exactly as we wanted for as long as we wanted without a word of cramp or complaint.

"I've missed you," I murmured, as his wings closed around us.

"I'm sorry, my love," Torion whispered, burying his face in my hair, breaths brushing through the strands to slide hotly down the side of my throat.

"I didn't mean it that way. You don't owe me an apology any more than I might owe you one for how much of my focus is on our daughter. I just wanted you to know."

"Mm. In that case, I've missed you too."

I smiled as Tylane nestled in my arms, my dress pushed aside for her to latch onto my breast. "I know you have." I'd felt it in the bond between us that had grown clearer by the day, stronger—a gentle longing, one born of appreciation and patience and awe.

Torion huffed out a laugh and we settled into quiet, little

sounds of suckling satisfaction and small gurgles lulling us both into contentment. As the rhythm of Tylane's nursing and the steady thump of Torion's heart soothed my exhausted nerves, I could almost drift back into another sleep here, warm and surrounded by the people I loved.

"I was thinking you might like to visit Bleake Isle, see what Mairwen is about there," Torion said slowly, words just stiff enough to rouse me from contentment.

My eyes, which had drooped, now opened again, searching the room for threats. When I found none, I glanced down to my baby, once more awed by the sight of her, by her existence, before Torion's suggestion took root in my thoughts. My gaze strayed over the top of Tylane's dark head to peek through the window of Torion's wings at the scraps of paper littering his desk.

"You've received word about Skybern?" I guessed.

Torion sighed, the movement of his chest a rolling wave of tension at my back. "Seamus and Ronson's men both reported the same. We're not long from Damian coming here himself."

I blinked at that. "To negotiate?"

The silence of Torion's refusal to answer turned into a high, glaring alarm in my mind.

I started to sit up, but Tylane's immediate scowl and fuss made me pause. Torion's hands stroked my arms and pulled me deeper into his hold. *Such a small person has total command over our actions*, I thought.

"Torion?" I pressed.

"We think he means to challenge me."

I choked and my head twisted, Tylane letting out a little wail of irritation at my unrest. "As *alpha*?"

Torion's left hand slid up my arm, fingers finding the back of my neck to distract me from my shock with a massage.

Part of me wanted to snap at him to quit coddling me, but it would've been a shame if he'd stopped, so instead I just tried to frown more seriously at him.

"Most likely," he said, nodding.

"How long have you known this?" And why hadn't he said anything?

"Just today. Well, I had considered that his challenging me would be a more direct solution if he really wanted a foothold here, but it's such an extreme route. It seemed too absurd for him to actually decide to do so."

"So taking Grave Hills into his territory really was his aim in asking you to sell estates to dragonkin from Skybern," I muttered, resting my head into Torion's working fingers.

"No doubt. Will you go?"

"Go?"

"To Bleake Isle. With Tylane."

"Absolutely not," I snapped, before I'd even considered another answer.

A small, cowardly part of me stirred restlessly, cried out, *Think of what happens to you if he loses the challenge. Think of Tylane.* But the moment I looked down at her face, my choice was already made. I'd desperately wanted a child—a daughter, if I was being entirely honest—but a child to love and care for. I had one now, and I would protect her with my life. But she wasn't just mine.

Torion hadn't just created her with me. He hadn't just stood at my side. He'd scooped me out of the ashes of my past that I'd buried myself in. He'd brought me back to life with care and *love* and patience. If the rut hadn't resulted in my pregnancy, I would still be deliriously happy, mated to a man who deserved the love he'd kindled in my heart. I owed Torion my loyalty, and I wanted Tylane to know that her mother knew how to love with everything she had.

"You won't lose," I said to Torion.

"If I am outmatched, I will surrender, and you and I will have to flee, *immediately*. Seamus will be on hand. But I can't guarantee Worthington won't insist on seeing me brought down fully to avoid further challenge from the dragonkin who might support me. We'll run in disgrace, but we may also be running into a life of hiding."

I was holding Tylane too tightly and I twisted on Torion's lap, trying to ease my grip on her, placing one hand on his chest and letting my fingers dig into his shirt. There was a ferocious, echoing roar of denial in my chest and heat in my throat, and I swallowed it down hard as I met Torion's gaze. "We will run if we have to, but you won't fall, Torion. If Worthington seeks to steal Grave Hills from you in this manner, then he isn't half the alpha you are. He doesn't have the fire in him to claim us. Tell me you won't fail."

Torion's eyes crinkled at the corners, a little line of worry between his brows. His gravity always surprised me, my young alpha who laughed with his whole heart and whispered sweet pleas in my ear at night and looked so startled when I was brave enough to answer his affection with some of my own.

"I can't refuse orders from you, mate," Torion said. "I won't fail."

I leaned down, grasping his jaw with a firm caress and planting my lips to his, sealing the promise with a kiss.

I PULLED the heavy velvet curtains closed in the alpha's suite, shutting out the cold wind that rattled the panes. I'd given birth to Tylane in the last gasp of summer, and in the less than two months since, the seasons had taken a sharp turn toward winter once more. It was almost a year since Torion's father had passed and he'd risen as alpha, and in all that time we'd never discussed the beautiful, towering rooms above ours, meant to be occupied by the alpha.

It was a bossy kind of surprise I'd fashioned for him, but he liked me bossy.

The rooms had been aired repeatedly over the summer, and I'd cleared them with Torion's permission months back. It'd been weeks since there were any lingering scents. When Torion had left yesterday to visit a northern conclave of betas —all descended from the same old laird who'd ruled as alpha centuries ago—Tylane and I stayed in a guest room as men of the keep dismantled and reassembled our bed in the alpha's suite.

Perhaps it was for Tylane's sake, so she would have her nursery and eventual bedroom in the same place Torion had, or perhaps it was my little ritual to defend Torion's right as Alpha of Grave Hills. It was his keep, his home, and his bed in the alpha's rooms. Someone might claim them from him someday, but it wouldn't be a lord of Skybern.

A knock sounded softly on the door, and I turned as one of Tylane's nurses appeared.

"She's in the bassinet," I whispered.

"Would you like me to take her down now? The alpha's just arrived."

I shook my head. "He'll want to say goodnight. Would you wait? It won't be—"

"Brigid?" I heard the shout, not urgent but seeking, and I smiled.

The nurse ducked back into the hall, and I glanced around the room for any last second adjustments.

The main room had a sitting area and a table, so we might take our meals here when we wished. There was an arched opening into the bedroom straight ahead, comfortably large enough for the alpha but still close. I'd restored our nest myself while Tylane had napped, putting the curtains back up, so that while Torion was inside he wouldn't even be able to tell we weren't in our old rooms anymore. Branching off from the bedroom was a bathing chamber and then a doorway into the dressing room which led back to the sitting room, so that staff could carry water to the bath without walking through our bedroom. I was already discussing the potential of getting pumped water up to our bath, and perhaps to a few chambers on the lower floors as well.

Torion had once said that I could claim any domain I wished to rule over—he'd been waggling his eyebrows up at me as I'd taken a seat over his lap—but I did like ruling over the keep, and no matter what changes I made, he'd never batted so much as an eyelash in protest.

"There you are," Torion declared, arriving in the sitting room, giving it barely a glance before marching forward and wrapping his arms around me.

I sighed, giving into the relief of being held by him for a minute or two before rousing myself to lean back and look up at him in expectation. He just smiled drowsily back at me.

"Well?" I asked, unable to pull my arms free of his embrace and settling for raising my eyebrows.

"It went well. They're quite enthusiastic about the prospect of mates, and—"

"Not that," I said, managing to poke him sharply in his ribs. I jerked my head over my shoulder. "What do you think?"

Torion blinked and looked around us, at the tapestries I'd ordered of scenes of Grave Hills, the heavy blue and green curtains hanging from doors and windows, the fires blazing, and our nest glowing silver and white through the archway.

"Ah," he said, smiling. "Feels like ours now. That's good."

I huffed and freed myself. Men. "Say goodnight to Tylane

for now. The nurses are going to take care of her so we can have at least a handful of hours of sleep to start."

"We'll be fine for the night, milady," the nurse assured me.

Torion snorted and went to the bassinet, lifting a wrapped bundle from within. "You will, but we might not," he told the young woman before kissing the crown of Tylane's head and releasing a long sigh.

"I bet you slept like the dead last night in the beta's keep," I muttered.

Torion laughed and passed our daughter to the nurse, waiting for them to leave the room and close the door before crossing back to me, wrapping me in an even tighter embrace.

"You did very well for us, mate," Torion said, purring through the word and nuzzling his face into my hair.

"You don't mind that I did it without asking?"

"No, it's better that way. It doesn't look or feel like it did when it belonged to my parents now. I wouldn't have thought that possible, but it's true. And it's our rightful place in the keep," he said, kissing my temple.

I wondered if that was something you heard a lot growing up in the shadow of an alpha, "rightful place." Torion said it in regards to my place at his side and his place here in the keep. It was a kind of surety I'd never had before in my life. I'd had no rightful place in my father's home, not when he'd replaced my mother with a new omega so quickly. And Malcolm had never really given me reign over his home either, likely knowing that I was only a temporary fixture, as the omegas before me had been.

Torion had given me leave to claim the keep, and himself, from the very start, and then made my place with him permanent, however unconscious the mating bite had been. He'd celebrated the accident.

I wiggled myself in his grip enough to rise up on my toes and graze a kiss over his mouth. "I love you," I said. I still didn't say the words often enough, but every time I did, Tori-on's face lit up and he would hold tight to me, rewarding the small offering with a great cresting wave of affection. This time, I slipped free before he could sweep me up, catching his rough hand in mine and tugging on it lightly.

"Come with me."

Chapter Thirty-Seven

BRIGID

"I see you're in an authoritative mood tonight," Torion said, grinning and following my lead through the dressing room. I hadn't lit the candles there, knowing we wouldn't need the room, but there was enough glow from the bath ahead of us and the sitting room behind to make our path clear. "Now *there* is a tub meant to be shared," Torion noted as we arrived in the room, warm from the fire and gently steaming bath.

"In the future, certainly. I've had mine for the night."

"Oh, have you? This feels familiar," Torion said, his eyes heavy lidded and his hand squeezing around mine, thinking of our first union. "I bet I could talk you in with me."

He likely could, but I had a plan and I was fairly sure I could persuade him into letting me have my way. I turned, clasping his other hand in mine and stopping by the bath. There were standing candelabras and a good roaring fire, the roof of the room rising from six points in beautiful stone arches. The curtains were closed to keep out the cold night, and rugs were layered over the floor to keep the stone from chilling our feet. The space was warm and romantic, a cocoon for us to share.

"Your wings need to be oiled, and I know you are sore after flying so much. Let me take care of you, Torion. You would do the same for me. You *always* do as much for me. Let me be the one to look after you for a night," I said, my voice low and coaxing.

His eyes narrowed, and his purr roared in his chest. "Witch," he murmured.

I smiled. I *had* tried to make the words into a kind of spell. There was lavender and rosemary oil in the water to soothe his senses, but there was only one magic word I really needed.

"Please."

Torion laughed, a sound of surrender, and spread his arms wide as I slipped my hands from his. Once, months ago, before I'd fallen in love, before the rut, I'd trembled with nerves as Torion had watched me touch him, afraid of failing to hold a man's interest once more. Now I trembled with an eager hunger. I had more than Torion's interest. I had his love.

Torion and I had touched plenty in recent months, before and after Tylane's birth. He'd washed me when I was exhausted, and I'd held him close as he'd talked about our future, but it'd been a patient affection, the love we shared without the lust. I'd never experienced that before and I'd relished in it, more secure with my mate by the day.

Knowing we would be alone for hours together, that Torion would let me have my way in taking care of him, I felt something between rising lust and bone deep satisfaction. This was my place in this world. This was my man, my mate.

I unbuckled metal and untied leather, unbuttoned shoulder plackets and peeled away fabric. His cheeks and knees were chapped by the cold wind, and there were dry, lightened patches on his wings. He *needed* me to do this for him, as much as we would both enjoy the process. He was mine to take care of now. He'd claimed me.

Had I ever really claimed him? I would tonight. I would every day forward.

"Step in," I murmured, circling to his back, positioning the table where I'd assembled more oil and dry clothes and lotions and a little wing wax. There was a comfortable stool for me to work from and a good lamp. The tub was double large, and each narrow end rose up in the middle and dipped at the corners to allow wings to hang out over the edges.

Torion hissed as he stepped into the water and groaned, shivering briefly as he sank into the water. It rose just to the low lip of the edge. I'd learned how he filled the tub perfectly, I realized, with an odd kind of pride.

"You know you always take care of me," Torion said, easing against the cool porcelain that rose up his spine and gave his head somewhere to rest.

His wings brushed my knees as I sat, warming oil between my hands. "I do, but I know my care is often expressed in practicalities. Managing the keep, maintaining our nest, planning dinners. You show me how much you love me with every gesture, Torion," I said, pleased with myself for not stumbling over the words.

"I happen to find your practicalities very romantic, witch," Torion rasped as I dug my hands into his shoulders and wing roots, massaging the knots there. He helped himself to a washcloth and soap, lathering over his arms and chest.

"You should know the very sight of you warms me from the inside out," I said softly, stroking my hands out from his back over the thick spines of his wings. "And that once I have set eyes on you, I ache to inch closer, just to feel your skin against mine."

Torion stilled in the water, head turning so I could see his eyes widen, his lips part.

"And you sh-should know that I feel safe here with you. I know myself better as your om—no, as your mate."

"Brigid," Torion murmured on a heavy purr.

"This is my rightful place, here with you, Torion. You are *right* for me," I said, echoing the words he'd offered me months ago.

He sat up, trying to twist toward me, but Torion had always given me too much power over him. I only had to pause him with a touch on his shoulder and gently pull him back to the tub, and he relaxed once more.

"I started fighting against falling in love with you the moment you claimed me as your omega, and I lost the battle far sooner than I wanted to admit," I said, leaning forward to kiss the nape of Torion's neck, smiling at his answering shiver. "I surrender to your love, Torion. And I promise to surrender my love to you, mate."

"I love you, Brigid," Torion answered, his voice thick with his purr and something richer. He cleared it softly, leaning back as I continued my work on his wings. "Wicked of you to say these things to me while I must behave and let you tend to me."

"You wouldn't have let me finish if we'd been in bed together," I said, and he laughed. Every time I repeated the vow since I'd first told Torion I loved him, I barely got the words out before he was kissing me. It took too little to please him, but I refused to grow complacent.

I loved the ritual of tending Torion's wings, rubbing in the oil that picked up dust and dirt, then wiping it away with a damp cloth in long strokes that made Torion groan and melt deeper into the bath. I'd asked him once if he found the process sensual when he had to do it for himself, and he'd said it paled in comparison to when I did the work. When his wings were dry and clean, I warmed a bar of lotion made from lanolin and the oils of walnut, lavender, and clove between my hands. We talked about Tylane, and then about how the betas of the Hills were adapting more easily to the idea of mating than they had in Bleake Isle. We'd given the tradition up later than other regions, as the historical records stated, although it had become a practice to tie families together rather than one made with the instinctive demand Torion had followed when he'd bitten me.

"I took Mairwen's advice and made sure the women of the household were always present when I discussed what a true mating would mean for them," Torion said. "I'd like to do away with the selection ceremony altogether. Dragonkin are slow to change, but I think it might be possible to prepare them before the next ought to take place. If mating does become more in fashion again, they'll hardly be relevant."

"Mm, you can always repeat the process from the most recent. Perhaps it's time to have the men of the Hills be the ones who are measured for their quality," I said.

Torion chuckled and then let out a soft moan as I started circling wing wax over the dense muscle and hide at his back. I knew this was always the part of the process that left him the most aroused, the cleaning and softening leaving him sensitive, the wax requiring the most massage. Water stirred in the bath, and I glanced over his shoulder to find his hand moving over his lap, working his cock in a similar fashion to the way I stroked the bones of his wings.

I leaned forward, brushing against the expanse of his wings, making them twitch, and then whispered into his ear, "I said *I* would be the one to care for you this evening, mate."

Torion huffed out a laugh and squirmed, lifting both of his hands above the water, spread in supplication. "Are you going to let me return the courtesy?"

"Perhaps," I said, a little shyly.

Torion had admired and worshipped my body at every point of the pregnancy and after the birth. The transformation hadn't given him any pause but to discover new and apparently pleasing changes. I'd healed over the weeks since Tylane's birth, but it was also the longest period of time of our acquaintance we'd gone without lovemaking. The majority of our time together, we were now too exhausted to really think of sex. When I did find myself aroused, the anticipation of waiting turned into nerves. Would it *feel* different now? My body had changed so much, and some days I felt more like I was designed for Tylane—her creation, her care, her feeding—than I was my own person.

Torion reached a hand back and I gave him mine, smiling as he drew it over his shoulder to kiss my knuckles and then the inside of my wrist. "I am yours to do as you please with," he said.

As I meticulously buffed and sealed the hide of his wings with the fragrant wax, Torion's breaths grew deeper, hitching in moments with a choked sound like he was swallowing a whine before he released a thunderous purr. With every sound he tried to stifle, my body grew a little more sensitive, heating at first, tender breasts pulsing as they brushed against the cotton of my shift dress, my core echoing the plea.

"Rise," I said, and my voice was lower than usual, rough, almost like I was mimicking Torion's growl.

His breaths were heavy as he pushed up from the edge of the tub, water sluicing off his body in a cascade that left me parched, my view now the beautifully muscled and rounded globes of his ass. I swallowed hard and pushed back from the tub, lifting the heavy linen sheet up as I rose.

"Come here," I ordered, and Torion stepped out of the tub and into my embrace, his cock prodding through the damp linen to plead against my stomach. I buffed him quickly and then pulled away. "Sit."

Torion glanced down at the cushioned stool and then back up at me with an eyebrow arched. I arched one back and he grinned, cheeks flushed, as he sat down, naked and still dripping. When I knelt before him on the layered rugs, his hands rose to cover his face, a plaintive groan buried in his palms.

"*Brigid.*"

All I had to do was nudge his knees, and he parted to make room for me.

His cock was standing high, bobbing against his belly and leaving a pearly drop against the dark hair that led down from his belly button. His sac was heavy and full and deep brown, and I thought it already looked like it was tightening, readying for release.

I ignored the area, focusing instead on his feet, pulling them into my lap and grabbing a softer lotion.

"Fang's fire," he laughed, breathless and fractured with need as I tended his body at my own pace, working on his feet and then up to his calves, over his knees. He twitched as I touched the sensitive, vulnerable skin at the back, and then his cock kicked for attention when I moved up his thighs. "You'll kill me, love."

"You're heartier than that, alpha," I teased.

He swallowed hard, smiling down at me with his blush spreading down his chest and his eyes the full dark of midnight in the new moon. "Not when it comes to you."

I stroked my hands over his hips, and he dripped a little precum right in front of my eyes. I glanced up at him, a wicked smile curving my lips, and he stilled, prey caught in my sights. I leaned forward and licked up his length, claiming his flavor on my tongue, my eyelids growing heavy as he swayed and then fumbled behind him, hands bracing against the tub.

"Fuck," he grunted, chest heaving.

I rested back on my heels for a moment, giving him a long, examining look, making my decision. I warmed more of the lotion in my hands and then reached between his legs, pulling and rolling his balls in my hands, stroking the dark crease of the inside of his thigh. Torion's head fell back on a hopeless cry for mercy, and his cock wept once more. I licked him again, fighting my own grin.

"Witch, *please*," he hissed through clenched teeth. "I won't last."

That was probably for the best because even through two rugs, my knees were starting to grow tired already. I released his sac from my grip and moved it up to steady the base of his cock, rising up on my knees and wrapping my lips around the head of his cock. He wet my tongue at the same moment that I felt dewy beads of arousal budding in my sex.

Torion shouted out a wordless sound as I mouthed and then licked at his head, wiggling my tongue to his tip and then along the rigid underside. Inside of my closed hand, his knot swelled, hard and quick. My cunt answered with a hollow ache, as if it knew exactly where that knot ought to have been. I put both hands to it, digging my thumbs in, and Torion's hips rose up from the stool to pump his length into my mouth, stroking it along my tongue and then deeper.

I wanted to laugh in giddy triumph, but the sound that came out was a moan, echoing down into his swollen shaft. I twisted my hands around his knot and bobbed my head in encouragement, approval of his use of my mouth.

There was a roaring in my ears, a rush of desire in my blood that I hadn't felt since before Tylane's birth, and the echo of one sound in my head—a dark chant of *mate, mate, mate*.

Except it wasn't just in my head. Torion was gasping the word, my name, *witch*, at the same tempo that his knot throbbed in my hands, thick with his pounding pulse, one that matched the drum of need in my core.

I lifted my head to catch my breath and found him staring down at me, feral with hunger, wild with pride and lust, and I knew my expression matched his. This was my alpha, mine for *life*. And I was his. He would never stray, mate bond or not. It wasn't in Torion's nature. He loved with breath and thought and the rhythm of his heartbeat. He'd taught me to do the same.

"I love you," I gasped out.

His wild expression softened. "And I love you, witch. Come here?"

I laughed and shook my head, then dove down, swallowing him deeply, squeezing hard around his knot with that same chant of *mate, mate, mate*, shamelessly starving and slurping at the warning of his release.

Torion roared, arching into my mouth, my hands, wings scraping at the floor and the tub, a splash of water from a slipping hand. I made a sound like a purr, as if our roles had changed in the past few minutes, curling my tongue as I retreated and returned, taking every drop of him as he quaked and fell back to the stool, flailed to right himself. I wished I could've watched us from the side. I had heard but not seen his collapse, but he was rich and salty and bitter on my tongue, and my whole body was moving, rocking, begging to be filled.

I sat up with a gasp and a whimper, my lips damp and my eyes wide.

"Tor—"

I didn't finish his name before Torion's hands were under my armpits, lifting me up as he stood, his expression slack with release but eyes dark.

"I have to taste you, mate," he rumbled, scooping me off the floor as his wings snapped around us, as if to prevent me from being stolen away from him. We rose unsteadily for a moment, Torion finding his balance after the rush of release. I thought briefly that I would have to work harder next time to leave him limp, but perhaps it was for the best that I hadn't succeeded so much this time. He shook himself, straightened, and then marched to the bedroom. "Say yes."

I smiled at his demand, at the gentle way he lowered me into our nest, not so much as blinking to see how it might've changed in the new surroundings. I stretched and watched him lick his lips.

My nerves and worries were gone, smothered under my desire and the urgency of Torion's touch.

"Taste me, alpha," I cooed, lifting my knees and letting my shift slide down to my waist.

Torion let out a growl of warning, and then I was his to devour.

"I'LL SPEAK WITH HER FIRST."

The words floated to me from a tunnel of sleep, the first clear phrase in the collection of soothingly familiar whispers.

"Don't push too hard. Wings or not, it may be better for you if she's in attendance."

My eyes opened as Torion hushed his partner in the conversation. The door to our suite groaned, the guest exiting, and I ran my hand over the sheets. They were still warm, so Torion's absence from the bed couldn't have been a long one. Even from the sitting room, his sigh was audible, and by the time he'd returned to the nest I'd pushed myself up to sitting, my shoulders back and chin raised in defiance.

It was just before dawn, light enough for Torion's grave features to be clear to me and my stubborn ones evident to him.

"That was Ronson. Mairwen is here as well."

"I'm not leaving, Torion."

"It might not even be a challenge. It could be a siege."

I didn't catch my wince fast enough, but Torion gave me the grace of not pointing it out. "I've made up my mind," I said. "We can trust Mairwen with Tylane. I will remain here, with you, until you put this matter to rest."

Torion stood frozen at the end of the bed, lips tense with objections, wings slightly spread at his back, shielding me from the approaching threat. Slowly, he unwound, bowing forward to the bed, spreading out there, his arms reaching above his head until he found my legs under our blankets, gently cupping warm fingers over my shins.

"If you're hurt—" he snarled into the bed.

"Ronson or Seamus will assure I am not," I soothed, leaning forward to cover his hands with my own.

"That is *my* responsibility," he said, voice growing even more tense and dark.

I took a silent breath. "It is, and that's what you'll be doing, Torion. Just as you'll be protecting Tylane, the Hills, the ungrateful betas, and the omegas who will be better off for your rule here. Using your allies is part of that. Speaking of—"

"Seamus is gathering the betas we trust," Torion mumbled, and then groaned, going limp on the bed.

If I'd been asked just a handful of months ago what I would do in this situation, it would've been to run with Tylane. Even now, a part of me demanded that action. I did trust Mairwen to keep my daughter safe—the woman had dragon's breath, after all. Even more so, I trusted Torion to *win*. Challenge, siege, argument, it didn't matter. He would be the victor.

"Mate, you are stronger and cannier than anyone realizes," I said, rubbing over his hands. His head stirred on the bed, one ear turning up to listen. "You will win a challenge—"

"If he brings an *army*—"

"If he brings an army, you will outwit him with diplomacy," I said. Torion snorted, and my eyes narrowed. "Don't tell me you think the way they do. Our land is rougher and we live in tune with it, but we are not simple folk."

Torion grumbled and rolled onto his side, glaring at me from under a dark, glossy curl of hair. "Of course not."

"Good. Then act like it. Poke at his pride. Mock him. Make it personal. Shame him for bringing a fleet of betas in a matter that should be settled between alphas," I said, snapping the words in a line, watching the spark light in Torion's eyes, the gentle twitch of his lips.

"Clever witch," he teased, words thick and warm with affection.

I smiled and sat up, letting the sheets fall to my lap, leaning over his face and kissing across his brow, down the length of his nose. His hands left my knees to circle around my ribs, thumbs brushing the underside of my breasts.

"All will be well, mate," I promised, flirting my mouth over his as his purr began to thrum. "Let's go greet our daughter and face what the day brings."

He took his time petting my waist and back, nuzzling up into gentle kisses, a private moment of soothing between us before we had to open the door to reality, the danger we truly faced.

You could lose everything, an old voice hissed to me.

It was and was not my voice that answered. *No. We'll win.*

Chapter Thirty-Eight

T hat danger became apparent midday as the sky grew heavy with great shadows of dragon wings soaring over the brown and gray hills, one after another. We stood in a crowd south of the keep, a few of the betas—including Samuel Cameron—already transformed into their dragons. Faces turned high to count the incoming arrivals, but Torion and I looked to each other, his whisky eyes solemn as I did my best to keep the gnawing worry from growing obvious in my expression.

"Nearly fifty," Niall murmured at Torion's left.

Torion's hand tightened around mine. We had thirty betas on the field with us, but it was just over half of them who could transform into their own dragons. We were badly outnumbered. My fingertips tingled as I tightened my grip on Torion's hand.

If Damian Worthington attacked without discussion, we likely stood no chance of winning. Torion had to make him demand a challenge.

"Keep close to Ronson and Niall," Torion murmured to me.

"We ought to have Mairwen on the field," Ronson said, his eyes scanning the approaching dragons. "She could bat most of those men aside like flies."

"All the more reason to keep her watching over Tylane," I said, but I directed the words to Torion—a reminder to us both that our daughter was safe and we had to keep our focus on the present threat.

I rose to my toes and pressed my cheek to Torion's, holding tightly to his shoulders, his grip firm on my hips. His nose turned to trail over my cheekbone as he took a deep breath. He'd told me once I smelled like "home" and refused to elaborate further. I forced myself to relax, to lean into him and pretend for a moment that we were alone, even as the cold wind of the hills struck my exposed side. Torion sighed as my scent bloomed for him, just a little.

"Go," I whispered, and he nodded, but neither of us moved.

What if I was wrong? What if I should've agreed to run, should've demanded that Torion come with us? What if I lost him today because I'd been too stubborn, yet again?

Unacceptable. The declaration was hard and thunderous inside of me, made of stone that ran deep down into the ground below me.

Torion and I leaned back at the same moment, and he nodded, as if he'd heard the word too. "Wait for me," he said, brow furrowing, lips parting as if to correct that, as if to tell me to run if I needed to.

"I will," I answered before he could say anything else.

And then a glossy charcoal gray and black dragon landed before us, sleek and lethal, gleaming and glittering with the shadows of the rest of Skybern's dragons churning above us. I assumed this was Worthington, as elegant as one might expect of the metropolis's alpha, but Torion frowned and stepped forward, tipping his head shallowly in greeting.

"What does he want, Reeves? To start a war?" Torion called, a deeper resonance filling his throat and chest, the authority of his alpha taking over.

The jet dragon shuddered, and the air shimmered like an oil spill, wind spiralling as the beast was replaced with a young man who looked as slumberous and dangerous as his dragon but was *not* Damian Worthington.

"Bennett Reeves," Ronson informed me in an undertone. "Rumor is he's Worthington's half-brother, and presumably right hand."

"Presumably?" I asked, not taking my eyes off Skybern's beta mouthpiece.

Ronson and Niall exchanged a glance, and Niall shrugged. "We're not so sure of his motives, but perhaps we're not meant to be. Time will tell."

"If he has to," Bennett Reeves answered, just loud enough to carry to us. A few more of our local dragons shifted in preparation, and Bennett's eyes skipped over them, likely doing the same obvious math we had.

"Then he's a coward," Torion said, looking up to the sky and making sure his words carried. Above us, a large dragon roared its objection. "Counting on others to conquer where he cannot."

I understood Niall and Ronson's uncertainty about this beta, as something in his eyes softened with amusement and he did something that could *almost* be considered a nod. Still, he remained silent.

"Ground your army and face me as you ought to, Worthington," Torion shouted up to the largest dragon in the sky, who hovered with his wings beating cold air onto us. "Alpha to alpha, in challenge. Or go down in history as the *snake* you are."

I shuddered at the answering roar, the way it made my skin crawl and my stomach turn restlessly. Impatient clawing in my chest wanted to answer that aggression and I stepped back, catching the eye of Bennett Reeves, any humor he might've exhibited now vanishing beneath blatant calculation.

"The Alpha of Skybern is here to help Grave Hills," Bennett Reeves said, in something like a monotone. "Lord Worthington has concerns over the perversion of tradition taking place here and...elsewhere."

"What the fuck is that supposed to mean, Reeves?" Ronson snarled, moving to bolt forward before his brother caught him by the shoulder.

Reeves ignored him. "With Skybern's leadership, Grave Hills would be cleansed of the questionable changes brought about in dragonkin society."

Rage bloomed in me, hot in my throat, my eyes on fire and my nails digging into my palms like claws. I snarled openly at the beta, baring my teeth like an animal.

"I'll see you dead first," Torion said to the sky, his wings spreading. "You're a half rate alpha. You've stood in your position this long because you're a useful tool for others. Fang to fang, wing to wing, you don't stand a chance of holding your succession."

Reeves's head ducked, and I knew he was smiling now. Above us, the Alpha of Skybern roared once more and took a dive down to the ground, headed directly for my mate.

Bastard, I thought. I was sick of these damn men. I was sick of hearing about *traditions*. So called traditions that hadn't lasted half as long as the ones before them. Traditions that served betas and no one else. Traditions that made girls like me disposable to the men around them.

I loved Torion. I loved my life with him. But I would've given anything to change how I was raised, how I'd lived before finding my mate, and I would die before I would see Tylane grow up in that same world.

Damian Worthington's dragon glittered like a jewel, arrowing down to Torion, who flexed, already starting his transformation. They would meet in the air above us, blood and claw and wing.

Would I really stand here on the ground and watch it happen? Was I a coward too, even after everything I'd faced already? Would I raise my daughter to stand on the sidelines too?

No.

All right, I thought, with something like surrender and something like welcome. *All right. Come to me.*

My dragon answered with a joyous scream of freedom, my head thrown back as I startled the men around me. Not Bennett Reeves, though. He grinned with dragon sharp teeth and then whistled to the sky. As my body blazed and grew and rose into the air, almost half of Skybern's battalion of dragons twisted in the air and began their retreat.

They didn't matter. The dragons of Grave Hills readying for flight behind me didn't matter. I dove up toward the sky, finding the air beneath my wings refreshing and shockingly natural, and darted for the iridescent dark dragon aiming himself toward my mate.

Weak, my dragon observed cooly as Worthington caught sight of me and reared back.

"Brigid!" Torion cried, his own transformation halting at the sight of mine. "Brigid, no!"

But it was too late. I met the large, lazy dragon in midair, catching its throat in my jaws, my long body whipping itself back and forth to dig my fangs in, jerk it side to side. When his claws reached for me in retaliation, I released him and darted away.

I let out a sound that wasn't a roar but a laugh. *I'm beautiful*, I thought, catching sight of my tail coated in daggers, venomous green with coal red tips. I flew like silk, turning easily, impossible to catch, too fast and sinuous. I spun over the top of the dragon and landed on its back, raking my talons over one wing and then leaping up.

This is why the betas were afraid of their omegas growing wings. We were beautiful, and *deadly*.

I flashed under the sun, blindingly bright, bile yellow and lit from within with my fire. I released it into the air, turning circles in greeting to my mate as his huge evergreen body lifted from the ground at last.

Slow, my dragon noted coolly, then grinned as Torion barreled into Worthington, hard enough to make the air quake. *But strong*, I added mentally, and she purred in agreement.

My wingspan stretched from one horizon to the next, and I spiralled up into the air, warning off the Skybern betas with a roar of fire that made them rear back in shock. I was a slimmer dragon, but long, with strong legs, feline in form and lethal to my prey. I swung my tail and laughed again as it scratched through the wing of a dragon that dared to challenge me. Sensibly, it changed its mind.

A cry of warning from the ground behind me caught my attention, and I noticed the odds in the sky were better now. I twisted and floated down, checking on Torion—he and Worthington were wrestling in the sky, but my mate would outmatch him in a moment—before looking out to the north, where more dragons appeared.

Torion's allies were already here, which meant whoever approached might be a new threat.

I snarled and darted forward, Ronson Cadogan's dragon leaping up from below to chase after me.

Too slow, my dragon cooed cheerfully, delighted to be loosed at last. She'd been patient with me, patient as I considered my future. She'd protected me during Tylane's birth, waited and watched as I'd adjusted. Now, after we'd learned to live with one another in secret observation, we were together. We were *free*.

I roared and behind me, unable to catch up, Cadogan echoed the sound.

Only a handful of dragons advanced, but one was especially familiar. Rust brown and massive. Heavy. Slow, slow, slow. I screamed in violent greeting, a sound the color of lightning, and grew faster, flying straight, defensive spikes flaring out from my body.

The dragon—*Malcolm*—balked, reared up, and beat his wings in retreat. Coward.

I circled the cluster of dragons. They were older, and they had slowed at my approach. I wanted to attack, but I resisted, waiting to see what their business was. Malcolm transformed and he was so small as a man, so weak, it made me laugh again.

"We came to help," he shouted, irritated and *nervous*. I could taste his fear, and it was surprisingly sweet.

Ronson reached us and transformed as well, nodding once to me as I continued to keep the dragons in line. "Help who?"

Malcolm watched me circling them and swallowed hard. Oh, yes. He recognized me now. Somehow, he knew who I was, and perhaps for the first time since we'd met, he knew he ought to have respected me from the start. Feared me.

"The Alpha of Grave Hills. I may not see eye to eye with the—with *him*. But I'll take a man of the Hills over those slimy Skyberners any day," Malcolm said, and then jerked his head to the other dragons. "That's why we're all here. To defend our home."

I grunted, snapped a lick of fire that would heat the air just enough to warn them, and then nodded to Ronson before turning back to the fight. I needed to check on my mate more than waste my time with dragons who flew at the speed of molasses.

Torion was watching me, trying to fight and keep an eye on me at the same time. Foolish. I didn't need *his* help. In fact—

I screamed as Worthington caught Torion by the wing. He would *pay* for that.

Chapter Thirty-Nine
TORION

It was hard to focus on the dragon in my grasp when I knew that my mate was running loose and wild, with *wings. Without me.* Her excitement flavored the air, sharp as citrus but sweet to me, sweeter than the scent of the other alpha's blood as it dripped to the ground below.

It was an old legend that a dragon's blood would nourish the land it fell on, one that had led to too much bloodshed in our history before the alphas were established. I wondered if there were any truth in the story. At least it would mean Worthington was good for something.

It was my fault for being distracted.

I was turning to search the sky for Brigid when I felt the talons shearing through my right wing. I let out a roar in unison with the numbing scream not far away, and my flight faltered. I had one paw on Worthington's chest, and I dug my claws in, but it wasn't enough to keep me airborne. The wound was bad, I could tell already, could see the bright rubies of my own blood in the air, falling. I would nourish the Hills too.

Damn.

Green as bright as a spring shoot, vivid as a creature that warned its predators *poisonous!*, shot through the sky toward myself and the other alpha. Brigid!

Mate! a silky voice called in my head as she neared. I bared my fangs up at Worthington, keeping him distracted, doing my best to tighten my body, kick my back legs into his stomach and do what damage I could, even as we began to sink through the air. I tucked my wings in before he could tear the other and let us fall.

Brigid barreled into Worthington from above, sleek and snarling, tail, talons, and claws all tearing at his wings. We screamed as one, and I thought the sound could've brought a mountain down. Maybe that was how the hills had formed, the old dragons bringing down the world around them in ancient battles.

Worthington gave up trying to down me, his claws retracting, trying and failing to free himself from Brigid's slashing onslaught. She was too fast, and while by no means small, she moved in a more liquid fashion than most dragons, her body curving and twisting and snapping out of reach. One of Worthington's wings was now as shredded as mine, and we were both struggling to fly. With him distracted, I managed to gain air, my good wing burning with the effort, my flight turning in an awkward curve.

It was enough. Brigid's long tail dangled in Worthington's face, and he fell for the bait, trying to snap his jaws onto her. She flicked it away again just as fast, grinning like a cat, and I took my moment. I leapt onto his wing with my full body, jaws clamping onto his joint, talon piercing the inside of my mouth as I bit down hard enough to feel it snap in my grip.

Worthington's roar was ragged, breathless, his fire too thin to catch us as I released him. He fell from the sky like dead weight, and figures on the ground scattered away. I was barely keeping myself in flight, but he needed to hit first for the challenge to be considered won. Brigid dipped in the air, her body coiling carefully around mine, taking some of the weight and holding us up with her massive wings. There were stains of blood on her tail and talons, but I was fairly sure they belonged to other dragons.

Dragons who were now retreating, fleeing back to Skybern, their alpha grounded below.

Do we kill him? Brigid asked in my thoughts, and my own chuckle answered warmly between us.

Only if he refuses to yield.

The other one is still down there. Reeves.

I grunted and Brigid and I began to fly down, with her supporting me into a halfway decent descent. *Stay a dragon*, I thought to her. She was safer that way. For that matter, so was I.

Ronson had told us about this phenomenon, being able to communicate between mates, but it was so much more intimate than he'd been able to express. I didn't just hear Brigid's thoughts. It was as if they were my own, tenored in her voice and the very flavor of her. Her dragon was energetic, playful, and *deadly*. Where Brigid was reserved, her dragon was impulsive and instinctive, sure of itself. Brigid answered me in a silent agreement, her softer reassurance mingling with her dragon's alert watchfulness, ready to pounce on the next threat that dared turn our way.

I transformed as my claws touched the ground, and Damian was already on the ground as a man, his left wing that I'd broken trying to tuck in close but unable. There was blood in my mouth from his talon, and my own right wing was torn, but the winner of the challenge was obvious. Damian was bleeding from almost every limb, and he would need a doctor as soon as possible. Standing over him, with undisguised derision now painting his face, was Bennett Reeves.

"By rights, you've lost Skybern," I said to the pair.

Damian was pale and sweating, and I was surprised by his own open shock. He looked up at his half-brother, staring wildly, as if it were the younger man who had landed him in this position. Which was interesting. Perhaps it had been. Could Bennett Reeves have goaded Damian the same way I had?

"Do you plan to take it?" Reeves asked me, eyes narrowed.

I ground my jaw. If I did declare myself the Alpha of Skybern, I had no doubt I would be facing another challenge. Possibly in a matter of seconds.

"I don't want it. I want you lot out of my hills," I said firmly. "I am the Alpha of Grave Hills."

Reeves relaxed infinitesimally and bowed low. "So you are, Alpha Feargus. Will you put down your challenger?"

Brigid snarled behind me and her tail swung forward, over my head, landing like a barrier in front of me, her spread spikes already red with fresh blood, warning others from crossing me.

"Get him out of here, Reeves," I said, glaring at the beta, who I was now *certain* had orchestrated this mess. "Clean up your own house. I'll not do the work for you."

Reeves's lips twitched and he stepped back, transforming into that thundercloud black dragon and mercilessly scooping up the former Alpha of Skybern in his claws. Damian howled in pain, crying out his brother's name, but his voice was snatched away on the wind as Reeves took flight.

He's dangerous, Brigid thought.

"He is if he hasn't gotten what he wants yet," I agreed. I hoped he had. Bennett Reeves could ascend as alpha for all I cared, as long as he didn't move toward my territory again.

Then I looked over my shoulder and smiled. No...he wouldn't. Any dragon would think twice before crossing

Grave Hills, crossing *me*, while I had Brigid at my side, gloriously vibrant and sharp and wild.

You need healing, Brigid prodded, and it sounded more like herself and less like the dragon now.

"You'll be sure I get it, but first, let's make sure our house is in order," I said, wincing as I turned and marched up over the crest of a low hill. I did need healing. Mostly, my wing needed to be plastered so it had time to scar over and hopefully seam itself back together. I thought one of my ribs was at least bruised if not broken, and I was sure Brigid would find more in her accounting and give me a lecture for every scratch. She was pristine, I noticed. Far too fast and sly to catch.

Go on, she purred in my head.

"I knew you'd make the finest dragon Grave Hills had ever seen," I said, grinning as we paused to look down below us to where a small crowd waited, only a few men still remaining as dragons. They transformed back quickly once they saw Brigid—smart of them. Better not to tempt her into battle by appearing as a threat to me.

Amongst the crowd was Malcolm Barr.

He said he came to protect Grave Hills from Skybern, Brigid informed me. *You should ride me.*

I would take her up on the offer but not just yet. "Better they see me able to move on my own," I said to her under my breath. She huffed, and the hot air ruffled my hair. Her dragon was impatient, the slow, plodding steps to match my pace boring her. Her tail thumped the ground behind us, like that of a cat that had spotted a colony of mice but was being told to remain put.

I found Malcolm's wary gaze and held it as we neared, until he visibly sighed and marched forward to meet us.

"Are you here to challenge me?" I asked, and behind me, Brigid snorted fire.

The answer was obvious before he even opened his mouth. He took one deeply horrified glance at Brigid and then bowed low. "No, Alpha Feargus." He stood straight, then seemed to consider something and bowed once more. "Omega Feargus."

Brigid's derisive disinterest was so profound in our bond, it thrilled me into a surprised smile. "That's enough, Barr."

He stood straight, but he kept his eyes on me, as if he ignored the huge and ferocious dragon—the woman he'd misused and discarded—at my side, she might vanish...or at the very least continue ignoring him.

"There is something I need to discuss with you," Malcolm said, clearing his throat nervously.

I was surprised he'd even mentioned it, but I decided he deserved to squirm, and we were far enough from the others not to be overheard. "The cottage," I guessed.

His eyes widened and his face went white, eyes bouncing up unavoidably to Brigid's dragon. "Y-you know?"

I did now. I nodded and watched him with narrowed eyes. Brigid had *not* known, and I was curious to see her reaction. If she decided to exact punishment, I wouldn't stop her.

"I was dead drunk. An idiot. Didn't mean for it all to go up like th-that," he gasped out. "It wasn't meant as a threat. I was just...mad. I swear, Alpha. O-omega."

Which matched what the tavern owner in the nearby town had told me of Malcolm's brief stay in the area. He'd taken off late, barely steady, with a bottle of whisky, and then come back for his horse reeking of smoke and looking green and terrified.

"There will be recompense," I said when Brigid remained patient and unconcerned at my side. "Showing up today to defend your own damn home doesn't count."

"Yes, Alpha. M-milord," he burst out, still struggling not

to look disgusted as he deferred to me. His eyes slid nervously up to Brigid.

"Unless you'd like some justice now, my love," I said, smiling up at Brigid and winking.

Malcolm stumbled back as Brigid snorted once more, this time managing to singe the grass where he'd just stood.

I don't care about him, Brigid thought to me. *Do as you see fit.*

"Fair enough," I said, reaching out to pat the rough hide of her leg. "We'll discuss it later," I told Malcolm, who looked as though he was just shy of pissing himself and fainting.

He apparently had enough dignity to keep from running outright, but he did do a strange sideways retreat, too nervous to give Brigid his back.

Can we go home now? Brigid asked.

"Why don't you go back to Tylane, and I'll join you soon?"

Brigid stomped restlessly and then shook her massive head. *I can feel her too. She's safe. Finish quickly.*

I opened my mouth to ask her more, how she could feel Tylane, but Brigid snarled a warning down at me. Even though I knew this was my mate, I still had the sense to obey, marching forward at a slightly more relaxed pace than Malcolm Barr.

"Ow." The sound escaped me, and I flinched, ducking my head.

"Stop it," Brigid snapped at me.

I pressed my lips hard together and stifled my groan as my body started to shake with repressed laughter.

On the bed, Tylane kicked her legs in the air and let out a gassy giggle. She'd apparently given Mairwen the lesson of a lifetime on baby dragons with wings, screaming her head off for the first hour and then managing to fly up to the rafters the second Mairwen had thought she'd calmed enough to be put to sleep. She'd been sticky and sleepy and hungry all at once when we'd finally made it back to the keep, and Mairwen had looked like she'd been caught up in a tornado. I suspected Ronson might have to wait a little longer for an heir.

Brigid snarled under her breath and yanked on the bandage, strangling my laugh under a fresh ache.

"Are you always this rough with patients?" I asked.

Brigid huffed and tossed her hair back to glare at me from where she was wrapping my ribs. "It's your own damn fault for not paying attention during the battle."

"I was paying attention—"

"To *me!*" she barked out.

I smiled at her and watched her eyes narrow to slits in warning. "Well, who could blame me, witch? You were magnificent."

Instead of her ire growing, it withered behind wet eyes and a fragile catch in her breath as she gasped out, "*Torion*."

Damn. I'd miscalculated.

"Oh, mate, come here now. It's all right. I'm being a beast on purpose—you know I love when you snap at me," I said, words tumbling over one another, my worry flaring as Brigid let me bundle her into my arms without so much as a squeak of protest. "The fight wasn't so bad. And you're right, I was distracted by you. Damian wasn't much of a threat, and he's gone now. No one else in Grave Hills is stupid enough to go up against me when I have you at my side. Hushhh, don't cry."

Brigid growled, but the sound hiccuped sweetly as she thumped her fist on my chest. I grit my teeth at the answering throb, and then she whimpered and soothed the spot with a touch that made *all* of the pain in my body go dull and distant.

"It's your own damn fault—"

"Of course it is," I agreed easily, wiping a tear off her cheek.

"—for making me so horribly, desperately, *stupidly*, permanently in love with you, you awful, beautiful, wonderful, perfect man," Brigid sobbed out.

I covered her ear and held her head to my shoulder so she couldn't hear my chuckle, kissing the top of her head and taking a great whiff of her. My home. My mate. My stubborn dragon witch. Brigid sniffled and snuggled deeper, and I stroked my fingers through the tangles of her hair, carefully unraveling them before they might pull and hurt her even the slightest bit.

"If you ever do anything to disappoint me, I will transform into my dragon and eat you," Brigid said, voice muffled and sullen.

"Good idea," I said, too outrageously happy to sound solemn.

"Don't agree with me. We both know perfectly well you never could stand to hurt me," she said, her voice going soft. My wing was coated in a mess of herbs and a plaster bandage. My ribs were wrapped, the rest of me was slippery with salve for bruising, and Brigid had made me rinse my mouth for the wound there, but thought it would heal faster than the rest.

She leaned out of my embrace, but only long enough to scoop Tylane up and enfold her between us, little snorts and snuffles of approval coming from our daughter.

"You can't even stand to disagree with me when I'm being unreasonable," Brigid said, kissing my jaw gently.

"You're never unreasonable," I said, entirely under her spell as usual, falling deeper as her eyes rolled.

"Silly man," she murmured, grazing her mouth over mine.

"Your man," I said, purring in a contentment too deep to

feel entirely real. Tylane's head thumped to my chest to listen to the sound.

"Oh, yes," Brigid purred back. "Undeniably mine. As I am undeniably yours, mate."

We curled up together, cocooned in our wings, Brigid's stretching to cover me protectively, brilliant green with talons tipped red. She would walk through Grave Hills as a warning to the men, and a promise to the women. So would our daughter. I would tend Brigid's wings soon. I was sure she was sore already.

"Everything will be all right?" she asked, but it was only a hint of a question.

Still, I answered. "Everything will be well, mate. I'll make sure of it for you, and for our daughter."

Brigid sighed and softened in my arms, nodding against my shoulder. She knew I would keep my promise, and I knew she was strong enough to stand by me through every challenge we might face, to conquer them with her hand in mine. Right where she was meant to be.

Epilogue

BRIGID

✤

"Have you got your bags? Bartlett, have you got the alpha's bags? There? Have you counted them all? You're sure?" There was a toss of black curls with a huff of breath, and our daughter's eyes rolled as she glanced at us before giving us a thorough once over and wincing. "Are you sure you wouldn't rather come and stay with me for a bit? Just till you get your feet under you again with the change."

I pursed my lips as Torion gave me a meaningful glance, his salt and pepper beard twitching uncontrollably. "We're perfectly able to keep our own house, love. We managed the keep for a century, after all."

"Aye, but it's meant to be your retirement now, and—"

"Tylane, you're driving them mad," a rough voice called from under a pile of screaming children.

Tylane, tall and proud and as fearsome a dragon as the Hills had ever seen, wheeled around and marched her way over to her brother, her large sage and blue wings flapping with irritation. "I am not, and you could do a great deal more to help today than you are, Lockie."

I sighed and leaned into my mate's side, felt him do the same to me in answer. "You always liked bossy women."

"Aye," Torion allowed, and then was quiet for a moment before adding, "Tylane's proof there can be too much of a good thing."

I snorted and turned, burrowing into Torion's broad chest. He'd grown thicker and softer in recent years, the perfect antidote to this morning's chilly spring air.

"She's gotten worse since her third," I said, muffling the words against him.

"Mm. What's the little one's name again?" He grunted as I pinched his side and laughed. "That's right, that's right, *Tormund*."

Torion was something like a *god* to our grandchildren, as plentiful as they were, and each one held his ever growing heart in their fist as he let them ride his dragon by the dozen, chasing rabbits and dogs and butterflies in the summer. And I —gallingly known as "Granny" to half the hills' children—had a bag full of sweets and bandages and seed crackers now constantly strapped to my hip.

A soft voice interrupted from behind, nearing our little huddle. "You are moving awfully far away from us all."

I pulled free from Torion to welcome our youngest, Bess, into the fold, her rounded belly pressing into mine. "Not away from you, my darling. But we've got to give the new alpha room to rise," I said.

"Think of it as just far enough away to feel like you're on a vacation when you come to visit," Torion said, brushing a hand down Bess's amber braid and kissing the crown of her head. "Anyway, we needed to make sure he found a place with room for the lot of you. You all keep multiplying!"

Bess snorted, and the sound was so familiar. Of all our

children, she looked the most like me. She reminded me of my mother somehow, little as I knew her—quiet, but direct in manner, sure of herself and her place in the world. She could be sure. Torion and I had fought every year of our long reign to give her and Tylane and all the other young women of Grave Hills that surety.

"Well, we had the pair of you as an example," Bess said as she untucked herself from between us, her own more recently acquired wings stretched behind her. She'd been born without them, but they'd appeared not long after she'd met her mate, Alec, beautiful and gleaming like brass.

"Your mother demanded at least three children from me when she claimed me," Torion said with a shrug. "She promised a son and demanded daughters. What could I do but obey?"

Bess wrinkled her nose, but Lockie loosed himself from the pile of nieces and nephews, and they ran off like a pack of puppies toward the approaching horses and carriages loaded with our belongings.

"Did you not want sons, Ma?" Lockie asked, feigning a scowl.

"If she hadn't, she'd've kept Pa off her after having me, wouldn't she?" Sebastian asked, ruffling the heads of the children.

"Not to mention me," Ben added, following after his twin and cuffing him on the back of his head.

I ignored the flush on my cheeks as I glanced up at Torion, whose beard did not manage to hide the smugness in his smile. I *had* suggested we not try for any more children after the twins. Then I...changed my mind.

And had not been able to keep my hands off my mate the year of the drought, when the contraceptive herb was in short supply.

"I wanted each and every one of you, as I've made

perfectly clear your entire lives," I said, not quite soothingly. Having five children had been a dream. It still was, but they were adults now and harder to distract away from a topic. "But now...your father has promised me a castle of our own, far out of reach of politics, for the remainder of our very happy lives. You all may come and visit us at your leisure...in a year or so."

"A year?!" the twins and Tylane scoffed.

"Aside from Bess and the new baby," I added.

"Ma!" Lockie cried out.

"Quick, now you've done it," Torion said, wrapping an arm around my waist and herding me forward through the crowd of our family, his grin bright.

"You won't last a year without us!" Sebastian shouted to our backs as we fled toward the carriages.

"Seb!" Tylane hissed before calling out, "Write me if you need anything at all! Or come and stay with—"

Someone cut her off, and as in a hurry as Torion and I were for the next chapter of our lives, we stopped at the carriages, lifting each of our grandchildren up in tight hugs full of kisses. By the time we made it into the dark quiet inside and the carriages were moving, I was exhausted, collapsed against Torion's chest.

Which was shaking with laughter. "A *year*?" he repeated finally.

I nudged him with an elbow, and he sat up, lifting me with him. "I know. It'll be a month at best. I just didn't want Tylane or Lockie following us there."

"Hmmm, you think a month... I'll have to do my best to keep you occupied, love. Let's make it two," Torion purred, lowering his mouth to mine.

Two months would be all right. Bess wouldn't be too close to delivering in two months. "Two months," I agreed, arching up for more kisses. "But not much longer than that. I do love them so."

"Of course. They're hellions, but they're our hellions, after all," Torion murmured.

"I didn't know then, Torion," I said, thinking of the conversation before we'd finally managed to escape the keep. We weren't Alpha and Omega of the Hills any more. Just Torion and Brigid. Just mates.

"Didn't know?" Torion asked.

"How much I really wanted what I asked of you. How much I would love our family. How much I would love you," I said, my eyes growing watery as I reached up to cup his familiar face, the soft beard soothing against my palm.

"No one could anticipate this kind of love, witch," Torion rasped, kissing my forehead. "It's never existed before."

Afterword

I really hope you enjoyed Brigid and Torion's story. I couldn't build a world where women can have everything they desire without giving a voice to Brigid. A lot of her story is outside of my usual patterns and comfort zones when it comes to writing but I hope I did her justice!

Bennett has snuck in and demanded his book next and I am absolutely looking forward to what his soon to be discovered love has in store for him! As is pretty typical for me, I already know that the moods and themes and nature of the characters won't always be the same across every book, but I hope you'll find more of what you enjoyed in the next one. I'll even keep my fingers crossed that I might even make you love each book a little more than the one before.

There are many ways to keep updated on my progress but the best places where are in my Facebook group and on my Patreon!

Also by Kathryn Moon

<u>COMPLETE READS</u>

The Librarian's Coven Series

Written

Warriors

Scrivens

Ancients

Standalones

Good Deeds

Command The Moon

Say Your Prayers - co-write with Crystal Ash

Secrets of Summerland

The Sweetverse

Baby + the Late Night Howlers

Lola & the Millionaires - Part One

Lola & the Millionaires - Part Two

Bad Alpha

Faith and the Dead End Devils

Sol & Lune

Book 1

Book 2

Inheritance of Hunger Trilogy

The Queen's Line

The Princess's Chosen

The Kingdom's Crown

Tempting Monsters

A Lady of Rooksgrave Manor

The Basilisk of Star Manor (novella)

The Company of Fiends

Sanctuary with Kings

<u>SERIES IN PROGRESS</u>

Sweet Pea Mysteries

The Baker's Guide To Risky Rituals

The Knitter's Guide to Banishing Boyfriends

The Florist's Guide to Summoning Saints (to be written soon)

Monster Smash Agency

Games with the Orc

Howl for the Gargoyle

Lessons with the Mothman

Sweet on the Swamp Beast (to be written soon)

Dragonkin Series

The Alpha of Bleake Isle

The Alpha of Grave Hills

The Alpha of Skybern (to be written soon)

About the Author

Kathryn Moon is a country mouse who started dictating stories to her mother at an early age. The fascination with building new worlds and discovering the lives of the characters who grew in her head never faltered, and she graduated college with a fiction writing degree. She loves writing women who are strong in their vulnerability, romances that are as affectionate as they are challenging, and worlds that a reader sinks into and never wants to leave. When her hands aren't busy typing they're probably knitting sweaters or crimping pie crust in Ohio. She definitely believes in magic.

You can reach her on Facebook and at ohkathrynmoon@gmail.com or you can sign up for her newsletter!

www.ingramcontent.com/pod-product-compliance
Lightning Source LLC
Chambersburg PA
CBHW021339310726

48971CB00001B/200